"Thou art fair, my love; there is no spot in thee," he said to her.

Rebekah opened her eyes a little and looked at him. This wasn't the way it was supposed to go. She had to make him stop.

"Is that more stuff from your heathen playwright, MacDougal?" she scoffed, although her voice sounded less than steady.

He smiled slightly. "No, my love. It's from the Bible."

She knew he was lying. "There's nothing like *that* in the Bible!"

"Oh yes, there is. In Song of Solomon. Maybe your father never let you read it."

She couldn't remember. She couldn't remember anything because he reached up and now he was stroking her hair and her face with fingers as gentle as the soft Texas breeze, and the touch was sending chills all over her body in spite of the lingering heat of the day.

"You really are beautiful, Rebekah Tate," he was saying. "Your hair is like spun gold when the sun hits it, and it feels as soft as silk. Your skin is soft, too, like satin." His rough fingertips brushed her cheek, and her breath caught in her throat. "Your lips are luscious, too, except I don't think anyone has ever taken the time to teach you how to kiss properly."

She opened her mouth to tell him she didn't want to know how to kiss at all, but just as she did, he ran his thumb across her lower lip, making her gasp at the intense pleasure the simple action caused. Then he traced her mouth all the way around, around and around, until her lips tingled and her breath came in tiny pants.

Just when she thought she couldn't stand it another second, he pressed his mouth against hers . . .

VICTORIA THOMPSON

WILD TEXAS WIND

ZEBRA BOOKS
KENSINGTON PUBLISHING CORP.

ZEBRA BOOKS

are published by

Kensington Publishing Corp.
475 Park Avenue South
New York, NY 10016

First printing: October, 1992

Printed in the United States of America

*To my husband Jim
and my two beautiful daughters,
Lisa and Ellen,
for helping me remember
I live in the real world, too.*

Chapter One

Sean MacDougal smiled to himself as he watched the squaws squabbling over the cheap trinkets he had brought as trade goods. The women would be thrilled with the colored beads and wool blankets for which their men would trade high quality buffalo robes and animal hides.

The other white traders in Sante Fe laughed at him for risking his life by venturing out onto the plains to trade with the Comanches himself. They stayed behind in their comfortable homes, trusting the Mexicans who worked for them to bargain for the best deal with the Indians. But Sean MacDougal enjoyed risking his life, and when it came to business, he trusted no one but himself.

Mentally calculating the profit he would make on this trip, he didn't pay much attention to the squaw who had approached him and who now stood waiting for him to glance up.

"You're a white man, aren't you?" she asked after a moment.

So startled at being addressed in English in the midst of a Comanche camp, Sean didn't at first understand the question. Looking up from where he was hunkered down beside the piles of trade goods, he saw the typical moccasins and beaded dress of a Comanche woman. The face above them was as brown as the other squaws', but the eyes staring back at him were shockingly blue, mirroring the brilliant Texas sky, and the cropped hair framing that face was the color of ripe corn.

Stunned, Sean rose slowly to his full six feet, looking the woman over again as he did so. She was as slender as a reed, in contrast to the Indian women whose bodies tended to thicken with age. Even still he could sense the tensile strength radiating from her. Weak women simply didn't survive in a Comanche camp.

"What did you say?" he asked when he was on his feet and gazing down at the golden head. He had to make a conscious effort to speak in English and not in the pidgin Spanish he used with the Indians.

"I asked if you're a white man." She spoke softly, probably so they wouldn't be overheard, although Sean doubted anyone in the camp could have understood them. "But I guess you must be," she added, gesturing toward the beard he hadn't trimmed since leaving Sante Fe. She used her chin to point, the way an Indian would. "I never saw a Mexican with red hair."

She was, he understood instantly, a white captive, and he tried in vain to recall any rumors of a white woman being with this band. "Who are you?"

She straightened her shoulders proudly and said the words that would change Sean MacDougal's life forever: "I'm Rebekah Tate."

Good God! Rebekah Tate was a legend even in far-off Sante Fe. "You're alive!" he exclaimed. The reply to this was so obvious, she simply stared back at him while he absorbed the astonishing information. "How long has it been since . . . ?"

"Seven years, when I was fifteen," she replied,

8

bitter anger flashing in her eyes. In that instant he caught a glimpse of all she had suffered during those years: pain and loneliness, humiliation and torture. Although few discussed it, everyone on the frontier knew the fate of captive females.

But as quickly as the flash of anger appeared, it was gone, and her expression became as blank as an Indian's, concealing all emotion. "You've heard of me?" she asked.

"Everyone's heard of Rebekah Tate, but it's been so long . . . Everyone thought you must be dead."

Once again emotion flickered in her eyes, but before he could read it, it was gone.

"My father, is he . . . still alive?"

"As far as I know. He offered a reward for you—"

Before he could explain, an Indian woman screeched something he didn't catch and grabbed Rebekah's arm in an attempt to pull her away from him. Her mistress, Sean thought, certain Rebekah Tate must be a slave in the camp, as most captives were, but Rebekah's response quickly changed his mind.

She screeched right back, shaking loose the old crone's grip and pushing her away. The older woman stumbled but didn't retreat. She started shouting in Comanche, a language Sean did not comprehend well, but he could tell everything he needed to know by the woman's tone. She didn't like Rebekah talking to him, and she was trying to drag her away. Rebekah was having none of it.

They argued for a moment, then Rebekah turned back to Sean. "Ransom me!" she cried, the words half-plea, half-command.

If only it were that simple. "But what—?"

"I'll find you later," she promised, finally allowing the woman to draw her away.

Ransom her! Did she know what she was asking?

9

The Comanche understood how desperately the whites wanted their own back, and they charged accordingly. Sean might have to pay the entire profit of this trip to free her, and who would repay him? He knew traders who had ruined themselves ransoming captives whose families had no means of reimbursing them.

True, the Rev. Zebulon Tate had offered a reward for his only surviving child, but that had been seven long years ago. The man might no longer be able to pay it, if indeed he ever had been. The man might be dead. The man might even have decided he didn't want the girl back after she'd been with the Indians so long. Few women were *worth* having back after even a short time in captivity. Charity was fine, in moderation, but only a fool would bankrupt himself for a woman he didn't even know. Sean MacDougal was no fool.

Unconsciously, he'd been watching her walk away. The tantalizing sway of her naked hips beneath the buckskin dress suggested a different kind of reward should he decide to help her. Sean felt his body stir in response, but he jerked his gaze back to the other squaws who were still picking through his goods, trying to decide what they wanted. He hadn't had a woman in a long time, and he'd known he'd end his celibacy once he reached the Indians, whose ideas of sexual morality were so different from the whites. Here he'd have his pick of the single girls who would be only too eager to sneak into his tent and lie with him in exchange for a pack of needles or a few colored beads. The whites had an evil name for such a barter, but the Indians were more practical.

Yes, he'd been expecting to have a woman, or more than one, which was why he'd had that momentary lapse in lusting after Rebekah Tate. Turning his interest to more promising quarters, he caught the eye of a buxom young girl. She couldn't have been more than fifteen, which meant she was most likely single. From the way she was smiling at him, he figured she must be. He smiled back, trying to concentrate on her face, but something was wrong. Her broad features, the high cheek bones and heavily lidded eyes, suddenly repelled him. All he could see were Rebekah Tate's fine features, the rounded chin, the turned-up nose, the satiny cheeks, things he hadn't even realized he'd noticed.

Rebekah Tate was, he thought, a beautiful woman. Or she would be if she were dressed properly and if she had been shielded from the sun so her skin was milky white as a lady's should be.

But Rebekah Tate wasn't a lady. She was a Comanche concubine. The sad thing was, she was probably better off here than she would be if he did ransom her and take her back. He wondered if she even suspected that.

Rebekah Tate allowed *Pipiku?,* Squeaky, to pull her away from the others, away from the tall man with the shoulder-length red hair and bristling red beard. Dear God, how long had it been since she'd seen a white man?

Seven years. Hadn't she told him so herself? Seven years since the awful day that still haunted her nightmares, when the Indians had come to the stockade where she and her family had lived with the other settlers for safety. The day when they'd swooped down on the defenseless women and children while the men were out working in the fields. When they'd slaughtered nearly everyone in sight, raping the women, then gutting them like hogs and leaving them to die in a fly-blown agony. When they'd taken her two-year-old brother by the heels and smashed his head against the side of a cabin. When they'd speared her mother to the ground and left her, naked and writhing, while they carried Rebekah away.

Rebekah had been terrified they would kill her, too. How silly that fear seemed now. There were worse things than dying, far worse things. Rebekah knew, because she had endured them all.

"My husband will not like you talking to the trader," Squeaky was saying in the shrill voice that had earned her her name.

"I was asking if he had any needles," Rebekah lied as they made their way through the camp toward their own lodges. "I lost my last one. The father of my son will be angry if he finds out you made me miss out on a good trade."

Squeaky scowled up at her. It was a game they played. Squeaky never let Rebekah forget she was the first wife of *Isatekwa*, Liar, and Rebekah never let Squeaky forget she was the mother of Liar's only child.

"You do not fool me," Squeaky informed her, squinching her wrinkled face until she looked like a dried potato. "I know you think the trader will take you away. I hope he does. Then I will never have to see your ugly face again! I should tell him to steal you in the night!"

Rebekah smiled benignly down at the woman who had done her best to make Rebekah's life miserable for almost six years, ever since Liar had taken Rebekah for his second wife. "Maybe the trader would rather have you instead. Maybe he will sneak into *your* lodge tonight. You will have to tell me if his hair is red all over his body."

"*Yaa!*" Squeaky squawked in outrage and would have started screaming again, but they both heard Rebekah's son calling her. Squeaky responded to the boy even before Rebekah could and hurried forward to meet him.

Sitū-htsił Tūkerū, Little One Who Hunts Away From the Camp, was running as fast as his short legs could carry him, his tiny breechcloth flapping against his thighs. He would, Rebekah knew, much rather have run naked like the younger children, even though he was old enough now to dress like a man. He argued with her every morning about putting on even this scrap of clothing, but Rebekah insisted, always looking toward the day when they would wake up in her father's house and she would dress him in trousers and a shirt and shoes and stockings.

Squeaky tried to catch him, crooning words of affection, but he masterfully eluded her clutching hands and flew on until he reached his mother. Oblivious of the murderous look Squeaky threw after him, he slammed into Rebekah's legs and began to chatter so fast she couldn't understand a word.

"Stop gobbling like a turkey!" she scolded, wishing he wasn't too big to scoop up into her arms. He hardly ever stood still long enough anymore for her to hug him. "What are you telling me?"

"The traders! They gave me something to eat, something brown and sweet. I want you to buy me some. This much!" he added, spreading his chubby arms as wide as he could.

She thought he must be referring to the brown sugar candy the traders always brought for the children. Since no one in Liar's lodge ever denied his only son anything, Rebekah felt safe in promising Little One Who Hunts his heart's desire.

But before she could open her mouth, Squeaky said, "I will get it for you, Little One. I will get you as much as you want. I have some painted deerskins I will trade, but you must show me which trader has it. Come."

She offered her gnarled hand and smiled as sweetly as she could, but Rebekah saw that Little One Who Hunts wasn't fooled. He knew how treacherous Squeaky could be, fawning one moment and screeching the next, depending on who was watching. The boy glanced around and, sure enough, saw Liar lounging nearby, sharing a pipe of newly purchased tobacco with his uncle.

"Let's ask your father," Rebekah proposed, taking the boy's hand and ignoring Squeaky's muttered imprecations.

But Little One Who Hunts was much too excited to wait for his mother. He slipped out of her grasp and raced over to where Liar reclined outside his uncle's lodge.

Rebekah followed more sedately, taking the time to look at the man the Indians considered her husband. No ceremony had sealed the relationship, nor did any bond Rebekah recognized unite them. Liar had simply taken her as his wife, paying her previous owner three good horses for the privilege because she was carrying a child likely to be born alive. Liar wanted a son, but his first two wives had both died barren, and his current wife, Squeaky, was childless, too. Although he most certainly wasn't the father of Rebekah's child, Comanches weren't particular about such matters, so now Liar had a son by virtue of having claimed him.

Seeing the two of them together, no one would believe for a second that Liar had actually sired the beautiful child who now stood before him, eloquently pleading his case for the purchase of candy. Even with his flat features softened to kindness, Liar was far too ugly to bear any relationship to the boy, and his wiry, bandy-legged physique stood in marked contrast to the boy's solid, sturdy frame.

"I want this much!" Little One Who Hunts

14

exclaimed, stretching his arms wide again. His light gray eyes glittered with excitement, the eyes that marked him as different from all the other Indian children.

Liar could not help smiling at his beloved son's enthusiasm. "How can one so small eat so much?" he teased.

"I won't eat it all at once!" the boy insisted earnestly.

Liar pretended to consider the request while his uncle, who had listened to the exchange with scowling disapproval, scolded the boy for being greedy. "Will you be like the wolf and eat and eat until you throw up so you can eat some more?"

Rebekah listened patiently. It was, after all, Uncle's job to discipline his nephew's son. Among the Comanches, the relatives took over this onerous duty so the bond between parent and child would not be damaged. The parents, Rebekah included, were free to spoil their children shamelessly. Consequently, no Comanche child ever rebelled against his parents, but rather held them in high esteem.

"And would you steal from your father?" Uncle was saying. "He must trade his hides for things your family needs, like cooking pots and iron for arrowheads, not waste them on—"

"But Uncle," Rebekah interrupted, "Squeaky has offered to trade for my son. She is too kind, but I know how much pleasure it gives her to give my son gifts." Rebekah smiled sweetly, remembering the time six years ago when Squeaky had kicked Rebekah's swollen stomach and screamed a prayer to her gods that the child inside would die. Taking a few deerskins from the woman would be just one more item on the balance sheet in Rebekah's campaign to make her pay for her cruelty.

Liar nodded his approval of this plan, and Little

One Who Hunts let out his piping version of a Comanche war cry that made the men laugh uproariously. Even Rebekah smiled, although she died a little inside each time she saw evidence her son was growing into an Indian.

For years she'd lived for the day when she would take him away from this awful place, back to civilization where he would learn to sleep in a bed and sit in a chair and read and write and take his rightful place in the world. She'd hoped she could take him away before he grew big enough to become one of *them*, but it had already happened.

Then she remembered the red-haired trader, the one who spoke English, the one who was a white man. No white man would leave a white woman captive with the savages. Soon she would be free, and so would her son.

Sean looked around carefully to make sure he was alone in the evening shadows before he stepped into the bushes to relieve himself. The Indian children— and even some of the women—had taken an inordinate interest in everything he did, and the fact that he had bodily functions just like they did seemed to delight them no end.

The day had been so busy, he'd hardly had time to consider his encounter with Rebekah Tate this morning. He still could hardly believe it. He well remembered the first time he'd heard about her from a freighter along the route from St. Louis to Sante Fe. In those days, Sean had made his living carrying other people's goods while saving up to start his own business.

The teamster had told him in graphic detail (probably exaggerated) about how a party of Indians had attacked a stockade of settlers while the men were out in the fields, killing most of the people inside and carrying away what captives they wanted. Two small boys had also been taken but had been ransomed within the year and returned to their families.

But no one had ever seen or heard of Rebekah Tate again. The kidnapping of children was bad enough, an outrage no white person could tolerate, but the capture of an innocent, pubescent girl who was doomed to be violated by savages was unthinkable. The horror of it inflamed every white man in the Republic of Texas and beyond, as far as the story spread. Everyone wanted to be the one to save her, reward or no reward. But no one had ever had the chance.

No one except Sean MacDougal.

"Psst, white man!"

The whispered call made him jump, and he hastily adjusted his clothing, cursing with surprise and chagrin.

"My father wouldn't have approved of your language, white man," Rebekah Tate informed him as she materialized out of the leaves. "He had a sermon about taking God's name in vain. I could probably remember some of it if I tried."

"Don't bother," he said, looking her over again and trying to imagine what she must have been like seven years ago. Younger, of course. Sweet and innocent. The blue eyes staring back at him now were as far from sweet and innocent as he could imagine, though. Instead, they were as hard and cold as glass, revealing nothing of what was inside of her and reflecting back only his own image. He glanced around to make sure they were still alone. "Is it safe for you to talk to me?"

"Not for me to be *seen* talking to you, which is why I followed you here. I want you to ransom me."

"It's not that easy," he protested.

"And you have to ransom my son, too. I won't leave here without him."

"Your son?" he echoed, looking her over again. No, she most certainly wasn't innocent.

"Yes, my *son*," she repeated, angry now. "What did you expect?"

Sean had no idea what he'd expected. He knew the Indians would have used a female captive, but for her to have borne a child . . .

"He's mine, and I'm taking him with me," she said, her eyes flashing. She was glorious in her anger, her sunburn and cropped hair not withstanding. Yes, she'd be a beautiful woman under the right circumstances. Too bad he'd never have her under the right circumstances.

"Like I said, it's not that easy."

"Of course it is! These savages would sell their own mothers for the right price!"

"And who's supposed to pay that price, Miss Tate?"

He'd spoken sarcastically, and for a moment he thought it was his tone that had surprised her. "A man could be ruined . . ." he began but stopped when she shook her head.

"Say it again," she urged.

"What?"

"My name. Call me by my name!"

"Miss Tate," he said, more disturbed by the strange glitter in her eyes than he wanted to admit.

"My whole name. Say my whole name!"

"Rebekah Tate."

She closed her eyes and a tremor shook her.

He stepped back instinctively. "Are you all right?" he asked suspiciously.

Her eyes flew open and the intensity of her gaze would have driven him back another step if he hadn't already gone as far as the bushes would allow.

"What's *your* name, white man?"

He hesitated, wondering if she was mad. It would be no wonder, considering all she'd been through, and it would certainly explain why she was so insistent on taking the kid with her.

When he didn't reply, she grabbed his arm with both hands. "Tell me your name!" she cried.

"MacDougal. Sean MacDougal," he told her quickly, wondering if he should try to break her grasp or just stand quietly and hope she didn't become violent. He'd never struck a woman before and didn't want to start now.

"MacDougal," she repeated as if trying to memorize it. "Is that Irish? Are you Irish?"

"No," he said, although he really had no idea.

"Then you aren't a Papist?"

He was, of course, at least technically. He'd had to convert in order to do business in Sante Fe. But in his heart . . . "No, I'm not."

She smiled, or at least her mouth curved upward. It wasn't a happy expression. "My father didn't approve of Papists. He said they were devils, but he was wrong. I know who the real devils are. I've been living with them for seven years."

"Listen, Miss Tate," Sean began tentatively, easing out of her grasp.

"You can't leave me here!" she cried, as if sensing his reluctance. "No white man would leave a white woman with the Indians!"

Sean wondered where that might be written. He was sure it wasn't a law. "How am I supposed to pay for your ransom?"

"My father offered a reward. You said so yourself! He'll make you a rich man!"

"In the story I heard, your father was a farmer who preached on the side. What makes you think he could pay me *anything?*"

The glitter in her eyes flared to cold fury. "Then *I'll* pay you. I'll sell *myself* if I have to, but I'll pay you somehow!"

Sean was feeling very uncomfortable. He didn't like feeling uncomfortable. "It's not just the money . . ." he hedged.

"But my father really will pay you, or somebody will. He's an old man, and someday everything he owns will be mine. I'll sign it all over to you. There's land, thousands of acres of it. You'll be rich—"

"I already *am* rich!" he said in exasperation. Instantly, he knew he'd made a mistake. Her eyes hardened again, this time with contempt.

"And you wouldn't spend a few dollars to save one of your own kind?"

"They'll want more than a *few* dollars, and I didn't get rich by throwing my money away!"

"Throwing it away!" she fairly shrieked.

Instinctively, he grabbed her and clamped a hand over her mouth. "Do you want someone to hear?"

She sank her teeth into the flesh at the base of his thumb, and he cried out in pain before he could stop himself.

"Do you want someone to hear?" she mocked when he'd jerked his hand away.

Nursing his injury—at least she hadn't drawn blood—he glared at her with pure hatred. "Give me one good reason why I should ransom you."

"Tell me first what's important to you, besides your precious money."

"Nothing," he answered more honestly than he might have under ordinary circumstances. "And no one."

She considered his claim, then smiled cunningly. "No one except yourself. And maybe your good name."

Surprise jolted through him.

Her smile widened at his reaction. "You said you'd heard of me. You said *everyone* had heard of Rebekah Tate. If that's true, then everyone will hear about the man who rescues her, too. You'd be famous, Sean MacDougal. You'd be the man who rescued Rebekah Tate."

That night as Rebekah tucked her son into his buffalo robes, she whispered to him in English.

"The red-haired man will save us, Little One. I told him. I told him he had to ransom us both, and he will because he cares more for his pride than he should. Your grandfather would probably preach a sermon about it, about how pride causes a man to fall. At least I think that's the way it goes. It's been so long . . ." She tried to recall her father's face, the way he'd looked standing in his rough-hewn pulpit on Sunday morning, but the image was fuzzy, faded by the years.

"Why are you making those funny noises to me?" Little One Who Hunts asked sleepily.

Rebekah shook off the memories. "It's special talk," she explained in Comanche. "My people's talk. Someday I will teach it to you."

"Then we can talk to each other, and no one will understand us," he said, pleased at the thought.

"The people who matter will understand us," she said, knowing he couldn't possibly know what she meant. Indeed, he closed his eyes, bored with the conversation, and was instantly asleep.

She kissed his brow and stroked the raven softness of his hair for a while. Then she moved over to her own pallet and stretched out. She and her son shared her lodge, her only sanctuary in the camp. She supposed she was fortunate to have a prosperous husband, one who could afford two wives to share the back-breaking labor and one who could provide lodges for each of those wives in addition to one for himself. The other two were close by, Liar's and Squeaky's, and a cord stretched from Liar's lodge to each of his wives' where the ends were tied to their bedclothes. When he wanted one of them to come to his bed, he need only pull the cord to signal her.

When he wanted an enthusiastic bed partner, he pulled Squeaky's cord, but he knew he would never get a child from her, so he sometimes pulled Rebekah's cord, still hoping to get her with child again. Rebekah glanced at the cord and shuddered. Soon, she would no longer have to lie in the dark and wait for that dreaded summons. Soon she and her son would be free, and she would never have to endure a man's touch again.

With a smile, she reached down and untied the cord.

The man who rescued Rebekah Tate.

The words had rung in Sean's mind all night. How could she have known? She'd never set eyes on him before yesterday, so how could she have hit upon the one thing that would tempt him?

His good name. Except Sean didn't have a *good* name. He didn't have a name at all. He'd heard the story too many times growing up in the orphanage in New York, about how they'd found him in a basket on the doorstep, a note pinned to his chest asking them to find him a good home. But no one had wanted a nameless, red-headed foundling, so he'd languished in the orphanage until he was old enough to run away.

Fourteen, he'd been, but tall for his age. He'd gotten work easily, common laborer's jobs at first, until he learned the ropes. Then he'd moved up and on, always westward, away from the place where he'd grown up, as far away as he could go. St. Louis had been his goal, but when he got there, he found it was only a gateway to the real West. A freighter's job on the Sante Fe Trail had led to his own freighting company until he decided his true gifts lay in trading goods for himself. Now, sixteen years after he'd left New York, his store was one of the finest in Sante Fe.

But no one truly respected a storekeeper, no matter how prosperous he became. And the name Sean MacDougal meant nothing to anyone, least of all to Sean MacDougal. It was just a name someone had chosen for him because it fit his red hair. Sean MacDougal had lived for thirty years as a nobody.

And now he had the chance to become *the man who rescued Rebekah Tate.*

Which explained why he was sitting in the Civil Chief's lodge with several other Indians, smoking tobacco he himself had traded to the chief the day before. One of these Indians owned Rebekah Tate and her son, and Sean was about to commence the most important barter of his life.

Sean itched to get on with it, but he knew the Indians would consider haste rude. They had nothing better to do than to sit and talk all day and wait for their women to bring them food. Unless he was hunting or raiding, the Comanche was the laziest creature alive, or at least that was what most whites thought. Sean knew better, of course, so he respected their ceremonies.

The tobacco he'd traded them was poor quality, not the kind he usually packed in his own pipe, but he savored the smoke just as the Indians did while they passed the pipe from hand to hand.

When they had smoked, Sean began the conversation by complimenting the Chief on the quantity of buffalo robes his people had to trade and the skill of the hunters who had brought them down. He spoke in the pidgin Spanish that was the language of trade. The Indians understood him perfectly well, but he had also brought Juan, one of his men who spoke Comanche fluently, to translate into their tongue, too, just to be sure there were no misunderstandings.

The Indians returned the compliments, and after a half-hour or so of exchanged flattery, Sean judged it was time to start dickering.

"You have a woman here who was taken from the whites," he said solemnly.

The Civil Chief, *Kebakowe?*, Coyote, nodded, and Sean could feel the sudden tension in the lodge. The man across from him, the man who owned Rebekah Tate, stiffened, but Sean pretended not to notice.

"Her people miss her," Sean continued to the Chief. "Her father still weeps for her. He is an old man, a chief among his people, and he wants to see her before he dies."

The Chief frowned. "But *Huuwūhtūkwa?* is happy among our people. Her husband is a good hunter. She is never hungry."

"But she misses her own people. She wants to see her father and live in his house again. You know how the whites are. No matter how happy their lives might be, they think they must be with their own kind."

Coyote had noticed this peculiarity. He nodded sagely, but Sean could sense the resistance still coming from the man called Liar. He looked at the wiry brave.

The Indian made a poor impression with his flat features and his skinny frame, but Sean knew that judging a Comanche on foot was like judging a fish out of water. Liar must be a skilled hunter because only such a man could feed more than one wife. And Liar must be intelligent. The Comanches respected a

24

man who could spin a tale, and to have earned his name, Liar must be far better than most.

Sean nodded to him. "The woman who is your wife is the daughter of a chief among her people. I do not expect you to give her up for nothing. You will need another wife when she is gone, and I will not leave you a poor man. I will trade you two mules for her."

The man called Liar suddenly looked less hostile. His beady black eyes narrowed cunningly. "I cannot buy a *good* wife with two skinny mules. *Huuwūhtū-kwa?* is strong and a good worker. It would take two women to replace her."

Sean smiled. The dickering had begun. It went on for a long time, during which Liar proved how he had gotten his name by trying to convince Sean that Rebekah Tate was the most industrious woman alive and worth more than her weight in gold. In the end, though, Sean was satisfied. He was out two mules and as much trade goods as they could carry, but in all, he felt he'd gotten a bargain. He wouldn't make much profit from this trip, but he'd bought himself a name. With it, he could move his operation to the brand-new state of Texas and become whatever he decided to be.

Then he remembered. She'd told him she had a child, a boy. All that talk about making Sean a hero had distracted him. She wanted the kid to go with her, although why she'd want to drag a half-breed bastard back to civilization, he had no idea.

"We have a deal then," he said, trying to sound casual. "I will bring the goods to your lodge this afternoon, and you will give me the woman and her son."

"*Yee!*" Liar cried, suddenly furious, and jumped to his feet, crouching beneath the slant of the tent. "You said nothing about the boy!"

Sean didn't like the disadvantage of still being seated while the Indian towered over him, but he remained calm and acted only slightly puzzled. "Didn't I? I thought I did. He's her son, so naturally I thought—"

"He's *my* son, you pile of coyote droppings!"

"Of course," Sean agreed amiably. "I didn't mean to insult you. Naturally, I'll pay extra for him. How about another mule?"

Liar began to shout in Comanche, and although Sean couldn't understand his words, he had no trouble at all sensing the changed mood inside the Chief's lodge. Suddenly, all the Indians were hostile, and Liar was the most hostile of all.

Juan, his interpreter, had paled. "Tell the chief you're sorry," he whispered to Sean. "Tell him you wouldn't think of taking a man's son away from him."

When Sean hesitated, Juan grabbed his arm urgently. "If you don't want him to cut off your *cajones* and stick them down your throat, you'd better do it!"

Sean apologized, although the words left a bitter taste in his mouth. It wasn't the most abject apology, but the Chief seemed satisfied even though Liar still glared at him from his beady black eyes.

When Sean had finished embroidering his speech with a lot of meaningless compliments, Liar grunted and muttered something else in Comanche before ducking out the door of the tent and storming off.

"What did he say?" Sean asked Juan.

"He say you cannot have the woman now, either."

Rebekah couldn't believe how the red-headed stranger had bungled everything. All morning she'd had to listen to Squeaky cackling her delight over the

26

story which had spread like wildfire through the camp. Liar had been willing to sell her for two mules—*two mules*— when he'd paid three horses for her. What an insult! He must be tired of his second wife. He must have seen how lazy she was. He would be happy to be rid of her. The jibes had gone on and on until Rebekah thought she might have to throttle the older woman.

Little One Who Hunts had been terribly upset, too, thinking his mother was going to be sold away from him and he would be left at Squeaky's mercy. It had taken ages to calm him down and convince him she would never leave him alone no matter what. Then Liar had come to their lodge and slapped her, sending her sprawling across the buffalo robes.

"You will never leave here now, and if you try to take my son away again, I will kill him with my own hand and give you his heart to keep as a reminder!"

It was, as he well knew, the only threat that would frighten her, and she stared up at him in mute horror, knowing he meant every word. He would much rather have no son at all than to give his son to the whites.

And it was all Sean MacDougal's fault. She was angry enough to kill him, but if she did that, she would have no hope left of escaping. Two days passed before she had a chance to sneak away from Squeaky's watchful eye and find MacDougal. She followed as he stole away from the camp at twilight, trying to elude the children who pursued him everywhere he went. Keeping to the shadows, she slipped past those strolling around the edges of the camp, then waited until she judged he had finished whatever business had led him to seek privacy.

When enough time had passed, she crept up to where he had disappeared into the bushes on the riverbank and found he wasn't there. She was cursing her luck when she noticed his clothes, carefully folded and concealed beneath an overhanging branch. Smiling to herself, she listened and heard the light sound of splashing.

Moving silently, the way an Indian woman would move, she reached the edge of the river where the willows clung to the bank and drooped into the water, providing a semblance of privacy. Sean MacDougal had taken advantage of that privacy to bathe himself.

He stood hip-deep in the swiftly flowing current, his back to her in the rapidly failing light while he scrubbed himself with sand from the river bottom. She had a moment to study him, to marvel at the whiteness of his flesh where the sun had never touched it, at the breadth of his shoulders and the narrowness of his waist. She'd seen hundreds of near-naked men in the past seven years, yet something about this man disturbed her.

The feeling wasn't fear. She'd known terror at the approach of a naked man, terror and dread and disgust and even resignation, but that wasn't what she felt when she looked at MacDougal. Instead she felt strangely unsettled, uneasy, as if she should run away even though she knew perfectly well he posed no threat to her at all.

Before she could figure it out, he turned abruptly. *"¿Quién es?"* he called.

She was so startled by the sight of the hair on his chest, for a second she couldn't answer. "It's me, white man," she called back in English finally, wondering why her throat felt so tight.

Did all white men have hair on their chests? She couldn't remember ever noticing before. Perhaps she'd never actually seen a white man's chest. The whites were so much more modest than the Indians.

MacDougal was cursing again, probably because

he was as modest as all the other whites, and he was splashing around, trying to cover himself. As if she wanted to see anything of his.

"What the hell do you want?" he demanded. He was crouched down in the water to hide the part of him men seemed to think was so important, and he'd crossed his arms over his bare chest.

"What the hell do you think I want?" she replied, taking a small pleasure in using profanity, something she'd never had the opportunity to do before. Her father most certainly would not have approved. "I want to know how you managed to convince *Isatekwa* not to let me and my son go."

"It was *your* fault!" he said, using typical male logic. "You should've told me he didn't want to let the boy go!"

"It was *your* job to *make* him want to!" she cried in frustration. "Didn't you offer him a good price? I should've known from that hair! You're a damn Scot, aren't you? Stingy and—"

"Do we have to talk about this *now?*" He sounded as annoyed as she felt.

"Why, no, you can call on me at my lodge tomorrow at three o'clock when we serve tea. Just ask your friend *Isatekwa* to let you in," she replied sarcastically. "Of course we have to talk about this *now!*"

"Well, maybe you wouldn't mind if I got some clothes on first. This water is damn cold, and my teeth are starting to chatter."

"Fine. Get out if it suits you."

Several seconds passed, but he didn't move. Rebekah was getting ready to ask him if he'd frozen solid when it suddenly occurred to her he didn't want to expose himself.

She almost laughed aloud at the thought. As if he had something she hadn't already seen or cared if she ever saw again. But then that uneasy feeling prickled up her spine again, and she suddenly realized she *did* care, and the thought of seeing Sean MacDougal completely naked brought her instantly to her feet.

"I'll . . . I'll throw your clothes down to you," she said, clamoring up the cutbank to where she'd seen his clothes hidden. Finding them easily, she tossed them through the trees. She could hear him splashing his way to shore and in a few minutes he climbed up the bank, still damp but dressed in a linsey-woolsey shirt and trousers.

He'd washed his hair, and it looked black in the dim light, slicked flat against his head. His beard was wet and limp, too, revealing the strong lines of his jaw. Once Rebekah might have thought him handsome, but she no longer cared about such things.

"Do you know you almost got me killed?" he inquired, obviously still angry as he pulled on his boots.

"If you made *Isatekwa* mad, it's your own fault! I thought an Indian trader would know how to trade with an Indian."

"I could have done a better job if you'd told me how much he wanted his son!"

Rebekah felt the familiar rage rising up in her. "Little One Who Hunts isn't his son!"

MacDougal started in surprise. "Well, why didn't you say so? Maybe his real father will be more reasonable. Just tell me who he is, and I'll ask the Chief to set up a meeting."

Rebekah glared at MacDougal in impotent fury. She could actually feel the rage burning in her face, or at least she thought it was rage until she realized she was *blushing*. Dear God! How long had it been since she had blushed? Or felt the shame that inspired it?

When she didn't reply, he planted his hands on his

hips impatiently. "Well?"

Her face felt as if it were on fire, and she hoped desperately he could not see it in the shadows. "I don't know who his father is," she said at last, although the words felt like shards of broken glass in her mouth.

"What . . . ?" he began, then stopped when the truth dawned on him. "Oh." He looked away, although she couldn't be sure if he were simply embarrassed or if he couldn't bear to look at her any longer.

"Well," he said after a moment, perhaps a little too heartily. "Since things didn't work out the way we wanted, I've come up with another plan."

For an instant, she felt the leap of hope, then immediately squelched it. Life with the Comanches had taught her never to get her hopes up. "What is it?" she asked skeptically.

"Well, since your husband won't sell you—"

"Don't call him that! He's not my husband!"

He looked as if he'd like to argue the point, but he shrugged and went on. "Since he won't sell you and the boy, your only chance is to escape."

"Oh, sure," Rebekah said, thinking she'd been right not to pin any hopes on this fellow. "We'd get about ten feet from camp before every brave here was on our trail."

"I said I had a *plan*," he reminded her irritably. "I know your hus—I mean, I know they'd come after you if they thought you'd escaped, so we'll fake your death."

"What?"

"We make it look like you died. I've been listening to the camp gossip. They say you wash yourself in the river."

Since the Indians cared nothing for personal cleanliness, Rebekah's bathing had always been

31

remarkable. "I try to remember I'm not a savage, Mr. MacDougal," she informed him coldly.

"Then all we have to do is make it look like you drowned, maybe even like you committed suicide."

"*What!*"

"You leave your clothes on the bank like you went in to take a bath. Do it in the evening, after everyone is in bed so it will be morning before they find out you're missing. Then you wade upstream where I'll be waiting with a horse and supplies. We'll be well away before they know you're gone, and they'll be looking downstream for your body, which will give us even more time to get away."

It was, she had to admit, a pretty good plan, but it had a few major flaws. "What happens when they don't find my body?"

"We hope they'll think some animal carried it away. Whatever they think, they'll never assume a woman just walked away from the camp, naked, with no food or horse. You could even make them think you can make yourself disappear, that it's some kind of white medicine. You know how superstitious they are. Just drop a few hints to some of the women that you've decided to move on to the next world or something."

Her respect for him was growing by the minute. She only had one other problem. "That will explain what happened to *me*, but what about my son? And I don't care how many hints I drop, *Isatekwa* will never believe the boy just disappeared. He'd hunt for him until the day he died."

MacDougal nodded. "Which is why we can't take him with us."

"*No!*" she cried, more loudly than she'd intended. MacDougal moved as if to clamp a hand over her mouth, then thought better of it.

"Be quiet, will you? God only knows what would

happen if your hus—if anyone found us together."

"I won't leave here without my son!" she informed him in a fierce whisper, fighting the sickening wave of panic that threatened to overwhelm her.

"He might be better off here, with his own kind. Have you thought about that?"

Her panic swelled into fury again. *I'm* his 'own kind'! I'm his *mother!* He's all I have, and I won't leave him here. Do you understand that?"

MacDougal frowned, but he said, "Perfectly. And I figured that's what you'd say, but there's just no way to get both of you out right now, so—"

"So you can forget the whole thing!" she cried as despair welled up in her, black and hopeless.

"So," he continued doggedly, "I'll take you out first, then come back for the boy."

"What do you mean?" she asked, not letting herself feel the slightest twinge of hope until she knew every detail.

"I mean, I take you away now, get you back to your father, safe and sound. By then the excitement will've died down a bit, and I come back with some Tonks and kidnap the boy."

The Tonkawas were a once-powerful tribe who were blood enemies to the Comanche. Although they no longer had the means to meet the Comanches in battle, they took whatever opportunity presented itself to defeat them in small ways, even to helping the whites.

"It'd be nearly impossible to take a child from the camp," she warned. "Without getting yourself killed, that is."

"Which is why I'll bring the Tonks with me. They could steal a topknot off a sleeping Comanche and never wake him up."

The plan was so crazy, it might just work, and Rebekah could hardly comprehend what it might mean. Freedom. Her old life back. To live among her own people, in a house with walls and a roof. To wear dresses and hats and shoes and stockings. To eat cake and pie and coffee and beans. To never again lie helpless beneath a rutting savage.

But she would have to leave her son behind, at least for a while. Weeks would pass while she traveled back to her father, then more weeks while Mac-Dougal returned. And what if he couldn't find the child? What if something went wrong and he was caught and killed? She might never see her son again.

As if sensing her fears, MacDougal grabbed her arms. "This is your only chance. You might never see another white man again, least of all one willing to help you escape. Your husband will never let you be ransomed now, and even if he would, he'd keep the boy."

He was right, although Rebekah couldn't help wondering why he sounded as desperate to convince her as she was to escape. "And you'll come back for the boy?"

"I swear," he said, "on everything I hold sacred."

She felt the strength of his hands and the strength of his will radiating from him. If anyone could do this thing, he was the man. She thought of leaving Little One Who Hunts, and pain ripped her heart like a dull knife, but she knew this was their only hope. If she refused . . . "All right," she whispered.

He sighed, as if in relief, and his grip on her arms instantly gentled. "Good."

They stood like that for a heartbeat, with Rebekah staring up into his eyes and noticing for the first time how strange they were, so light brown they were almost yellow.

Then, as if suddenly realizing the impropriety of holding her like that, he cleared his throat and released her, moving back a step. Rebekah felt the loss of his touch, although she could not have said what she had lost. For an instant there, she'd been back in civilization, and he was her link. Perhaps that was it, although she didn't think so.

"When will you take me?" she asked to break the silence.

"We'll have to wait until the new moon."

"That's weeks away!" she protested.

"I'll be here for another week at least, and I have to go back to Sante Fe to close out my business and make some arrangements."

"But—"

"And we have to let some time pass. If you disappeared the day after I left, somebody would figure it out and come looking."

She had to admit he was right again.

"On the night of the new moon, you go to the river and leave your clothes on the bank. I'll bring you some new ones, everything you'll need. Then wade upstream until you find me."

"And what if you aren't there?" she asked, voicing her worst fear.

"I will be."

She shouldn't have trusted him. Nothing in her life, at least for the past seven years, had given her any reason to trust another living soul. Yet she found herself nodding.

"And you must see my son before you go so you'll know what he looks like when you come back for him."

"I've already seen him. He's the one with gray eyes."

"Yes," she breathed, feeling a tiny warmth deep in her chest. Although she still fought it, she knew what it was. It was hope struggling for life, and for the first time in seven years she had reason to believe it might survive.

"You'd better go before somebody comes by," he was saying. "And don't try to speak to me again. It'll be better if no one remembers ever seeing us together."

She nodded, thinking there was something else, something she should say, but unable to remember what it was. Only when she was back at her lodge, lying next to her son in the darkness, did she remember. She should have thanked him, but it had been so long since she'd had something for which to be grateful, she no longer even remembered how.

But once they were free, once she and her son were safely in her father's house, she'd learn how to once more.

Sean waited until the woman had time to get back to the village and settle into her tent before making his own way back. He couldn't help smiling as he walked through the darkened camp. Things had gone even better than he'd hoped. He'd known she would argue, that she wouldn't want to leave the boy behind, but she'd been a lot easier to convince than he'd expected.

Getting her away would be tricky, but Sean had long ago learned all the skills he'd need to sneak up on a Comanche camp and spirit away a woman who was more than willing to go. The Comanche didn't post guards around their camps, figuring no one in his right mind would attack a whole nest of them. Usually, they were right, and their lax security would enable Sean to accomplish his goal. He never doubted for a moment that the woman would be there when he came, either. He was, as he had said, her only chance.

Most people would consider him crazy for doing such a thing, and most people would be right. Sean

36

himself would only do it for the kind of reward he expected to receive once he reached civilized Texas with Rebekah Tate.

Of course, only a damn fool would try to do it twice, and Sean had absolutely no intention of coming back for her kid. She'd probably be upset about it when she found out, but Sean wasn't going to tell her until she'd been back for a while and she'd had a chance to see the kind of welcome she got. Once she understood what she'd be facing back in civilization, she'd forget about the boy. He was better off with the Indians anyway.

Chapter Two

As she had watched the comancheros leave, Rebekah had fought the urge to run after them and beg Sean MacDougal to take her with him. In the weeks since, she had cursed herself a thousand times for a fool for trusting him. Why should he come back for her? He had nothing to gain and everything to lose, and if the Comanches caught him, he would die a death too horrible for words.

Of course, she reminded herself just as often, he'd told her his plan for rescuing her. He'd had no reason to think of such an elaborate lie if he didn't plan to carry it out. She *had* to trust him. She had no other choice.

As the moon waned, day by day, Rebekah grew tenser, like a cat on a hot stove, skittish and jumpy and obsessed with her son. She wanted to spend every possible moment with him, not knowing how long it would be until she saw him again, if she ever did. Life, as she had learned, was an uncertain thing.

But Little One Who Hunts had no intention of being smothered by his mother's attentions.

"I want to shoot arrows with the other boys," he complained when she tried to keep him by her side.

"It's too hot," he protested when she tried to hug

him close.

"My father wants to show me how to track an antelope," he argued when she wanted to tell him stories of her own childhood.

Only at night, when he came to her exhausted and ready for sleep, could she cherish him the way she wanted. In the darkness of their lodge she snuggled him while he slept and whispered in English of the wonders she would show him and of the grandfather he had never seen. When she ran out of words, she would stare at him in silence, memorizing every feature for the lonely weeks ahead, and she would wish she could still pray because she would have asked God to keep him safe while she could not.

And during the day she dropped the hints MacDougal had suggested.

"Did I ever tell you?" she asked Squeaky one afternoon as they worked over a deerskin. "A white medicine man once taught me how to disappear. If I wanted to, I could vanish into the water and cross over into the other world where the dead live."

Squeaky made a sound of disgust. "Why don't you do it then?" she asked.

Rebekah pretended to consider. "I would except for my son. I wouldn't want to leave him with you."

"Your son is safe as long as Liar lives," Squeaky told her. "And if you were gone, he would be *my* son. If that is all that is keeping you, be gone!"

Rebekah shuddered at the thought of Squeaky raising Little One Who Hunts, but she nodded solemnly. "Sometimes I get so tired I do not think I can live another day, and the other side calls to me so sweetly."

Squeaky had snorted again, ending the discussion.

Finally, the last, tiny sliver of moon disappeared completely, and Rebekah stared at the night sky dotted only with stars, knowing the time had come at last. She had spent the final moments of daylight looking over her meager possessions—meager by white standards, but not by Indian standards. Among her peers in the camp, she was wealthy, having several beaded dresses and all the cooking pots she could use. Taking any of her possessions with her would be far too dangerous, of course, because it would be a clue that she had not really died. There was nothing here she cared to keep, though, even if she could have. She wanted no remembrance of her time in this place except her son.

As she tucked him into his bed that night, she held him to her until he cried out in protest.

"I can't breathe!" He pushed her away with grubby fists.

"Do you know how much I love you, Little One? More than earth and moon and stars all rolled into one. More than life itself."

"I know," he said with the confidence of one who has never doubted his position in the world.

"And I would never leave you unless I had no choice. Do you believe that?"

"Is my father going to sell you?" he asked, his beautiful face crinkling into a worried frown.

"No, my darling. He promised he would never sell me. Don't you remember?"

He nodded slowly, suspiciously.

"But if . . . if something happened," she tried, not knowing exactly how to tell him without telling him. "If I wasn't here tomorrow, you'd know that I wouldn't be gone long. I'd never leave you forever. I'd come back for you, and we'd be together again. You believe that, don't you?"

He nodded uncertainly. "Are you going away?"

"Oh, no," she lied to reassure him. "I'm only talking about *if* I did. You don't need to worry, because everything will be fine."

40

Fortunately, he was too weary to argue or to question her further. In a few more seconds he was sound asleep. Rebekah gazed at him for a long time, until she thought her heart would burst from the pain of leaving him, and when she couldn't stand it another second, she gathered her things and left the tent.

Squeaky was outside, huddled in a blanket beside the fire. The late summer night was only mildly cool, with just a hint of the coming autumn, but Squeaky's bones were growing old and she could no longer bear the least chill. Although she was only about thirty by Rebekah's reckoning, Squeaky was already an old woman and might not last the coming winter. Rebekah looked upon her for the last time, remembering the countless little cruelties the woman had performed and thinking how little she would miss her life here, then turned away.

"Where are you going?" Squeaky snapped to Rebekah's back.

"To the river to bathe."

Squeaky snorted in disgust. "You will catch a chill and die and then I will be rid of you."

Rebekah smiled mysteriously. "Maybe I will disappear tonight and *then* you will be rid of me."

"I hope you do."

"And if I do, remember that I went across of my own will, and I can come back the same way, so if you are cruel to my son, I will haunt you."

Squeaky spit into the fire to show her contempt, but Rebekah saw the fear flicker in the woman's eyes. All the Comanche feared ghosts and spirits. Perhaps she had bought her son a few weeks of peace until the red-haired trader returned for him.

Forcing herself to walk slowly, as if she had no life-changing purpose in mind, Rebekah moved through the camp. All around her people went about their normal tasks, eating, sleeping, talking, playing. The ever-present smell of wood smoke hung in the air, masking the underlying odors of spoiled food and unwashed bodies. This was, she thought, the last time she would ever see a Comanche camp. At least she hoped it would be.

Although she may have appeared outwardly calm, her heart was hammering so loudly, she was afraid it might give her away. Over its thundering, she listened for familiar sounds, familiar voices, that would tell her the whereabouts of the one person she most feared.

There, she heard it, a familiar shout as Liar won at the game some of the men were playing. Then the rattle as the hunks of bones were thrown again in the game that was strangely like dice. She smiled in spite of herself to think what her father would say about the gambling. He had a sermon about that, as he did about every vice known to man. Perhaps he had missed his calling. The Indians were so much more corrupt than any of the whites she had ever known, and they could certainly profit much more from her father's messages than the straight-laced, viceless folks she remembered from his congregation. She would be sure and mention this to him when she saw him.

The thought lightened her step and before she knew it she was fairly running to the trees that lined the riverbank. Arriving there out of breath, her pounding heart threatening to burst from the added strain, she hugged a willow trunk until she was somewhat calmer. When she was no longer deafened by the beating of her heart and the rasping of her breath, she listened again, this time for silence.

The night had closed softly around her, and the only sound was the whisper of the wind through the leaves and across the surface of the river. Even

42

the water itself made no sound as it moved inexorably onward.

Then she waited, counting to a hundred in English as she had often done so she wouldn't forget how. Still no one came. The women wouldn't be hauling water at this time of night, and no one in the camp would think of taking a bath. The wind stirred the willow branches, and they brushed against her, making her jump.

Calling herself an idiot, she laid down the things she had brought, the square of blanket she used as a towel and the comb made of porcupine quills. She'd look strange to her people when she returned, with her sun-browned skin and her short hair, but she'd hide away for a few months until the tan had faded and her hair had grown enough to pin up. And she'd make herself some real dresses, out of calico with flowers printed on it. And she'd wear shoes and stockings and petticoats with lace on them. Then no one would ever be able to tell what had happened to her because she'd look just like every other white woman.

And no man would ever touch her again.

With a shudder, she began to unlace her moccasins. Kicking them off, she reached for the hem of her dress, ready to pull it over her head. She hesitated for just a moment, as she always did before undressing, on the off chance that someone might be nearby watching. But when she listened again, she still heard only the murmur of the night wind. Quickly, before she lost her nerve, she stripped off the dress.

The breeze instantly raised goosebumps on her naked flesh, puckering her nipples and causing her to instinctively press her thighs more tightly together to protect her greatest vulnerability. The water would be even colder, she knew, but she wouldn't feel it. What was a little cold compared to what she had endured during the past seven years?

Carefully, she folded her dress so no one would think someone had torn it from her body and taken her away by force. Then she left it in a neat pile with her moccasins and other things. Suddenly, an owl hooted, and she shivered at the forlorn sound.

"Whooo?" it asked again, and Rebekah lifted her face to the wind. "It's me, Papa, and I'm coming home."

With one last look over her shoulder at the quiet camp, she climbed down the cutbank and stepped into the water. She gasped at the first icy touch, then steeling herself, plunged in up to her knees and began to walk upstream.

With long strides, ignoring the bite of rocks against the soles of her feet, she moved against the gentle current. The water splashed softly with each step, but gradually she learned how to glide without the splash, as silent as a duck, or almost.

Still she listened, straining for any sound that might mean discovery. In the distance a coyote howled, and she shivered again, hugging her arms against her bare breasts and the pounding of her heart. If they found her, what would she do? Would she endure the punishment and hope for another chance, or would hope die with capture? Should she kill herself and end this suffering once and for all?

How often had she asked herself that question? How often had she begged God to take her? Often enough to know prayers weren't answered. Often enough to lose all the faith her father had so diligently taught her. And often enough to know she could never take her own life, no matter how bad things got. No, she would endure, no matter what happened, and she would live for the next opportunity to escape.

Suddenly she realized she had no idea how far she'd walked. Her body had warmed a little with the exercise, but her feet were thoroughly chilled. How far away would MacDougal be? Surely, he wouldn't take a chance on being seen by someone in the camp, so he must be a fair distance. But how far? She began to count her steps. A hundred. A hundred-fifty. Two hundred.

And what if he wasn't there at all? What if he'd been hurt or killed? What if he'd been taken sick. Life was, she knew, dangerously uncertain and could be snuffed out in an instant. And what if he'd simply decided, after considering the matter more carefully, not to come back at all? She could understand that. He'd be a fool to risk his life for her, a woman he didn't even know. Any man would be.

But how would she know? How far should she walk before giving up? An hour? Two? A hundred more steps? Until morning? And if she never found him, then what? Go back to the camp? Back to Squeaky and Liar and slavery and humiliation and—

"Pssst, white woman!"

Rebekah cried out in surprise and froze, looking around frantically, but she couldn't see a sign of whoever had made the sound.

Sean MacDougal watched her from his hiding place among the willows. At first she had been just an indistinct blur, like a ghost hovering over the surface of the water, wafting toward him like a vapor. Then, gradually, she had materialized in the faint starlight, a porcelain goddess skimming along, more perfect in her nakedness than he had ever dreamed a woman could be.

Desire stirred in him, hot and urgent, as he watched the gentle sway of her full breasts. It roared when his gaze drifted lower, to her belly where the golden curls crowned her womanhood. For a moment he imagined how her skin would feel, how she would taste beneath his eager hands and ravenous mouth. For another moment he imagined sinking into her velvet depths, her arms and legs clasping him to her, her lips calling his name. His fist tightened convulsively around the branch he was holding, and it snapped with a pop that sounded like a rifle shot in the dark silence.

She saw him then. "MacDougal," she said. Her voice sounded odd, and he tried to guess what emotions she might be feeling, surprise or relief, wonder or joy, perhaps all of them together. Or perhaps something else entirely.

He rose from his hiding place. "You made it."

"So did you."

They stared at each other for a moment in the faint light of the stars. He was almost invisible to Rebekah there in the shadows, but she knew he must be able to see her plainly, naked and vulnerable as she was. The old urge to cover herself caused her hands to twitch, but there was too much to cover for her hands to do any good. And she had learned never to betray shame. It was a tool others could use against her.

Lifting her chin in silent defiance, she said, "What would you have done if I didn't come?"

"I should be asking you that question," he replied. She heard the huskiness in his voice, the unmistakable grate of lust. Her blood ran cold, but she steeled herself against the instinct to flee. He was a white man, after all. He would never force himself on her the way an Indian would. Still, she couldn't bring herself to move one step closer to him, at least so long as she was naked.

"Did you remember to bring me some clothes?" she asked as nonchalantly as she could. "It's getting cold out here."

"Oh, yeah. Right here." He sounded a little

disconcerted, as if he'd been caught doing something he shouldn't have been doing. Rebekah smiled slightly as he disappeared back into the bushes and at last felt comfortable enough to take the final few steps to where he stood.

She had reached the water's edge when he reappeared holding a small bundle. *Clothes.* For an instant she pictured a calico dress with flowers on it and petticoats with lace and real shoes. Her heart leaped but came thudding back down when he handed her the leather bundle.

"I brought Indian things," he was saying. "I figured they'd be more practical for the trip."

He was right, of course, and she swallowed her disappointment. The rest would come in time, *if* they got away. Clutching the bundle, she looked up, expecting him to turn away, but he continued to stare, his eyes shadowy wells from which burned a flame that seemed to scorch her right across the space that separated them. For a moment she stared back defiantly, certain she could make him flinch, but he didn't move, didn't even blink.

In disgust, she pushed past him into the willows, turning her back while she untied the rawhide string holding the bundle together. She heard a smothered oath and smiled.

Sean swore his frustration. Dear God, she was as beautiful going away as she was coming toward him. He stared, mesmerized, at the roundness of her hips, the alabaster globes of her bottom, and the tantalizing cleft between. Closing his hands into fists, he could almost feel the soft flesh yielding to his fingers and smell the sweet musk of her scent.

Then the fringed skirt of the dress drooped down and over her, concealing all her charms, and Sean shook himself as one coming out of a dream. Better concentrate on what's important for now, he told

47

himself sternly. Acting like a deer in rut would get him killed, and her, too. He certainly didn't want Rebekah Tate getting killed. He had plans for her.

He waited until she'd laced up her moccasins, then said, "The horses are hidden over here." He led the way.

Rebekah followed, slightly unnerved because of the clothing he had brought. "You got this in my village, didn't you?" she whispered as they pushed through the trees.

"Sure, why?"

Rebekah didn't answer. He probably thought he'd done well, purchasing a finely beaded gown that was the Comanche equivalent of somebody's Sunday best. Unfortunately, Rebekah recognized it as having belonged to a young woman who had recently died in childbirth. She tried to shake off the feeling of foreboding, telling herself it was just the Indians' superstition playing on her mind, but she wasn't quite successful.

They found the animals tied under a live oak tree, lazily chomping the summer-dried buffalo grass. MacDougal had brought two fine horses and a pack mule loaded with supplies.

Seeing her looking at the mule's load, he said, "We won't be able to fire a gun to kill game for a long time, so I brought enough food to last us."

She nodded, knowing food would be only the second of their concerns. Then she noticed several large skin bags of water, and she realized he'd provided for them.

"I doubt they'll figure out you've run away, but just in case, we'll ride all night and all day tomorrow to put as much distance as possible between us," he said.

She nodded. "Just like a Comanche would do," she said with a trace of irony.

He smiled grimly. "Yeah, just like a Comanche."

She looked over the horses and, picking the one with the shorter stirrups, she untied it, stuck her foot into one and swung up. It was a bay gelding, a well-made animal with what the Texans called "bottom," the ability to go on running long after an ordinary horse would have petered out.

MacDougal's horse was also a bay, chosen no doubt because the drab color would help them blend into the equally drab, late summer landscape. She noticed he'd tied feed sacks to the hooves to disguise their tracks. The sacks would wear out after a few miles, but by then, with any luck, they'd be too far away for the Indians to pick up their trail. At least she'd chosen a man who knew what he was doing.

They rode slowly at first, warming the horses, then gradually sped up until they were running, skimming over the ground as fast as the lead mule would allow. After a while they slowed again to rest the animals, and the night passed in a bone-numbing ride that left even Rebekah, who had been hardened by the unceasing labor of a Comanche squaw, sagging in the saddle.

"We'll rest and eat something before dawn," MacDougal told her, his words drifting across the night as if from a dream.

Rebekah nodded wearily and reined in, dropping from her saddle onto legs that wobbled dangerously. Still, she instinctively began to unsaddle her horse so the animal could rest and cool off in the interval. As she pulled the heavy saddle onto the ground, she caught MacDougal watching her, having paused in the act of unsaddling his own mount, a strange expression on his face.

"What's the matter?" she demanded.

"I'll do that," he said gruffly. "Just sit down and rest."

49

For a moment she didn't comprehend. She was only doing what a woman should do, care for the animals, gather wood for the fire, prepare the campsite . . . Then she realized what was wrong. She was doing what a *Comanche* woman would do, not what a white woman would do.

Instantly she dropped the saddle and stepped away from it as if it had suddenly grown a head. No wonder he was looking at her as if she were demented. A white woman would never unsaddle her own horse. She would wait for a man to take care of her and serve her, never soiling her lily white hands.

Except Rebekah's hands weren't lily white. And she and MacDougal had a long way to go before they were safe. It would be foolish to expect him to do all the work. Besides, she'd forgotten how to be a helpless female. With a shrug, she bent down, pulled a handful of grass, and began to rub the sweat from her horse's back.

Acutely aware that MacDougal was still watching her, she kept doggedly on until he finally turned back to his own tasks. Within a few minutes, he'd unloaded the mule and rubbed the other two animals down while Rebekah hobbled her horse with the rawhide MacDougal tossed to her.

With the animals cared for, Rebekah turned back to MacDougal. "Should we have a fire?"

"No, although I'd kill for a hot cup of coffee. I've got some pemmican. That'll keep us going for a few days until it's safe to build a fire."

He pulled a sack from among the load the mule had been carrying, and opened it, offering her first choice. She dug into the mixture of dried meat, nuts, and berries some Comanche woman had spent days making last spring in preparation for the coming winter and wondered how much MacDougal had paid her for her hard work.

Scooping out a handful, Rebekah squatted on the ground and began to shovel the mixture into her mouth with two fingers of her other hand. Water drunk afterwards would cause the pemmican to swell in the stomach, staving off hunger for hours. MacDougal had planned well.

She was almost finished with her breakfast when she noticed MacDougal was still standing. She looked up to find him staring at her again, that strange expression still on his face.

She froze, her fingers halfway to her mouth, and stared back, wondering what she had done now to shock him. For a moment she couldn't imagine, then to her horror she saw herself through his eyes: a squaw squatting on the ground, gobbling her food as if there were no tomorrow. In a Comanche camp, there often wasn't. Food was consumed instantly and eagerly when available and longed for when it was not. She was acting like an Indian again.

Frantically she tried to think how a white woman would sit to eat, but she failed. White women didn't sit on the ground. They sat on chairs or benches or sofas, and they didn't eat from their hands with their fingers. They used plates and forks and spoons and knives.

She closed her mouth and slowly chewed the last scoop of food she had taken, looking away from MacDougal who suddenly got very busy eating his own meal. He, too, hunkered on the ground, but he picked up his food with the ends of his fingers and placed it in his mouth, chewing slowly. Rebekah knew because she watched him covertly until she'd seen enough to have mastered his technique. Then she finished her own meal the same way.

When he was done, he offered her one of the water skins. There was only one way to drink from one, by holding the skin balanced between two hands and squirting the water into one's mouth, so that's what she did. At least when she handed the skin back to MacDougal, he wasn't gawking at her as if she were a calf with two heads that he'd paid a nickel to see.

Exhaustion weighed heavily on her, but she knew how to keep going long after common sense and every aching muscle insisted she'd gone far enough. She looked at the saddle and wondered if she would have the strength to lift it back on the horse.

"We'll rest for an hour, until sunup. Here." He handed her a blanket from the pack and took one for himself. She waited, watching what he would do so she wouldn't do the wrong thing, but all he did was spread the blanket on the ground, lay down on one end, grab the edge and roll up in it. Then he caught the end of his horse's trailing rein and wrapped it around his wrist. If the animal sensed any danger, it would warn him immediately. By the time Rebekah was wrapped in her own blanket with her own horse securely tethered to her wrist, MacDougal was snoring softly. She only had time to curl her lip in distaste before sleep claimed her, too.

By the time the sun peeked over the horizon, they were in the saddle again. They hadn't gone far when MacDougal drew them to a precipitous halt.

"What is it?" she asked, searching the area for a sign of what had alarmed him.

"I thought I saw something," he said, pulling a long, brass cylinder from his saddlebag. He pulled it out even longer, lifted it to his eye, and began to scan the area.

"What's that?" she asked and could have bitten her tongue when he gave her one of those shocked looks of his.

It was gone in a second, though. "A telescope. Some call it a spy glass. You can see things far away with it. Here, try it."

Rebekah took the thing gingerly, hefting its weight experimentally before lifting it to her own eye. Instantly, the world jumped toward her, and she jerked the thing away from her face with a startled cry, almost dropping it.

"Careful," MacDougal warned, but when she glanced at him, he was smiling in amusement at her reaction. His teeth shone white through his ginger beard, and she might have thought he looked attractive if she hadn't wanted to smash his spy glass right through those teeth.

Glaring at him until his smile disappeared back into his whiskers, she again lifted the glass to her eye carefully this time, so the world's jumping wouldn't surprise her so much. This time she didn't start, but she couldn't help gasping to see the distant ridges zooming in so close she could count the rocks on them. Slowly she scanned the area as MacDougal had done, marveling at how clear everything looked, the rocks, the scrubby mesquite bushes, the browning grasses.

The Indians. She cried out again, this time in terror and panic until she jerked the glass from her eye and they disappeared.

"You saw them, did you?" MacDougal asked with maddening calmness.

"How could they be so close? They must have followed us all night!" How could they have tracked them in the dark? MacDougal had been so careful. *She* had been so careful. Surely no one would even have noticed she hadn't come back to her lodge until dawn this morning. Poor Little One Who Hunts would have awakened, looking for her to fix him something to eat, and by now he would be crying because they would have found her clothes beside the riverbank . . .

But she couldn't think of that now, not if she

wanted to live to see him again. Desperately she looked around for a place to hide, forgetting for a second that the Indians she had seen so clearly were still miles away, not even dots on the horizon.

"They aren't following us," MacDougal said, but she hardly heard him.

"We can cut through that wash," she was saying, pointing off into the distance. "And wait there until they— What did you say?"

"I said they aren't following us."

"But they must be! They're so close. They must have set out late last night and—"

"Even Comanches can't track on a moonless night," he reminded her. "It's a hunting party. Didn't you notice?"

She hadn't, of course. Reluctantly, she lifted the glass to her eye again and felt a new wave of panic as the Comanches burst into view. They didn't look at her, though, probably because they couldn't possibly have seen her with the naked eye. And they were carrying meat. It was the hunting party that had left the village a few days earlier. "We still have to make sure they don't see us," she said, annoyed that he had seen her momentary fear.

"Yeah, I was thinking maybe we could go through that wash," he said with a sly grin. "Get around them. We'll be fine unless they cut our sign, which isn't likely with the ground as hard as it is."

"We'd better get started then," she said crisply, handing him back his cursed spy glass. She turned her horse and led the way. Damn him. The days ahead with him at her side would be a trial, but she had endured much worse. And when she was home, she'd never have to see Sean MacDougal again.

They rode all that day across the sun-bleached landscape, resting every few hours so the animals wouldn't wear out and watching their back trail carefully to make sure the Indians they had seen hadn't turned to follow them. At sunset MacDougal called a halt, and they ate for the first time since that morning. Rebekah's stomach was gnawing at her, but she'd learned to ignore such minor inconveniences as hunger pangs. MacDougal seemed impervious to pangs of any sort. He didn't even act as if he were saddlesore.

When they'd eaten and it was dark, they mounted and rode for another hour to fool anyone who might have seen them making camp and planned to surprise them in the night. Certain at last that they were safe, they rolled up in their blankets for their first long rest.

Rebekah shut her eyes and instantly she was in her lodge with Little One Who Hunts beside her, snuggling his small body against her for a goodnight hug. Pain lanced her heart as she pictured his small face the way she had last seen it, angelic in sleep. For a moment she wondered if she even wanted to be free without him, then reminded herself of MacDougal's promise. Although she'd been certain at the time he made it that he was able to keep it, now she knew it for a fact. If anyone could steal her son for her and bring him out safely, MacDougal was the man. With that thought, she surrendered to sleep.

Sean shifted on the sun-baked ground, trying to find a more comfortable spot. He couldn't remember ever being so tired, and every muscle and bone in his body was screaming with exhaustion, but there was still *one* part of him ready for action even though he knew perfectly well the rest of his body couldn't possibly have followed through with it.

Damn it to hell. He'd been watching Rebekah Tate all day, watching the way that sweet little bottom bounced in the saddle and the way her strong thighs hugged the sides of her horse and imagining what it would be like to feel those thighs hugging him while he did a little bouncing of his own. It was almost enough to make a man forget all about Indians and danger. Almost. He wasn't so far gone that he'd risk his scalp for a little poontang.

No, he could wait until it was safe. Another day in the saddle should do it. Now if he could just convince a certain part of his anatomy to calm down, maybe he could get a little sleep so he'd be able to carry through with his plans for tomorrow evening.

They rode east all the next day without incident and without sighting any more Indians or Indian sign, and near evening they found the water Sean had been sure they'd encounter soon. It was nothing more than a trickle at this time of year, but the widely spaced banks—dry now and growing young trees—showed that at others times of the year it was a raging torrent.

There was more than enough water for their purposes, however, and they made a small, smokeless fire from the deadfalls beneath the willows and cottonwoods lining the banks. The willow branches concealed any hint of the fire, and they enjoyed their first cooked meal. Even though it was nothing more than boiled cornmeal, bacon, and hot coffee, Sean savored it as if it were manna from heaven.

Rebekah might have enjoyed it more if she hadn't started eating her mush with her fingers before she caught herself. MacDougal had handed her a spoon without comment, but she had felt the unfamiliar heat in her cheeks. Damn him to hell. And for the life of her, she couldn't remember exactly how to hold the spoon. Even when she copied MacDougal's technique, the thing felt awkward. Slow, too, when she thought of how quickly she could have devoured the meal with no utensils at all.

The coffee was heavenly, though. She'd forgotten how rich and black it tasted. MacDougal made it so strong she thought it might dissolve the tin cup that held it, but she drank it all anyway.

When they had eaten, she took the utensils down to the water and scrubbed them out with sand. By the time she got back, MacDougal had put out the fire and scattered all traces of it, covering the spot with dead leaves and branches. The camouflage wouldn't fool anyone who was tracking them, but at least the spot wouldn't be discovered accidentally.

"Do you want to get cleaned up before we move camp?" he asked as he watched her packing the utensils away.

She did, of course. They'd been riding for two days and a night and were covered with trail dust and sweat. Still, there was little cover here, and the thought of taking her clothes off in front of MacDougal brought back the same uneasiness she had felt that night she'd met him beside the river. "Yes, but . . ." She looked around, searching in vain for some way to create some privacy.

"If you're shy, I'll go downstream a ways," he said, a little irritably. She couldn't read his expression behind the red beard, but his brown eyes narrowed. "I could use a bath, too, you know. That'll save time anyways."

"All right," she said. Without another word, he picked up a blanket to use as a towel and headed off downstream.

Rebekah waited until he had stopped. He hadn't gone far, but he kept his back conspicuously to her as he stripped off his butternut shirt. Looking quickly away—she had no desire to see him—she snatched up her own blanket and walked a ways in the other direction. She glanced back just long enough to make sure she had gone far enough, not long enough to get a good look at him, then quickly peeled off her own clothes.

Night was coming on, and the evening breeze whipped around her, touching her in sensitive places, places she would never willingly let another human hand touch again. Her nipples puckered, but she hardly noticed. She made a habit of ignoring her body, particularly its responses to pleasant sensations. Pleasure was a dangerous lure that could make a woman weak and vulnerable if she surrendered to it. Rebekah had no intention of ever being vulnerable again.

Kneeling in the ankle-deep water, she quickly scrubbed away as much of the travel dirt as sand and elbow grease could remove, paying particular attention to the areas her horseback riding had rubbed raw, then poured handfuls of water over her to rinse.

Down river, Sean performed the same ritual, carefully keeping his back turned so she couldn't see how excited he already was. Not that he didn't sneak a peek at her now and then, just to keep his interest up. She'd moved upriver, but he could still see her plainly, even in the fading light. Her perfect body, alabaster where the sun never touched it, berry brown on her arms and face. Skin like silk.

Sean could hardly believe his luck. A white woman who'd make love with all the abandon of an Indian. She'd said herself she didn't know who the father of her son was. That meant she'd been with lots of bucks before her marriage to Liar, and *that* meant she'd had a good education. She'd probably be glad to have a white man, too. And grateful that he'd gotten her out of that hellhole of a village. It was all he could do to keep from rubbing his hands together in glee. He settled for scrubbing himself nearly raw until his flesh tingled with anticipation.

When he got back to their camp, she had already

saddled both horses. God, it was a relief to be with somebody who pulled her weight. He'd imagined this trip would be a lot harder, what with having to care for all the animals and her, too. He should have remembered what a help a well-trained squaw could be. Even better than traveling with another man, especially under the blankets at night.

He quickly loaded the mule again, and they rode off with the last rays of sunlight at their backs. They rode as long as Sean could stand the wait, then he called a halt. He thought she seemed a little surprised to be stopping so soon, but she didn't protest. In a few minutes they had the animals unsaddled again.

Rebekah figured MacDougal must be tired, which was fine with her. She could keep going as long as he did, but she wasn't going to go any farther if she didn't have to. When they had the camp ready, she noticed to her chagrin that the coffee she'd drunk at supper was going to force her to make one last trip to the edge of camp before she settled in.

"I'll be right back," she said, figuring that was enough explanation.

"I'll get your bed ready," he said to her back.

She smiled grimly. That's how white men were, always helping the helpless females. She'd have a time getting used to it again.

When she returned, the sliver of moon was casting just enough light for her to see MacDougal sitting up in his own blankets.

"Where did you put my bed?" she asked.

"Right here." His voice sounded odd, strained, but she didn't pay much attention.

"Where?" she asked, looking around but seeing nothing that looked like the darker shadow of a blanket.

"Right here, I said. By me."

She'd taken a step toward him before his tone

registered with her. She'd heard that tone before. Her heart thudded to a stop, and gooseflesh rose on her arms.

No, she told herself, she must be wrong. She was too suspicious. White men were different from savages. MacDougal would never . . .

But then she saw he wasn't wearing a shirt. The pale moonlight glinted off his naked shoulder, and when she looked lower at the legs he'd drawn up in front of him, she saw they were bare, too.

Her stomach clenched and her blood turned to ice. It couldn't be, but it was. He might be white, but he was just like the other animals who'd taken her before. That was all they ever wanted.

Fury boiled up in her, scalding her throat and her skin and her eyes. She hated him with a loathing purified by years of torment and humiliation, and the urge to kill him, to plunge a knife into his throat and feel his warm blood pouring over her hand, was nearly overwhelming.

She couldn't kill him, not any more than she could run away to escape him. If she did, she would be a woman alone in the wilderness, helpless and vulnerable. She would never get home to her father, and she would never, *ever* see her son again. Fighting would do no good, either, as she well knew. They always won in the end, and they hurt you more if you struggled. She could not resist him, and he knew it, and she despised him for it.

"Come on," he coaxed, patting the blanket next to him. "We'll have a good time, and then you'll sleep like a baby."

She could already feel herself drifting away. Her body moved only with great effort. Somehow she took another step toward him, then another, on legs that felt as dead as tree stumps.

He was smiling, or she thought he was. The

darkness turned his beard to black, and she thought she saw the flash of his teeth. It was hard to tell, though, because everything was getting hazy.

"Take off your dress," he urged when she was next to him. "It's more fun that way."

Somehow she got her arms to move, to pull the dress over her head until she stood naked. But she felt no shame, not the slightest trace of embarrassment to have someone looking at her naked body, because she wasn't in it anymore. She was someplace else, someplace secret and safe.

He held out a hand to her, but she couldn't take it, couldn't lift her arm again. Woodenly, the woman bent her knees and lowered herself to the blanket beside him. Rebekah could see what she was doing because she was watching her, watching everything that happened to her.

MacDougal rose up on his knees, too, facing her, and he put his arms around her. He tried to kiss her, but she never let them do that and she turned her face away. So he kissed her neck instead, moving his hands over her back, then down lower, down to where he shouldn't touch her.

His mouth moved, too, over her shoulder to the swell of her chest. He shouldn't do that, either, shouldn't, shouldn't, shouldn't. Someone should stop him, but nobody did, and he didn't stop himself. Instead he did other things, worse and worse, touching her in nasty places, and pretty soon Rebekah couldn't bear to watch anymore, so she drifted some more, farther away. Up to where the stars were, cold and distant, far, far away from men and their hands and their pushing and their thrusting. Away to where she was alone and no one could touch her ever again.

Chapter Three

At first Sean was too lost to know anything was wrong. She felt exactly the way he'd expected only much better, much softer, much sweeter. Oh, so sweet, he could hardly think for wanting her. He touched her everywhere, exploring the body that had haunted his dreams both waking and sleeping since he'd seen it coming toward him across the water. Wildly, he remembered every trick he'd ever heard for arousing a woman, where to touch and how to touch. Stroking, caressing, he worked to raise her to a fever pitch to match his own. Out of all her lovers, *he* would be the one whose memory alone could cause her breath to catch and her body to dew with wanting.

At first he was too busy to notice how passively she endured his kisses and caresses. At first he thought she was simply submitting, coyly allowing him to pay her the tribute she knew she deserved and to earn the passion she held in check to torment him into greater frenzy. At first.

But then he lay her down and reached between her thighs to cup the center of her wanting and to discover the secret desire even her passive response could not stop. Except he found no hint of desire, secret or otherwise. She was as dry as the earth over which they had traveled that day, and when he teased against her sensitive flesh, she didn't react, didn't flinch, didn't even sigh. In fact, her breathing was perfectly regular, as if she were *asleep*. What on earth?

Aggravated at having his best efforts unappreciated, he raised up on one elbow. "Look, if something's wrong..." he began, then stopped when he could think of nothing else to say. Having never discussed such a thing, he had no idea how to go about it.

Still she didn't respond, and her breathing didn't change. All he could hear was the slow, rhythmic inhale and exhale as if she were deep in sleep, except her eyes were wide open and... Dear God! He suddenly realized she was staring up at the sky like a dead person.

"Rebekah!" he said sharply, leaning down to see her more clearly. Still she didn't blink, and he began to panic. *"Rebekah! Rebekah Tate!"*

He practically shouted in her face, and still she didn't react. Frantic now, he grabbed her shoulders and shook them, calling her name, but she lay limp in his hands, her eyes blank and staring, until finally, in desperation, he slapped her cheek. At last she flinched, starting from the sting.

"Rebekah Tate! Can you hear me?" This time he did shout, heedless of how the sound might carry across the prairie night and what ears it might reach.

She blinked and shook her head in confusion, or perhaps it was denial. "Wha...?" she murmured vaguely, looking at him but not focusing. "Who...?"

"It's me, MacDougal. Can you hear me? Are you all right?"

Suddenly, she stiffened in his grasp and jerked

63

away, sliding across the blanket and grabbing the edge to pull it over her. Now it was Sean's turn to ask, "What?" except the question died on his lips when he saw the look on her face, the expression of naked loathing glittering from eyes so bright they seemed to be lighted from within. He felt the force of that hatred like a blow and drew back instinctively.

"What the hell's the matter with you?" he demanded.

She continued to inch away, taking the blanket with her, pulling it more tightly as she went. Slowly he began to realize she was trying to get away from him, that he repulsed her. What he couldn't understand was *why?* What had he done that was so repulsive? If she hadn't wanted him, all she had to do was say so.

He watched her uncertainly, wondering what, if anything, he should do or say. Then he saw she was shaking. Although the night was far from cold, he thought she might have gotten a chill.

"Do you want your dress?" he asked lamely.

She might not have even heard him for all the reaction she gave. While her body continued to shake, her eyes continued to stare, and Sean knew with an awful certainty that if she could, she would kill him where he stood.

Carefully, watching her all the time, he found her dress and carried it to her, offering it gingerly. "Here it is," he said softly as if he were trying to soothe a wild thing. A *dangerous* wild thing.

Her arm snaked out from the blanket, and she snatched the garment from his hands. He backed away instantly, holding his hands up to show her he meant no harm. Still she kept staring and made no move to put on her dress. Finally he became aware of his own nakedness. Feeling strangely vulnerable, he moved to where he'd left his own clothes folded

64

nearby and began to put them on, turning his back to her as he did so out of some instinctive modesty.

Only then did she move. He heard the rustling of cloth and the clacking of the beads on the leather gown as she pulled off the blanket and pulled on the dress.

When he was clothed again, he turned and found her swaddled in the blanket once more, her eyes still staring wildly as her body quaked.

"Maybe we should try to get some sleep," he offered, still speaking softly, soothingly. From the corner of his eye, he saw her saddle sitting next to his where he'd optimistically expected her to pillow her head beside his all this night. Quickly he scooped it up and deposited it beside her, then just as quickly backed away again.

Still watching her, still not certain she wouldn't do something untoward, he rolled up in his own blanket and lay back against his saddle. There he pretended to sleep, although he knew he probably wouldn't close his eyes all night, not when he thought about the murderous glare in Rebekah Tate's blue eyes. And even if he wasn't afraid for his life, his body still ached from thwarted desire so badly he wondered if he would even be able to ride tomorrow. If only he could figure out what in the hell had set her off.

After a while he heard her lay back against her saddle, and after a much longer while, the faint click of the beads of her dress fell silent as whatever ague had shook her subsided. Her breathing grew slow and steady again, and when he glanced over, he saw her eyes were finally closed.

Just when he thought it might be safe to go to sleep, he heard a strange sound, like a kitten mewing piteously. It was so faint at first that he didn't know from where it was coming. He sat up, wondering if some wild creature had wandered into the camp, and he listened intently, trying to trace the sound to its source. After a minute, he knew, although he could hardly credit his own senses. The sound was Rebekah Tate. The sound was Rebekah Tate *crying*.

For an agonizing moment, he didn't dare move. Sean MacDougal had precious little experience in dealing with a woman's tears, but even if he'd been an expert in the matter, he wouldn't have wanted to deal with Rebekah Tate's, not after what had happened tonight. But after a few minutes, as he watched her contorted face and the tears seeping out from under her tightly closed eyelids, he understood that she was asleep. She wouldn't know if he made a fool of himself.

When he could stand the noise no longer, he crept over to where she lay. Beneath the blanket, she had curled her body into a ball as if to protect herself from a blow or blows. She was shaking again, but this time from wracking sobs that were all the more terrible because they were choked back behind her tightly clenched teeth and escaped only as a thin, blood-curdling wail.

Sean watched helplessly. No one had ever comforted him, so he didn't know how to offer it himself. Although he had no idea what he had done, he was fairly certain he had somehow caused this outburst, and pride compelled him to end it somehow.

Tentatively, awkwardly, he stretched out a hand and laid it on her trembling shoulder. "It's all right now," he whispered, saying the words no one had ever said to him, not even when he would have sold his soul to hear them. "It's all right. You don't need to cry anymore."

She didn't stop, of course, at least not right away. She shuddered beneath his touch, but she didn't waken or shrug away, so he left his hand where it was, feeling her warmth through the layers of leather and cloth. Desire teased at him like the echo of a shouted summons, faint and far away, but he ignored it, slightly shocked that he could even think of that now. The wanting was part of being a man, he supposed. He just had to make sure it didn't get the better of him again.

Although God knew how he would manage it. He and Rebekah Tate would be alone on the trail for days, perhaps weeks. He'd been so certain she wouldn't mind a little roll in the hay now and then to pass the time, but he'd been dead wrong on that one.

As her sobs subsided and she settled into an uneasy sleep, Sean stared off into the night and wondered what in the hell he was going to do now.

Rebekah awoke slowly, reluctantly, to the feeble light of dawn. For some reason, her body was curled into a tight ball, her knees pressed to her chest, and she felt stiff and sore all over, as if her muscles had been tensed all night.

Carefully, deliberately, she relaxed each one and unfolded herself. Only then did she open her eyes, prepared to see the walls of her lodge around her. Instead she saw the pinkening sky of morning above her head. Memory returned like a slap in the face, suddenly and painfully, and she recalled it all, her escape with MacDougal, their furious ride across the prairie, and last night. *Last night.*

She didn't remember it all. She never did, not when she was able to drift away so she didn't have to be there, but she knew what must have happened. Had he hurt her? Was that why she felt so awful this morning? Closing her eyes against the memories, she flexed her limbs experimentally beneath the blanket and found everything in working order. She didn't even hurt down there, where it hurt when one of them forced her. In fact, the flexing had relieved even her stiffness, so now she felt no physical discomfort at all. No, the pain went much deeper. He may not have injured her body, but MacDougal had hurt her far worse: he had betrayed her trust.

She'd thought him different from the others, from the savages. White men weren't animals, or so she'd always believed, but she'd been dead wrong about that one. They were all the same, red or white. It was a good thing she'd learned it now, before she got back to civilization, so she would be on her guard. In a way MacDougal had done her a favor, although she couldn't quite feel grateful.

Listening intently, she heard the regular rhythm of his breathing and knew he still slept. Quietly she rose and stole away to the edge of their camp for a few moments of privacy, still marveling at how little discomfort she felt. If only her anguish didn't weigh on her like a lead casing around her heart, she would have been fine.

When she returned to the camp, MacDougal was sitting up in his blanket, knees pulled up, arms resting on them, just as he had been last night, and Rebekah stopped instinctively, fear surging through her before she could stop it. But he wasn't naked, nor did he look the least bit lustful. Instead he glared at her warily through bloodshot eyes.

Rebekah's own eyes felt gritty and swollen. Probably they'd been up late last night, although she would have no way of knowing. Without a word, she went to where the water skins lay, opened one, and filled her cupped hand. Carefully, with one finger, she used the liquid to bathe her aching eyes, then drank the rest, swishing it in her mouth before swallowing it. It was lukewarm and brackish, tasting of the skin, but it was all they would have until the

68

next watering place. She wanted a bath, wanted to wash away the remnants of last night, the feel of his skin against hers, but that would have to wait, too. Meanwhile, she could endure. She always had.

MacDougal continued to watch her, and she continued to ignore him. He'd want to get going as soon as possible—Rebekah had no argument with that—so she found the bag of pemmican, scooped herself a handful for breakfast, and tossed the bag over to where he sat.

Conscious of those light brown eyes on her, she ate slowly and carefully, pinching it up with her fingers the way a white woman would. Still MacDougal made no move to feed himself, and when she was finished, Rebekah forced herself to look at him at last.

Brushing the crumbs off her hands with what she hoped was disdain, she studied his face, trying to read his mood. She'd faced other men after they tried to have their way with her: the men who'd captured her, the young bucks who'd caught her unawares in the camp in those first few months before she'd learned to be careful, and the man who'd called himself her husband for the past six years. But none of them had looked at her like this. She would, she decided, make him look away first, and refused to lower her gaze.

A full minute passed, or at least it seemed like a full minute. MacDougal studied her, and she studied him back, growing more furious with each passing second. How dare he look at her? How dare he touch her? How dare he violate her? What gave him the right? What gave any man the right? She hated him, hated *them*, every member of that despicable sex. If she could, she'd kill them all, one by one, slowly, the way the Comanches did it, cutting off their . . .

"Are you all right?" he asked suddenly.

"*Ai!*" she cried in Comanche, forgetting herself in

69

her rage. She jumped to her feet. *"All right?"* she screamed. "When I was fifteen, I watched the Indians butcher half my family, then was carried off to be a Comanche slave for seven years, and when I finally get away, I have to leave my son behind, thinking I'm dead, and then you . . ." She gestured helplessly, speechless with rage and because she couldn't remember the English words to describe what he'd done to her. Perhaps she'd never even known them. Certainly, she'd never needed to know them until now.

"I didn't do anything to you," he replied just as fiercely.

She laughed bitterly. "Nothing that a Comanche warrior hadn't already done, you mean."

He flinched, but he didn't back down. "No, I mean I didn't do *anything* to you. If you hadn't passed out, maybe you'd remember."

Passed out? She hadn't . . . But she *had* gone away. Was that what it looked like, like she'd lost consciousness? Which was, of course, what really happened because she was no longer conscious of what was going on.

She stood gaping at him, not knowing what to reply. After a moment, he swore in disgust and started to get up, but he stopped abruptly and groaned.

"What's the matter?" she asked in alarm. Even though part of her wouldn't have cared if he'd died on the spot, the sensible part of her knew how important he was to her survival.

"The *matter*, Rebekah Tate, is that I really didn't do anything to you last night, and now I'm paying the price." With elaborate care, he hoisted himself to his feet and started off toward the edge of camp, walking with a decided limp and swearing under his breath at each step.

She didn't believe him, not for a minute. All men were liars. She'd lived with a man whose very name was Liar, so she knew. Yet she couldn't help thinking that if things had gone the way he'd intended last night, *she* would be the one in pain this morning.

He was gone a long time, long enough for her to get the horses saddled. She would have loaded the mule, too, but she didn't know how to do it the way MacDougal did, so she waited. While she waited, she tried to make sense of what MacDougal had said, but she couldn't.

When he returned, he wasn't limping quite as much, but he didn't seem to be in any better temper. He served himself some pemmican and ate it in silence. When he was done, he loaded the mule, then carefully obliterated any sign of their cold camp while she sat her horse patiently.

Then he mounted—gingerly, she noticed—and they rode into the rising sun. As usual, MacDougal spent the first minutes scanning the horizon, pulling out his spy glass from time to time to check on anything he thought looked suspicious. When he was finally satisfied they were alone on the prairie, he settled down some, although Rebekah couldn't relax at all because now she knew she couldn't trust him. Now she knew she had two enemies to watch for: the Comanche and MacDougal.

They'd ridden a mile with MacDougal out ahead when he pulled his horse up and let hers come alongside. She pretended indifference when he fell in beside her, but every nerve in her body had bristled to attention. He didn't speak for another few minutes, and by the time he did, Rebekah was tense enough to scream.

"What happened to you last night?" he asked.

Rebekah felt the blood boiling in her veins, but she gave him a mirthless grin. "How should I know?

You said I was unconscious."

"That's what I mean. What happened?"

She wasn't going to tell him, wasn't going to explain how she had learned to escape the Comanches even though she couldn't get away from them. She wouldn't have told *him* even if she could have explained it at all. She shrugged and stared straight ahead.

"It scared the hell out of me, I can tell you," he went on when she didn't reply. "If you hadn't been breathing, I would've thought you were dead, and when you started to cry—"

She turned on him in rage. *"Liar!* I didn't cry! I *never* cry! In seven years the Comanches never saw me cry, and you never will either!"

He was shocked. Probably no woman had ever put him in his place before. She glared at him until he looked away again, obviously uneasy.

They rode on in silence, automatically scanning the far reaches of the prairie. Suddenly a jackrabbit bounded out in front of them. Rebekah's horse shied and almost bolted, but she held him with iron hands and brought him back under control.

Beside her MacDougal was swearing, his pistol in his hand. He jammed the gun back in its holster. "Almost fired it off before I thought," he said in disgust. "Fastest way to let folks know we're in the neighborhood." The noise, as they both knew, would have traveled over the prairie for miles, drawing Indians from all directions.

Rebekah's nerves were tingling from the fright, and when she thought of how close MacDougal had come to giving them away, she shuddered. When her horse had finished dancing out his skittishness, they continued. The rising sun sent mirage puddles racing before them on the scorched ground. To the untrained eye, the landscape looked exactly the same

72

as it had the first day of their journey, miles of flat land broken by an occasional ridge or dry wash and dotted with scrubby mesquite and cactus. But Rebekah noticed the subtle changes that told her they were moving closer to home, to the part of Texas where rain fell with much more regularity, where the hills rolled gently and the river bottoms were dark and fertile, where trees grew in abundance and where she would never again hear a Comanche war cry.

MacDougal interrupted her musings. "I just need to know if that happens often and what I'm supposed to do if it happens again."

"If *what* happens often?" she asked irritably.

"If you get . . . I don't know, unconscious, or whatever you call it. Do I have to watch you don't fall off your horse or something?"

Once again the rage welled in her. She hadn't felt so much anger in years, not since the very early days when she'd first decided she would survive her captivity and knew she would have to control her fury in order to do so. "You don't have to worry about me at all so long as you keep your filthy hands off me."

His temper flared, too. "Look, I never would've put my filthy hands *on* you if I'd known you didn't want it."

"Ha!" she laughed in disgust. "You were probably just waiting for me to object so you could slap me or punch me or kick me. Is that what you wanted? It is, isn't it? That's why you're so mad this morning. You wanted me to cry, that's why you said I did, but if the Comanches couldn't make me cry, one skinny Scotsman isn't going to do it."

His eyes stared at her steadily across the space separating their horses. In the sunlight, they looked like a wolf's eyes, dangerous and cunning, and Rebekah felt a prickle of unease.

"You cried in your sleep," he told her baldly.

Had she? Was it possible? Her eyes had felt gritty this morning, and swollen. But did people really cry in their sleep? Was it even possible? And if she didn't cry when awake, what would make her cry when asleep? He was lying again. He *must* be.

But when she looked into his wolf's eyes, she knew he wasn't. "Why are you talking about this?" she demanded.

"I told you. I want to know what to expect. Damnit, I *need* to know what to expect from you. If you're going to start acting crazy—"

"I'm not crazy! I know what happens to women who're taken by the Indians. I've seen some of them, the empty eyes, the stupid stares. But that didn't happen to me. I'm just as sane as you, Scotsman, and I told you, you don't have to worry."

"Your eyes were pretty empty last night."

There it was again. Was that how she looked when she drifted away, like one of those crazy women? Was that what happened to them, they learned how to escape and then decided not to come back? But Rebekah wasn't like that. She always came back when it was over. "Just stay in your own blankets, white man, and it won't happen again."

She could have sworn his neck grew red, but it was hard to tell since he was already pretty sunburned. Even the broad-brimmed sombrero he wore couldn't completely protect his redhead's complexion.

Certain she had silenced all discussion of the matter, she rode beside him in quiet triumph for a while. Then he said, "I know what you think, but nothing happened last night. I wanted you, but I didn't want you like that, like you were dead or something."

Rebekah didn't look at him. She couldn't, especially when she felt her own neck heating up. The heat spread over her face and down her chest, and for the life of her she couldn't imagine what was causing it. She wasn't embarrassed or ashamed. She'd done nothing to be embarrassed or ashamed of. Unable to figure it out, she rode until the Texas wind had cooled her cheeks again. Only then did she realize she was waiting tensely for him to speak again. He hadn't retaken his lead position; instead he still rode beside her, sociably close.

If she wasn't careful, he would say something else she didn't want to hear. Out of desperation, she brought up a topic of her own, one she thought safe. "How long will it be until I'm home?"

"I don't know. I don't even know where you lived."

This forced her to look at him, if only to make sure he was serious.

"Then where are we going?"

"To civilization, or at least to the edge of it. To a town or a trading post. When we get there, I'll ask directions."

"To where, if you don't know where we're going?" she asked sarcastically.

He grinned, showing her his white teeth through his beard. "To where Zebulon Tate lives. I figure everybody in Texas knows, or just about."

Was it possible? How would they know? And why would anybody care where one poor farmer lived?

Her confusion amused him. "Your father is a famous man, Rebekah Tate, almost as famous as you. He used to argue with Sam Houston something fierce. Houston wanted to make peace with the Indians, give them title to their own land and keep the settlers out of it. These were the Indians in the east, you understand, the peaceful ones, not the Comanche. But your pa, along with a lot of others, didn't feel too kindly toward any redskins, no matter what tribe they belonged to. They fought Houston and they won. No Indian is ever going to own one square foot of Texas."

"They fought him? What do you mean?" she asked suspiciously, knowing he couldn't be talking about her gentle father.

"In Congress. Your pa got himself elected."

Now she knew he was lying. Her father would never have done such a thing. He would never neglect his family to go running off to . . . Then suddenly she remembered: Zebulon Tate no longer had a family. His wife and son had been murdered, his daughter carried off. He'd been left alone except for some nieces and nephews who had come to Texas with them just after the Texas victory at San Jacinto had won Texan independence from Mexico and opened the place for Anglo settlers. Rebekah didn't even know how many of her cousins had survived the raid in which she had been captured. Perhaps none of them had.

Still, she couldn't imagine her father as a politician in the new Republic of Texas.

"Who's the president now?" she asked, thinking surely Sam Houston must be long out of office.

"President of what?"

"Of Texas," she replied in annoyance.

"Nobody. There's a governor now."

She tried to make sense of this. "You mean . . . ?"

"Yes, Texas is a state now. Just happened the first of this year."

"*Just?* You mean the United States didn't take them until just now?"

"That's right, made them wait almost ten years to get into the Union. Seems they had some problems in Congress about admitting another slave state, but they finally got it settled. Mexico isn't too happy about it, though. They've been threatening war all summer."

"Mexico? What've they got to say about it?" she asked contemptuously.

"A lot, since they never really recognized Texas independence in the first place."

This was all too much for Rebekah, who had been sheltered from politics all of her adult life. "For a Sante Fe trader, you know an awful lot about it."

"It's important news in Sante Fe since the U.S. captured the city about a month ago and claimed all of New Mexico for its own. Didn't even have to fire a shot to do it, either. Seems the U.S. government figures it has a right to *everything* Mexico owns above the Rio Grande. They've sent some general named Taylor to the river. He's been sitting there all summer with his army, just waiting for the greasers to do something'd give him an excuse to cross over and start a fight."

"Another war," she sniffed. "You'd think the greasers would've learned after we whipped them the last time."

"Careful," he warned. "You're talking about my people."

"*Your* people? Don't expect me to believe you're a Mexican."

"By adoption," he said, an oddly bitter expression on his face.

"You don't look too happy about it."

The bitterness vanished, and his face grew impassive. "I have no feelings one way or the other. Besides, I guess I'm an American again, and a Texan for the first time."

"What do you mean?" she asked with a frisson of alarm.

"I mean I'm going to settle in the fair state of Texas."

This was the last thing Rebekah wanted. When this was over, she wanted Sean MacDougal as far away as he could get. "What about your business? You said you were a rich man."

"I was. I am, and I'm even richer because I sold my store. Selling it was amazingly easy, too, since the new government has lifted the tariffs that kept prices so high in Sante Fe. That's why I had to go back before I took you away. I told you I had some things to take care of."

"What are you going to do now?"

"I told you, I'm going to settle in Texas and open a store there. Take advantage of the reward you offered me for rescuing you."

"What reward?" she asked, her apprehension growing. All she could remember was some talk about the money her father had offered years ago, and MacDougal had ridiculed that.

"My new reputation, as the man who rescued Rebekah Tate." Rebekah flinched, but he didn't seem to notice. "I figure people will come from all over the state to see me, and while they're there, they'll buy something at my store. That's what I'm good at, you know, buying and selling, bartering and trading and—"

Rebekah couldn't help her snort of derision. It stopped him cold, and this time there was no doubt his neck turned red. So did the rest of his face.

"I usually do a much better job than I did trading for you," he said.

"You'd have to," she judged.

He didn't reply, and Rebekah thought she'd silenced him again. She certainly hoped she had. Then she remembered what he'd said about settling in Texas and felt renewed alarm. Texas was a big place, though. He'd want to put his store in some town, too. There wasn't a town within a hundred miles of where the Tates' stockade had been. Somewhat comforted at the thought, she didn't notice at first that he was studying her.

When she did, she flashed him a look of annoyance. "What are you staring at, white man?"

"Nothing," he said with maddening cheerfulness. "I was just thinking you still speak English awfully well for somebody who hasn't spoken it in seven years."

"I practiced," she told him without a trace of cheerfulness. "I talked to myself whenever I was alone, and I talked it to my baby after he was born. I didn't want to forget. I didn't want to come home babbling in Comanche like some squaw."

This made him frown and look away.

"What's the matter?" she demanded.

"Nothing," he said, not very convincingly, and once again she felt the prickle of alarm. No subject, it seemed, was completely safe.

"Is it me? Is it the way I talk? Can you tell . . . ?"

"No," he assured her. "It's not the way you talk."

Was he thinking about the way she ate? The difficulties she'd had handling the spoon? Heaven knew her table manners could use some improvement, and probably her other manners, too. She could hardly remember the things her mother used to tell her were proper behavior for a young lady, but she'd relearn them just as soon as she was back. If she could adapt to life as a slave in a Comanche camp, she could readapt to life in the world into which she had been born.

Meanwhile, she'd watch MacDougal more closely and pick up as much as she could. Her father would have no reason to look at her the way MacDougal had that first few days.

"It won't be easy," MacDougal said, as if reading her thoughts.

"What won't?" she scoffed, knowing he couldn't have known what she was thinking.

"Going back. Things have changed. People change. *You've* changed."

She wanted to deny it. The words trembled on her tongue, but she couldn't utter them because she knew it was true. Seven years ago she'd been an innocent child, dreaming about her cousin Andrew Nelson, a lanky boy two years older than she on whom she had a youthful crush. Back then the greatest tragedy she could imagine was not marrying Andrew when she grew up. Now she didn't even know if Andrew was still alive. God knew his mother wasn't. Her scalp had been hanging in a Comanche lodge for seven years now. And God knew—or at least He would if He really existed—that Rebekah was no longer innocent and she now understood what real tragedy was.

For a moment she tried to imagine what Andrew might be like today, a grown man scarred by the loss of his mother at the hands of savages. He'd been fond of his younger cousin, the girl who had insisted on tagging after him when they were children and who had mooned over him shamelessly when they no longer were. Perhaps they might have married if Rebekah hadn't been taken. Now, of course, it was out of the question. Rebekah had no intention of marrying anyone, and besides, there was Little One Who Hunts to consider. Few white men would want an Indian bastard for a son, and Rebekah wasn't about to give any of them a chance to reject him. And how would Andrew look at her now, knowing she'd been an Indian squaw?

MacDougal was right: it wouldn't be easy. But she wasn't going to give him the satisfaction of telling him so.

Sean took more frequent rests that day. The animals were starting to need it, and Rebekah Tate certainly did. Her face was almost gray with fatigue when they stopped for their evening meal. Even still, she didn't complain, didn't even groan when she slid from her saddle, although Sean knew every muscle in her body must be screaming in agony. And from somewhere she found the strength to unsaddle her horse and rub him down, too.

A man would certainly have realized that the animal's comfort was much more important than his own, since his life depended on the horse's ability to carry him across this barren land. Few women would have, though, and all the women Sean had known would have been far too concerned for their own comfort to worry about some beast. Rebekah Tate was like no one he had ever known, male or female, and his admiration for her was growing right along with his wariness of her as he continued to watch for more signs she might not be in her right mind.

Because they were out in the open again, they didn't risk a fire and ate a cold meal. Sean had spotted a sheltered place a few miles ahead, and when the sun had set, they rode there to camp for the night.

Some cataclysmic event eons ago had thrust a body of rocks out of the flat earth, and now they stood starkly, a darker shadow against the night sky. The two travelers spread their blankets nearby, with the rocks serving as a wind break against the relentless Texas breeze, and fell asleep instantly.

Sean awoke first in the early moments of dawn. He glanced at Rebekah Tate and was surprised to see how sweet she looked with her face relaxed in sleep, all traces of anger and wariness gone. She was, he thought again, a most beautiful woman, and he almost laughed aloud at his body's automatic response.

Swearing silently against the pull of desire, he climbed up the rocks to take a look around. Using the glass, he scanned the area for miles around and saw not one sign of human habitation. Of course, that only meant there were no large Indian villages around. A small band, out hunting or raiding, wouldn't risk a fire any more than he would. But at least he had no reason to suspect they were being followed. It was beginning to look as if he and Rebekah Tate had fooled the Comanches. Soon he'd have her safely back in her father's house.

Grinning in satisfaction at the thought, he climbed back down, making enough noise to wake his companion, or so he'd thought, but she didn't move. She must, he reasoned, have been even more exhausted than he'd thought, but he couldn't let her sleep any longer no matter how tired she was. They had to spend every moment of precious daylight traveling if they hoped to get out of Indian country with their hair.

"Hey, Rebekah Tate," he called. Her eyelids fluttered but remained closed. Chuckling, he strode over to where she lay, caught the corner of her blanket and gave it a sharp pull, rolling her over onto her stomach.

"Damn you, MacDougal!" she cried, flopping back over and thrashing angrily free of her blankets.

He caught a glimpse of naked thigh and was thinking he'd have to console himself with little things like that when she suddenly cried out in pain. That's when he saw the snake, writhing in the folds of her blanket, too tangled to even rattle a warning but not too tangled to have sunk his fangs into Rebekah Tate.

Rebekah knew in an instant what had happened. The snake must have been in the rocks during the heat of the day, and when night had cooled them, he'd come looking for another source of warmth. He'd found it in her blankets.

Now she stared at the two puncture marks just above her knee and with abject terror felt the life draining from her. How often she had prayed to die when death would have been a welcome relief, but now she had so much to live for . . .

"Don't move!" MacDougal shouted. In an instant he'd drawn a knife from his belt and plunged it into the snake, severing its head.

"Thanks," she whispered, smiling at the irony. At least he'd gotten revenge. An eye for an eye, a life for a life. Her father would have approved such justice. "Tell my father what happened. Tell him . . ." She thought frantically, trying to use the precious seconds she had left to compose a message that would tell the old man everything she wanted him to know, but seconds flew by and her mind seemed numb, unable to form any coherent thoughts.

MacDougal wasn't paying attention anyway. He was skinning the snake, cutting the skin away from the moist flesh, but she was too busy with her own problems to even wonder what pagan ritual he might be performing.

"And my son, MacDougal," she began and stopped when he sliced off a chunk of the still-quivering meat and slapped it against her wound. She watched in detached fascination as the meat turned green. It was all very interesting, but she had to finish telling him before it was too late, before the poison raced through her body and stopped her pounding heart. "Promise you'll go back for my son, MacDougal," she said desperately. "Even if I'm dead, I don't want him growing up with the Indians. Please, swear you will!"

"Shut up!" he growled. "You aren't going to die!" He tossed aside the green meat and slapped a new piece over the wound. It, too, began to change color.

"Promise me you'll take him to my father! Tell

him I want my boy raised as a white man. Tell him that's all I ever wanted. My boy is the only one of the Tates left now. You have to get him, MacDougal!"

But MacDougal was busy applying a fresh piece of meat to her leg since the second had already turned completely green. The snake was long, almost three feet, and Rebekah wondered absently if he intended to use up the whole thing or if he'd stop when she was dead.

"Why now?" she wailed in despair. "I was so close! Only a few more days and I would've been home. Maybe there is a God after all, and He's just been waiting for this moment so he could kill me when it would hurt the most!"

"A snakebit person shouldn't be blaspheming, Rebekah Tate," MacDougal warned. He discarded the green meat and applied a fresh piece. "If I were you, I'd be telling God how sorry I was for all the bad things I'd ever done."

"I'm not sorry for anything I've done," she replied, not certain if it were true but no longer caring. What did it matter? What did anything matter? She didn't believe in heaven anymore, and if there was a hell, it couldn't be worse than what she'd already endured. In fact, she could probably teach the Devil himself a little about suffering.

"Aren't you even sorry for all the mean things you've said to me?" he inquired.

"Why should I be?" she challenged. Naturally he'd think of himself at a time like this.

"Because I've just saved your life," he informed her, tossing aside yet another greenish chunk of rattlesnake and applying a fresh piece. "Did you think I cut this snake up for something to do while I wait for you to die?"

Fear had left a metallic taste in her mouth, but she swallowed it and considered his claim. She wasn't

84

dead, at least not yet. Her heart was still beating—violently, in fact—and she was still breathing and talking and thinking. How long had it been? Some people died instantly from snakebite, while others lingered for a while, feverish and comatose, but they died, too, eventually.

"I could've sucked the poison out," he was saying, "but the snake meat works better if you can catch the snake." He tossed aside still another greenish chunk of flesh and applied a new one. Even Rebekah could see they were no longer turning quite as green.

"Is that what you're doing, drawing out the poison?"

His light brown eyes flicked up and his gaze held hers for a moment. "Sure. I'm surprised you didn't learn that from the Indians."

She was surprised, too. She'd learned an awful lot about the Indians' methods of medicine, most of it superstitious foolishness but some of it quite effective, like the way they used cactus poultices to treat bullet wounds. Many Comanche warriors proudly carried the scars of wounds that should have killed them, *would* have killed them if they'd been treated by a white doctor.

But she'd never seen anyone treat a snakebite like this. By now the area around the wound should have become swollen and purplish, but it was only mildly tender to MacDougal's ministrations. She watched in grim silence as he continued to treat her until the meat no longer turned green, proving all the poison had been drawn.

At some point her heart had ceased to pound and her terror abated, leaving her strangely calm. It could have been the lethargy before death, but she didn't think so. Watching MacDougal's hands working, she had the strangest feeling that he simply wouldn't let her die, that he would keep her alive by sheer force of will, if necessary.

"Do you feel cold?" he asked when he had finished and flung the remains of the snake away.

She shook her head. She simply felt numb, like she wanted to sleep for a hundred years or until she could remember this as a bad dream. "I'd like to lay down for a while before we start, though."

His teeth flashed in a quick grin beneath his moustache. "We aren't going anywhere today, and you can't lay down, at least not for a while. Here." He moved around behind her and sat down alarmingly close, spreading his legs on either side of her.

"What are you doing?" she croaked, recoiling instinctively from his nearness.

"Not what you obviously think," he replied. "You can't lay down in case there's any poison left. We don't want it getting to your heart, so you have to sit up. Here, lean against me."

He clapped his hands on her shoulders and pulled her back against his chest, brooking no resistance. His warmth and his scent engulfed her, that horrible male muskiness she'd learned to hate, except for some reason this time she felt strangely comforted by the smell. She leaned stiffly against him, growing even more rigid when he wrapped his arms around her waist, enveloping her completely. For a second she could hardly breathe, as if someone had pressed a pillow over her mouth and was suffocating her, and the urge to shut off her mind and drift away to a safe place where no men could touch her almost overwhelmed her.

But she'd almost drifted away once already this morning, to a place from which she'd never return. If she was yet going to die, she wanted to know it, wanted to be aware of every second as her life drew to a close, so she fought the urge to escape.

"Relax," MacDougal commanded, his breath hot

on her cheek, his beard tickling her ear.

She would have fought him, would never have consented to *anything* he demanded, if she hadn't noticed something quite strange at that very instant. The arms encircling her waist were trembling. And so was the chest against which she leaned, however resentfully. And so were the legs stretched out beside hers. Reaction had set in, and he was shaking like a leaf.

"MacDougal?"

"Hmmm?"

"Were you afraid I'd die?"

"Damn right."

"Why?"

"Because you got bit by a snake," he said irritably.

"No, I mean why were you *afraid?*"

He hesitated a moment before answering, and she thought he might deny it. Most men would have. "That's a stupid question," he said at last. "Why do you think?"

She didn't know, didn't even want to guess. She'd been afraid, too, so terribly afraid that she would never see her son or her father again. What a waste, what a terrible waste to have endured for seven years just to die on her way home.

Only when MacDougal's arms tightened around her did she realize she had also begun to tremble. At some point she had relaxed, too, and was now leaning fully against him. She should have felt repulsed to be so close. Instead she felt oddly comforted. In seven long years, no other human had ever offered her comfort, not even when she'd suffered the most agonizing losses a woman could endure.

The sensation was so foreign, she didn't know what to do with it, and when her throat tightened, for a moment she panicked, thinking perhaps the poison was going to work after all. Then she noticed the strange stinging sensation behind her eyes, something she hadn't felt in so long she almost didn't recognize it for what it was.

When she did, she wanted to laugh in relief. She might have, too, except she didn't laugh, either, not anymore than she would surrender to the tears that now threatened. Swallowing the lump in her throat and blinking away the burning in her eyes, she stared straight ahead at the slowly brightening sky and the vast reaches of land over which they had just come and the vultures circling lazily in search of something dead.

Not today, she told them silently. She would not die today. Instead she would let MacDougal hold her while they both trembled, like two leaves clinging to each other for strength against the threat of the autumn wind. Together, she knew, they could survive.

"You could thank me, you know," MacDougal said after a long time, after they'd both stopped shaking and Rebekah had fallen into a light doze.

"Maybe I will later," she replied sleepily, her lips twitching into what felt like a smile. "It's a little too soon, though. I might die yet, and I wouldn't want to waste any gratitude on the likes of you, Scotsman."

He sighed against her cheek, and it felt like a caress that raised gooseflesh on her arms. She hoped he didn't notice.

"That's a relief," he said. "That snake didn't seem to have taken any of the spunk out of you. In fact I'm starting to wonder who poisoned who."

"Maybe you'd like to bite me yourself and find out," she suggested.

He chuckled, the sound like music in the barren stillness. "Not likely," he said, "although I expect you'd taste mighty sweet."

Rebekah flinched. She hadn't meant it like that, not at all. She'd forgotten lovers sometimes bit each other in the heat of passion, or at least the Indians did. She had no idea what whites did, although she was fairly certain MacDougal hadn't bitten her the other night. At least she'd found no marks.

"I reckon I owe that snake something," he went on, oblivious to her reaction. "If it hadn't been for him, I doubt I ever would've got my arms around you again."

She jerked upright, breaking his hold, and scooted forward, away from his arms and the warmth of his body.

"What's the matter?" He sounded more concerned than annoyed. Rebekah hugged herself in a vain attempt to recapture the comfort of his embrace. She was shaking again, although she could not have said from what.

"Is that all you think about?" she snapped.

"What?" he asked, genuinely puzzled, but after a moment, he figured it out. "You mean sex?"

Sex was not a word Rebekah had ever used in her brief life as a white woman. The very sound of it sent the heat rushing to her face, and she looked away, no longer able to meet his eye.

She hadn't answered his question, but she hadn't had to. He made a disgusted noise. "It didn't used to be all I thought about. In fact, I hardly spent any time on it at all until I met up with you. Now I've got to, because I'm trying to figure out why it makes you go crazy."

"I'm not crazy!" she shouted.

"Next thing to it, then, and I can't figure it out at all. It's not like you're some spinster virgin or something. You were married, for God's sake."

"I wasn't *married* to that bastard," she shrieked, "and if you ever say that again, I'll *kill* you!"

He didn't seem too frightened by the threat. In fact, his eyebrows lifted in open skepticism which only made her more furious. "You lived with him as his wife," MacDougal clarified doggedly. "Nobody made you do that, or did they?"

He wasn't going to leave her alone until she told him, so she might as well get it over with. "He bought me from the bastard who captured me because he wanted my son," she explained through clenched teeth.

"I didn't think the Comanches forced women to marry against their will."

"Which shows how much you know about it." She glared at him, but he refused to flinch, so she went on. "But you're right, they didn't force me. Going with him was the lesser of two evils."

"What was the other evil?"

Rebekah felt the bile rising in her throat as the memories came flooding back on a tide of filth. She'd blocked them for so long, she'd thought they were gone for good, but they'd only been waiting until she was too weak to resist them anymore. Images streaked across her consciousness, terrors too horrible for words, humiliations too awful to bear, unspeakable pain and torment.

She heard MacDougal's voice calling her, but he sounded far away, so she knew she was drifting, escaping from the unthinkable as she always had. She was almost gone, but MacDougal wouldn't let her go this time. His hands were on her, holding her, shaking her. His voice was shouting her name, compelling her back, and like a half-drowned person being pulled ashore at the very last second, she gasped and sputtered to consciousness.

His wolf's eyes were mere inches from hers, his red hair and beard a fiery halo around them as if he peered at her through fire. *"What was the other evil?"*

he demanded, and she knew she must reply.

"The other evil was *everyone*." Her voice broke, but she choked the rest of it out, even though each word was like a shard of glass tearing at her throat. "The other men, at least. If any of them caught me alone someplace, they would force me, and I had no recourse because I was just a slave. But if I married, I'd be safe from them. Only one man could have me then."

She felt sick, so sick she thought she might die, and she thought maybe the snakebite was working after all. But she didn't die because MacDougal was holding her, his arms like iron bands wrapped around her so she couldn't shake even though she was trembling violently.

He stroked her chopped-off hair and said things she couldn't hear because his heart was thundering in her ears, drowning out his words. She didn't want him to hold her, didn't want him to be stronger than she, but she needed his strength, and miraculously his strength drove the other demons away until all the awful faces disappeared and they were alone again on the windswept prairie.

She must have slept then because the next thing she knew, she smelled coffee and MacDougal was shaking her awake and telling her to drink some of it. She did, and it tasted wonderful. It was half gone before she realized something very important.

"You built a fire!"

"A little one. Out of buffalo chips. It hardly made any smoke at all."

The prairie was littered with the dried droppings of the shaggy beasts that roamed the western reaches, although she and MacDougal had seen few so far in their travels. The animals' droppings provided fuel for the inhabitants of this desolate land, however, even when the animals themselves had migrated to distant parts.

She frowned at MacDougal. "You shouldn't have taken the chance, though. If somebody saw the smoke—"

"I told you, there wasn't much. Besides, we'll move on at nightfall like we usually do. You should be feeling well enough to travel a few miles by then."

"I'm well enough now," she insisted, feeling the familiar fear at the thought of being overrun by savages.

"Better eat something first." He'd prepared her a bowl of cornmeal with slivers of jerky in it.

The delicious smell made her remember she hadn't eaten at all today, having been distracted from any thought of breakfast by her encounter with the rattlesnake. As she maneuvered the awkward spoon, she thought of what had transpired so far today. She'd looked death in the face, and MacDougal had snatched her from its very jaws, but even more, she'd allowed MacDougal to see inside her soul, into the horrible blackness that haunted her. He should have been revolted. Anyone would have been. Instead he'd held her and soothed her and saved her once again.

And as a result something had changed between them. They were no longer strangers, but it was more than that, although she could not have said what. It was in the way he spoke to her and in the way she spoke back to him. Where once they had been careful with each other, now they were at ease. More than that, they shared an intimacy Rebekah had never felt with anyone, particularly not with other men who had taken her body, not even with the one who'd considered himself her husband.

She had no name for what she felt toward MacDougal, but she felt it, just as she knew he did, too. The strangeness of it colored even the ordinary words they said as they broke camp and rode on, painting their speech with a strange glow, like a new dawn.

That was why, when they'd ridden for a while, Rebekah knew it was time to say the words she hadn't yet said to him. She looked over at where he rode beside her, waiting until she'd caught his attention. "Thank you, MacDougal."

He didn't ask what for. He didn't say anything at all, but Rebekah knew he was smiling underneath his mustache.

Chapter Four

The next few days passed in a comfortable routine, at least for Rebekah. The soreness in her leg gradually eased until she could actually forget how close death had come. She and MacDougal worked well together, traveling, making camp, preparing food, caring for the animals. They had gotten so used to each other, they hardly even needed to speak anymore, and to Rebekah's great relief, he no longer seemed sexually interested in her either. The way he treated her, he might have been traveling with another male. For the first time since she could remember, Rebekah actually began to feel comfortable with a man.

Even the dreams stopped. In the early days of the trip, as she'd always done when she was disturbed or nervous about something, she'd dreamed about the raid, her family and friends' deaths, and her own fate afterwards, the things she never allowed herself to remember in the light of day. But for several nights now, she'd had no dreams at all, or at least none she remembered. Perhaps, she reasoned, she was simply too exhausted from the constant riding.

As they lay in their blankets that night, Rebekah stared up at the stars and the crescent moon, and listened to the familiar sound of the horses chomping on the summer-dried grass. They'd found water again late that afternoon, and they'd stopped to bathe and wash their cooking utensils. Now, hours later, after another ride through the darkness to a new spot for camping, Rebekah allowed herself to feel a small measure of contentment.

As if sharing her feelings, MacDougal said, "We'll probably be coming to a settlement soon. Another day or two, I figure. We should be watching for smoke."

She, too, had seen the changes in the landscape. As if they'd crossed some invisible barrier, suddenly the level plains were giving way to gently rolling hills, and the vegetation was growing lusher. They'd even seen a few straggling trees, which meant the land here received enough rainfall to allow farming.

But Rebekah didn't think she was quite ready to see other people just yet. "People won't have settled out this far, will they?"

"Not if they're smart, but there'll be some traders set up to deal with the Indians, maybe even a fort, or at least that's what I was told back in Sante Fe by some men who should know. We can stop in for supplies, maybe even trade in our horses for some fresh ones, though I hate to do it. Those crooks'll probably skin me alive, knowing I don't have any choice but to deal with them."

Rebekah smiled at his dismay. "I thought that's what you liked, dickering and dealing."

"Not when I'm the one at a disadvantage."

"You like to have the other fellow by the short hairs, is that it?"

He simply grunted, but Rebekah knew she was right. MacDougal always liked to come out ahead. A few days ago, she would have derided him for it, but now she was glad to have a man like that beside her.

With a lesser man she might be lying dead some-where this night, her bones picked clean by the scavengers, and no one would ever have known what became of Rebekah Tate.

She stared up at the night sky until her eyes closed and sleep settled over her like a feather comforter. When she woke up a long time later, it was still dark and she was lying on the buffalo robes in her lodge again, all comfortable against the nighttime chill, and Little One Who Hunts was beside her. She loved him so much she wanted to cry, but of course she'd forgotten how to cry, so she simply reached for him to pull his small body close to hers.

It felt wonderful to hold him again. The warmth from his body heated her blood, so she felt vibrant and alive, her heart pounding with happiness. Except the body next to hers wasn't small anymore. It was as big as hers or bigger, and the warmth suffusing her changed dramatically, touching her breasts and her belly with a fire that didn't burn but left her wanting.

Then she knew it was a dream, a dream she'd had before. She wasn't in her lodge and Little One Who Hunts wasn't here, anymore than the man's body she felt beside her was there. It wasn't a man at all, because she wanted it to hold her and she never wanted a man to hold her. She wanted to press the aching, burning parts of her against it, against its solid strength, but when she did, the flames only burned hotter, searing and throbbing until her whole body vibrated with need.

Her nipples strained with agony, and the fire in her belly roared, but when she tried to tighten her hold on whoever was beside her, he was gone and she was alone. *No!* she moaned, wanting him back, whatever he had been. Only he could soothe this aching. Only he could make it stop. But he wouldn't.

She knew it, because he never had before. He always left her like this, and she would awaken with the same aching need. She would carry it for days, feeling raw and edgy, longing and yearning for something she couldn't have.

No, please, she begged, reaching, reaching.

And then he was there, filling her arms again, holding her close, his weight crushing her. But she didn't care because he was touching her, touching her breasts and her belly and her throat and her thighs and everywhere the fire burned and other places, too, until her whole body blazed with wanting.

With wanting *him*, whoever he was, whatever he was, her ghost lover, the man who had always eluded her and left her empty. But this time he wouldn't leave. This time, he was hers, fully and completely. She looked up into his face and saw that he, too, was wreathed in flame, the red of his hair and the red of his beard, and even his wolf's eyes smoldered, and she knew who he was but she didn't care. She only wanted and needed.

"Please," she whispered again, not knowing for what she pleaded but certain only he could give it.

And he gave, filling her aching emptiness, filling *her*, fuller and fuller until she thought her heart would burst from the sheer joy of having, and then it did, and the convulsion rocked her, sending wave after wave of ecstasy flooding her body, drowning her senses, drowning *her* in rapture too great for any human to endure. She would die of it, she knew, or perhaps she was already dead and this was the heavenly bliss of which her father had always preached except no one could possibly bear such pure pleasure for eternity.

Indeed, it was already fading. The aftershocks rippling through her were each less violent than the last until they faded into a simple, golden glow that would have enveloped her in its rapturous warmth if something else hadn't suddenly started shaking her and far less pleasantly this time.

"Rebekah Tate!"

She knew that voice and responded instinctively to the summons, opening her eyes to see his wolf's eyes and his fiery hair in the feeble light of dawn, and just as instinctively she knew what he had done to her.

"No!" she cried in horror, lashing out at him with all her strength. The blow sent him sprawling backwards with a grunt of pain, and Rebekah scrambled upright, throwing off the blanket, ready to hit him again. But throwing off the blanket had been a mistake because her dress was rucked up around her waist, completely exposing her, so she had to struggle frantically to cover herself again.

Only when her skirt was in its proper place once more did she dare look over at him, and she found MacDougal sitting on the ground, glaring at her through sleepy eyes while he rubbed his rib cage. "What's the matter with you?" he inquired grumpily.

"What do you think is the matter with me after what you just did?" she demanded.

"All I just did was wake you up, which I can see now was a mistake, but I didn't really have much choice because you were making enough noise to attract the whole Comanche nation. That must've been a hell of a dream," he added, rubbing his ribs again.

"Liar!" she cried, jumping to her feet. "You were . . . you were attacking me! I should cut your heart out!"

"*Attacking* you?" he echoed incredulously. "I was sound asleep, minding my own business, all the way over there," he pointed to where his blankets lay, "and you started moaning and groaning and . . ."

His voice trailed off and his eyes narrowed speculatively. "Just what do you think I was doing to you?"

Rebekah opened her mouth to say something contemptuous, but then she recalled the burning and the wanting and . . . Oh, God! She remembered the excruciating pleasure, too! Her stomach dropped as if she'd fallen from a great height, and her heart lurched up to her throat and the burning was now in her face. "You . . . know . . ." she stammered, mortified.

"No, as a matter of fact, I don't," he replied. "You said I was 'attacking' you, which would explain why you punched me when I tried to wake you up, but from the way you were moaning . . ." He considered the problem for a moment. "When you said 'attacking,' what exactly did you mean?"

Rebekah refused to answer, refused to give him the satisfaction of making her say it aloud.

But her stubborn silence didn't seem to bother him. Quite the contrary, it seemed to amuse him. "Did you think I was trying to make love to you, Rebekah Tate?"

Make Love. Those words didn't sound as if they could describe anything men and women did together in the dark, or at least anything with which she was familiar. "What does that mean?"

He seemed genuinely surprised at the question and more than a little disconcerted. "Uh, well, you know," he stammered, plainly at a loss. "When a man and a woman . . . come together . . ." He gestured vaguely toward his male part, and Rebekah's blood ran cold.

"No!" she cried, hugging herself and dropping back down to her blankets. That was most definitely not what had just happened to her! She'd endured

99

that act more times than she cared to remember and never experienced one moment's pleasure from it. She'd certainly never experienced the kind of pleasure she had just now, or at least the kind of pleasure she thought she'd experienced just now. It couldn't possibly be the same thing. "No, not *that*," she denied emphatically.

But MacDougal was nodding with infuriating assurance. "Oh, yes, Rebekah Tate, I think so. I think you were dreaming you were making love, and from what I heard, you were having a good time, too. Or should I say *we* were having a good time. It *was* me you said was 'attacking' you, wasn't it?"

Was it true? Could it have all been just a dream? Rebekah was so mortified, she thought she might actually go up in smoke. "Shut your filthy mouth! I hate you, MacDougal," she told him through gritted teeth.

"Why?" he inquired, not bothering to hide his amusement. "Because I didn't really make love to you? Knowing you, I'd expect you'd be grateful. I guess it's like they say, 'How sharper than a serpent's tooth . . .'"

Well, she *was* grateful, or at least relieved. Or at least she thought she was. But, "What does that rattler have to do with any of this?" she demanded, thoroughly confused and even more angry to be so.

For a second, MacDougal looked confused, too, but then his expression cleared. "I wasn't talking about the snake that bit you. I was quoting."

"From what? The Bible?" She remembered lots of things in the Bible about serpents.

But MacDougal was shaking his head. "From Shakespeare."

"What's that?"

"William Shakespeare. He was a playwright, from England," he added by way of explanation.

"You mean he wrote plays?"

MacDougal nodded.

"Then no wonder I never heard of him. My father always said plays were sinful."

MacDougal started rubbing his mustache, and Rebekah thought he might be covering a smile at her expense, although she couldn't imagine what he thought was so funny.

"They probably are, too, if *you're* quoting from them," she insisted.

"You may be right," he agreed with mock solemnity which made her angry with him all over again.

But they were getting off the subject. "And you never did tell me what serpents have to do with anything."

"Oh, yes," he agreed, still solemn. "The entire quote is, 'How sharper than a serpent's tooth it is to have an ungrateful child,' although it's not exactly appropriate because you're not my child, but you are ungrateful, even after all I did for you, even if it was only a dream, and—"

"Stop it!" she screamed as panic welled up in her. She jumped to her feet again, knowing she couldn't accept any of this, dream or not, because if she did . . . Well, she didn't know what would happen, but it would be terrible, of that she was certain.

In her fury, she snatched up her blanket and began to shake out the dust and dirt, making certain that it was all going right on MacDougal. MacDougal was on his feet in an instant, swearing and dodging the flying dirt. He called her a few names she'd never heard in English before and wondered how they translated into Comanche, if they did. She was beginning to realize her English vocabulary had been sadly lacking, a lack she was beginning to miss because she was in sore need of a few choice names to call Sean MacDougal.

"You . . . you . . . heathen!" she cried in retaliation, drawing on her Biblical training. "You blasphemer! You . . . you . . ." Then she remembered the worst word she'd ever known, the one the children had always giggled over, although she'd never quite understood why. "You *whoremonger!*"

He started at this and even stopped trying to brush the dirt out of his hair and beard. He stared at her for a long moment, and just when she'd begun to believe she'd delivered the ultimate insult, he started to laugh.

To her horror, he not only laughed, he whooped, doubling over with it until she slashed at him with her blanket in frustration and knocked him over completely. He didn't seem to mind though, because he just rolled around on the ground for a while, howling.

Rebekah watched him in helpless fury for a few minutes until finally, not knowing what else to do, she turned her back and began to break camp.

MacDougal stopped laughing after a while and began to help her, although every now and then he'd snicker as if he'd just remembered what he'd thought was so funny and couldn't help himself. Rebekah ignored him, hunkering down to devour her breakfast of pemmican with her back to him. He joined her after a moment, but she didn't deign to look at him for fear he'd be grinning over the joke she didn't get. She ate slowly, feeling his gaze upon her, so he finished before she did.

From the corner of her eye, she saw him brushing the crumbs off his hands and pushing himself to his feet again. Grateful that he was leaving again, she was totally unprepared when he reached down, clamped a hand on her shoulder, and squeezed affectionately.

"Oh, Rebekah, you're wonderful," he said, and then he was gone, striding over to pack the mule.

He was gone but his touch lingered, scorching her like a hot brand, burning where he'd touched and sending the fire racing over the rest of her like a fever. Her nipples had hardened, and she felt an odd little spasm between her legs.

Dear God, what *had* he done to her?

When she rose, she found her legs trembling and the rest of her was, too, although for the life of her she couldn't figure out why. Sean MacDougal, she decided, must be some kind of devil.

But if he was, he gave no other sign of it as they rode off that morning. He finally stopped chuckling every few minutes, too, as if the joke had worn thin or worn out. For that Rebekah was glad, but after a while she began to notice his mood had truly gone somber, and she felt her own nerves tense as she began to scan the horizon for signs of danger.

After a while, he said, "Do you see it? Off over there." He pointed, and only then she realized to what he was referring. It looked like a cloud from here, except there were no other clouds in the sky, and it was in the east. An approaching cloud would appear in the west.

"Smoke," she said in some relief. "A trading post?"

But MacDougal shook his head, and her relief died. "That's what I figured at first, but there's too much for a chimney."

As she studied the smoke, she saw what he meant. A chimney would have sent up a thin trail that would be lost on the wind. This smoke was billowing up, as if something large were burning, like a building . . .

The way the cabins had burned at the stockade the day they'd taken her. She'd been thrown over the back of a horse and tied, the stench of death and dying choking her along with the smoke that billowed up like the fires of hell.

"It's probably a small raiding party," MacDougal was saying. His voice sounded very far away, and Rebekah had to force herself back to the present. "We'll find a good spot where we can't be seen and wait it out today." He managed a grin. "We'll lose a day's travel, but we don't want to ride right into them on their way home, now do we?"

Rebekah shook her head numbly, forcing herself to breathe normally when her heart was pounding in mute terror and her lungs burned with the need to gasp, almost as if the distant smoke were suffocating her.

They probably wouldn't hurt her, she told herself. She was wearing Comanche dress and she could speak their language fluently. She could tell them she was from Coyote's band, that MacDougal had kidnapped her to be his woman.

They wouldn't kill her, but they'd kill MacDougal after they'd tortured him in unspeakable ways, and then they'd take her back. She'd be with her son again, but what would it matter because her soul would be dead. If she couldn't be free, she didn't want to be alive anymore, and if she had to live with MacDougal's death on her conscience . . . She shuddered.

"Are you all right?" he asked.

"Yes. Do you see a place where we can hide?"

He did, of course, and he led her there. There was no true cover anyplace among the gently rolling hills and sparse vegetation, but MacDougal found a spot behind one of those hills where they wouldn't be visible from riders coming from the other direction but where MacDougal could climb up and take a look every now and then to see what was going on.

They didn't risk a fire, and they kept their horses

saddled, just in case. The morning sun was hot, but Rebekah still felt chilled as her mind's eye saw things she didn't want to see.

"Who do you suppose it is?" she asked at one point late in the morning.

"I told you, just a small raiding party. We might even be able to outrun them if we have to since our horses are rested and—"

"No, I mean . . ." She gestured vaguely, not knowing what to call the ones she knew now lay slaughtered by the ruins of their home.

He understood. "I don't know."

"Traders, maybe? Would they attack a trading post?"

MacDougal shrugged. "Who knows what a Comanche would do, but my guess is no, they wouldn't. Too much risk. There'd be a lot of men inside and a lot of guns. It's probably a settler."

"Out this far?" They'd seen no signs of settlement at all.

"Who knows?" was all he said.

They waited as the sun inched its way up the sky and started its descent. Neither of them were hungry, but MacDougal made her drink some water every now and then.

At midafternoon, MacDougal crawled up the hill to take one of his periodic looks around. For a while now he'd been watching the cloud of dust that marked the passage of the Indians as they made their wild escape. After a raid, they would ride at top speed for hours and hours until their mounts threatened to collapse to put as much distance between themselves and any pursuit as possible. They'd stop for nothing, except possibly the chance to collect a few unexpected scalps along the way.

Rebekah's nerves were stretched taut at the enforced waiting while every muscle in her body ached to run and hide, even though she knew she was far safer just where she was. At least she'd thought she was safer until she heard MacDougal swearing as he scrambled back down the hill, holding his spy glass clutched to his chest.

"They're heading right toward us," he told her as she leaped to her feet.

She had one foot in her stirrup when he caught her around the waist and pulled her back. "Whoa! Not so fast! If we ride out of here, they'll see us for sure."

"Let me go!" she cried, struggling in his grasp. "I won't let them take me again, and if you try to stop me, I swear—"

She stopped when she heard the thunder of hooves and knew it was too late to run anywhere. She turned terrified eyes to MacDougal, who was already running to the mule.

He's cutting the animal loose, she thought, except he didn't. Instead, he threw the beast onto its side. It brayed loudly in protest and started thrashing its feet, but MacDougal quickly tied its jaws together, then caught the thrashing feet and bound them with a piece of rawhide.

Rebekah was shaking, her heart beating wildly against her ribs, terrified to run and terrified to stay, and the roar of the Comanche's war horses grew louder with each passing second.

"Throw your horse," MacDougal shouted, "and get down. Lay flat and for God's sake don't move!"

She couldn't move at all, not for a moment, not until MacDougal threw his own horse and shouted her name again. The next few seconds passed so slowly, Rebekah would remember them in perfect detail for the rest of her life. Somehow she forced her paralyzed body to move, and she grabbed her horse's halter. Using all her weight, she forced the animal to the ground, then tied the trailing reins around its feet

106

so it wouldn't thrash.

The first Comanche topped the hill just as she collapsed onto her horse's head. The ground shook and dust filled her nose and her mouth along with the stench of Indian. She gagged and clenched her teeth against it, closing her eyes to the flying dirt and the sight of the savages' ponies racing by, almost close enough to touch if she'd reached out her hand.

But she didn't reach out. She didn't move, didn't blink, didn't even breathe until her lungs were screaming for air and she was forced to take a gasping breath. It sounded like thunder to her ears, and only then did she realize how silent the world around her had become.

She opened her eyes a slit and saw nothing but swirling dust and open space.

"Don't move yet," MacDougal cautioned. "Give them another minute or two to get over the next rise."

At the sound of his voice, her horse shivered and tried to lift its head, but she held it fast in a white-knuckled grip. Minutes later, MacDougal had to pry her hands from the leather halter to get her to release the animal.

"They're gone," he told her over and over again before she finally heard him. "I won't let them get you, I swear it."

He put his arms around her, and for once she didn't resist, couldn't have resisted even if she'd wanted to because her whole body was numb with some mysterious cold and she desperately needed his warmth. She clung to the front of his shirt with both hands, shivering uncontrollably while he patted her back and swore over and over again that she was safe now.

The Indians wouldn't be back. She knew that, but the terror of their nearness lingered over her like a miasma that took a long time to clear. When it finally did, she shuddered again to remember how very close they had come.

"Why didn't they see us?" she asked MacDougal through chattering teeth.

"People see what they expect to see, and I figure none of them was expecting to see two unsuspecting travelers on the other side of that hill. Our horses are brown and our clothes, so we blended right in with the grass as long as we didn't move. Now if we'd been riding away, that would've been a different story."

She liked the way his voice rumbled in his chest when he talked, even if she couldn't quite bring herself to believe his words. Her father would have called what happened a miracle. He would have said God had protected them. Rebekah no longer believed in God's protection, so she was thankful she had MacDougal instead.

"How'd you get so smart, MacDougal?" she wondered aloud.

Although she couldn't see his face, she could actually feel him smiling. "I used to be a freighter along the Sante Fe Trail. You learn a lot about Indians."

He'd learned a lot about a lot of things, she mused, then remembered the dream she'd had last night and wondered if he'd learned *that*, too. She stiffened instantly, realizing she was holding onto him as if they were lovers.

He released her at once, although he frowned at her sudden withdrawal. Before he could ask her about it, she said, "Let's get out of here. It smells too much like Indian."

He didn't argue, although he did look as if he wanted to say something to her. They rode cautiously, careful not to skyline themselves on top of any hills so an Indian looking over his shoulder could catch a glimpse of them. Progress was slow, and at first Rebekah paid little attention to the direction in which they were headed. When the setting sun illuminated the horizon, though, she saw the lingering cloud of smoke dead ahead and knew where they were going.

She reined up instantly, a new kind of terror clutching at her throat, and turned accusing eyes to MacDougal.

He stopped, too, and shrugged his shoulders. "It's the safest place, the one sure place we know they won't be."

He was infuriatingly right again. Whatever the whites might fear, the Comanches never returned to the scene of a raid, recognizing the danger of doing so, but Rebekah wasn't afraid of the Comanches. "There's nothing we can do for the people," she reminded him. "They'll all be dead."

"Then we can bury them."

It was a gesture she wouldn't have expected from MacDougal, although she should have known by now not to be surprised by anything he did. "They probably have neighbors who'll do it," she offered.

"I don't think so. Look," he said, his wolf's eyes amazingly gentle, "you don't have to go in with me. I know it won't be very pleasant for you. You can go downstream and make camp and wait for me there."

The settlers had chosen a spot beside a winding stream which they'd seen even though the cabin itself—or what was left of it—wasn't in sight yet. But the thought of being alone was worse than the thought of facing what they'd find at the settlers' cabin, so Rebekah shook her head. "I'll go with you."

They rode on in silence, although MacDougal kept glancing over at her warily. Probably he was making sure she didn't drift away to her secret place, a prospect that was tempting but to which she would not surrender.

The smell of smoke carried to them, bringing with it memories Rebekah didn't want to relive, so she steeled herself against it, shutting off her emotions the way she did when things became too awful to bear.

And things at the settlers' cabin were too awful to bear. Only the house stood intact because it was just a dugout in the side of a hill fronted with lumber probably taken from a wagon. Whisps of smoke still curled from the remains of what had been a log barn and from a pile of smoldering refuse that lay in the yard, the remnants of furniture dragged from the house, no doubt. The Indians always destroyed what they couldn't take with them, and when the house wouldn't burn, they'd made a bonfire of the furnishings.

Bags of flour had been ripped open and the contents covered the ground like snow. Two bodies lay in the midst of the chaos, a man and a woman.

They looked even whiter than the white flour, their naked, untanned bodies made even paler by death except where the Indians had slashed them. It was impossible now to judge their ages. Scalpless, their faces sagged, making them seem old and sad, but they had probably been young. The woman was pregnant, or had been until the Indians had ripped the unborn child from her womb. The infant had been horribly mangled before some heartless savage had laid it across its dead mother's mutilated breast.

Rebekah thought of her own son and pain stabbed her chest like an Indian's arrow. For a moment her throat burned and her eyes stung and she almost welcomed the blessed relief that tears would bring. But they didn't come, and slowly the burning subsided.

The man had also been mutilated. The Indians

believed an enemy who had been emasculated would be no threat to them in the afterlife, so of course they had cut off his genitals along with his ears and his nose and various other parts of him. There was surprisingly little blood, which meant the mutilations had taken place after death, a small mercy, at least.

"Damn fool," MacDougal said when they'd sat their horses long enough to have seen everything. "What in the hell possessed him to settle way out here? Probably not a neighbor in a hundred miles and he goes and brings a woman, too, like he'd never even heard of Comanches. Damn fool."

MacDougal's voice quivered with fury at the dead man for getting both himself and his woman killed so needlessly. As if by taking care a man could prevent death from finding him. Rebekah knew better. "Do you think . . . ?" She swallowed at the dryness in her throat. "Could they have carried off some children?" Her heart turned to stone at the thought, but MacDougal was shaking his head.

For a second she thought he was denying it, but he said, "We'll know when we've had a look inside the house."

He started his horse, then stopped and turned back to her. "You don't have to stay here with me."

She shuddered, but she said, "You'll need help."

"There's just the two of them. The ground's too hard to dig, so I'll just collapse the dugout over them. It'll keep the varmints away from them anyways."

Rebekah looked at the woman's body spread so obscenely and cradling the remains of her child. "You'll need some help," she said again and kicked her horse into motion.

MacDougal followed. The animals protested the stench of death, but Rebekah hardly noticed it. She forced herself not to notice anything. She'd seen worse, she kept telling herself. She'd seen the women butcher an enemy warrior once, skinning him alive before cutting off everything they could cut off and letting him choke on his own manhood. These people were the lucky ones. They'd been killed by arrows before the Indians got ahold of them.

MacDougal checked out the dugout while Rebekah stood in the yard and tried to imagine what the place had been like before the massacre. Quiet and peaceful, just like now, she thought. They'd had horses in the corral which the Indians had stolen, and maybe a milk cow or two. The woman had scratched out a garden, although everything in it was dried up now. The man had planted corn and probably harvested most of it long since. Probably the crop had burned up in the barn. She knew what they'd wanted, a good life, a fresh start in a new land. The same thing her people had wanted when they'd brought her to Texas ten years ago.

Damn fools.

"No sign of any kids," MacDougal reported when he returned from the house. "Only one bed inside, or what's left of it. If they'd had a little one small enough to still sleep with them, the Comanche would've probably killed it, too. They don't like to take real little ones. They cause too much trouble."

Rebekah nodded, remembering how they'd murdered her brother because he'd been too young to carry along. The wind across the smoldering fires was scorching, but Rebekah felt cold again.

"Let's take care of them," she said. "Is there a blanket or something to wrap them?"

There wasn't, of course. The Indians had stolen all the blankets, but they'd left the feather mattress after ripping it open to scatter the feathers. Tearing this up, MacDougal fashioned a shroud for each of the stiffening bodies, leaving the child with its mother.

Together, he and Rebekah carried them into the house and laid them on the ruined bed.

Rebekah didn't look around. She didn't want to intrude on their privacy, didn't want to know anymore about these people than she already did. When they were laid out, she walked away, down to the stream to wash the smell of death from her hands while MacDougal rode his horse up to the top of the dugout and after a time was finally able to collapse the roof, creating a makeshift tomb.

When he came back, Rebekah saw his face looked unusually pale, even under his sunburn, and wondered if she looked equally shaken even though she felt completely numb.

"We should say a few words over them," he said.

"Why? They're dead. They'll never know."

MacDougal looked at her strangely. "I thought you were a preacher's daughter."

"What does that have to do with anything?"

Plainly, he wasn't sure. "I guess you don't remember much about it."

"I remember *everything!*" she cried, suddenly furious. "I remember everything that happened to me before I was captured and everything that happened after, so now I know that everything they told me before was a lie. There is no kindly Heavenly Father watching over us all, giving us each our daily bread and delivering us from evil. If there was, He wouldn't let *this* happen, now would He?" She gestured toward the ruined house where the dead now lay.

"God didn't do this, the Comanches did," he reminded her.

"But He didn't stop them, either. Do you know how many times I prayed to God after I was captured? Do you know how many times I prayed to be rescued or prayed just to die because nobody should have had

113

to live through the things I lived through? Do you?"

"I can imagine," he said, but she shook her head.

"No, you can't imagine. Nobody can imagine unless they've been through it, so don't talk to me about your God. And if you want to pray over the dead who're beyond help anyway, go right ahead, but don't expect me to join you."

He looked at her for a long time, the expression in his wolf's eyes unreadable, the wind teasing at his long hair and his fiery beard. Then he turned and walked away toward where they'd left the horses. She thought for a moment he meant to mount up and ride away. Instead he went to the mule and dug into the pack the animal carried. After some searching, he came up with a black book which Rebekah immediately recognized as a Bible.

MacDougal with a Bible? How strange, and how strange he would have chosen to carry it with him all the way from Sante Fe. Now he carried it across the yard and stopped beside the dugout. There he opened the book and began to read something that sounded vaguely familiar, something about Judgment Day when the dead shall rise and be taken up into heaven.

The words sent chills racing over her, and she could almost hear her father's voice in the deathly stillness, echoing MacDougal's. How many times had she heard him saying those same words, standing beside some grave, first back in Tennessee and then in the new country of Texas? Among countless others, they'd buried two of her sisters and one brother before they'd come here. She'd been the only Tate child left until her mother had given birth to the baby at the stockade.

Had her father read those words over the graves of her mother and brother, too? And over the others who had died in that raid? And what good had it done? What good had it ever done?

When MacDougal finished, he pulled off his sombrero and bowed his head. He was praying, she supposed, and another chill swept over her. She only wished she still believed. If she did, she'd ask MacDougal to pray for the living instead. They were the ones who needed it.

When she saw him walking back to the horses, she went there, too, and met him. She felt unutterably weary, but she had no intention of camping anywhere near this awful place, so she forced her foot up into the stirrup and mounted her horse. MacDougal led off, downstream, and as if he shared her sentiments, he didn't stop until the house was well out of sight.

Darkness had fallen by then, and MacDougal risked a fire, knowing the raiding party would be too far away by now to see it. There might be other Indians around, of course, but neither Rebekah nor MacDougal thought so. Besides, they both needed a hot meal and some warmth to chase away the chill of death.

When they'd eaten, Rebekah huddled in her blanket, holding her hands to the fire as if she were fighting a frigid December wind instead of a warm September breeze.

"They must be celebrating by now," she mused.

"Who?" MacDougal asked. He was reclining on the opposite side of the dying fire.

"The Indians. It was a perfect raid. They killed two enemies and probably didn't lose a single man. And with all the stuff they stole, they'll be rich."

MacDougal snorted derisively. "They didn't get much from that place."

"Shows what you know, MacDougal," she replied just as derisively. "An Indian don't need much to be rich. A few pots, some cornmeal, and a new blanket, and he's a king . . . Dirty, murdering savages."

115

"I know you don't have any reason to like them, but you can't really blame them for what happened back there."

She gaped at MacDougal across the fire, unable to believe her ears. *"Can't blame them?* Didn't you see what they did to those people? To that woman and her baby? To that man?"

"Those people had no right to be there," he argued. "They knew it was Indian land. They were trespassing, and they paid the price."

"And a pretty high price it was, too! Besides, who says it's Indian land. The whites have just as much right to settle here as anyone else. More."

"Why?"

"Because . . ." She hesitated. She'd never had to defend herself before, and she realized she didn't really have a reason. "Because we're white and they're savages. They're animals who'd butcher a human being and never even flinch. A white person would never do a thing like that!"

"You don't think so? You don't know much about history, then. Do you know how they used to execute people in England? Drawing and quartering? Burning them at the stake? And people would come to watch like it was a show. Not much different from the Comanches, if you ask me, except the Comanches don't kill their own kind the way the whites do."

Rebekah stared at him in horror. "Whose side are you on?"

"I'm not on any side. I'm just telling you, the Indians have a right to protect what's theirs. They were here a long time before the whites ever even heard of Texas, and it's a big country, big enough for all of you if the whites don't get too greedy."

"I should've known you'd side with them," she said in disgust. "They made you rich, didn't they, and money's the only thing you care about."

116

"Not the only thing."

"Ha!" she scoffed. "Name one other thing, except your stupid pride, of course."

"You."

Rebekah gasped, the shock as great as if someone had punched her in the stomach. She gaped at him for a long moment, waiting for him to sneer or laugh or somehow show he was just making fun of her, but he met her gaze steadily and solemnly. She felt both hot and cold, as if she wanted to slap that serious expression off his face and run away and hide all at the same time. But even as she longed to escape, her body tingled from half-remembered delights, drawing her to him in spite of everything.

Then she realized what he'd really meant. He didn't care about *her*, he only wanted her body. He wanted to climb on top of her and . . .

"No!" she screamed, jumping to her feet and clutching the blanket around her. "If you lay a hand on me, I'll kill you, MacDougal!"

To her surprise, he smiled at the threat. "It might kill me *not* to lay a hand on you, too. Have you thought of that?"

She didn't know what he was talking about. She glared at him in helpless fury.

At last he said, "Calm down. You're safe, from me at least. Now lay down and go to sleep." He threw some dirt on the fire to extinguish it, then took up his own blanket, wrapped it around him, and lay down himself.

Watching him, she felt her anger bubbling away into frustration. Realizing she looked foolish standing there in the dark glaring at a sleeping man, she adjusted her own blankets and took his advice. For a few minutes, her annoyance with him insulated her from thought, but as her weary muscles relaxed, so did her resistance, and visions of the dead they had

117

buried today shimmered before her.

She fought them, trying to drive them away, but she was too tired to resist. The dead woman rose up, cradling her mangled infant, and when she held it out, Rebekah saw it was her own child, Little One Who Hunts, beaten almost beyond recognition, but she would have known that beautiful face anywhere. She tried to scream, tried to call his name, but no sound would come out of her throat, and the woman vanished, taking Little One Who Hunts with her.

But there were many more dead to take her place, their naked bodies glowing white against the crimson slashes of their wounds. Cousin Esther, Andrew's mother, with her hair gone and her insides hanging out. Rebekah's baby brother with his head smashed. Her mother, her dear mother, mangled by a Comanche lance. They were everywhere, all around her, writhing on the ground and reaching for her, trying to pull her down, trying to make her one of them.

She tried to scream, tried to fight, but her body wouldn't move. It was as if she were stuck in molasses, unable to struggle, and the hands were pulling her down . . .

Sean wasn't really asleep. He'd been waiting, wondering if today's horrors would have any effect on her. While they'd been at the settler's cabin, she'd been in shock. He could tell from her pale face and her dilated eyes. The shock was wearing off now, and no matter what she said, he knew the sight of those people had horrified her.

Any other woman would have wept, but Rebekah Tate didn't cry. At least she didn't cry when she was awake to know about it. So Sean was waiting, and sure enough, after a while he heard that terrible mewling sound of strangled sobs.

He hesitated a moment, remembering her reaction

the last time he'd tried to wake her from a dream, but then he remembered what that dream had been about. Like it or not, admit it or not, Rebekah Tate was warming to him. It was just a matter of time now before she started wanting him when she was awake, too. And until then Sean would take care of her, whether she wanted him to or not.

Picking up his blanket and his saddle, he carried them over to where she lay and made his bed beside hers. Then he pulled her gently into his arms, blanket and all, and held her while her tears soaked his shirt and her body quaked with sobs.

He'd told her he could imagine what she had been through, but as he held her, he knew she'd been right to deny the claim. He could imagine nothing terrible enough to reduce so proud and strong a woman as Rebekah Tate to a sobbing child. Whatever horrors she had endured, he could never hope to understand. All he could do was help her forget them.

And, he swore as he stroked the golden softness of her hair and held her precious body next to his, he would do exactly that.

Chapter Five

The adobe stockade sat beside a winding stream in the middle of a barren plain that had been stripped of all vegetation that might possibly provide cover for marauding Indians. Sean and Rebekah stared down at it from the top of a hill, watching for the signs that would reveal the character of the place to them. They were careful not to skyline themselves, so the people in the fort wouldn't see them until they were ready to be seen.

"They're some of the traders I heard about in Sante Fe. They do business with the Indians," MacDougal said after they'd studied the place for a while.

Rebekah tried to picture what the place would be like inside. Would it be like the stockade where her family had lived, with barefoot children playing in the dirt? She shuddered at the thought. "Who's down there?"

"How should I know?"

"I don't want their names, MacDougal," Rebekah replied in annoyance. "I just want to know what kind of people are there. Are they settlers?"

MacDougal shook his head. "No, just crooks like me, trying to get rich off the poor savages."

She ignored his sly grin. "Will they have women

with them?"

"Women?" She knew he was thinking this over, trying to guess her reason for asking. She had no intention of explaining herself, however, so she waited. "Maybe some squaws," he said at last, then added, "to use as whores."

Rebekah had never heard the word before, but she instantly understood its meaning. Everyone thought Indian women were immoral, good for only one thing. Suddenly, she also realized what the word *whoremonger* must mean and knew why MacDougal had laughed so hard when she'd shouted it at him.

He saw the color coming to her cheeks and misunderstood the reason for it. "Men get lonely, and only that stupid sodbuster we buried the other day would be crazy enough to bring a white woman way out here. You can't blame them."

He was making excuses, but Rebekah didn't care about the why's and wherefore's of it. She was too busy thinking about what kind of place it was down there and about riding into it. The very thought made her blood run cold.

"I'm not going down there," she said after a moment.

"What?"

"I said, I'm not going down there."

MacDougal frowned at her from underneath his mustache which was getting quite long. The ends caught in the breeze and whipped around his face. "We need to get some supplies and some fresh horses," he argued. "We also need to get some directions. Somebody down there is bound to know where your father is or at least have a good idea."

"I didn't say *you* couldn't go," she explained with more patience than she felt. "I just said *I'm* not going to."

"What the hell am I supposed to do then? Ride off

121

and leave you sitting here?"

"No, I'll make camp and wait for you," she said.

"Oh, fine," he replied, far from pleased at the prospect. "And when I come back, I'll find out you've been bitten by a snake or carried off by some raiding party or—"

"I'm not going down there!" she cried, shaken by the very real dangers he'd named but even more frightened by what she might face at the stockade.

"Why the hell not?" he shouted right back.

"Because . . ." How could she explain?

"Because why?" he prodded, obviously determined to get the truth out of her.

She tried desperately to think of a plausible lie, but none came to mind. When it looked as if he was going to take hold of her and shake the truth out of her, she blurted, "I'm not going down there dressed like a squaw!"

He opened his mouth to argue, then closed it with a snap. His frown deepened as he plainly tried to think of a way to convince her she was being silly. "Nobody will think *you're* a whore," he said at last.

She gaped at him incredulously. "I've been with the Indians for seven years. What *else* would they think?"

He thought this over for a few seconds. "You'll be with me. Nobody would dare lay a finger on you."

"I know they won't because I'd kill any man who tried," she replied. "I just don't want them looking at me, thinking their filthy thoughts and talking about me behind their hands or maybe even to my face. I know the kind of men who're down there, and I won't go down there with them."

She knew he had no argument for that because she was perfectly right. Still, "I can't just ride off and leave you here alone."

"Leave me a gun and a knife. If anybody comes, I'll

122

fire off a shot. You'll be able to hear it."

They argued some more, but in the end Rebekah won because they really did need supplies and fresh horses, and short of tying her hand and foot, MacDougal wasn't going to get her anywhere near the fort.

He found her a sheltered spot not too far away where she wouldn't be visible. Then he started unsaddling her horse.

"I'm going to leave your saddle here. I don't want them to see it and guess I've got somebody with me, especially a woman," MacDougal explained. "If they get the idea I've brought a woman along, they might want to take a look at you."

This was fine with Rebekah since that was the last thing she wanted.

"I'm also going to leave most of the stuff I've got on the mule. Some of it's valuable, and I don't completely trust the honesty of whoever's down there."

"If they're traders like you, you shouldn't," Rebekah replied archly.

He didn't dignify her remark with a response, but his disgruntled glare made her smile.

"I've got some books here, too. If you get bored, you can read."

Her smile vanished. Could she still read? She wasn't sure she wanted to find out.

MacDougal made a pile of small sacks, most of which Rebekah had never seen him open during their journey. "What's in those?" she asked.

"Gold."

She gasped. "In all of them?"

He nodded. "I told you I was rich, but I probably won't even be alive if the folks down at the fort suspect I've got my fortune with me. So I'm just going to be a poor traveler. I'm leaving you most of the food, too. I won't stay long," he continued. "I'll tell them I'm in a hurry to get home and don't want to take the time. When I leave, I'll head east, like I'm going ahead with the journey, then I'll circle back for you. Watch for me."

She nodded, feeling a new kind of apprehension. When MacDougal left, she would be more alone than she had ever been in her entire life, stranded afoot in the middle of nowhere. She hugged herself against a sudden chill and resisted an insane urge to throw her arms around him. It was crazy, she knew, but for some reason she desperately wanted to feel his body pressed against hers. For reassurance, she told herself, and hugged herself more tightly.

As if sensing her need, he laid a hand on her shoulder and squeezed as he had done once before. And just as before, her body reacted instinctively. Her breath caught and that familiar heat surged through her, settling in the strangest places. For one horrible second, she actually thought she might cry, of all things, then he dropped his hand back to his side and scowled at her and said, "Rebekah Tate, if you let anything happen to you, so help me God, I'll murder you."

She blinked in surprise, then saw the twinkle in his eye and knew he was trying to lighten the moment. She managed a smile. "I'd never give you that satisfaction, MacDougal."

He nodded once, as if his faith in her had been confirmed, then mounted and rode off, leading the extra horse and the mule.

Rebekah watched him go, crawling to the top of the hill behind which she was hiding so she could see. He didn't look back, not wanting anyone who might be watching from the fort to see and wonder what he might have left behind. He sat his horse as one born to it, she thought, and she wondered for the first time where he had come from and what forces had conspired to bring them together and to this place.

Not that it mattered, of course. He wasn't important to her. He was just a man who was taking her from her old life back to her older life so she could start anew. And after he'd brought her son back, too, Sean MacDougal would disappear from her life just as suddenly as he had appeared in it. She would never have to wonder about him or think about him or see him looking at her with his light brown eyes again.

The thought should have brought relief. Instead she found it disturbing, almost as disturbing as the man himself. As she watched his figure grow smaller and smaller until she couldn't even make out the fiery red of his long hair, she told herself she was just letting the situation spook her. It was the solitude making her so morbid, not the thought of losing MacDougal for good. By the time he'd disappeared inside the fort, she'd almost convinced herself it was true.

MacDougal was wishing he was a more religious man. If he had been, he would have felt a little more confident offering up prayers for Rebekah Tate's safety. Damn, he hated leaving her alone like that. Anything could happen. All the things he'd predicted and a hundred more he didn't even want to think about. Still, if they were ever going to get where they were going, he had to find out where that was. He also needed fresh horses and some supplies, too, since the chances of finding another place to trade within a week's ride were remote at best.

As he'd expected, his approach had been noticed, and all the occupants of the stockade were waiting just inside the gate to greet him. A motley bunch they were, too. Some white men in buckskins, hunters most likely; a few Indian bucks looking dissipated from their contact with the white man and his whiskey; three Indian women, looking even more dissipated in their ragged calico dresses; and one white man in homespun who was obviously the leader of this unsightly crew.

He stepped forward, wiping his hands on the large bib apron that stretched over his round stomach. He looked like a greenhorn with his bald head and wire-rimmed glasses, but MacDougal knew the impression was false. No greenhorn could have accomplished what this man had accomplished in this place, nor could he have lasted five minutes in the company of these rough men unless he were even rougher than they.

"Welcome to Hopewell's Fort, stranger," the round man said, smiling broadly. "Josiah Hopewell, at your service." His voice was high, almost effeminate, but the pistol on his hip looked very masculine indeed.

"Thank you, sir," Sean replied, returning the smile although he was still keeping a cautious eye on the men in buckskin. "I don't suppose a man could get a drink of real whiskey around here, could he?"

"For the first white man to ride in here in over two months, I would break out champagne, if I had any," Hopewell assured him. "Since I do not, I will treat you to a taste of my personal stock. Get down and I'll have one of my boys take care of your animals."

"I'll take care of them myself, if you don't mind," MacDougal said, eyeing the "boys" warily. "I'd also like to look over your stock and see if we can work out a trade. My animals are about played out."

"So I see. I've got some fine saddle horses. You look as if you might be low on supplies, too. I'm sure we can accommodate all your needs."

Sean didn't miss the shrewd gleam in the man's eyes as he sized Sean up, and he bit back a smile. This would be enjoyable.

As they led the animals across the open area of the fort toward the corrals, Sean took in his surroundings. The place was typical of other stockades he'd seen. Made of thick adobe that formed a protective wall, the enclosure was lined inside with buildings of various sizes, all of which used the stockade as their rear walls. One large building housed Hopewell's mercantile. Another served as the livery stable. The rest were one and two-room hovels in which the various residents of the fort lived.

An hour later, Sean and Hopewell had come to what Sean considered very unsatisfactory terms over two new horses and a mule, and Sean had purchased enough foodstuffs to see him and Rebekah to the end of their journey. Sean had paid far more for everything than it was worth, but Hopewell knew he was the only game in town and charged accordingly. As a comfort, Sean reminded himself he'd at least managed to bargain Hopewell down as far as he could go.

"Transportation charges, my friend," Hopewell explained for the third time. "Everything must be hauled thousands of miles. That's what makes the merchandise so dear."

Sean nodded over the meal one of the Indian women had prepared for him. He found himself wishing Rebekah could be here to enjoy the buffalo steak and gravy with fresh biscuits. Of course, it was her choice not to be here, and he wasn't going to allow her absence to affect his own pleasure.

"How long have you had this place?" Sean asked between bites.

"Almost a year. The frontier is moving quickly, my boy. Soon we'll have a regular town here."

127

"Did you know you already had some neighbors a day and a half's ride west of here?"

Hopewell frowned. "Fellow name of Zeth and his woman. She's simpleminded, and he's crazy. Told him so myself. Going to get him and his woman killed, you mark my words."

"He already did. Comanches got them day before yesterday. We buried them."

Hopewell's shrewd eyes narrowed behind his glasses. *"We?"* he echoed curiously. "I thought you were alone, stranger."

Sean's heart went cold in his chest, but he was careful not betray his true emotions. Instead he chuckled in self-derision. "Did I say 'we'? Damn, I reckon I've been talking to my horse so long, I'm starting to think we're a couple."

Hopewell smiled politely, but Sean hadn't convinced him. He'd already questioned Sean about why he insisted on trading for two saddle horses when he could have saved a lot of money by getting only one.

"Anyway," Sean continued, "your neighbors are dead."

"Knew it would happen." He shook his head sadly, probably mourning the loss of a customer more than the loss of life. "I suppose you think we ought to get up a party and ride after the heathen bastards who did it."

But Sean was shaking his head. "You know as well as I do that they're long gone. You'd never find the ones who did it, and you might get your own scalp lifted for your trouble."

Hopewell grinned, happy to have met another sensible man. "Now what else can I get for you, stranger? Will you be wanting a bed for the night? And maybe a companion, too?" He gestured to where the three Indian women squatted against the far wall, their flat eyes staring blankly at nothing. "You can

128

have your pick or maybe you want all three."

Sean couldn't imagine any circumstances when he'd want *any* of the women, although the prospect of sleeping in a real bed was tempting. "Can't stay the night, I'm afraid. I've got some urgent business, and there's half a day of light left I can't afford to waste, much as I'd enjoy the company," he added politely.

Hopewell knew better than to ask what sort of business. Men riding alone through Indian country were seldom doing anything they liked to discuss openly.

Sean, however, was only too happy to explain himself, or at least to explain the story he had decided to tell. "I could use some information, though, if it's not too expensive."

Hopewell smiled at the jab. "As a matter of fact, most of it's free."

"My business is with a man called Zebulon Tate. Ever hear of him?"

"Who hasn't? He's made quite a name for himself, and of course everybody knows the story of how his daughter got took by the Comanche that time they raided Tate's fort."

Sean nodded solemnly, betraying nothing. "Like I said, I've got some business with him. Trouble is, I'm not sure where to find him. I was hoping you might give me an idea."

"Might be I could, but that all depends. He should be home, but since we're at war with Mexico, he might be in Austin with his fellow legislators, wringing his hands and arguing."

Sean grinned at the picture. "You don't really call all this marching up and down along the Rio Grande a war, do you? Hell, they took all of New Mexico without firing a shot." United States troops had been camped in South Texas for a year, just waiting for the Mexican army to provoke them into a fight, so far as Sean knew, without success.

"It's heating up finally. They say old Zachary Taylor is going to take Monterey, or at least try."

"I wish him luck. I wouldn't want to march an army through Mexico this time of year."

"Or any time of year," Hopewell agreed. "But all this talk isn't getting you any closer to Tate, is it?"

"No, it isn't. I think I'll try his home first, if you can give me some idea where that might be. If he's not there, they'll surely be able to tell me where to find him."

Hopewell knew exactly where Zebulon Tate's home was and gave him the sort of vague directions that had served to pilot pioneers across vast reaches of wilderness for centuries. Sean had no doubt he could ride straight to Tate's front door on the basis of Hopewell's instructions.

By then Sean had finished his meal and sipped the last of the whiskey Hopewell had provided. It wasn't the best Sean had ever drunk, but it was definitely a step above the sheep dip usually served at such outposts.

Sean leaned back in his chair and tried to think of anything he might have forgotten in the way of provisions. It might be a long time before they came upon a real town. Sean wondered if he could get Rebekah to accompany him to it when they finally did or if he'd again have to leave her hiding away for fear someone would think she was a squaw and . . .

Suddenly, Sean thought of one more purchase he needed to make.

"This might seem like a peculiar question, Hopewell, but I was wondering if you've got any dresses for sale."

Hopewell couldn't quite hide his amazement, although he made a valiant effort. "Women's dresses?" he asked. Sean nodded. "Well, now, we don't have what you'd call a big selection, but I might have something. Let's take a look."

He disappeared into a storeroom, and Sean stole a glance at the squaws. None of them had moved so much as a muscle, and if they had understood his conversation with Hopewell, they gave no indication. Sean wondered who might be outside the door listening, and figured whoever it was would report on every word exchanged. News was scarce in a place like this, and every stranger was a curiosity.

When Hopewell reappeared, he clutched two bundles of material and laid them down on the table in front of Sean. "This here is all I've got. Only things come in are what I get from the Indians, and if there's no blood on the clothes, I don't ask no questions."

Sean nodded, examining the two garments. One was made of homespun linsey-woolsey, coarse to the touch and dyed an ugly brown. The other was hardly better, although it was made of gingham and the dark blue color was at least a tiny bit more cheerful. Both garments were in need of washing and ironing, but Sean couldn't very well ask for laundry services without arousing suspicion, even if he'd had the time to spare.

He picked up the blue dress and shook it out, trying to judge its size. It would be long enough, he supposed, and wide enough, too. The fabric was in fair condition, even though he couldn't do anything to make it more attractive.

"How much for this one?" Sean asked, bracing himself for the reply. When it came, he whistled and shook his head, laying the garment back on the table.

"But you won't find a ready-made dress anywhere within two hundred miles," Hopewell protested. "And obviously, you've got a particular young lady

131

in mind to give it to. Now I think on it, I might even have a petticoat to go with it. I'll throw that in."

Sean shook his head again and made a counter-offer. The dickering had begun. In the end, Sean paid about three times what the dress and petticoat (which turned out to be a worn bit of muslin hardly worth using for a rag) were actually worth. More even than a silk gown would have cost him, but when he thought of how pleased Rebekah would be, even with a dress so ugly, he decided it was worth it.

"You're a crook, Hopewell," Sean informed the merchant as he counted out the coins to pay him.

"And you, my friend, drive a hard bargain. I am tempted to offer you a partnership in my enterprise here."

"I'm flattered, but I've got my sights set on someplace a little more civilized," Sean replied.

"Someplace near where Mr. Tate lives, perhaps," Hopewell suggested.

"Perhaps."

Hopewell studied him for a long moment, obviously trying to think of a way of obtaining some more information about his visitor without offending him. At last he said, "I hope it's good news you've got for Mr. Tate."

Sean debated, then decided he could divulge at least a part of the truth. "I may have some information about his daughter Rebekah."

"The girl's alive?" Hopewell didn't bother to hide his delight. "Have you seen her?"

"I don't want to say anything more," Sean hedged. "At least not until I've talked to Mr. Tate."

"Rebekah Tate, still alive," Hopewell mused. "Who would've believed it? She'll be a sorry case by now," he predicted. "Being with the Indians all those years. You know what they do to white women. It's a sin, but they don't know any better. Been doing the same thing for years, so I reckon it's too late to stop them."

Sean nodded, biting his tongue to keep from refuting Hopewell's theory about Rebekah's state of mind.

"Will you be going after her?" Hopewell asked, and Sean noticed his shrewdness was back.

"If it's her," Sean hedged again.

"I'd like to help," Hopewell said. "You can't just ride into a Comanche camp and take her back, you know. I've dealt with the Indians, and I could help you make a deal for her release."

"I appreciate the offer," Sean said noncommittally, knowing Hopewell had seen the same opportunity to make a name for himself that Sean had.

"You'll need scouts, too. Those boys out there are the best around. You just tell them where you want to go, and they'll take you right there."

"If I decide to go after her, I'll take you up on that," Sean promised, feeling no guilt at all for the lie. If Hopewell thought he was going to get a share of the glory for rescuing Rebekah Tate, Sean's chances of riding away from the fort unmolested and unfollowed were greatly increased.

Hopewell was full of plans which he expounded to Sean as he loaded his purchases onto his new mule and saddled his new horse.

"Maybe you ought to just go after her right now," Hopewell suggested. "I mean, no use in wasting a month or two tracking down her daddy."

"Like I said, I'm not sure it's her. I'm not even sure he'll want her back after all this time. There's a lot of things to consider."

"Like what size reward he's going to offer," Hopewell suggested slyly.

Sean nodded just as slyly. "Getting her out could be an expensive proposition what with paying her ransom and all. I doubt your scouts will work for free, either, and I want to make sure it's worth my trouble."

Obviously Hopewell thought he'd met a kindred soul. "I understand perfectly. I'll be watching for you to come back this way, stranger. Maybe you'd like to tell me your name."

Why not? Sean thought. "MacDougal," he said and shook hands with the trader.

Hopewell and his people gathered again to see Sean off on his journey. Sean could tell the others were coveting his goods. They looked like the sort who would cheerfully murder a man just for the clothes on his back, but of course such activities would never take place within the fort itself since Hopewell would be cautious about giving the place a bad name. No, if they'd targeted him, they would follow and ambush him somewhere else. He was pretty sure Hopewell would let him go unmolested, however, even though he intended to watch his back trail just in case.

With a wave and a promise to return soon, Sean left the fort, heading east even though he'd left Rebekah behind him. He'd waste the rest of the day circling back to her, but by then he'd know if anyone had followed him, and in the morning they could travel on in safety.

The time passed slowly for Rebekah. She'd spent most of it watching the fort as if by doing so she could hurry MacDougal on his way. Judging the time by the progress of the sun across the sky, she guessed he'd been in the stockade only about two hours when he rode out again, although the time had seemed to her like the better part of a day.

Even though he'd warned her he would start out in

the wrong direction, Rebekah's heart froze in her chest at the sight of him riding away without her. She'd watched until he was out of the range of the spy glass, which, for all its wonders, could not see through hills. Then she continued to watch to see if anyone followed him, but nothing stirred through the long afternoon except the buzzing insects in the brittle grass and the sun that moved inexorably across the broad Texas sky.

She was alone, more alone than she had ever been in her life. How often she had longed for just such solitude in her chaotic life. First in the crowded cabin in Tennessee where she'd grown up with too many brothers and sisters squeezed into two small rooms. Then in the stockade in Texas where so many families lived cheek by jowl, supposedly for safety although they'd learned to their sorrow that such safety was an illusion. Many times she'd wandered outside the walls of the fort, searching for some peace and quiet, only to be followed by some of her young cousins or her baby brother. What a nuisance they had seemed at the time. Now she wondered if any of them were even still alive.

Then, of course, she'd been with the Indians when to be alone meant to be free of the torment only a Comanche could administer. The first year her life had been an unrelenting series of humiliations and degradations, both large and small. Then Liar had bought her, and while the humiliations and degradations hadn't ceased, they had diminished, since only Liar and Squeaky were then allowed to torment her. Still, she'd had to be constantly on guard against a kick or a slap and braced for the constant barrage of insults Squeaky heaped on her.

And she was never allowed to be alone, not for years and years because they were afraid she'd run away. Even when they'd begun to trust her, she'd found solitude elusive since life in a Comanche camp was even more crowded than life in the stockade had been. So she should have welcomed this time when she had no need to be alert or aware of those around her, ready always to protect herself as best she could.

Instead, she felt lost and abandoned, acutely aware of her insignificance and her vulnerability in this vast barrenness. If MacDougal didn't come back for her, her choices would be to walk down to the fort and there become one of the Indian whores or else to walk away from the fort and die somewhere on the prairie. At the moment, she couldn't decide which would be a worse fate.

Overhead she saw some hawks circling, taking advantage of a current of air to swoop and soar. They looked so free, her heart ached with envy. When had she ever been free? When had she ever been able to make a decision about her own life? Even now she was at the mercy of someone else, someone she didn't like or trust, someone whom she feared might be even more dangerous than the Comanches had been.

Why she felt that way, she couldn't imagine. He'd never harmed her in any way, had never struck her, and had hardly even spoken a harsh word to her. Still she sensed he was somehow a threat to her. Since she had been with him, all the defenses she'd so carefully created to protect herself these last seven years had begun to weaken. He'd said she cried in her sleep, something she was certain she had never done before, and several times she'd almost cried while awake, too.

And then there was that dream, the one where he'd made love to her, whatever that meant. Rebekah suspected it was just a set of beautiful words to describe something she knew was sordid and ugly. Except it hadn't felt sordid and ugly. But then, it had only been a dream, too.

And, she reminded herself once again, he certainly hadn't rescued her out of the goodness of his heart. Sean MacDougal was nothing but a greedy opportunist, and he had every intention of profiting from this opportunity. She was nothing to him but a chance to make a name for himself. And he was nothing to her but a means to an end, a way to escape the horrors of hell and return to a normal life. When this trip was over and he'd brought her son back to her, he'd be gone.

And she would be alone again.

She shuddered at the thought, but before she could even wonder why, she heard a noise that sent her scrambling for the pistol MacDougal had left her.

"Rebekah Tate! Don't shoot!" MacDougal called.

She sighed with relief, lowering the gun. Her heart was pounding, but she told herself it was only the fright he'd given her. "What took you so long, MacDougal? Did you get lost?"

He came trudging around the hill, leading the animals and grinning that obnoxious grin of his. "That's a fine welcome. I could've left you here, you know. You should show a little gratitude."

"You'd never leave me," she countered. "You can't be the man who rescued Rebekah Tate without Rebekah Tate."

"Too true, I'm afraid, so I guess I'll have take you along even though you refuse to show me the proper respect. Now come and give me your opinion of my purchases."

He drew the horses and the mule up closer, offering them for her inspection.

"They must've seen you coming, MacDougal, and pegged you for a greener. I've never seen such a sorry bunch of livestock!" she said when she'd looked the animals over.

"Don't judge by appearances, my dear girl," he

137

cautioned, not noticing her flinch at the endearment. "I will allow that these are singularly ugly beasts, but I didn't select them for beauty. They are strong, healthy animals, perfectly capable of carrying us to our destination."

Rebekah blinked, wondering at the subtle change that had come over him. He seemed quite happy about something, and she didn't understand half the words he was using. Probably words he'd gotten from that heathen playwright he'd told her about.

"I hope you at least had sense enough to ride them before you bought them. If you've picked me a horse with a gait that jars my teeth loose, so help me—"

"I'm wounded that you would think me so heartless, fair lady," he said, laying a hand over his heart in a manner Rebekah found ridiculous. "Of course I rode your horse, and he has a gait so smooth, you will probably find yourself nodding off as if you were being rocked in a cradle by the hand of a loving mother."

All this cheerfulness was beginning to get on Rebekah's nerves, but she thought she knew a way to sober him. "How much did you have to pay for these plugs?"

He gave her a disapproving look and said, "Money is no object where your comfort is concerned." He started to unsaddle his horse. "And if you can't be properly grateful, I might decide not to give you the present I bought you," he added offhandedly.

Rebekah hated the way her heart lurched in her chest and her breath caught in her throat. He was only teasing. She knew that perfectly well. He hadn't bought her a present. Why would he? And even if he had, why should she care? She didn't need anything from him. She didn't need anything from anyone.

Still, she couldn't seem to control the frisson of excitement tingling along her nerve endings or the

138

way her heart was fluttering in her chest. She'd die before she'd let him know, though, so she laced her fingers tightly together and pressed them against her stomach so she wouldn't fidget impatiently.

He glanced at her once when he'd finished unsaddling his horse. Then he went to the mule and began to unload it. "Aren't you even curious about what it is?" he asked.

Suddenly she realized he was setting up camp. "Are we going to spend the night here?"

"We've only got about an hour of daylight left. I figured we might as well stay here as anywhere."

For some reason she had been looking forward to getting out of there. Maybe it was the nearness of the fort that disturbed her. Or maybe it was just MacDougal with his silliness.

"I brought you some biscuits and some cold meat," he said before she could object to his plans. "Figured you'd enjoy it for a change."

She would, of course. How long had it been since she'd eaten a biscuit? Her mouth was watering at the very thought, and she realized she hadn't eaten since he'd left her this morning.

"If that's the present you brought me, I promise to be grateful if you'll stop messing with that mule and give it to me."

"That's not it," he said, rummaging through the pack for the sack he wanted, "but I'll remember how easy you are to please."

When he'd found the sack containing the food, he tossed it to her, and she tore into it more eagerly than she knew was seemly. Still, she couldn't seem to help herself, and when her fingers closed around the first biscuit, her mouth puckered painfully in anticipation.

The biscuit was hard and cold and probably hadn't been very good even when hot and fresh, but Rebekah lifted it reverently to her lips and bit into it, savoring the bitter sourdough as it crumbled on her tongue. Memories came flooding back, her mother kneading dough and cutting out circles, showing her how to space them so she didn't waste any. The silky feel of the flour on her hands. The smell of baking bread. The taste of it warm in her mouth.

Only when she'd swallowed the dry crumbs did she realize she'd closed her eyes. When she opened them again, she saw MacDougal watching her, a strange expression in his light brown eyes.

"There's some buffalo steak in there, too," he said. "I figured we could make a meal on it."

She nodded, aware that she was making a spectacle of herself over a biscuit. Still, she took another bite before moving to the blanket upon which she had been sitting for most of the day. There she sat again and spread out the food MacDougal had brought.

The buffalo meat was no treat since she'd eaten it almost exclusively for the past seven years, but she couldn't seem to get enough of the biscuits. Only when they'd finished eating did she notice Mac-Dougal had let her eat them all.

Embarrassed, she quickly cleaned up the remnants of the meal and tried to think of some way to express her gratitude for his gift without making too much of it.

Before she could, he said, "Are you ready for your present now?"

"What?" she asked before she remembered he'd already told her the food wasn't the gift. "Oh," she murmured, even more embarrassed. "I suppose."

Her heart was fluttering again, and she felt like a fool for being excited over what was probably some trick MacDougal had thought up to annoy her. But it had been so long since anyone had given her anything, she couldn't help herself. Visions of

140

Christmases past in her father's house teased at her memory. There'd never been much, but there'd always been something, a hair ribbon or an orange, and that last year a Bible of her very own because her father had said she was almost grown up and would need it. Where was it now?

MacDougal was digging through his pack once more, and Rebekah felt her nerves tingling again. Even though she called herself a fool, she couldn't stop the reaction. At least she didn't feel the least bit like smiling back when he walked toward her grinning like an idiot. He was holding something behind his back so she couldn't see, and she was too proud to try to peek. She sat like stone, even though inside she was quivering like a leaf in a strong wind.

Still grinning, he brought his prize from behind his back and laid the bundle of cloth ceremoniously in her lap. For a moment, she couldn't imagine what it could be.

"Don't you want to look at it?" he inquired, his strong, white teeth still visible through his fiery beard.

Willing her hands not to tremble, she gingerly grasped a corner of the blue fabric between two fingers of each hand and lifted. Instantly the bundle fell open. For another instant, she couldn't quite figure out what it was, but then she did and she cried out in surprise.

"A dress!" she exclaimed, scrambling to her feet and shifting the fabric so she could hold it up full-length by the shoulders. It was probably the ugliest dress she had ever seen. The dark blue color had faded at the seams, and the material was frayed at the neck and cuffs. One of the bone buttons down the front of the bodice was missing, and even a good washing probably wouldn't remove all of the ground-in dirt, but Rebekah adored it.

"Oh, MacDougal!" she cried in delight.

"I know it's ugly," he said, frowning now, as if he might be worried she didn't like it. "But he only had two, and believe it or not, this was the prettiest. It's dirty, but I figured we could wash it downstream a ways. I got some soap . . ."

Rebekah hardly heard him. She was clutching the dress to her, trying to judge whether it would fit and running her hands over the softness of the fabric at the same time. A dress! A real, white woman's dress!

She looked up to see MacDougal staring at her again. "Get out of here!" she commanded, grabbing his arm and giving him a shove in the right direction.

"What?" he asked in outrage.

"Get out of here! I want to put it on! Go down there with the horses and turn your back. Hurry up!"

His mustache twitched as if he were smiling behind it or trying not to, but he did as she had ordered, even though he was shaking his head as he went. He kept looking back over his shoulder, too, as if he were trying to catch a glimpse of her, but she didn't make a move until he was with the animals.

"Now don't look until I tell you!" she called, and she thought she saw his shoulders shake, as if he were laughing, but she no longer cared how foolishly she was behaving.

A dress! A real dress!

"There's a petticoat, too," MacDougal called, startling her, but when she glared down at him, she saw he still had his back to her.

She looked around and saw the scrap of white fabric that had fallen free when she had shaken out the dress. It was little more than a rag, but it would serve the purpose. Quickly, with hands less than steady, she peeled off the hated buckskin gown and tossed it aside.

The "petticoat" was actually the remains of a

chemise. The well-worn muslin was soft against her skin, like a loving hand, and her body tingled in response to the almost-forgotten sensation. The dress slid easily over her head, smelling of the dust that had accumulated in its folds, but Rebekah didn't care. She didn't care that the button was missing. She didn't even care that the dress was too large and hung loose on her slender frame. Nothing about the dress itself mattered at all. What mattered was what it stood for. Her freedom. Herself.

The sleeves were full and reached all the way to her wrists. The skirt was full, gathered at the waist, and when she twirled around it flared out like the petals of a buttercup. Joy exploded inside of her, sharp and sweet, a flood of it that bubbled up past her lips with a small bark of sound.

The hoarse sound startled her, and she covered her mouth in surprise, but another escaped, then another, until she recognized the sound as laughter. And she was twirling and laughing, around and around, the joy overwhelming her, the world whizzing past until MacDougal caught her in his arms, and his arms felt so strong and the world was spinning out of control, so she clung to him desperately, still laughing because she couldn't stop, the laughter raw in her throat, an agony, yet she couldn't stop, couldn't stop.

And MacDougal held her. He was saying something, but she couldn't hear what because she was laughing too hard, laughing until the tears rolled down her face and she wasn't laughing anymore because the pain of it had made her cry and she was sobbing, sobbing out the hurt and the rage and the anguish and the fury.

And MacDougal held her, rocking her until her legs wouldn't hold her anymore, then lowering her to the blanket and lying beside her while the sobs wracked her and she thought of her brother who was dead and her mother who was dead and all the others who were dead and of her son who was so far away and the years she had lost and the things that had been done to her and she thought she might never stop crying for the pain of it all.

But of course she did stop finally, simply because she was too exhausted to cry anymore. While an occasional hiccup shook her, she lay limp in MacDougal's strong arms. She hated him for being so strong when she was so weak, but she needed his strength because she had none of her own anymore, and she was afraid that if he let her go, she would fall into a million pieces.

He'd stopped talking to her, and she missed the comforting sound of his voice even though she hadn't heard a word he'd said. At least he was still stroking her hair and cradling her against his chest. She didn't want him to let her go, but she knew he would soon, now that she'd stopped crying. He would let her go, and then she'd be alone again, so terribly alone, and she couldn't bear to be alone, not again, not yet. The thought made her shudder, and MacDougal murmured something soothing.

She had to do something to keep him with her. She knew what to do, too. She knew exactly what would make him stay with her all through the night so she wouldn't have to be alone.

She'd have to start it herself, though, because MacDougal wouldn't do it. She wasn't sure how she knew this, but she did. The only problem was that she didn't know how to. It shouldn't be hard, though. Men always wanted it. If she just let him know she was willing, surely that would be enough. Then she could drift away, and she didn't even have to be afraid because MacDougal wouldn't hurt her. He hadn't hurt her in the dream, had he?

But when she thought of the dream and that one moment of intense pleasure, she shivered.

"Do you feel cold?" MacDougal asked. "I can get another blanket."

He tried to pull away, but she wouldn't let him, couldn't let him. Instead she slipped her arms around him and held him close. He stiffened a little in surprise and went completely still when she started to caress his back, running her hands over the coarse fabric of his shirt.

Squeezing her eyes shut so she wouldn't have to see his face, she kept her hands moving, tracing the firm muscles through the shirt. It wasn't working, though, and she knew a moment of panic before she remembered what else she could do.

Finding a spot where his shirttail had pulled loose, she slipped her hand inside. The warmth of his naked flesh startled her for a second, but she forced herself to touch him, to stroke the satiny skin, and when she heard his gasp of pleasure, she knew it was working.

But only a little bit. He still held himself from her, tense and wary, and when she moved her hand around to his stomach he grabbed her wrist.

"Rebekah—" he said, but she never knew what else he intended to say because in desperation she pressed her mouth over his. This was what they always wanted, the only intimacy she could deny them, but she would grant it this time because she didn't want him to talk because if he talked he would spoil everything.

But he was too strong for her, and he pushed her away and held her away, forcing her to look at him. When she saw his face and the glitter in his wolf's eyes, she knew he wanted her, knew she had won, but he said, "Do you really want this?"

No, she thought, but she said, "Yes," because it

was the only thing she could do. "Please," she whispered, desperate now because she was afraid he would know she was lying.

Clutching at his shirt, she tried to press her mouth to his again, but he held her off. "All right, then, we'll do it right this time," he said, and in an instant he was on his feet, pulling off his shirt.

The sun was a crimson ball on the horizon, painting everything with a fiery haze and making MacDougal's hair even redder than before. The hair on his chest was red, too, and she stared at it, fascinated, as he pulled off his boots. But when he started on his pants, she closed her eyes, knowing if she saw his arousal, she might panic, and she couldn't panic, not if she wanted to keep him with her.

By the time he lay down beside her again, she was trembling even though she didn't think she was afraid.

"I know you hate to give up your beautiful gown," he was saying as his fingers worked the buttons between her breasts, "but I want to see you."

Of course, she thought. They always wanted the woman completely naked and completely vulnerable. It didn't matter, she told herself. It wouldn't make any difference because in a few minutes she wouldn't be here anyway. She didn't help him, but she didn't resist either when he pulled the dress and then the chemise over her head and even removed her moccasins.

When she was naked, she braced herself for the onslaught, but it didn't come. Instead he simply lay beside her, silent and still. The Texas breeze teased at her sensitive flesh, stirring her nipples to hardness and brushing softly against the curls on her mound, and still he didn't come to her.

At last, compelled by the suspense, she opened her

eyes a little and looked at him. He, in turn, was looking at her, his eyes caressing every inch of her, from the top of her head to the tips of her toes. Acutely aware that every inch was completely exposed to him, she should have felt humiliated. She should have felt the degradation she'd always felt when one of them violated her body.

But none of the others had ever looked at her the way MacDougal was looking at her. Instead of lustful, the expression on his face was almost worshipful, very like the way she'd seen men look when they spoke to the God in whom she no longer believed.

When that worshipful gaze had made its way back to her face, he said, " 'Thou art all fair, my love; there is no spot in thee.' "

The words sounded familiar, as if she should have heard them before, although she knew she hadn't, and they made her tremble even more.

" 'How beautiful are thy feet, O prince's daughter!' " he continued, his voice reverent. " 'The joints of thy thighs are like jewels, the work of the hands of a cunning workman. Thy navel is like a round goblet, which wanteth not liquor: thy belly is like an heap of wheat set about with lilies. Thy two breasts are like two young roes that are twins. Thy neck is a tower of ivory; thine eyes like the fishpools in Heshbon; thy nose is as the tower of Lebanon which looketh toward Damascus. Thine head upon thee is like Carmel, and the hair of thine head like purple. How fair and how pleasant art thou, O love, for delights!' "

This wasn't the way it was supposed to go. He wasn't supposed to talk to her at all, let alone talk gibberish, especially gibberish that called her his love and made her stomach knot with apprehension. She had to make him stop.

"Is that more stuff from your heathen playwright, MacDougal?" she scoffed, although her voice sounded less than steady.

He smiled slightly. "No, my love. It's from the Bible."

She knew he was lying. "There's nothing like *that* in the Bible!"

"Oh, yes, there is. In Song of Solomon. Maybe your father never let you read it."

She couldn't remember. She couldn't remember anything, because he'd reached up and now he was stroking her hair and her face with fingers as gentle as the soft Texas breeze and the touch was sending chills all over her body in spite of the lingering heat of the day.

"You really are beautiful, Rebekah Tate," he was saying. "Your hair is like spun gold when the sun hits it, and it feels as soft as silk. Your skin is soft, too, like satin." His rough fingertips brushed her cheek, and her breath caught in her throat. "Your lips are luscious, too, except I don't think anyone has ever taken the time to teach you how to kiss properly."

She opened her mouth to tell him she didn't want to know how to kiss at all, but just as she did, he ran his thumb across her lower lip, making her gasp at the intense pleasure the simple action caused. Then he traced her mouth all the way around, around and around, until her lips tingled and throbbed and seemed to swell and her breath came in tiny pants.

And just when she couldn't stand it another second, he pressed his mouth against the throbbing, but only for a instant, as if he were drinking and had taken just a tiny sip. Then he took another, and another, little nibbles that did nothing to relieve the ache, so she arched her neck, offering her mouth to him, silently pleading with him to take it completely, except she wasn't so silent because soft little

148

sounds whimpered past her hungry mouth, entreating him.

But still he wouldn't come, so in desperation she reached for him, clasping her arms around his neck and pulling his mouth to hers. This time he surrendered, covering her lips with his own, devouring her, but if she'd thought his kiss would end the wanting, she was very wrong because it only made the wanting worse. The more he kissed her, the more she wanted him to kiss her. She didn't even mind when his tongue swept over her lips, then plunged into her mouth to tangle with her own. She loved the taste of him, so different yet somehow familiar, as if she'd been waiting for him all her life.

They kissed for a long time, until Rebekah could hardly breathe and she thought her heart might burst from her chest. When he finally raised his lips from hers, they were both gasping for air, and she noticed irrelevantly that his beard was tickling her face.

Now he would take her, she thought, and she didn't really care except she didn't want it to be over quite yet, not until . . . Well, until something else happened, although she didn't know what.

He didn't take her, though. Instead he pressed his mouth to her throat and began to nibble, as if he were tasting her flesh and finding it delicious. His mouth found the sensitive spot behind her ear and the delicate lobe itself and the place at the base of her throat where her pulse was beating wildly.

But he didn't stop there. Oh, no, he went on, his beard like a third hand, caressing her along with his mouth while his palms stroked her sides, up and down, up and down, almost tickling but not quite so that her skin tingled but she didn't want to draw away.

At last he'd worked his way down to the swell of her breasts. He slipped one arm beneath her, forcing her to arch her back while his other hand cupped a breast.

"'His left hand should be under my head, and his right hand should embrace me,'" he murmured against her skin. "'Thy breasts are like clusters of grapes.'"

He took one puckered tip into his mouth and suckled gently, sending a jolt of pleasure zinging through her. She cried out in surprise and the sound became a moan as his avid mouth continued to work and his hand kneaded and teased and tormented and wave after wave of pleasure washed over her.

Vaguely she realized her body had passed out of her control but she no longer cared. She would let MacDougal control it now. She would let him do whatever he wanted. There was still time for her to drift away, and she would, too, in a moment, before he entered her, before he took her, so that even when he had her body, he wouldn't have her soul. But not just yet. Not just yet.

His hands were magic, weaving spells wherever he touched, and he touched her everywhere. His lips left a trail of stinging kisses across her belly, stopping only to dip into the goblet of her navel as if he would taste the wine he'd said was there. And as his mouth moved down, his hands were moving up, stroking her thighs, sliding between them, finding the sensitive spots and sending shivers racing over her until she instinctively opened her legs to him, opened herself to him.

Even still, she started when he touched her womanhood but not because she wanted to escape his touch. Oh, no, she didn't want to escape at all. She wanted him to touch her again and again, and he did, his fingers exploring the warm, moist center of her, his soothing strokes igniting burning needs even stronger than her need to have him kiss her, stronger than her need for food or water or even air.

"Do you want me, beloved?" he whispered.

"Yes," she breathed, and this time her answer was not a lie. She inhaled the sweet scent of him, drawing it in as she longed to draw all of him inside her body.

"Tell me, love. Tell me you want me."

She couldn't, of course. She didn't know how. Instead, she whispered, "Please," desperate now for the ending, whatever that might bring.

At last he came, moving over her, his body warm and hard along the length of hers, his manhood even harder, prodding against the ache he had created. She opened to him, lifting herself, offering him sanctuary, and she sighed, mingling her sigh with his when he entered her, filling her with his strength.

"Yes," she said or thought she did in the instant before his mouth closed over hers, shutting off speech. Then she locked her arms around him, holding him to her as if she could take him completely into herself.

But relief didn't come. Oh, no, instead the need grew more intense with each stroking thrust until she felt as if she were standing on the edge of an abyss, teetering, but afraid to fall, afraid to surrender to the tempting, beckoning oblivion because if she did, she knew she would lose a part of herself and she had so little of herself left.

No, she thought. *I can't!* And even as the blissful oblivion beckoned, she drew away, closing her eyes to drift off into the other oblivion where she knew she would be safe. Slowly, reluctantly, she relinquished her body and all the tantalizing sensations coursing through it.

"No!"

She heard the cry from far away and someone calling her name, calling her back.

"Damn you, Rebekah Tate! Come back here!

Don't you dare do this or so help me God, I'll wring that beautiful neck! Rebekah Tate!"

He was shaking her now, slapping her cheeks, not hard but making them sting, ordering her to open her eyes until she could no longer resist. But when she did open her eyes she wanted to close them again because MacDougal's face was only inches from her own, his wolf's eyes terrible in the dying sunlight.

"Look at me!" he commanded when she tried to shut him out again, and she was afraid to refuse even though he was too close and everything was so real she didn't think she could bear it.

And MacDougal was inside her, pushing and pushing, but it felt so wonderful, just like her dream, and after a moment she realized she could surrender to the sensations instead, to the raw pleasure washing over her and over her, and she wouldn't have to think at all. So she did surrender, immersing herself in the billowing passions, and soon she was teetering on the brink again, clinging and clawing at him to keep from falling, even though she wanted to fall, wanted to drown, wanted to plunge into the rapture she knew was waiting, but she was so afraid.

Then MacDougal called her name and called her his love and drove her over the edge, plunging her into the swirling maelstrom of ecstasy. The spasms shook her to the very soul she had protected for so long, and she knew she was lost, completely lost, but she simply didn't care.

Chapter Six

Sean looked down into Rebekah Tate's sleeping face and knew he'd never seen a more beautiful woman. He'd been holding her now for a long time, afraid to move, almost afraid to breathe lest he disturb her. Now the breeze had turned cooler with the coming night and would soon chill their naked bodies. So, with great care and even greater reluctance, Sean released her to fetch the other blanket to spread over them.

She murmured a protest but did not waken, and when Sean returned with the other blanket, he hesitated, taking one last look at the body that had just given him the greatest pleasure he had ever known.

He'd lied when he'd said she had no mark on her. Although her creamy flesh was gorgeous, it was also marred here and there by scars from old wounds, burns and cuts and God-only-knew what. Sean didn't even want to imagine how those wounds had been inflicted or the pain they had caused her. Besides, these scars weren't the ones that mattered. The important ones were the scars on her soul, the ones that had made her afraid to feel either pain or pleasure anymore.

Only when he'd seen her laughing and crying a little while ago had he begun to understand how very real her fears were. Sean suspected that if she ever really allowed herself to feel the anguish of the past seven years, it might destroy her.

So Sean would simply not let her feel it. From now on, she was his, and he would protect her, and she would never have to be afraid again.

He smiled at the thought. The task would have its rewards, too, he decided, admiring the gentle curve of her full breasts with their pink tips, now puckered from the touch of the evening air, and the long slender legs that had so recently been wrapped around his own. Just remembering her passion stirred renewed desire so that he wanted her all over again, and he shook his head at his foolishness. Quickly he covered her before his imagination could run completely wild, then he slid into the makeshift bed beside her.

Drawn by his warmth, she curled into his side, sighing contentedly when he took her silken length into his arms again. Yes, Rebekah Tate, this is where you belong, he thought with a shaky sigh, stroking the golden hair off her forehead, then pressing his lips to the soft flesh. Her fair lashes made tiny fans against her sun-darkened cheeks, and he thought of how blue her eyes had looked in that instant when her body had convulsed in climax, how blue and how surprised.

Well, Sean MacDougal had lots more surprises in store for her since he intended to spend the rest of his life with her.

The thought startled him, but when he examined it more closely, he realized it was true and wondered if what he felt for Rebekah Tate might be love. He'd never been in love before, wasn't even sure what love was or even if it existed. He did know that he respected her and admired her and lusted after her, and hell, he even liked her, at least most of the time. She would be a challenge, but Sean MacDougal enjoyed challenges. The rest of his life promised to be very interesting indeed.

This time when Rebekah woke up in the dawn light and felt the warmth beside her, she knew it wasn't a dream. She knew who her phantom lover was and even why he was there. He was there because she'd wanted him there, because she hadn't wanted to be alone and so she'd bartered her body for the comfort of his.

Except the trade hadn't gone exactly the way she'd expected, and she shivered at the memories of his hands and his lips on her and the mind-numbing pleasure that had consumed her. Dear God, her dream hadn't been a dream at all but rather a portent of things to come. MacDougal really had made her feel things she'd never believed she could feel. He'd made her laugh and made her cry, and worst of all, he'd made her lose control. He'd brought her back from her safe place, forced her to feel emotion, and now she knew why she'd feared him right from the first moment she'd seen him. He was the most dangerous man she had ever known.

And now she hated him, too, because he'd seen her weakness and proved he was stronger than she, because he'd looked into her eyes at *that* moment and known what was happening to her and known he was responsible. She would never forgive him, not as long as she lived, and she would hate him for much longer.

Only when she felt the hot track of a tear sliding down her face did she realize she was crying. In near panic, she blinked the moisture from her eyes, remembering how she'd wept last night and what the result had been. She couldn't let herself cry, not now, not ever again. And she couldn't let MacDougal touch her again either, not if she expected to stay strong.

Except he was touching her right now. They were lying side by side, his front to her back all the way from her shoulders to her heels, and his breath was stirring the hairs on her neck. His arm lay over her, his hand cupping a breast as if he had every right to any intimacy he chose to take. The worst part was she could feel his arousal hot and hard against her buttocks and felt an answering heat in her own loins.

No! she thought, and using the utmost care, eased herself away from him, lifting his arm and sliding out from under it, then slipping quickly out from between the covers. Robbed of his warmth, her body instantly puckered in gooseflesh in the cool morning air, but she found her Indian dress and hurriedly pulled it over her head, as much for protection from MacDougal's eyes as from the chill. Then she shook out her moccasins and put them on, lacing them clumsily in her haste to be completely covered when MacDougal woke up. He'd never see her vulnerable again. Never.

When she was dressed, she hazarded a glance at him and jumped to find his wolf's eyes staring straight at her. How long had he been watching? How much had he seen? She decided she didn't really care and squared her shoulders defiantly.

"It's late," she informed him, jerking her chin toward the risen sun. "Are you going to sleep all day?"

He raised his rust-colored eyebrows. "Good morning to you, too," he drawled, rolling onto his back and locking his hands behind his head. "You aren't wearing your new dress."

Rebekah felt the heat in her cheeks and hoped fiercely that she wasn't really blushing. "It's dirty," she snapped, snatching the garment from the ground where it had lain all night after MacDougal had removed it from her body. She wadded it up into a ball, stuffing the rag of a chemise into the center. "It's ugly, too. It's about the ugliest dress I ever saw in my life."

"You seemed to like it well enough last night," he reminded her. "You were a lot more grateful last night, too."

Now her face was scalding, and she knew he must see the color in her cheeks, but she just glared murderously at him. "Just be sure to keep track of everything you spend on me. My father will pay you back for it."

"He doesn't owe me anything for the dress. I've already had my reward for that."

Rebekah fairly choked on her rage, so she turned away, afraid to look at him another moment for fear of what she might say or what she might do. She was stuffing the accursed dress into her pack when she heard MacDougal fling back the blanket and haul himself out of his pallet.

Her breath caught in her throat and she slammed her eyes shut because even though she wasn't looking at him, she could see him clearly, the long, lean body dusted with the fiery hair, broad shoulders and narrow hips and gentle hands and tender lips . . . Her eyes stung behind her tightly clenched eyelids as if she might cry although she could never let herself do such a thing, and her throat clenched so that she could barely get her breath.

Then he was behind her, the heat of his body reaching out to her across the narrow space that separated them. "What's wrong with you this morning?" he demanded, and his hands came down on her shoulders in a caress.

As if he'd struck her, she wrenched away, whirling to glare at him until she saw he was still naked, then turning away just as quickly. "Don't touch me, MacDougal! Don't you ever touch me again!"

"You didn't mind me touching you last night," he reminded her angrily. "In fact, you practically begged me to."

She covered her ears, wishing she could truly shut out the sound of his voice. "Leave me alone!"

From the corner of her eye, she saw him reaching for her again, and she darted away, frantic to escape. Desperate now, she snatched up one of the blankets and began to shake it furiously. "We need to get out of here," she said, still not daring to look at him. "I don't like being so close to that fort. What if they see us? What if somebody decides to go hunting or something?"

"Then they'll see us," he replied with maddening calm. "You've got a white woman's dress now, so what does it matter if someone sees you?"

How could she explain? How could she tell him *he* was the one she wanted to get away from, especially when she knew there was no hope at all of that?

"Are you going to get dressed or are you just going to let your privates hang out all day?" she asked him through gritted teeth as she concentrated all her attention on the task of folding the blanket.

MacDougal swore eloquently and started stomping around the camp, but at least he was stomping over to where he'd left his clothes, and in another moment he was putting them on, still swearing. He kept swearing until he was dressed again, and Rebekah couldn't help marveling that he'd kept going all that time and hadn't repeated himself once. She'd hardly understood a word of it, but she was impressed, nonetheless.

At last she could look at him and give him the full weight of her contempt. "Now maybe you can get the horses saddled without worrying one of them'll bite off something you consider important."

"I'm not even going to try to figure out why you're in such a foul mood this morning, but why're you in such an all-fired hurry?" he snarled as he stomped into his boots.

"Because the sooner we get started, the sooner we'll get where we're going and the sooner I'll get shed of you, MacDougal." She found the bag of pemmican, scooped out a handful from the dwindling stores, and squatted down to eat it.

"Is that what you think?" he asked, his voice dangerously soft. "That when we get to your father's, you'll be rid of me?"

Every nerve in her body tensed and her hand stopped halfway to her mouth. She forced it to continue and forced herself to take the pemmican into her mouth and chew and swallow it before she replied. "Your job'll be done. I expect you'll be anxious to start up your new business someplace," she said carefully.

He didn't answer for a long time, so long she wondered if he'd even heard what she said, or cared. She kept eating, although the dried mix tasted even more like sawdust than usual. At last she had to look up to see if he was even paying attention to her anymore. Unfortunately, he was. His wolf's eyes were locked on her, his expression stony. "What about what happened last night?"

Suddenly her mouth felt like it was stuffed with cotton and the world looked fuzzy, as if she were seeing everything under water. MacDougal's image blurred, like he might actually disappear, but of course he didn't. Instead he planted his hands on his hips, silently telling her he expected an answer and was prepared to shake it out of her if necessary. She swallowed dryly and forced the words out. "Like you said, I was paying you for the dress."

MacDougal didn't seem to notice how difficult the words had been for her to say. His cheeks above his beard grew crimson, and fury fairly radiated from him. Rebekah braced herself, ready for the blows she knew would come, the blows which always came. when she'd annoyed some male. He took a step toward her, and instinctively she threw her hands over her head and ducked her chin into her knees, tucking her body into a protective ball.

MacDougal swore again, even more eloquently than before, striding toward her while she tensed, ready for what would come, hoping against hope he wouldn't kick her with his boots because surely he would break her ribs and maybe even kill her.

But instead of hitting her, he grabbed one of the arms with which she was shielding her head and yanked her to her feet, then grabbed her other arm and held her upright, leaning down until their noses almost touched.

"What in the hell is the matter with you?" he shouted into her face.

She opened her mouth to reply, but no words came out, so she closed it again.

"God, you're shaking," he marveled. "Did you think I was going to hit you?"

She hadn't known she was shaking, and she most certain *had* thought he was going to hit her, but she shook her head no.

He knew she was lying, though. "You did, didn't you? You thought I was going to hit you, probably because that's what you deserve, but I'm not going to, so you can stop being afraid of me. I've never hit a woman yet, and I don't intend to start now, no matter how you provoke me."

160

Rebekah swallowed again. "And what if I don't want to share your bed again, white man? Will you hit me then?"

The question was no more than a whisper, but he heard it perfectly. She knew because his eyes narrowed and the hands holding her tightened painfully. For a moment, she held her breath, certain she had pushed him too far. Then, suddenly, he relaxed and underneath his mustache, he smiled, his eyes twinkling. "I didn't have to hit you last night, did I?" When she gasped in outrage, he chuckled. "No, I didn't have to even ask. In fact, you were the one doing all the asking. I reckon I can just wait until you ask me again, and you will, Rebekah Tate. You will."

Once again she wrenched free of his grasp, so furious she couldn't even speak to deny his outrageous prediction. She would die before she'd let him lay a hand on her again, and she'd certainly never *ask* him to.

"You stinking, conceited . . ." She cast about for an insult awful enough and had to settle for a Comanche phrase. ". . . pile of coyote droppings!"

He didn't seem phased by the barb. He was too busy getting his own breakfast, and when he squatted down to eat it and looked up at her, his eyes were dancing with silent laughter.

"You hypocrite!" she tried, using all the English epithets she knew. "Your blasphemer!" She deliberately avoided "whoremonger."

"I can see your vocabulary of profanity needs some improvement," he observed in amusement. "Just listen more carefully to what I say the next time you provoke me. Meanwhile, you can curse me in Comanche if you want. I understand it pretty well even though I can't speak it much."

But Rebekah was too angry to speak at all, much

less think of names to call him in any language, so she continued packing up the camp, her movements so furious she knew she didn't dare approach the animals for fear of frightening them into a stampede.

"Have I mentioned how much I appreciate all the help you've given me during this trip?" he asked when he had watched her working for a while.

"I'm just doing what any squaw would do," she snapped back, not wanting him to think she was helping because she wanted to please him.

"Well, you're doing a fine job, *Huuwūhtūkwaʔ*," he informed her.

She whirled on him in renewed fury. *"Don't call me that!"*

He blinked in surprise. "Why not? It's your name, isn't it?"

"Not anymore it isn't, not ever again, and if you call me that again, I'll . . . I'll cut your tongue out!"

He looked as if he were trying not to laugh at her threat, and he dropped his gaze when she continued to glare at him. Satisfied that she had won this engagement, she went back to her packing.

But after a few minutes he said, "What does it mean?"

"What does what mean?" she snapped.

"That name you don't allow me to call you. What does it mean?"

"Nothing," she said, but they both knew she was lying. They both knew all Comanche names had meaning and were only bestowed as the result of some event in the person's life. Consequently, a Comanche's name might change several times through the years to commemorate momentous occurrences. Reluctantly Rebekah remembered the event that had given her her name and smiled in spite of herself.

"All right, white man, I'll tell you what it means. It

162

means 'Take a stick and hit someone,'" she announced triumphantly.

"And who did you hit with a stick to earn it?"

The memory was old and faded now. She couldn't even remember what had led up to the incident, but if she concentrated, she could still feel the stick in her hand and the shock of it striking solid flesh. "The woman who owned me," she said softly, hardly able to recall the woman's face anymore. She'd been dead for several years. "The Comanche men are horrible, of course, but in many ways the women are worse because they keep after you all the time. A slave can't hit a Comanche brave back unless she wants to die. I didn't know I could get away with hitting a woman, so I just let her beat me and scream at me until I couldn't stand it anymore and I didn't care if I died or not. Then I picked up a stick and broke it over her head."

She smiled at the memory, although she'd been terrified at the time because she thought she'd killed the woman and that when the Comanche killed her in return, she'd burn in hell for doing murder.

"But of course they didn't kill you," MacDougal said, speaking just as softly as she had. "In fact, they treated you better afterwards, didn't they?"

They had, too. They hadn't treated her well, certainly, but better than before. And the beatings had stopped, probably because the woman was afraid of her now. "I thought the man who owned me would cut my throat, but he only laughed when he saw the blood running down her face and . . ." She glanced at MacDougal and stopped abruptly, realizing she had forgotten for a moment that she hated him and had no intention whatsoever of ever speaking a civil word to him again. "Aren't you finished eating yet?" she demanded.

He grinned—just to annoy her she was certain—

and brushed the crumbs off his hands. "I suppose I'd better get moving before you find a stick," he remarked, pulling himself to his feet.

Rebekah didn't see any humor at all in the remark because if she'd had a stick, she would have been sorely tempted to use it on him. Maybe he knew that because he wasted no time in saddling the horses and loading the mule. In a matter of minutes they were on their way, leaving Hopewell's Fort behind.

After that the days and nights passed in a blur of sameness and routine. She and MacDougal spoke only when absolutely necessary. They worked well as a team, however, and once Rebekah decided he wasn't going to sneak into her blankets in the middle of the night, she was able to relax in his presence again.

But having lost one source of concern, she gained another, because each day's travel brought them closer and closer to civilization. They frequently saw isolated cabins now, smoke rising from the chimney to indicate human habitation, but instead of making Rebekah happy, the sight struck an icy fear in her heart.

The first time they'd encountered such a cabin, MacDougal said, "Shall we go down and pay our respects?"

"No," she'd replied, fighting panic at the thought. "I don't want to see anyone."

"But you've got your dress now," he'd reminded her gently. Too gently, she'd thought at the time and still did. "And you can't complain it's dirty because you washed it and—"

"No!" she'd cried in desperation. "I don't want to. If you think you've got to go down there and jaw with some stupid farmer, go right ahead, but you'll have to go alone."

He'd stared at her for a long time as if he were

trying to see inside her head and figure out what she was thinking. Then, without another word, he'd ridden on, passing the cabin by as he'd passed all the others since. And as he'd passed a real town that morning.

The place had been pathetic by Eastern standards, but the tiny collection of buildings had included what MacDougal judged to be a store and a livery stable/blacksmith shop and some houses. A thriving metropolis by frontier standards.

That night as they lay in their blankets, staring up at the stars, MacDougal grumbled, "I could be sleeping in a real bed tonight. I could've had a homecooked meal today, complete with raised bread and buttermilk. I could've—"

"How do you figure all that, MacDougal?" Rebekah challenged him. "I didn't see no hotel in that town."

"No, but one of those folks would've doubtless offered his own bed to the man who rescued Rebekah Tate."

He was joking, she knew, but hearing her own words repeated here in the shadow of white civilization gave them an entirely new meaning. That meaning made her stomach clench and caused her nerves to tingle. Rebekah Tate. That's what MacDougal always called her, both names together as if it were an official title or something. As if it were really as famous a name as MacDougal always insisted. As if rescuing her really would make him as important as she'd promised.

She hadn't expected that it would, of course. Oh, no. Who would know or care about a young girl long ago given up for dead? And who was Rebekah Tate anyway? The girl the Indians had taken no longer existed, and the woman the Comanche called *Huuwǔhtǔkwaʔ* no longer existed either. The person

165

MacDougal called Rebekah Tate didn't know who she was or where she belonged. At the moment, she was a stranger between two worlds who belonged in neither.

Would her father think that, too? Would he want her now that she'd been defiled by the savages? Now that she had borne an Indian bastard? Now that she'd forgotten almost everything she'd been taught as a child until she hardly even knew how to use a spoon anymore? Now that she no longer believed in his God?

And what about the rest of the Tates, whatever relatives were still alive, and her father's friends? What would they think of her? What would they say about her?

Although the night was warm, Rebekah found herself shivering in her blankets.

"Are you all right?" MacDougal called from where he lay.

She wasn't sure she trusted her voice, but she had to answer because if she didn't, he might come over to see what was wrong. "I was just wondering," she said, her voice sounding hollow even to her ears, "how close we are now."

"Pretty close," he said, striking renewed terror into her heart, "if that was the town I think it was. I'll have to stop at the next place we come to and ask, but I'd say we're no more than a day or two away."

Tomorrow or the next day she would be home. She tried to picture the stockade and imagine what it might look like today. What would it be like to live there without her mother and her baby brother, and without all the others who had died? To live inside walls after living on the open prairie for so many years? To live with white people who would be watching every move she made?

By now she was shaking so hard, her teeth wanted

to chatter, so she clamped them tightly together lest MacDougal hear and come over to investigate. If he were to touch her now when she was feeling so desolate, she didn't think she could resist the comfort of his arms, no matter what else went with it.

But MacDougal didn't come over, and soon she heard him snoring softly. It was a long time before she fell asleep.

Sean didn't like leaving Rebekah alone, but once again she'd given him no choice. Late that morning they'd seen the smoke from a cabin, and Sean knew he'd have to stop there and inquire about the exact location of Zebulon Tate's home. She, at least, had come most of the way with him, stopping just before the cabin itself came into sight and making a dry camp to wait for him.

So Sean had ridden on alone, covering the remaining distance in less than an hour. He paused on a small hill overlooking the place to get an idea of what he might be riding into. It looked safe enough, just like all the other farmer's houses he'd ever seen in Texas. The log house was the typical "dogtrot," four rooms built two by two with a covered walkway between them called a "dogtrot," probably because dogs liked to sleep in the shade there.

The barn and a few smaller outbuildings were also built of logs and stood off to one side with the corrals. Sean saw a few saddle horses and a milk cow penned up in them and a lone man in the yard, chopping wood. The sound of the ax came to him faintly, like an echo. All around, the fields showed the remains of the harvest, and he thought he saw some men working out there, probably gathering the sheaves for winter fodder.

Kicking his horse into motion, Sean rode down the

gentle slope to where the farmer worked. The man saw the approaching rider when Sean was about halfway there, and he stopped his work and waved, welcoming him in and coming forward to meet him.

"Howdy, stranger," the man said, smiling broadly. "Looks like you've come quite a ways." He was a young man, probably no more than twenty-five, tall and strong and handsome with the same blue eyes and blond hair that marked at least half the settlers in Texas. Hatless, he was sweating profusely from his labor, having soaked through his home-spun shirt and the waistband of his homespun britches. He wiped the moisture from his forehead with his forearm.

"You're right. I've come straight through Indian country from Sante Fe," Sean replied.

The farmer whistled appreciatively. "Get down and come inside. You've just missed dinner, but I'm sure we can scare up something for you to eat."

"Thanks, but maybe another time. I'm in sort of a hurry, and somebody's waiting for me. All I need right now is a little information. Could you tell me where Zebulon Tate lives?"

The farmer's smile disappeared. "Do you have some business with Mr. Tate?"

"Yes, very important business." He could understand the farmer's caution. Sean knew he must look like some sort of desperado.

"Is he looking for you?"

Sean smiled. "No, but he'll be happy to see me. I've got some news about his daughter."

The farmer's face lighted instantly. "Rebekah? You know something about her? What? Is she alive?"

Now it was Sean's turn to be suspicious. The man was simply too interested. "Yeah, I reckon she's alive," he allowed.

The man strode over and grabbed Sean's stirrup,

his eyes alight. "Have you seen her yourself? Where is she? *How* is she?"

Sean shifted uncomfortably in his saddle, wondering how he should react. "That's information I intend to give to Mr. Tate," he said stiffly.

The farmer's handsome face reddened in embarrassment. "I'm sorry," he said and obviously he was. "It's just . . . I'm her cousin, Andrew Nelson." Belatedly, he stuck out his hand.

Sean nodded again, wondering how much he should reveal, how much Rebekah would *want* him to reveal.

"How is she?" Nelson asked, and the farmer's face concealed nothing. At the moment he looked as if he might actually weep out of concern for the long-lost girl. "Is she . . . well?"

"Perfectly well," Sean said, still trying to decide what to tell him.

"Is she . . . in her right mind?"

At least he could reassure him on that score. "Yes, she's in her right mind." At least most of the time, he thought, remembering how he'd almost lost her again when they'd made love.

"And you know where she is!" he exclaimed. "Can we get her? Are you going to go back for her? Well, of course you are, that's why you're here, isn't it, to get help? I can get a hundred men to go with you, maybe more. The problem will be in *keeping* men from going with you. Everyone who's ever heard the story will—"

"It's a little early to be making plans," Sean cautioned, hoping to calm Nelson's enthusiasm. "First I need to talk to Mr. Tate."

"Yes, yes, of course! It'll be a shock to him, I guess, although a pleasant shock. He still prays for her every Sunday before the entire congregation. Nobody has forgotten her. But maybe you shouldn't go alone.

169

Maybe it would be better if somebody from the family went with you. My father's out in the fields working. I can go get him and—"

"I'd really rather go alone," Sean said quickly, wondering how he would explain it to Rebekah if he rode back with a passel of her cousins. "I've got some private things to tell him," he improvised.

"But the Tates don't have any secrets from each other. He and my father are as close as brothers, even though my father isn't even a blood relative. It was my mother was a Tate, Uncle Zeb's niece. She died in the raid when Rebekah was taken, so you see, we've all got a stake in this. If there's any hope she's still alive and we can bring her back . . ." His voice broke, and he covered his face with one hand for a moment while he regained his composure.

"You must've been pretty fond of her yourself," Sean guessed, thinking he might just have to confide in this man if he hoped to get Rebekah home with a minimum of fuss.

Nelson nodded, wiping at his eyes with his fingers before looking up at Sean again. "We grew up together. She was like my little sister." He smiled sadly. "I think everybody expected us to marry someday."

Sean felt as if somebody had punched him in the stomach, not hard but hard enough to give him an unpleasantly hollow feeling deep in his belly. He forced himself to return Nelson's smile. "Then you'll want what's best for her, won't you?"

"Anything I can do, anything at all," he agreed eagerly.

Sean looked off into the distance while he considered his options. He didn't know if he could trust this man, but if he cared for Rebekah as much as he seemed to . . . "I'm going to tell you something, but you'll have to promise to keep it a secret, at least

170

for a while."

"Something about Rebekah?"

"Yes. Can I have your word?"

"Yes, yes, anything. What is it?" His cheeks were pale and his knuckles were white where he still gripped Sean's stirrup.

"Not only is Rebekah Tate still alive, but she's here. I've brought her home."

"Where?" he demanded, peering anxiously off into the distance as if he might catch a glimpse. "Where is she? What have you done with her?"

He smiled at the accusation. "I haven't done anything with her. She's just a little shy about seeing other people, at least until she sees her father." Sean hoped that much was true, although he as yet had no way of knowing for sure. "She wouldn't come with me to your cabin, even though she didn't know it was your family down here. If she had . . . Well, I've got to be honest with you, I still don't think she would've come. She's . . . I think she's a little scared about the way people will treat her."

"That's crazy! We're her family! Look, I'll go to her and explain—"

"No!" The steel in Sean's voice caught him up short and a flush rose in his face as he glared up through narrowed eyes. "I'm trying to explain," Sean said patiently, "it's the people she cares about most that she mostly doesn't want to see, at least not yet, not until she's ready. She's been through an awful lot, more than anybody will ever know. The least we can do is not force her to do anything she doesn't want to do."

Nelson wasn't happy, but he nodded. "Are you going to take her to her father now?"

"Yes, just as soon as I find out where the stockade is. Rebekah doesn't really remember and—"

"He doesn't live in the stockade anymore," Nelson

said, placated but still unhappy with the situation. "Nobody lives there now and they haven't for a long time. Uncle Zeb has his place just over there." He pointed to the east. "It's not more than a few hours' ride. You can be there before dark if you leave now."

Sean nodded. "I'm much obliged. Rebekah will be, too."

"You want me to keep this a secret, though." The prospect disturbed him greatly.

"Only for a few hours until it's too late for anybody to get over there tonight. Give her and her father a chance to be alone for a while."

Nelson nodded, unhappy but understanding. "I'll wait until morning. No matter how late it is, my stepmother would be sure it was her Christian duty to go right over to see her, so I'll make sure Rebekah has tonight alone with Uncle Zeb."

"Thanks." Sean offered his hand again, and Nelson shook it firmly, his expression grim. Somehow he looked much older now than he had when Sean first rode in.

"You're the one who should be thanked, Mr. MacDougal. You're the one who rescued her, after all." He smiled slightly. "I'm real anxious to hear how you did it."

"I'll be happy to tell you the whole story, or maybe Rebekah will," he added generously, although Sean didn't think he liked the idea of Rebekah spending any length of time with this handsome young man whom she might once have married.

"God Almighty, I just can't believe she's alive and *here*. It seems so sudden after all this time of waiting."

"I think it seems sudden to her, too. That's why she needs some time to get used to it."

Nelson nodded. "Give her my love, will you? And tell her I'll see her tomorrow. Oh, and how happy I

172

am she's home!"

Sean agreed, however reluctantly, and took his leave. When he turned to wave, he saw a woman on the front porch of the cabin, probably the stepmother of whom Nelson had spoken. Shading her eyes, she was trying to make out who the rider might be. He wondered vaguely what lie Nelson would tell her. He just hoped he could trust the farmer to keep the rest of the family away at least until morning.

Rebekah had spent her time nervously pacing in the shade of the scraggly cottonwood tree under which she had made her camp. At first she had been too tense to notice, but after a while the incessant click of the beads adorning the fringe of her once-fine buckskin dress began to annoy her. With the annoyance came the realization of how she would appear to anyone who might happen to ride by. Although the chance of encountering someone was slim, she and MacDougal had seen enough human habitations in the past few days to ensure the possibility.

And MacDougal had said he would have her home within a day or two. She glanced down at the garment that had served her so well during the grueling trip from the far Texas plains and knew she couldn't stand it another second. Digging into her pack, she found the awful dress MacDougal had given her.

Most of the dirt was gone now, having been cleansed away in the alkaline water of a tiny stream they'd happened across several days ago. She'd draped the garment and the ragged chemise on a mesquite bush to dry overnight, then folded them carefully away. In spite of her care, however, the dress was terribly wrinkled, which did nothing to improve its appearance. Still, it was a white woman's dress, the only one she had, and she wasn't going to ride up to her father's house looking like a squaw.

By the time she saw MacDougal returning, she was wearing the blue gingham, her hair combed with the porcupine quill brush MacDougal had provided for her, and her moccasined feet tucked carefully under the skirt so she would present as demur a picture as possible.

She'd expected some smart remark or at least a little teasing, but MacDougal's expression was grim as he climbed down from his horse and looked her over critically. "Well, now, don't we look fine," he said sarcastically.

"I can't speak for me, but you look a long way from fine," she replied, more annoyed than she wanted to admit that he hadn't seen fit to compliment her appearance. She jerked her chin toward his head in the Comanche way of pointing. "With all that hair all over your face, I've been thinking I probably wouldn't even recognize you if you shaved."

He reached up and touched his beard which now hung down onto his chest. "No, you probably wouldn't," he agreed somberly. Then, without another word, he went over and started loading the mule.

Rebekah had been braced to hear what he had learned. Now, it seemed, he had no intention of telling her. He was also unhappy about whatever he had discovered, and Rebekah couldn't imagine why.

Or at least she couldn't imagine why until she started trying to, and then she could imagine all sorts of things. Had they come the wrong way, to the wrong place? Had that man Hopewell sent them off on a wild goose chase? Or worse, had they come to the right place and MacDougal had found her father and learned that . . . what? That he no longer wanted

174

his daughter? That he couldn't bear the sight of her? That he wanted to send her back to the Indians where she belonged? Or even, oh, God, what if MacDougal had found out her father was dead?

The hand she laid over her pounding heart was trembling as she watched MacDougal performing the all-too-familiar task of breaking camp.

"MacDougal?" she ventured, using every ounce of her strength to hold her voice steady.

He stopped what he was doing, although he didn't turn to look at her.

"What . . . what did you find out?"

He still didn't look at her. "I found out we aren't far. We should be at your father's house before nightfall."

Her pounding heart made a painful lurch, but she forced herself to go on, knowing there was something more, something MacDougal didn't want to tell her. "And . . . ?" she prodded.

"And nothing. We'll be there tonight. Oh, yeah, I almost forgot," he added, not very convincingly. "I ran into an old . . . friend of yours."

So far as Rebekah knew, she had no old friends. "Who?" she asked in alarm.

Now, finally, he turned to look at her, his wolf's eyes narrowed. "Your . . . cousin Andrew Nelson."

Andrew! She must have cried out in surprise, and she certainly jumped to her feet. "You saw him? You talked to him?"

MacDougal nodded, grudgingly, she thought.

"How is he? What's he like? Where was he?"

"He's a farmer," MacDougal said, as if that answered her questions.

"But is he all right?" she demanded, hurrying to confront MacDougal so she could demand answers.

"Why shouldn't he be?" MacDougal snapped, stopping her in her tracks. "He wasn't the one taken by the Indians."

Which was true enough, although Rebekah couldn't imagine why that made MacDougal so angry, and no question about it, he was furious. "What did he say? What did you tell him? Oh, God, MacDougal, you didn't tell him I was here, did you!" Now she really was terrified and gazed frantically off into the distance, trying to see if anyone had followed MacDougal back to their camp.

But she saw no one and nothing, and MacDougal grunted in disgust, drawing her attention again. "I had to tell him you were with me. Otherwise, he was going to get a hundred men together to go into Indian country after you. Cousin Andrew's quite a hero."

"But he's not . . . not coming *here?*"

"No, he's not coming here. I asked him to wait until tomorrow to tell his family you're back so you and your father would have some time together alone first."

Her heart softened toward MacDougal instantly, but terror still throbbed through her veins. "What . . . what did he say when you . . . when you told him about me?"

MacDougal's beard hid most of his expression, but she could still easily read his fury. "He said he'd see you tomorrow, and he sends you his *love.*"

MacDougal's tone was so harsh that it took a minute for Rebekah to comprehend the gentleness of the words.

Andrew had sent her his love! He didn't hate her. He didn't hold her in contempt. He wanted to see her. He wanted her back. And if he felt that way, her father must, too. Oh, surely he did!

She covered her mouth with both hands and blinked furiously against the sting of tears, although why she should want to cry now when for the first time in seven years she was actually *happy* she had no idea. But the urge lasted for only a moment, and when it passed, she lowered her hands and glanced at MacDougal to find he was still watching her closely.

"What . . . did he say anything about my father?" she asked anxiously.

"He seems to think your father will be happy to see you, so maybe we'd better get moving if we expect to get there before nightfall."

Rebekah no longer cared why MacDougal was so grouchy. She was going to see her father. She was going *home*.

Within minutes they were on their way. As they rode, Rebekah scanned the horizon, looking for something familiar, something that would tell her she was almost home, but everything looked the same as it had looked for days and days. Too much time and too many miles had passed for her to remember.

"I guess Andrew's family doesn't live at the stockade anymore," she remarked after a while.

"Nobody does," MacDougal replied, his voice still gruff. "I guess they stopped worrying about Indian attacks. They've all got their own places now."

At least she wouldn't have to live under the watchful eye of all her relatives within the confines of the fort, she thought with relief. One less thing to worry about. Of course, tomorrow she would have to face Andrew and his father, but she wouldn't think about that now. First she had the meeting with her own father to get through.

She wondered vaguely why he'd gotten his own house. Had he remarried? Perhaps he had other children by now. Would she fit into his new life? And what about her son? Would there be room in her father's heart for him? Suddenly she realized she was being ridiculous, just making up things to fret over.

Beside her, MacDougal rode in silence, glancing

over every now and then as if he were required to keep an eye on her, and his mood hadn't improved at all. She would have thought he'd be elated to find he'd reached the end of his journey and was about to receive the acclaim he expected. Instead, he seemed annoyed. Very annoyed.

Well, maybe Cousin Andrew hadn't been appropriately awed by his accomplishment. Maybe MacDougal was wondering if all this work would be for nothing.

Or maybe he had realized that once she was back with her family, he would never be able to touch her again!

The thought startled her, and she glanced at MacDougal to find him once again watching her through narrowed eyes.

She couldn't ask him, of course, because she'd be far too embarrassed and besides, he'd never admit it even if it were true. She found the possibility intriguing, though, especially when she recalled that relaying Andrew's affectionate message had made MacDougal the most angry. Could he possibly be jealous?

No, the very idea was ridiculous. To be jealous would imply that MacDougal cared about her when she knew he only wanted her body. That's all men ever wanted, especially men like MacDougal. If he was upset about anything it was because he'd realized he would no longer have any power over her whatsoever.

Never again would he touch her and force her to feel things she didn't want to feel. Never again would he draw her out of herself and make her lose control. From now on, no one would ever have that power over her.

The knowledge should have been comforting, which was why Rebekah couldn't understand the hollow feeling of loss that settled in the region of her heart.

MacDougal hadn't spoken to her in hours, and she had been only too glad for the opportunity to lose herself in her thoughts. A hundred times she imagined the meeting with her father and each time it was a little different. Too many times it was awful, too, because he wasn't what she remembered or she wasn't what he wanted her to be or . . . But there was no use in imagining, she told herself over and over just before she imagined it yet again.

At last MacDougal said, "That must be it."

The buildings were small specks on the horizon, but the curl of smoke was unmistakable and had probably been visible for an hour or more if she had been paying attention.

They rode inexorably onward as Rebekah's heart began to pound in increasing apprehension. The buildings grew bigger, giving the illusion that they were coming toward the riders instead of the other way around. It was a typical setup, the dogtrot house, the barn and outbuildings, the corral. She saw what looked like a second cabin, although she could not imagine who might be living here with her father. Maybe he had someone to help with the farming. That would be logical, she supposed, since her father was getting to be an old man.

He'd married late in life, as she'd often heard him explain. He'd been almost forty when he'd taken a bride barely twenty. She'd given him much happiness and many children, but only one child had survived their mother and perhaps none of the happiness had.

Would Rebekah's return restore some of that lost happiness or would she be a constant reminder of the old tragedy? Would her father expect the innocent child he had lost or would he accept the woman who was returning? And how would he feel about his grandson? So many questions, and not one single answer.

Rebekah felt her nerves tingling, making her want to jump off the horse and run the rest of the way to the cabin, or perhaps run just as fast in the other direction, but of course she didn't do either of those things. Instead she sat sedately in her saddle, one leg hooked over the horn to give the illusion she was riding sidesaddle the way a white woman would.

Slowly the details of the buildings grew clearer. The individual logs took shape. The animals in the corrals chewed lazily. Two rib-thin dogs of indeterminate breed rose up from the shade of the dogtrot and began to bark a warning. The Negroes on the porch of the smaller cabin whittled.

Negroes? What would Negroes be doing here? Her father had never owned slaves, hadn't even believed in it. There must be some mistake. They'd come to the wrong place after all.

But then she heard one of the black men calling, "Massa Zeb! We gots company!" and every hair on her body prickled.

Blindly now, she rode for the house, her blood thundering in her head, her fingers clenched on the reins, her heart hammering against her ribs.

An old man emerged from one side of the dogtrot house, his hair snow white, his beard hanging halfway down his chest. He'd once been tall, but the years had stooped him, and his homespun clothes hung loose as if he'd lost flesh since having them fitted. The evening breeze whipped his hair about his head as he stood in the open area between the two sides of the house and shouted the barking dogs to silence.

As if it knew the way, her horse carried her right up to where the old man stood waiting. He was smiling uncertainly, as if he sensed the strangeness of the visit but had no idea what that strangeness was.

"Welcome to my home, young lady," he said, and while she hadn't recognized the man, she recognized the voice, the one she'd heard every day for fifteen years, the one she'd heard in her dreams for seven more. It had lost none of its resonance, and it stirred her to her soul.

Numb now with tension and fear, she unhooked her knee from the saddle horn and slid to the ground. Her knees felt like jelly, but somehow she walked the remaining few feet until she was close enough to touch the old man.

She didn't touch him, though, couldn't make her arms move. All she could manage was to push the words past her fear-clogged throat.

"Don't you know me, Papa?"

Chapter Seven

The old man blinked, then his faded blue eyes narrowed as he studied her face in the fading sunlight.

"Rebekah?" he whispered in disbelief.

She wanted to cry. She wanted to laugh. She wanted to run away. Instead, she nodded, unable to speak because of the tremendous lump in her throat.

He lifted one large callused hand slowly, tentatively, until he touched her cheek. "Am I dreaming?" he asked in wonder.

"No, Papa," she managed in a husky whisper. "It's me."

"Rebekah!" he cried, and in the next instant she was in his arms. He crushed her to his chest as if afraid she would evaporate if he didn't hold her tightly enough. He smelled of wood smoke and pipe tobacco and himself, just like the Papa she remembered. She didn't cry, she didn't dare, but he did, sobs wracking his body as he held her against the thundering of his heart.

He was speaking, too, although she couldn't understand the words at first because she was too overwhelmed by the onslaught of his emotions. After a while the words began to make sense to her, though, and she realized he was praying, pouring out his joy and his praise to the God he had always worshiped.

"'When the Lord turned again the captivity of Zion, we were like them that dream,'" he said, quoting some passage of scripture she had long forgotten. "'Then was our mouth filled with laughter, and our tongue with singing: then said they among the heathen, The Lord hath done great things for them. The Lord hath done great things for us; whereof we are glad.' The Lord hath done great things for us! Praise the Lord God Almighty who has brought my child out of captivity!"

At last he released her, holding her out at arm's length so he could look at her again as if not quite trusting his own senses. "Praise God, Praise God," he murmured as he took her in from head to toe.

But Rebekah wasn't too interested in praising a God who had been so tardy with His help, even if she had really believed He'd had any hand at all in rescuing her. "You'd do better to thank the person who really brought me home," she said, getting control of her voice at last. She glanced over her shoulder to see that MacDougal had followed her up to the house and now sat his horse a respectful distance away, waiting to be acknowledged.

"Papa, this is Sean MacDougal."

Her father pulled himself up straighter, although he didn't let go of her shoulders, and looked past her to MacDougal. In spite of the tears still glistening on his cheeks, he looked exactly the way Rebekah had always pictured the Old Testament prophets of which she'd heard him preach time and again. "Welcome to my home, Mr. MacDougal. Please get down and come inside so I may thank you properly for the wonderful thing you have done. Dan and Enoch! Take care of the horses, will you?"

Rebekah turned to see the two Negroes who had been sitting on the porch of the other cabin. They'd come forward to see what was happening, and now they were staring at her with unabashed curiosity.

"Rebekah and Mr. MacDougal, I want you to meet my right hand and my left hand, Dan and Enoch. Boys, this is my daughter Rebekah whom the Lord has restored unto me at last."

The "boys" were actually young men. Rebekah judged them to be in their late twenties, although she couldn't be exactly sure. They smiled shyly, bobbing their heads in acknowledgement of the introduction.

Rebekah turned back to her father in horror. "Slaves, Papa? You own slaves?"

"I bought them out of slavery, yes," he said, "But I do not consider them my property. I had to have someone to help me with the farm, you see, and—"

"What's going on out here?" a female voice demanded, and Rebekah looked up to see a tall, coffee-colored woman standing in the doorway to what must have been the kitchen. Her hair was completely covered by a red bandana and a stained white apron hung over her homespun dress, below which her brown feet were bare. Still, she held herself with the stateliness of a queen.

Indeed, even Zebulon Tate seemed sensitive to her authority. He beamed up at her. "This is my daughter, Jewel, returned from the dead!" he informed her.

For a second, Rebekah wondered if he might be right, if she had been dead and in hell all these years, but the thought passed just as quickly as the smile appeared on the black woman's face.

"Do tell! Not Rebekah her own self! Glory be! Well, don't be keeping her standing out in the dust! Get her inside so I can give her a good meal!"

MacDougal had by then alighted from his horse

184

and now stood beside Rebekah, the two dogs sniffing at him curiously. Her father released her at last in order to offer his hand to the red-haired stranger.

"Mr. MacDougal, unless you have a child of your own, you cannot know how I feel at this moment," he said as he pumped MacDougal's hand. "At last to see the daughter for whom I have prayed each day for over seven years. God sent you, my boy, and kept His hand upon you, and now He will reward you."

"I don't think that's the kind of reward MacDougal had in mind," Rebekah observed, earning a black look from MacDougal and a puzzled one from her father.

The woman named Jewel saved the moment. "Now get yourselves inside here. The boys'll take care of your animals. You just bring their possibles up here," she directed Dan and Enoch, pointing to a spot in the dogtrot. "We'll sort it all out later. Don't you worry about a thing," she added to MacDougal, who looked far from worried.

At last her father released MacDougal's hand and turned back to Rebekah. He took her in again from head to foot, noting the cropped hair, the shabby, ill-fitting dress, the worn moccasins peeking out from beneath her skirt.

His faded blue eyes filled with tears again, and he laid an unsteady hand on her shoulder. "What have they done to you, my child?"

For an instant all the horrors of the past seven years flashed before her, but just as quickly they were gone, and she was with her father again, safe and free. She managed a small smile. "Nothing, Papa," she lied. "I'm fine. I really am."

"Except that she's pro'bly half-starved," Jewel observed caustically, "and you're keeping her from her supper. Now are you gonna let her come inside or do I have to take a stick to all of you?"

185

Rebekah was shocked. No one in her memory had ever spoken to her father like that, least of all a servant! She fully expected a lightning bolt to crash down and burn the woman to a cinder.

Instead, her father chuckled affectionately, slipped his arm around Rebekah, and led her inside after shooing away the curious dogs. MacDougal followed.

The room was, as Rebekah had guessed, a kitchen, a large comfortable room full of delicious aromas and furnished with a big, round, homemade table around which sat a half-dozen equally crude chairs. A massive stone fireplace covered one wall and over it hung an assortment of cooking utensils, polished brightly. Bunches of drying herbs dangled from string in the corners, and a large pot was suspended over the dying fire.

"Set yourselves right down here. I'll have you something to eat in no time at all."

Zebulon seated Rebekah in a chair facing the fire. The sensation of sitting in a chair was odd, but she adapted quickly, and she kept looking around, hoping against hope that she would see something familiar, something she remembered from her other life, but everything here was strange and new. Perhaps all her mother's things had been stolen or destroyed in the raid.

"You must have an interesting story to tell, Mr. MacDougal," her father was saying over her head as MacDougal took the chair next to hers.

She thought MacDougal smiled behind his beard, but he said, "I guess it will be interesting to you, although it was pretty dull while we were going through it. I met your daughter when I was trading with the Indians a few months ago."

"Trading with the Indians?" Zebulon echoed, obviously disapproving. He had taken the chair on Rebekah's other side while the woman named Jewel

186

bustled about the kitchen.

"I'm a trader from Sante Fe. The New Mexicans have no quarrel with the Comanches, and we've been trading with them for a long time," MacDougal said.

"Ah, yes, I've heard how the New Mexicans have made a treaty with the savages that for some reason the savages have chosen to honor, even though they honor none they make with Texans."

This time there could be no doubt MacDougal smiled. "They keep their treaty with us because we've kept our promises to them, unlike the Texans, Mr. Tate. We haven't sent settlers into their land after promising not to or—"

"The savages have no right to any land at all! They own nothing but the horses they steal. We're the ones with the legal rights and—"

MacDougal held up his hand to stop the tirade Rebekah knew was coming. "There's no point in us arguing about all this. Besides, you want to hear how I got your daughter away."

Rebekah had had enough of their sparring. "He came to the camp where I was," she explained. "I saw him and asked him to ransom me." She glanced disdainfully at MacDougal. "He made a botch of that, so the Indian who owned me wouldn't sell me, so I had to escape."

But MacDougal wasn't going to let her get away with her jibe. "*I* worked out a plan for her to escape," he clarified. "She staged her own death by drowning so the Indians wouldn't follow us, then I spirited her away."

"You did this alone?" Zebulon marveled.

"Sneaking up on a Comanche camp is pretty easy," Rebekah explained, unwilling to let her father think too well of MacDougal. "They don't post guards because they know, and so does everyone else, how stupid it would be to attack a whole nest of

187

Comanche warriors."

"But still, if he'd been caught . . ." Zebulon shook his head, determined to be impressed by MacDougal's exploits. "And they didn't follow you?"

"No, although we did almost run smack dab into a raiding party once on our way back," MacDougal said.

Rebekah was waiting for him to tell how he'd saved her life after she got bitten by the snake, but he fell silent when Jewel set a plate down in front of him. She set another down in front of Rebekah who suddenly felt faint at the heavenly aroma of beans and fatback and cornbread.

"That's just what I got leftover from supper," Jewel informed them apologetically. "If I'd knowed you all was coming, I'd've fixed something proper." She gave them a look that plainly said she did not like being taken by surprise and having to offer guests second best. Rebekah felt absurdly guilty for coming home so unexpectedly.

But she quickly forgot the guilt when she started to eat, remembering to use the spoon Jewel set beside her but hating how slowly it scooped up the wonderful food, things she hadn't tasted in so many long years, things she couldn't swallow fast enough. When the beans were gone, she broke the cornbread and stuffed it into her mouth as quickly as she could, desperate for the melting sweetness.

Only when the last crumb was gone did she raise her head to find three pairs of eyes watching her, two pairs in horror. MacDougal just seemed curious, but Jewel and her father couldn't seem to believe their senses. What had she done? She'd used the spoon, hadn't she?

Then she realized she was leaning over her plate, encircling it with her left arm as if afraid someone were going to take it away from her. Her face was practically in the plate, her chin greasy from drips, her hands covered with crumbs. Dear God, she'd been eating like an animal. No, even worse, she'd been eating like an *Indian*. She felt her cheeks burning as she wiped her chin with the back of her hand.

"Maybe you'd like to wash up," Jewel suggested. "There's a pan of water just outside the door."

She pointed and Rebekah fled. On a bench outside was a basin and a bucket of water, a wedge of lye soap, and an old flour sack hanging on the wall for a towel. She scrubbed her face and hands until they tingled, silently cursing herself for forgetting. How could she have been so stupid? Her father must think . . . She had no idea what he must think and didn't even want to know. She couldn't even stand to imagine what the slave woman's opinion of her must be.

The slave men had carried hers and MacDougal's belongings to the shelter of the dogtrot where her father's two mongrel dogs kept watch, and looking at the bundles now, Rebekah had an irrational urge to gather her things and escape again, this time to a place where she would belong.

Except there was no such place. She no longer belonged anywhere. She'd been too civilized for the Indians, and now she was too uncivilized for the whites. The knowledge was like a lead weight on her heart as she forced herself to go back into the house.

Inside, everyone was making a concentrated effort not to look at her. The supper plates had been cleared away, and Jewel had set out pie and coffee. A wedge sat at Rebekah's place, a mouth-watering hunk of flaking crust and oozing sweet filling. Rebekah's jaws ached from just looking at it, but she managed to sit down stiffly, take up the fork Jewel had provided and ever so sedately cut off a mouthful and raise it to her lips.

By the time the luscious dessert touched her

tongue, her eyes were watering from the strain. She chewed and swallowed it, savoring every tantalizing crumb as happy memories of her life before the raid swirled in her brain.

When she had swallowed, she looked up and caught Jewel's dark eye. She seemed to be pleased with the improvement in Rebekah's manners. "I can't tell you how delicious this is," Rebekah said. "I haven't tasted apple pie in seven years."

Jewel pretended the compliment hadn't affected her. "It's nice somebody appreciates my cooking around here," she muttered, going back to her work.

After the pie was gone and Jewel had cleared the dishes—refusing Rebekah's offer of help—her father led them into the other room on that side of the dogtrot. This room was furnished as a parlor, albeit crudely, but at least here Rebekah saw some familiar things.

Her mother's sofa had survived the raid, although one of the cushions showed an obvious mend. One of the tables looked familiar, too, but the rest had been fashioned by an unskilled hand to fill in the blank areas of the room. A few straight-backed chairs completed the seating arrangements. A large fireplace covered one wall, but no fire was lit. The heat from the kitchen was more than enough on such a warm night.

Zebulon silently indicated she and MacDougal should sit on the sofa, although MacDougal opted for one of the chairs, which he turned backwards and straddled. Her father took another after pulling it close to where Rebekah sat.

Rebekah was running her hand over the brown velvet of the sofa, now crushed and faded, even threadbare in places, but still familiar enough to stir memories of sitting in that very place on a Sunday afternoon, her legs stretched straight out in front of her because they were too short to bend over the edge while she listened to her father reading a story from the Bible. All those stories. She should be able to remember at least one of them.

After a moment, she looked up to find her father waiting expectantly. What did he want her to say? Surely he didn't want her to tell what had happened to her. Even if he did, she had no intention of doing so. No one would ever know the things she had endured.

To forestall any questions, she asked, "Who . . . who all survived the raid that day?"

Her father winced. Plainly, discussing the tragedy still pained him, but he told her, first listing all the dead, most of whom she had already known about. Then he listed the survivors, mostly the men who had been out in the fields when the attack had come, and told her what had become of each of them. Surprisingly, none of them had fled Texas for safer territory after the raid.

"And Andrew and your Uncle Cecil," he finished, his voice weary from recounting the aftermath of the tragedy. "Cecil was better than a brother to me after . . . after it happened," he said. "I never understood what Esther saw in him. He never seemed like much account, but he was stronger than I'd figured, or maybe he just had to be. I don't know. Anyhow, he come through and helped hold the settlement together when I . . . when I might've given up."

"Oh, Papa, you didn't really want to give up, did you?"

Zebulon smiled bitterly, stroking his long white beard. "I wanted to die after I lost my wife and children. I kept thinking if we'd stayed in Tennessee, this never would've happened. The only thing kept me going was knowing you might still be alive out there. I had to stay alive, too, so I could pray for you, and so some day I'd see you again in this world."

His eyes were moist, and Rebekah didn't think she could stand to see him cry again. MacDougal must have shared her reluctance, because he said, "I saw Andrew today. He's the one gave me directions to your place." Rebekah could tell he still wasn't happy about the encounter, although she didn't think her father could.

"Then you've seen him?" Zebulon asked Rebekah. "He knows you're back?"

"No," she said, looking to MacDougal to make the explanation.

"Rebekah didn't want to see anybody until she'd seen you. I told him about her, though," MacDougal admitted.

"Prudence knows Rebekah is here, and she hasn't come over yet?" Zebulon exclaimed in amazement.

"Who's Prudence?" Rebekah asked, wondering if she could have forgotten one of her relatives.

"Your Uncle Cecil's wife," her father explained. "I forgot, you couldn't've known her. She and her first husband settled here after . . . after you were gone. The husband died, and she married Cecil. Fine Christian woman. She's been a good wife to Cecil. Just wish she could've done more with Andrew. He hasn't been much use at all since . . . well, since his mother died."

"What's the matter with him?" Rebekah asked in alarm. Andrew was the relative she'd remembered most fondly. She'd wanted him to be happy.

"Nothing wrong exactly," her father clarified. "He just . . . I don't know, he can't seem to settle down to anything. His father's got the best farm around these parts, but Andrew doesn't want any part of it. He just sets and dreams most of the time. Like I said, he's not much good for anything."

Silence fell as Rebekah considered her father's

judgment and tried to reconcile it with the boy she remembered. What had happened to him? And was it possible the raid had affected even those who had survived unscathed?

After a few moments, her father cleared his throat, and she saw him looking expectant again. "Rebekah," he said gruffly, "I . . . I want you to tell me what happened to you, where you've been all these years. Everything . . ."

His voice broke, which told her he'd imagined at least some of the horrors she had endured. Everyone knew what happened to white women captured by Indians. But she would not confirm his fears, not even if she could have brought herself to speak them aloud.

"They carried me back to their camp," she said, neatly skipping over the ordeal of that nightmare journey. "The Indian who captured me gave me to his wife as a slave. That's the way they treat their captives, even the Mexicans and Indians from other tribes that they kidnap. So I was a slave for a while."

Her father's faded blue eyes were bleak. "Did they . . . mistreat you?"

Mistreat. What a kind word to describe unspeakable acts, she thought, but she said, "The woman would beat me, but never very badly. They wanted me to work, so they couldn't really hurt me. The beating was mostly to keep me too frightened to run away or disobey. After a while . . ." she glanced at MacDougal and saw by the twinkle in his eye that he was remembering her story about hitting the woman with a stick, "the beatings stopped. I guess they started to trust me."

MacDougal coughed, covering his mouth with his hand, but she ignored him.

"Then, after about a year . . ." She stopped, suddenly panicked as she tried to think of how to

193

explain what had happened next without revealing to her father how she had conceived her son. "One . . . one of the men bought me. He . . . he wanted a wife." The word almost choked her, and she didn't dare look at MacDougal after chastening him so often for calling the man Liar her husband. "He already had one wife, but she didn't have any children, and he wanted a son and I was young and healthy and—"

"Heathen savages!" her father exclaimed, his cheeks mottled and his gnarled fists clenched with suppressed rage.

If he only knew, she thought, but smiled because now she would tell him her *good* news. "I have a son, Papa. He's a beautiful little boy, tall and strong, with hair as black as midnight and gray eyes. His name is . . ." Quickly, she made the translation. "Little One Who Hunts Far From the Camp. He's a wonderful child. He's your grandson."

She'd expected him to be shocked. She hadn't expected him to be horrified. He gaped at her, dumbfounded, his face white and his eyes blinking rapidly as if to keep from weeping.

"A son," he murmured at last.

"Yes, and he's the smartest thing you ever saw, so clever and—"

"He's . . . he's not with you," Zebulon interrupted gruffly.

"No," she said, feeling the stabbing pain. "We couldn't take him because nobody would have believed we'd both drowned, but MacDougal is going back for him just as soon as he can."

Zebulon glanced at MacDougal in surprise, or perhaps he was aghast. "You're going back there? To get an Indian boy?"

It *was* hard to believe that a man would voluntarily return to Indian country when he had once escaped

194

with his scalp intact. Rebekah told herself that was the only reason her father looked so shocked. "He's not 'an Indian boy'! He's my son!" Rebekah reminded him. "And of course he's going back. He promised. He swore to me."

She glared at MacDougal, daring him to renege now. His wolf's gaze darted from her father to her and back to her father again. After a few seconds, he simply shrugged fatalistically.

"See, I told you," she said triumphantly. "Mac-Dougal may be many other things, but he's a man of his word."

Zebulon stared at MacDougal for a long moment as if seeing him for the first time. "You are far more courageous even than I thought, Mr. MacDougal. I do not know how I can ever repay you for bringing Rebekah back."

"Yes, MacDougal, how can my father repay you?" Rebekah prodded him, anxious to change the subject to something other than herself.

"I promised a reward," Zebulon said hastily, "right after it first happened. A hundred dollars. It was a rash promise then because I had nothing with which to pay it, but I, too, am a man of my word. I'm afraid that I don't have much cash on hand right now—cash money is pitifully scarce in Texas even now that we're a state, and most of the money I received from selling my crop went to pay bills from the previous year—but I can give you a promissory note until I sell next year's crop. The only other source of cash I have is my colored people, but I've promised not to sell them, you see, and—"

"I don't want any money from you, Mr. Tate," MacDougal said.

The old man stared at him in surprise, and Rebekah opened her mouth to remind him he should at least ask to be repaid for the things he had bought her. Then she remembered what he'd said about already having been paid for the dress she was wearing and closed her mouth again, flushing furiously.

"What do you want then, young man?" Zebulon asked after a moment.

"I . . ." He glanced at Rebekah, then smiled at her father. "Perhaps we should discuss this privately, man to man."

Rebekah was just about to tell MacDougal exactly what she thought of his suggestion when the door to the kitchen opened and Jewel stuck her bandana-wrapped head in.

"Miss Rebekah, don't you think you oughta be in bed? You've had a mighty hard time of it lately and looks like you be needing some rest."

A hard time? If only she knew the real hardships Rebekah had endured. The simple ride across half of Texas had been more like a pleasure trip.

"I'm not really—"

"I moved all your stuff into your room, and I done fixed you a nice hot bath and made up your bed with clean sheets," Jewel announced.

"My room?" Rebekah asked in confusion.

"When I built this place, I built a room for you, too," her father said softly, his faded eyes misty. "I always knew you'd be back someday."

Rebekah covered her mouth to keep the emotions from escaping. She wouldn't cry, not now, not yet. She still didn't feel safe enough, and she didn't know if her father could bear to see her cry either.

But she knew she had to escape. Her nerves were simply too raw to stand anymore of this.

"I . . . I think I'll go to bed now."

Her father nodded, rising when she did and reaching out to touch her, as if he needed to reassure himself that she was really there. Knowing if she stayed another second, he would take her in his arms and shatter what was left of her fragile defenses, Rebekah fled, following Jewel's stately figure out through the kitchen and not even looking back to bid good night to MacDougal.

Why should she worry about MacDougal at all? she reasoned. She was free of him now. She was home.

Jewel led her across the dogtrot to the other side of the house and opened one of the two doors in the log wall. Inside was a small bedroom with a bunk built into one corner. It wasn't the same bunk in which she had slept at the stockade, but it was remarkably like it as was the quilt that covered it.

The wardrobe along one wall was the one in which she and her sisters had kept their clothes back in Tennessee and which they had carried in a wagon all the way to Texas. A crude washstand stood on another wall, completing all the regular furnishings. In the center of the room sat a tin washtub filled with steaming water, and once again Rebekah felt almost faint at the thought of actually lowering her saddle-weary body into the warmth.

"Now you get that dress off and let ol' Jewel take care of you," the black woman commanded.

Rebekah would have protested, but Jewel was already unbuttoning her bodice, muttering imprecations at the ugliness of the dress.

"MacDougal bought it for me," Rebekah explained with a smile.

"That man don't got no taste at all," Jewel said as she pulled the offending garment over Rebekah's head. "Didn't he know it was big enough to hold two of you? And look here at this rag!" she exclaimed in outrage at the sight of Rebekah's undergarment.

Oddly, Rebekah felt the need to defend MacDougal's choice. "It was all they had. He'd stopped at a

197

fort way out on the frontier. Hopewell's, I think it was called. They don't have much in the way of women's fashions out there."

"I reckon not," Jewel said, swiftly removing the raggedy chemise from Rebekah's unresisting body as well.

Before she knew what was happening, Rebekah stood naked, but Jewel was much too competent to allow for such a thing as modesty even if Rebekah had remembered how to feel it. Indeed, Jewel seemed hardly to look at her at all even as she helped her into the tub.

The warm water was so exquisite, Rebekah moaned aloud with bliss as she lowered herself into it. "Oh, Jewel, do you know how long—?"

"Yes'm, Miss Rebekah, seven long years," Jewel replied briskly, dipping a rag into the water to moisten it. "I've got some soft soap here. I figure to wash your hair, and you can wash the rest of you. This lye soap'll take care of lice and any other little critters you might've collected."

Rebekah winced, knowing she'd carried just such little critters with her from the Indian camp and hating that Jewel knew, too. But once again, Jewel didn't give her time to feel any humiliation, especially not after her strong fingers started rubbing the suds into Rebekah's scalp, sending delicious chills racing over her body. Dear God, how could she ever have taken such luxury for granted? How could she have actually resented the Saturday night baths of her youth?

"Why'd they cut off all your hair?" Jewel asked as she rinsed the soap from Rebekah's shorn locks.

"That's the way the Indians wear it. It's easier to take care of."

"I always thought they wore them long pigtails," Jewel observed.

"The men do. For them, long hair is a . . . I don't know, a sign of strength or something."

"Like Samson in the Bible."

Rebekah had never made the connection. "Yes, I suppose so."

When she had finished with Rebekah's hair, Jewel picked up the clothes from the floor as Rebekah scrubbed away the years of her captivity, savoring the scrape of the rough cloth and the silken suds on her abused flesh.

"I'll wash these out tonight," Jewel said, "and see if I can't mend 'em a little, too." She shook her head in disgust at the garments.

Rebekah thought Jewel might leave then and wondered at her own reluctance to see the woman go. She certainly had no reason to want her to stay. Perhaps she just wasn't ready to be alone yet.

But once again Jewel surprised her. "So you got yourself a son, have you?" she said. Plainly, she'd been eavesdropping, and just as plainly, she didn't care if anybody knew it.

Rebekah had never spent any time with a colored person before. She didn't know if it was appropriate for her to discuss something like this with a slave. Jewel seemed intent on discussing things with her, however, and Rebekah did need to talk about her boy.

"It almost killed me to leave him, but MacDougal was right: they never would've let us get away if we'd taken the boy with us. I guess they think I'm dead. Getting the boy will be harder, of course, because he won't know he's supposed to go. He might even be frightened at first, at least until MacDougal tells him I'm alive."

"You're really gonna bring him here, then," Jewel said, her voice offering neither approval or disapproval.

But Rebekah recalled her father's shock and

199

wondered if the black woman was equally shocked, only hiding it better. "Don't you think I should?" she challenged.

Jewel looked down at her, her eyes bright in her dark face. "If he's your flesh and blood, don't you let nobody keep him from you," she said fiercely.

Jewel's sudden passion raised gooseflesh on Rebekah's wet skin, and in spite of the difference in the color of that skin from Jewel's, Rebekah felt an instant kinship with the woman. "You must have a child, too," she guessed.

To her surprise, Jewel's expression hardened instead of softened. "I had me four babies once at the place where I was before your pappy bought me and I come here. That was my job there, making babies. It was what they call a breeding farm."

"What's that?" Rebekah asked, although she was pretty sure she didn't want to know.

"It's a place where they raise slaves. They gets a whole bunch of young nigger girls and a few bucks and sets 'em to making babies. Then they sells the babies like they was a crop. They sold all four of mine, one by one, soon's they was weaned, and I ain't never gonna see a one of 'em again."

Rebekah stared at the woman in horror, wondering how she could even bear to remember such pain, much less speak of it. To have lost *four* children forever when Rebekah could barely stand the pain of simply missing her one for a few weeks. Her eyes filled with tears, and she reached out instinctively and took Jewel's hand.

The black woman started at the touch, then her fingers closed over Rebekah's for just an instant before she seemed to shake off the pall of the past and return to the present. "Don't you listen to anybody says you shouldn't get him," she said crisply, releasing Rebekah's hand and moving quickly away, as if she had important tasks to perform, although Rebekah noticed she didn't seem to be doing anything very vital, just straightening the already straight quilt on the bed and checking for dust on the top of the wardrobe and centering the chipped basin on the washstand. "They'll tell you he ain't nothing but a red nigger bastard. They'll tell you you'll be happier if he ain't here to remind you of what happened to you with the Indians, but don't you listen. It'll be hard, but I'm telling you, there ain't nothing worse than having a baby off someplace and not knowing if he's dead or alive or happy or miserable. If you want him, you get him here. You hear me?"

Rebekah heard her and believed her. When she thought of her baby left to Squeaky's tender mercies for the rest of his life, she wanted to scream. She nodded, not trusting her voice.

As if she were uncomfortable with having revealed so much emotion, Jewel continued to bustle around the room, not looking at Rebekah or speaking again until Rebekah was finished with her bath.

"I always tried to keep clean," Rebekah remarked, reaching for one of the flour-sack towels Jewel had laid on the floor near the tub and wrapping it around her damp hair. "But washing in a cold creek with only sand to scrub with just isn't the same."

"No," Jewel agreed. "I don't reckon it is."

Rebekah rubbed the towel over her hair, reluctant to leave the lingering warmth of the tub until she absolutely had to. "Jewel, how did you get here? I mean, how did you get away from that place?"

Jewel stood with her back to Rebekah, and Rebekah saw the squared shoulders droop a bit. Instantly she regretted her question, seeing it had caused pain, but when Jewel turned to face her, she saw the woman didn't mind the telling.

"I stopped having babies. They didn't have no use for a woman who couldn't breed anymore, so they sold me down the river. I thought sure I'd die in some cotton field. That's what slaves hear happens to them what's sold down the river. Nobody lasts long in the deep south, with them fevers and all. But your pappy buys me in N'Orleans. He says he needs a housekeeper. I figures I knows what he means by that." She smiled with bitter wisdom and for an instant Rebekah had visions of her father and Jewel . . .

Then Jewel shook her head. "He won't even let Dan or Enoch bother me, not unless I wants to marry up proper with one of 'em, and I don't. I ain't never gonna lay under no man again. He'd have to kill me first."

Rebekah shivered at hearing her own thoughts spoken aloud and dropped her gaze when she remembered how quickly she had forgotten her pledge in MacDougal's arms. The memory of his hands on her body made her shiver again.

"You're gonna catch a chill," Jewel declared, seeing her reaction and misinterpreting. "Better get out of there now and get into bed. I don't have nothing for you to wear, but it ain't cold and there's plenty of blankets if you need 'em."

Brooking no argument, Jewel drew her out of the tub and helped dry her off, then turned the blankets down and tucked her in between the crisp sheets as if Rebekah had been a child. The straw mattress crackled underneath her as it gave to her weight. For a moment, she surrendered herself up to the sensuous luxury of it all, of lying in a bed up off the ground that didn't smell of animal skins and wood smoke, and looking up to a real ceiling instead of the inside of a tent or a brush arbor, and knowing she could close the door and no one would come in, not ever, ever again, not unless she wanted them to.

"Oh, Jewel," she whispered in awe.

"I know," Jewel said, and Rebekah believed she did.

As soon as the women were gone, Zebulon Tate turned to Sean, a thousand questions in his old eyes.

Sean said, "Mind if I smoke?"

Tate shook his head. "Could use one myself," he said. He got up from his chair and crossed the room to a small crudely built cabinet that sat against the far wall. Inside was a collection of pipes. Tate selected one and began to fill it from a tin humidor of tobacco. "Help yourself," he offered. "The tobacco ain't the best, although it's dear enough, but it's all we can get out here."

As Sean selected a pipe from Tate's collection and filled it, he nonchalantly inquired about where Tate got his supplies and how he disposed of his crops and what the prices were like.

Having answered all the inquiries, Tate studied Sean when they were seated again, puffing on the pipes. "Sounds like you might be interested in settling around here yourself," he observed.

"I am, Mr. Tate. Most interested. You asked me before what kind of reward I wanted for rescuing your daughter, and the truth is, I believe for a man like me, having rescued her will be a reward in itself. I'm a businessman, Mr. Tate, and having the respect of the community is perhaps the most important element in building a successful business."

"You're a trader, you said."

"A storekeeper," he demurred. "I traded with the Indians because it was acceptable in Sante Fe and because I made a lot of money from it. Now I want to open a store in Texas."

"Where everyone will know what you've done for

203

Rebekah." Tate frowned in disapproval.

"That's part of it," he admitted. "The other part is so that I'll be close to Rebekah."

The old man's frown deepened. "What do you mean, close to her?"

Sean leaned forward earnestly. "I mean, I admire your daughter, Mr. Tate, and I've become very fond of her during the past few weeks. I'd like to marry her."

The old man's surprise was almost comic, but it quickly turned to suspicion. "If you want her because you think I'm rich—"

"I'm rich, Mr. Tate. I don't need anyone's money. I don't need anything from anyone, so I'm free to go after what I want. Back there in that Indian camp, your daughter offered me a way to make a name for myself. That's important to me because I'm an orphan, Mr. Tate. The only name I have is the one they gave me in the orphanage. I have no idea who my people were or what they were. All I have is myself, and by rescuing your daughter, I had a chance to make my name one people would respect. I thought that was going to be enough, but that was before I got to know Rebekah. Now I want her, too."

"And that's why you've decided to go back out there and get her . . . that child." Plainly, mention of the child disturbed him even more than it disturbed Sean.

"Don't you think that's a good idea?" he tried.

"No!" Tate cried, his eyes anguished. "Do you know what that would mean? It'll be bad enough for her as it is! People will pity her, some will even despise her. I've had folks tell me they knew Rebekah was dead because any decent woman would kill herself before she'd let an Indian touch her. There'll be some who'll think she should've killed herself, who'll think she's unclean. It will be bad at first, but

204

after some time, after they get used to her, people will learn to accept her and even to forgive her."

"*Forgive* her?" Sean echoed incredulously.

"Yes," he replied wearily. "For surviving when so many others didn't. For coming back healthy and whole when so many others never came back at all. For enduring what they do not believe themselves capable of enduring, and for being stronger than they think a woman should be. But they will forgive her eventually and come to accept her, and if she were to marry a respectable man . . ." He smiled slightly. ". . . if she were to marry a respectable man, she might even have a fairly normal life."

"And you don't think she could have a normal life if she had a half-breed child?"

A spasm of pain flickered across Tate's face. "The child would be a constant reminder of what happened to her, proof that the savages had defiled her. No one could pretend it hadn't happened, and no one would forget."

"And no one would forgive her, either," Sean guessed.

"Not for bringing one of those animals to live in their very midst. So many of our people have lost loved ones to the Comanche, seen them slaughtered, butchered . . ." His voice broke and he looked away, as if seeing his own loved ones again. Sean drew him back.

"You don't think they'd have any sympathy for an innocent child?"

Tate's eyes burned with some inner fire when he looked back at Sean. "They would never consider an Indian 'innocent,' not even a child. And I'm afraid they'd turn all the hate they feel for the entire Comanche race onto the one living representative of it that happened to be in their midst."

"Then you don't think I should go after the boy?"

Tate's eyes were bleak. "The child is my grandson, Mr. MacDougal. My own flesh and blood, so I hope you know how much it costs me to say this, but my loyalty must be to my daughter whose welfare will always come first to me. No, Mr. MacDougal, I do not think you should go after the boy."

Sean sighed. "That's good, because I never had any intention of getting him."

"What!"

"It's was the only way I could get her away. She'd still be out there if I hadn't promised her I'd go back for the boy, but I agree with you, she'd be a fool to bring him here. He's half wild, like all Comanche children. It would be cruel to bring him here, like trying to housebreak a wolf. Besides, there's no way to get him. His father will never let him go voluntarily, and only a crazy man would sneak up on a Comanche camp to steal a child who didn't want to be stolen. One peep out of him and . . ." He shrugged expressively, knowing he didn't have to explain any further.

Plainly Tate did not approve of Sean having lied to his daughter, but he also couldn't argue with the logic of his decision. "When do you plan to tell Rebekah you aren't going back for the boy?"

This was something Sean had been trying not to think about. "I guess I'll wait until she's had some time to get used to being back, until she sees what it's going to be like."

"You mean until she sees how people are going to treat her," Tate said with a troubled frown. "I just pray they won't be too cruel to her."

"Your daughter is a strong woman," Sean said. "She's survived things that would have destroyed most people. Her friends and relatives can't do anything worse to her."

Zebulon Tate puffed pensively on his pipe for a

moment. "I certainly pray you're right, Mr. Mac-
Dougal."

When Rebekah awoke the next morning, she knew
instantly that she was home. Her naked body was
encased in the warm cocoon of a real bed with real
sheets and real blankets in a real house, and nothing
would ever hurt her again. If only her son were here,
everything would be perfect. Longing for him
throbbed through her, but she reminded herself that
soon she would hold him in her arms again.

She wondered how quickly MacDougal would be
leaving and guessed he'd want at least a few days to
rest and to enjoy some real food before hitting the
trail again. In any case, it wouldn't be long, perhaps
only a month, before she had her boy and she could
allow herself to be truly happy. If only she still
remembered how.

She lay there for a while, wallowing in the almost
sinful luxury of the bed. Even without opening her
eyes, she knew she'd slept long past dawn. Talk
about sinful, wasn't laziness one of the seven deadly
sins? She couldn't quite remember, but neither did
she care. For once she had no place to go, nothing to
do, no firewood to gather, no food to prepare, no
child demanding attention, no master to please.

Was this why people liked having slaves? If so, she
could certainly understand how the institution had
gotten started. How blissful to lie there knowing
someone else was taking care of all the chores she'd
been doing ever since she could remember. And if she
got up and went to the kitchen, Jewel would prepare
her breakfast and serve it to her, and afterwards Jewel
would wash up the dishes, too. If Rebekah weren't
careful, she might become totally corrupted.

Except, she suddenly realized, she couldn't even

consider going to the kitchen because Jewel had taken her clothes last night. Oh, well, she supposed she would just have to wait until Jewel brought them back again. With a contented smile, she stretched sinuously and opened her eyes.

The room was flooded with sunlight, and Rebekah guessed it must be close to noon. How long since she had slept so late? Probably never in her entire life. She adjusted the covers around her naked breasts and considered what the day (or what was left of it) might hold. More questions from her father probably, questions she would never be able to answer. And MacDougal would be there.

How odd that the thought of his being there should give her comfort. She'd never considered MacDougal's presence at all comforting. In fact, he usually had the opposite effect on her. Except of course the time she'd cried and he'd held her and . . .

But she wouldn't think about it, wouldn't remember her lapse because it would never happen again. She was strong now, and she would never need a man's shoulder and even if she did, she'd have her father. As soon as MacDougal brought her son back, she would happily banish him from her life.

Happily? Yes, *happily*, she insisted to herself although the reaction she felt at the thought wasn't a bit like happiness or even relief. It felt strangely like regret, although she knew she'd feel no regret over losing MacDougal.

Before she could completely convince herself, however, the door to her room began to open very silently. Rebekah's heart leaped into her throat and she snatched the covers to that throat, certain she would see MacDougal's insolent grin beaming through his red beard and his wolf's eyes glittering across the room.

But the face she saw peering around the door was

brown and female, and Rebekah knew a strange sense of disappointment.

"You awake?" Jewel asked unnecessarily.

"Yes, and I was wondering how I was going to go anywhere without any clothes."

Jewel smiled and came completely into the room. She carried a tray made out of a plank of wood. On the tray was Rebekah's breakfast. Over her arm she carried Rebekah's dress.

"I hated to wake you up, but I knowed your Aunt Prudence would be here 'fore long and figured you'd want to be up and dressed."

"Prudence?" Rebekah couldn't remember anyone by that name.

"Your Uncle Cecil's wife," Jewel reminded her. "Or maybe he ain't your uncle. I ain't too sure."

Rebekah nodded, remembering now. Her father had told her Cousin Cecil had remarried. "She's coming here?" Rebekah asked, dread a cold lump in her stomach.

"Don't know for sure, o'course, but if she knows you're here, I don't reckon anything could keep her away." Rebekah thought she detected a faint note of criticism in Jewel's tone.

Jewel set the tray down at the foot of Rebekah's bed, and the delicious aromas reminded her she hadn't eaten in quite a while. She certainly hadn't eaten flapjacks in quite a while.

"Here, put this on," Jewel said, handing her something white that she had carried in with the dress. "It ain't much, but it'll do until we can get you something better."

Jewel had obviously stitched a few flour sacks together to make Rebekah a decent shift. It certainly wasn't much in the way of beauty, but Rebekah felt an odd stinging in her eyes at the thought of Jewel sitting up last night, sewing by candlelight to make it.

"Jewel, you shouldn't have!" she said, wondering if she was going to want to cry every time she received an article of clothing. At least she wouldn't have to worry about Jewel taking advantage of her the way MacDougal had.

"Can't have you going around in rags," Jewel said briskly, helping Rebekah slip the garment over her head. "Miss Prudence wouldn't approve."

Again Rebekah heard the tone of disapproval, and this time took it as a warning. "What's she like, Jewel?"

"A fine Christian woman," Jewel pronounced, helping Rebekah sit up and placing the tray of food in her lap. In Jewel's mouth, the words did not sound like praise as they had in her father's. Suddenly, the food no longer smelled quite so delicious and Rebekah's appetite was gone.

"You eat now," Jewel commanded. "We gotta get some meat on them bones or you're likely to blow away in the next big wind."

Rebekah smiled politely, and equally politely, she picked up the fork and awkwardly began to struggle with the flapjacks. "You're a good cook, Jewel," she said after the first mouthful, although she hadn't actually tasted it.

Jewel grunted in acknowledgement. "I pressed off this dress," she said, holding the garment up for Rebekah to see. "Didn't seem to help it none, though. It's still as ugly as it can be." It was, too, although it looked considerably better than it had the night before.

"Thank you, Jewel," Rebekah said sincerely.

Jewel grunted again and laid the dress across the foot of the bed. Then she began to needlessly straighten the room just as she had the night before while Rebekah ate.

After a few more mouthfuls of the food, Rebekah's

body began to appreciate it even if her mind could not, and she started to eat with more enthusiasm. At least until she thought of something else. "Will . . . will my Cousin Andrew be coming today, too?"

"I expect so," Jewel said. "Mr. Cecil, too. They'll prob'ly think it's their duty to see you and welcome you home. Miss Prudence'll prob'ly bring a cake." Jewel raised an eyebrow. "She thinks I don't know how to feed my folks."

Rebekah smiled in spite of herself. "I'll reassure her."

"You can try," Jewel said. "We'll have to get Massa Zeb to put on another room for your boy when he comes," she continued. "Can't have him sleeping with his mammy, 'specially not after you and that Mr. MacDougal get married."

Rebekah nearly choked on a mouthful of flapjack. "*What?*" she cried when she'd managed to swallow it without strangling.

Jewel's expression was completely innocent. "That man means to have you, Miss Rebekah. Anybody with eyes can see that. I just figured you knew."

For a moment, Rebekah's brain refused to function, refused even to understand Jewel's statement, and then they heard the commotion in the yard, the dogs barking furiously, a wagon rattling up, and voices calling a greeting.

Jewel sighed resignedly. "I reckon you got yourself some visitors, Miss Rebekah."

Forgetting all about MacDougal, Rebekah felt an emotion she'd never expected to experience again: sheer terror.

Chapter Eight

If given a choice, Rebekah would have stayed in her room all day, but of course Jewel didn't give her a choice. While Zebulon Tate took his guests inside the other half of the house, Jewel helped Rebekah wash and dress. She even produced a comb with which Rebekah unsnarled her cropped hair.

At least the dress looked more presentable today. In addition to ironing it, Jewel had taken in the seams so it actually fit, and she'd also turned up the frayed cuffs and hem.

"You're a wonder, Jewel," Rebekah marveled when she had the repaired garment on. "How do I look?"

Jewel considered her for a moment. "All right, 'cept for them shoes," she concluded, indicating Rebekah's moccasins. "Reckon Massa Zeb'll have to send off for some real ones. 'Cept for that, you look fine, though. Maybe you oughta see for yourself." She pointed to the washstand, above which hung an ancient, foggy mirror that Rebekah remembered had once hung in her parent's bedroom.

Rebekah hadn't even glanced in it when she'd washed her face there a few minutes earlier, having completely forgotten the small vanity that white

212

women took for granted. Comanches feared mirrors, considering them demon possessed or something like that, so Rebekah hadn't seen her reflection except in water for many years.

"It won't bite you," Jewel chided when she hesitated.

Not wanting to appear a coward, Rebekah forced her reluctant feet to move toward the washstand. The image reflected back at her was a stranger, a woman where she had remembered a girl, short hair where she had remembered long, experience where she had remembered innocence. Her skin was dark, so dark she might have actually been an Indian except for her blue eyes and yellow hair.

She touched the shorn ends where they touched her earlobe.

"It'll grow," Jewel assured her. "And we can get you a bonnet."

But not in time, Rebekah thought, not before Andrew saw her, and the mysterious Prudence. What would they think? Would they know simply from looking at her what the Indians had done to her? Would they ask her about it? And if they did, what would she say?

"They'll be waiting," Jewel reminded her.

Rebekah laid a hand over her churning stomach and regretted sampling Jewel's delicious breakfast. "I guess I can't put it off anymore."

"No, you can't," Jewel agreed. Without hesitation, she went to the door and opened it, waiting for Rebekah to step through. For one fleeting second Rebekah wished MacDougal were with her. Perhaps if she asked Jewel to fetch him . . . But no, she could never let MacDougal know she needed him, even if she would have sold her soul at that moment to have his strong arm to lean on.

Sucking in a deep breath, she walked out the door,

realizing too late that Jewel had no intention of going with her. While the black woman went back for the breakfast tray, Rebekah stood for a moment in the shade of the dogtrot, listening to the rumble of voices from the kitchen opposite. The words were indistinguishable, but she knew what they were saying nonetheless. They were talking about her, and the only way she could stop them was to make her feet carry her over to the door and up the small stoop and into the kitchen where all those eyes would turn to her and . . .

She let out her breath in a tremulous sigh and took the first step and then the second. By the time she reached the kitchen door, she felt strangely detached, as if all this were happening to someone else. It was a feeling she recognized. She was drifting away to her safe world. Not all the way, not yet, not unless it was just too awful to bear, but far enough so that they couldn't hurt her.

The rumble of voices grew louder as she approached the door, and she could make out the words. MacDougal was telling how he'd rescued her, and the others were marveling, asking questions and expressing their amazement. She stepped through the doorway and suddenly the room grew silent.

Her eyes weren't yet accustomed to the dim interior light, so for a few seconds she couldn't quite make them out. Then they materialized, and she saw them clearly, or at least she saw their eyes. She saw their surprise and their curiosity and their wariness, as if they didn't know quite what to expect but were ready for anything.

Then her father said, "Rebekah," and the spell was broken. Chairs scraped across the plank floor, and everyone stood up to greet her. "You remember your cousins, don't you?" Zeb asked gently, as if afraid of startling her.

214

Cousin Cecil stepped forward first. The years had thinned his yellow hair and stooped his shoulders, and grief had carved new lines into his face. He wore a black broadcloth suit instead of the work clothes she remembered, but she recognized him easily enough.

He repeated her name, as if confirming her identity, but he made no move to embrace her, for which she was grateful. "We're very glad to have you home," he added awkwardly. He seemed painfully aware of how inadequate his greeting was.

"Rebekah," someone else said and when she looked up, she saw Andrew, grown taller now, a man instead of the boy she remembered, but Andrew still. He took her hands in his, his grip fierce as if he wanted to crush her to him but didn't dare. His eyes glistened, brimming with emotions Rebekah couldn't possibly allow herself to share, not if she wanted to preserve her dignity. In spite of the threatening tears, he was smiling at her with such unabashed joy she could hardly bear to look at him. How could he possibly be so happy to see her?

"Andrew, where are your manners?" a female voice chided after a moment.

Andrew started and dropped her hands instantly, leaving her fingers aching. He stepped back to make way for the woman. "Rebekah, this is my step-mother, Prudence Nelson."

Prudence exhibited none of the hesitancy of the males of her family. She stepped forward and took Rebekah's hand and shook it firmly. "I'm happy to meet you," she declared. "We would have been here sooner, but Andrew didn't tell us until this morning that you were back." She gave Andrew a disapproving glance, and he dropped his eyes sheepishly. "You seem remarkably well," she told Rebekah, looking her over in frank appraisal. "A little thin, perhaps, but that's not surprising, I suppose."

Prudence Nelson was a few inches shorter than Rebekah, perhaps no more than five feet tall, but no one would ever accuse her of being thin. Her well-padded figure was encased in a brown, shadow plaid dress of linsey-woolsey. The fan folded bodice draped over her full bosom and cinched in at her surprisingly narrow waist to fan out again into a full skirt that covered equally full hips. A matching bonnet framed her plain face and covered graying brown hair that had been scraped back into a bun, and a delicate lace collar adorned her throat, drawing attention away from her double chin. Nothing, however, could draw attention from her gimlet eyes which missed no detail of Rebekah's appearance and which told her far more than the mirror had how pathetic she looked.

"We'll have to do something about your complexion," Prudence declared. "It's fair ruined, but you're young enough, maybe it will improve with some care. If you rub on a mixture of buttermilk and lemon juice, it'll lighten the skin, although where we'd get lemons, I don't know. I've heard stump water works just as well, though I've never tried it myself, and those hideous things you've got on your feet! Zeb, we'll have to find her some shoes immediately! We can't have her looking like a savage another day!"

Rebekah gaped at the woman, aghast at being discussed as if she weren't actually there, but before she could think of a thing to say in response, everyone jumped at the crash of tin dishes hitting the floor.

They all turned to the doorway to see Jewel grinning back at them, the contents of Rebekah's breakfast tray scattered at her feet. "Sorry, Massa Zeb," she said, although she didn't look the least bit repentant. Plainly, she'd dropped the tray on

216

purpose to draw attention from Rebekah. "I'll clean this up right away."

Prudence rolled her eyes and shook her head so that her chins quivered. "I just can't get used to having *them* around," she confided without bothering to lower her voice. "Cecil needs them for the fields, but I won't have one in the house. I've told him. I don't care how hard the work is."

Rebekah glanced at Jewel to see how she was reacting to being talked about in just the same disparaging way Rebekah had been, but Jewel was busy picking up the mess and shooing away the interested dogs, apparently oblivious to the comments. It was a skill Rebekah suspected she would have to develop herself.

Turning back to Prudence, Rebekah tried to think of something to say since that seemed to be what everyone was waiting for. She couldn't, and she wished fervently that she could go back to the security and solitude of her room. Or at least that she could find a friendly face among those gathered in her father's kitchen. Desperate, she scanned the room for the only person with whom she would feel comfortable, the only one who really understood what she had been through and who would protect her now. But he wasn't there, even though she'd heard his voice just a moment ago. She saw only the Nelsons and her father and a stranger still sitting at the far end of the table even though everyone else had risen to their feet. Wondering vaguely who the strange man might be, she glanced into the corners, hoping to see the familiar red-bearded face grinning at her from the shadows, but she saw no sign of him. No sign of anyone else except the stranger and . . .

Her gaze darted back to him, back to the face she hadn't recognized at first because the red beard was gone, as was most of the hair which someone had

217

trimmed to a respectable length. He wasn't smiling, at least not with his mouth, but his wolf's eyes were mocking her surprise. Or at least they were at first. After a few seconds the mockery flickered out, and he raised one hand self-consciously to touch his naked cheek. Was he afraid she didn't like what she saw? She smiled slightly at the thought. If anything, he was more handsome than ever with his lean cheeks and square jaw exposed, even though they were pasty white as compared with the upper part of his face that had been burnished by the sun. He didn't have to know she thought so, though.

Their gazes held for a heartbeat, his uncertain, hers now mocking, then Prudence said. "Rebekah? Maybe you'd like to sit down?"

Her strident tone had mellowed into something gentler, and she spoke slowly, carefully enunciating each word, as if afraid Rebekah couldn't understand. Rebekah looked at the shorter woman in surprise, trying to determine what had caused the change in her.

Prudence stared back, her small eyes wide now with what could only be alarm. "Can she understand what I'm saying, Zeb?" she asked, actually backing up a pace.

"Of course I can understand," Rebekah snapped, and from the way everyone jumped, she realized this was the first time she had spoken. "Did you think I forgot how to talk English?"

Prudence smiled, although the effort was strained. "I'm sure no one thought that, dear," Prudence said, and the men confirmed her statement with unintelligible murmurs.

Good God, Rebekah thought, do they always let her do the talking? Don't they have anything to say for themselves? She glanced at MacDougal who was no longer holding back his grin and for a second they

218

shared amusement.

"I haven't forgotten how to sit in a chair either," she informed them and jerked out the one nearest her and sat down.

Everyone else hastily followed suit, then another awkward moment of silence fell during which everyone just looked around and tried to pretend they weren't ill at ease. Finally Prudence saved them. "Mr. MacDougal was just telling us about your daring escape. I'm sure I don't know how you did it. Riding all that way on horseback, all alone in the wilderness with Indians all around." She shuddered delicately.

"It wasn't so bad," Rebekah said, feeling an irrational anger at them for their awkwardness. "Not compared to the way I went out, tied naked to the back of a horse and getting beaten every night and hardly getting enough food or water to keep me alive." She bared her teeth at the woman in the semblance of a smile. "Compared to that, my trip home was almost fun."

Feeling satisfaction at having shocked Cousin Prudence, whom she had decided she didn't like one bit, she looked around to see the effect on everyone else. Instantly, she regretted her impulse. Cousin Cecil looked stunned, Andrew aghast, and her father . . . Well, her father looked as if she'd slapped him in the face. The pain in his eyes tore at her heart. Only MacDougal seemed unaffected, and Jewel, of course, who was working over by the fire and had her back to everyone although Rebekah knew she was listening to every word. MacDougal rose from his seat, however, and said, "Maybe you gentlemen would like to join me in the other room for a smoke. We'll leave the ladies alone for a while so they can get acquainted."

Rebekah shot him a black look—the last thing she wanted was to get better acquainted with Cousin

Prudence—but he ignored her. The other men scrambled to their feet, pathetically grateful for the opportunity to escape what was becoming a very uncomfortable situation. MacDougal herded them into the parlor and closed the connecting door, but before he did, he caught her eye one last time as if to warn her to behave herself while he was gone.

Feeling angry and embarrassed and not a little frightened at being alone with the formidable Prudence, Rebekah clasped her hands tightly together in her lap and forced herself to meet her adversary's eye.

Prudence's smile was more than strained now, but she was making a valiant effort to pretend nothing untoward had happened. "You must have had quite a time of it out there," she remarked in astonishing understatement.

"Not as bad as some. I'm still alive."

"You want some coffee, Miss Rebekah?" Jewel asked in a voice Rebekah had never heard her use before. She sounded subservient, the way a slave probably should.

Rebekah didn't think she could swallow anything at all, certainly not with a civilized white woman watching her every move, but she nodded. "Thank you, Jewel."

Prudence waited until Jewel had poured Rebekah's coffee and refilled Prudence's cup, too.

Then Prudence took a deep breath. "I know your father would want me to minister to you just the way your own mother would if she were still alive, God rest her soul."

"Minister?" Rebekah echoed suspiciously.

"Yes, help you get adjusted to being home." She smiled more sincerely. "Be a friend to you."

Heaven knew, Rebekah would need friends. If only she trusted Prudence more. "That's very kind of

220

you," she said evasively.

"I know you've suffered," she said, although Rebekah figured the woman had no real idea. "I've heard things. The men don't like us to know, but we ladies overhear and we discuss the dangers. You were just a child when you were taken, but . . . Well, we're both women and we know how men are. I'm sure the Indians are no different. In fact, I've heard they're much worse. I assume you are no longer . . . innocent?"

She folded her hands on the table and leaned forward earnestly, but if she expected Rebekah to bare her soul, she would be disappointed. "If you're asking me if I've been with a man, the answer is yes, and if you want to know if I've been with more than one, the answer to that is yes, too, but if you want me to tell you all about it, I won't."

Prudence seemed a little taken aback. "I must say I'm surprised, Rebekah."

"By what?"

"By . . . by your attitude. I would expect a young woman in your situation to be more . . ." She groped for the proper word.

"Ashamed?" Rebekah suggested bitterly.

Prudence blinked and straightened up in her chair. "I'm sure you have nothing to be ashamed of, although one does wonder . . ."

"Wonders what?" Rebekah prompted angrily.

"How . . ." The gimlet eyes darted away, and now it was Cousin Prudence who seemed embarrassed. Her plump cheeks reddened in unbecoming blotches. Then she pursed her lips and squared her shoulders as if she were mentally chastising herself for being weak. "One can't help but wonder how you survived. How you . . . how you bore it. Oh, I know God gives His grace to those most in need of it but . . ." She forced herself to look at Rebekah. "You

221

seem almost unaffected."

If only she knew how very affected Rebekah was, but Rebekah had no intention of letting anyone know that, least of all Cousin Prudence.

When Rebekah did not respond, Prudence went on, her voice a little less steady than it had been before. "What I mean, I've always wondered, could *I* have survived? If one of those savages touched me . . ." She shuddered at the mere thought, and Rebekah wanted to shudder at the memories.

"They don't let you die," Rebekah said without meaning to.

"What?" Prudence was confused.

"I said, they don't let you die. It doesn't matter how much you might want to or even how much they torture you. If they want you alive, they keep you that way. They never have enough women in their camps to do the work, and the women they do have never have enough babies. That's why they steal children, because they always need more than they have."

Prudence's small eyes grew wide with comprehension. "And why they steal women, to have more babies for them."

Plainly, the idea horrified her, and Rebekah had no comfort to offer even if she'd felt inclined to offer it, which she didn't.

"I'd kill any child of mine before I'd let them have it," Prudence said after a moment.

"No, you wouldn't," Rebekah said. "You'd keep it alive because you'd hope against hope that someday you'd get it away again."

Prudence studied her for a moment. "You talk like you have a child of your own."

"I do," Rebekah said, shocking her again. "A son."

Prudence started, then looked around as if she expected to find the child hiding somewhere nearby.

"He's . . . Your father never said . . . Where is he?"

"He's still out there, but MacDougal is going back for him just as soon as he can."

Prudence's expression was difficult to read, but Rebekah thought she sensed relief. "Your . . . the boy," she ventured. "He's white?"

"He's half white, if that's what you're asking. Like you said, I was only a child myself when they took me. How could I have a white child?"

"And Mr. MacDougal plans to go back for him? Isn't that dangerous?"

"Yes, very," she admitted, and seeing Prudence's amazement, she began to entertain her own doubts for the first time. "But . . . but he promised me."

"Mr. MacDougal is a very courageous man, although one must certainly question the character of anyone who does business with savages."

"MacDougal is a man of his word," Rebekah said, as much to convince herself as to convince her companion.

"I'm sure he is," she said, although her tone implied otherwise. "But have you thought this through, Rebekah? I mean, the child is an Indian. He must be nearly wild, with no understanding of Christianity or even civilized behavior. How can you possibly hope to bring him here, away from everything he's ever known?"

"He's my son!" Rebekah cried, frightened because Prudence's arguments seemed alarmingly logical.

"And I'm sure you love him with a mother's love, but how will others see him? Rebekah, he's a savage. Those who do not hate him will fear him. Do you want him treated that way?"

"No one would be that cruel to a child!" Rebekah insisted, although even as she said the words, she knew they weren't true. "And I won't leave him with the Indians. You just said you wouldn't leave your

223

own child with them!"

"Yes, a white child, but your child isn't white. I think *you* would be the cruel one to take him from the only life he knows."

Now Rebekah was certain she didn't like Cousin Prudence. In fact, she could no longer stand the sight of her. Without another word, she jumped up from her chair and bolted from the room. Outside, she hesitated a moment before deciding she had best seek the sanctuary of her room. She had reached the door when she heard someone softly calling her name.

"Rebekah!" Andrew was hurrying toward her, his face anxious. "Is anything wrong?"

Anything wrong? Rebekah was wondering if anything would ever be *right* again, but she couldn't say such a thing to Andrew, especially not when she saw the blatant anguish in his eyes.

"Did Prudence say something to upset you? She's not a very tactful person, but she means well, and she'd never hurt you intentionally." He smiled sadly. "I'm afraid she sometimes hurts people unintentionally, though."

"She didn't hurt me," Rebekah assured him. "She only made me angry."

"Well, she's pretty good at that, too." He glanced down at where her hand rested on the latch to her bedroom door. "Where were you going?"

Rebekah looked at her hand, too. "I guess I was going to hide."

"Would you sit with me for a few minutes instead? I want . . . I've been wanting to talk to you for a long time."

"Since yesterday when MacDougal told you I was back," she guessed.

"No, since seven years ago."

The pain in his voice stunned her, and she did not resist when he took her arm and led her down the length of the dogtrot and around to the rear of the house. There, in the shade of the eaves, was a bench made out of a split log. They sat down on it.

Neither of them spoke at first. He seemed content just to look at her, and Rebekah looked back for once not self-conscious because she saw no criticism in Andrew's expression. After a few moments, she decided that Andrew was a very attractive man. Although he was now in his mid-twenties, he had retained a sort of boyish innocence that she found appealing. His hair, as golden as her own, was longish and curly, and his clear blue eyes were open and honest. Or at least they would have been if he hadn't been so troubled.

Unable to bear his distress, she glanced away and studied the landscape while Andrew continued to study her. After a few more moments, he said, "You've grown into a beautiful woman, Rebekah."

She would have laughed if she'd remembered how. "You've changed, Andrew. You never used to say nice things to me."

"That's because you were a pest," he countered, making her smile.

"I was a pest because I was in love with you, and I wanted you to notice me."

"I know, and I did notice you, which is why I tried to stay as far away from you as I could. It wasn't easy with all of us living together in the fort, either."

"You managed."

His eyes grew bleak. "I loved you, too, 'Bekah."

She didn't know whether it was the confession or his use of her old nickname that brought the lump to her throat, but for a few seconds she didn't trust herself to speak. When she was finally able to swallow it, she said, "Now's a fine time to tell me."

"They wanted us to get married. Did you know?"

She nodded, trying to recapture the innocent

pleasure the knowledge had given her then, the delicious longing combined with the thrill of romance. How long ago it all seemed now, and try as they might, they could never bring it back.

"I was scared to death," he said. "I didn't want to get married yet. I was only seventeen, and I had dreams of doing something with my life, something besides pushing a plow for the next fifty years. I didn't want to be tied down."

"I can understand," she said. She smiled as sadly as he had smiled before. "But it doesn't matter anymore, Andrew. None of it matters now."

"But it does," he insisted, taking her hands in his. His fingers were surprisingly cold. "I should have been there that day. If I'd been there . . ." He closed his eyes, and his boyish face twisted in agony.

"Been where?" she asked in confusion.

"At the fort when they . . . when the Indians came." He opened his eyes and they brimmed with anguish. "I should've been there. I could've protected you. I could've saved you."

"Don't be silly!" she exclaimed, tightening her own grip on his fingers. "There was nothing you could've done! You would've gotten yourself killed for nothing!"

Plainly he had considered this possibility. "I would've gladly died that day if I could've saved you, 'Bekah."

Her heart ached for his pain and for all the futile suffering and regret. "Oh, Andrew," she whispered.

"Did they hurt you?" he asked, his voice ragged with grief. "Oh, God, the nights I've laid awake imagining—"

"No!" she told him fiercely. "I'm fine! Can't you see? Can't you tell? I'm fine. They didn't hurt me at all!" she lied.

He pulled her hands to his face and pressed his lips

226

first to one and then the other. When he looked up again, his eyes were wet with unshed tears. "I'm so glad you're back," he breathed.

Then, seeing the consent in her eyes, he took her in his arms, cradling her to him as if she were a precious treasure for which he had been searching his entire life. She lay against his chest, overwhelmed by memories of the life they'd known before, of the happiness they might have shared, of everything now lost to them.

A sob shook him, and she whispered, "It's all right, Andrew," and patted his shoulder. Sadly, she realized she always seemed to be comforting her loved ones when it was they who should have been comforting her.

For a second she thought she might weep, too, but she heard a growled profanity, and Andrew quickly pushed her away.

"Hope I'm not interrupting anything," MacDougal snarled.

Poor Andrew jumped up from the bench and turned his back, obviously afraid MacDougal would see he had been crying, and Rebekah jumped up, too, compelled to defend him from humiliation.

"What do you want?" she demanded, planting her hands on her hips.

Sean glared down at her. "Jewel sent me to find you. She says it's dinnertime."

"I just had breakfast," Rebekah scoffed, and Sean resisted an urge to shake her. What in the hell did she think she was doing, sneaking off with another man the minute his back was turned?

"Not everybody sleeps half the day. It's nearly noon for the rest of us," he informed her.

The color came to her beautiful cheeks, but she refused to back down. "Fine. We'll be along in a minute."

227

As if he'd leave her alone with her long-lost lover another minute! He was just about to remind her to whom she now belonged when Nelson said, "I think I'll go wash up."

Sean watched him go through narrowed eyes, noticing the boy was careful not to face him. Probably afraid Sean would see the bulge in his pants. Damn him to hell.

"I think I'll go wash up, too," she said and would have walked away, but he grabbed her shoulders and held her in place.

"Not so fast," he said and took some satisfaction in the fury that sparked in her lovely blue eyes. The sun was shining on her silken hair, turning it to pure gold, and he longed to touch it and to press her face to his and taste those luscious lips. But he figured if he did, she'd bite him, so he settled for just holding her shoulders and looking at her. "Just what did you think you were doing out here with that young pup?"

She looked genuinely surprised. "Andrew?"

"No, General Santa Anna," he snapped sarcastically. "Of course Andrew. I guess you're going to tell me you're kissing cousins."

"Kissing? Are you crazy, MacDougal?" She tried to shake his grasp, but he held her fast.

"Listen here, Rebekah Tate, if you think I risked my hide to carry you across hell and half of Texas just to turn you over to another man, then you're the one who's crazy."

This time she looked more shocked than surprised and not a little frightened. "What do you mean?"

He could feel the tension radiating from her. "I mean that . . . that capon lost whatever right he might have had to you a long time ago."

Anger flashed in her sapphire eyes. "*No* man has a right to me, not now and not ever."

Sean felt an answering fury. "You've got a short memory," he said. "Maybe you need a little reminder of how things are."

He hauled her into his arms, needing as much as wanting to feel her mouth under his, to wipe away the taste of Andrew Nelson from her lips, to restake his claim and prove to her once and for all that she was his and his alone.

Except, as he quickly learned, even a very strong man can't kiss a woman against her will, especially if she was intent on hurting him as well as resisting.

"Ouch!" he cried when her teeth sank into his lower lip, and he shoved her away when her knee very narrowly missed colliding with his groin. "What in the hell is wrong with you?" he demanded, gingerly touching the wound on his mouth, then drawing his fingers away to look for traces of blood.

"Nothing's wrong with me now that I'm not being attacked," she replied, arms akimbo. Her eyes glittered like diamonds in her tanned face, and her teeth were bared in a near snarl. For a second he remembered experiencing that heat as passion, and his body quickened in automatic response.

"I wasn't attacking you," he informed her indignantly, trying to ignore the surge of desire. "I was just trying to kiss you. You didn't seem to mind when young Nelson was doing it," he added bitterly.

"Not that it's any of your business, but Andrew wasn't kissing me."

He snorted in derision.

"And even if he was," she added haughtily, "I don't see how you've got anything to say in the matter."

"Maybe you forgot what happened between us out there," he said, pointing westward, "but I haven't."

Once again he saw the flicker of what might have been fear in her eyes, but she hardened herself against whatever it was and glared back at him. "I had to do whatever you wanted when we were out there. I couldn't take a chance you'd get mad and leave me, could I?"

He felt as if she'd slapped him. "Are you saying you didn't want it, too? That you were just pretending when you arched yourself and wrapped your legs around me and clawed at me like a wild thing and—"

"Stop it!" she cried. She looked so stricken he felt an absurd urge to comfort her. He might even have done it if he hadn't so recently tried that very thing without success.

"No, I won't stop it. You wanted me then, just like I wanted you, just like I still want you. I'll give you a little time to get used to the idea, but sooner or later—"

"Never!" she fairly shouted. "Not as long as I live!"

"Never is a mighty long time, Rebekah Tate, especially when you know how it can be between us." Her eyes were wide with emotions he couldn't name, and she looked so vulnerable that he couldn't resist reaching out to touch the satin of her cheek. "Did you forget what it was like?" he asked softly, his own need pulsing through him. He wanted to strip away that ridiculous dress and lay her down and make love to her until she screamed his name and begged him never to leave her again.

She flinched slightly at his touch, but she didn't resist, so he slid his fingers into her hair, feeling the stilken strands caress his fingers as he cupped the back of her head and drew her to him.

"No," she whispered, but she came, trembling slightly when he took her gently into his arms, and when he lowered his mouth to hers, she met him with parted lips. When he plunged his tongue into her moist depths, she seemed to melt against him, and he crushed her to him, desperate to feel every curve and angle of her precious body, to feel it and know it and possess it, to take her into himself so she could never deny him again.

Desire roared in him, blocking every coherent thought except the vague knowledge that her arms were around him now, clinging with the same fierce need he felt, wanting, wanting . . .

At last he released her, holding her at arm's length so he could see her reaction. It was everything he could have wanted, too. Her blue eyes were dazed, her lips moist, her cheeks flushed, and her breath came in ragged gasps, just as his did.

He didn't know how long they'd stood there, staring into each other's eyes, when suddenly they both realized they were no longer alone. They broke apart guiltily, but Sean kept his hand on her arm, unable to let her go completely as he turned to see who had interrupted.

There stood Andrew Nelson, his handsome face creased into a worried frown as if he'd seen something he hadn't wanted to see and couldn't quite believe. "Is everything all right, Rebekah?" he asked, not even looking at Sean.

"Yes," she answered, somewhat breathlessly. She sounded like a woman who had been thoroughly kissed, and when Sean glanced at her flushed face, he was gratified to see she still looked that way, too. So there, Andrew Nelson, he thought.

And Andrew Nelson frowned more deeply, wanting to believe her but knowing he shouldn't. "You'd better come on to dinner before somebody else comes looking for you."

"I will," she said.

He waited for a long moment, obviously expecting her to come with him. When she did not, he flushed, turned on his heel and left.

Neither of them moved for another moment. Sean was too busy thinking of ways to inform Cousin Andrew that Rebekah Tate belonged to Sean Mac-Dougal, so he'd better not get any ideas in that direction.

Then Rebekah said, "We'd better go." She sounded more like herself this time, but when she started to walk away, Sean tightened his grip on her arm instead of letting go.

"Wait a minute," he said, knowing he had to get a few things straight between them.

She looked like she wanted to argue. Instead she said, "Your lip's bleeding, MacDougal." He was too startled to stop her when she shook off his hand and strode away.

And when he realized he wasn't bleeding, he swore.

Rebekah sat at the kitchen table with the others all around her and stared at her full plate, knowing she didn't dare pick up a fork and eat in front of the Nelson family. If she'd shocked Jewel and her father, she'd put the Nelsons into apoplexy with her table manners. Besides, the mere thought of food made her stomach turn. All she could think about was the little scene outside just now with MacDougal.

Damn him to hell. Why couldn't he leave her alone? He'd gotten what he wanted from her, what they always wanted from her. Why couldn't he be satisfied with that and go away like the others always had?

In the early days at the Indian camp, she'd been very careful not to be caught outside alone, and now she knew she'd have to be just as careful not to let MacDougal catch her alone either. Although she knew he'd never take her against her will, he was even more dangerous because he seemed able to take her will instead.

She wanted to kill him for having such power over her, but of course she couldn't even think of it because he was the only one who could get her son for her. As soon as he did, though, as soon as he did . . .

No one spoke as they ate the smoked ham and gravy Jewel had set before them. Eating was serious business in the West, and everyone attended to it accordingly. This left Rebekah with nothing to do but try not to look across the table at where MacDougal sat and remember the taste of his mouth and the sensation of his newly shaven cheeks and the feel of his hard body pressed against hers.

Damn him to hell and back.

And then there was Andrew, dear sweet Andrew, who was understandably dismayed to have found her in MacDougal's arms. And he'd obviously thought the worst, that she and MacDougal were . . . But that was silly. She'd have to tell him so, too, at the first opportunity.

Dear, sweet Andrew, so different from MacDougal in every way, which of course made Andrew much more attractive to her. If she had to marry someone, better it be someone with whom she'd feel safe, someone who would never threaten to destroy the fragile barriers she had erected around her soul.

But that was silly. She didn't have to marry anyone at all, safe or otherwise. She just had to get her son back. As soon as he was here, everything would be fine.

When everyone had finished eating, the men went outside to smoke, although before they left they all looked at Rebekah as if not quite sure about leaving her alone with Prudence. Rebekah wasn't sure about it either, but they gave her no choice.

Rebekah tried to get up and help Jewel clear the table, but Jewel clamped a strong hand on her shoulder and forced her back down into her seat. Reluctantly, she glanced over at where Prudence still sat.

"You didn't eat very much," Prudence observed carefully.

"I just had breakfast," Rebekah replied.

Prudence waited until Jewel had taken her plate. Then she said, "Andrew was always very fond of you."

"I was fond of him, too."

"He . . . he's never married, you know," she ventured.

Rebekah wondered where she was going with this and decided to play along. She had nothing else to do. "I know."

"I . . . I can't think he'd want to raise an Indian boy as his son," she said stiffly, plainly uncomfortable but determined nevertheless to make her point.

Rebekah felt her cheeks burning, but she refused to drop her eyes and let Prudence think she was ashamed of her child. "Maybe Andrew is the one who should make that decision," she said, knowing she was being cruel to mislead the woman but unable to stop herself. Of course, if Rebekah had any desire at all to marry Andrew, it was Prudence who was being cruel.

Prudence's face splotched with red again. "Men are noble creatures, Rebekah. He might take you both out of a sense of duty, no matter what he really wanted. Is that fair?"

"Fair to whom?" Rebekah demanded. She'd certainly never been impressed with the nobility of men.

"Fair to any of you," Prudence continued doggedly. "If you truly care for Andrew, you will release him from any pledge he might have made you before . . . Well, before you both changed so much."

234

"Before I was defiled by the Indians, you mean," Rebekah snapped, furious now. How dare this woman take it upon herself to decide what was best for either Andrew or herself?"

Prudence, however, did not seem cowed by Rebekah's outrage. "You cannot deny the . . . the experiences you had with the Indians have changed you, Rebekah. You aren't . . ." She paused, obviously at a loss for words.

"I'm not what? Not fit for Andrew anymore? Or maybe you don't think I'm fit for anything, is that it?"

"Rebekah, please," Prudence begged, increasingly distressed with this turn of the conversation. "I'm sure you're a fine person, in spite of . . . I mean, your mind doesn't seem to have been affected by your ordeal, for which we can only be grateful to God and—"

"Let's leave God out of this," Rebekah interrupted.

Prudence gasped in surprise and her face grew even redder. Plainly she was having second thoughts about the state of Rebekah's mind, but she somehow managed to recover herself. "You've only just returned to civilization," she pointed out. "It's much too soon for you to be making any decisions about your future, isn't it?"

Suddenly Rebekah felt infinitely weary, much too weary to continue this argument. "You're right, Cousin Prudence," she said dully, and they both jumped as a cast-iron pot crashed to floor behind them.

Rebekah was too tired to even turn around, knowing Jewel had just been registering her disapproval of Rebekah's capitulation.

"Good heavens," Prudence murmured, laying a hand over her heart. "Do try to be more careful," she scolded Jewel who muttered something in reply.

When she turned back to Rebekah, her homely face was set into what Rebekah supposed was a look of deep concern. "We all want what's best for you, Rebekah. You must believe that. You may not understand how I as a virtual stranger could care about you the way your family does, but I assure you that I have prayed for your safety through the years just as earnestly as those who knew you have done." She reached out as if she would take Rebekah's hand, but something in Rebekah's expression stopped her, and she snatched her own hand back again. "We want you to be happy," she concluded lamely.

"And you want Andrew to be happy, too," Rebekah guessed.

"Exactly," Prudence agreed, apparently under the impression they had reached some sort of understanding. Rebekah thought they had, too, except she was fairly certain they understood things a little differently.

Prudence was babbling on, something about the ladies of the church wanting to welcome her home, but Rebekah wasn't really listening. She rose to her feet. "I think I'll go lie down for a while. I'm a little tired."

"Oh, of course, my dear. I understand perfectly. You've been through so much . . ."

If she only knew, Rebekah thought, and wandered out of the room. The men were sitting on benches in the shade of the dogtrot, and they all looked up when she came out, stopping their conversation abruptly. She didn't look at them, though, not wanting to encourage them to question her. The dogs lazily noted her presence with pricked ears, but they didn't bestir themselves from their resting places.

She thought someone called her name, maybe Andrew or her father, but she pretended not to hear and quickly crossed the dogtrot and entered her room, closing the door firmly behind her. None of them would follow her, so she was safe. She leaned against the solid wood of the door and sighed, feeling the last of her strength ebbing away.

Why did no one understand? And why were they all so certain they did? All she wanted was her boy. Her arms ached with the need to hold him to her heart and lavish on him the love she dared give no one else. As if in a trance, she shuffled across the room to the bed and collapsed onto it, clasping the feather pillow to her bosom as she would have clasped her son.

"*Sitū-htsi2 Tūkerū*, Little One," she murmured to herself and settled into sleep.

Rebekah awoke to Jewel's scolding. "You wake up now, you hear? Can't sleep your life away."

Sunlight still filled the room, and Rebekah wondered how long she had slept. "Are they still here?" she asked groggily, deciding the answer to that question would determine her response to Jewel's command.

"Lord, no, they left yesterday after I told them you wouldn't wake up 'til morning."

"Yesterday?" Rebekah echoed in confusion, pushing herself up on one elbow.

"Yes, yesterday," Jewel confirmed. "You done slept all day and all night and now it's morning again. Or rather it's almost noon. I reckon you'd starve to death if I'd let you sleep. Now set yourself up and eat this food before it gets cold and I have to give it to the dogs."

Rebekah couldn't quite accept that she had slept so long. She must have been far more tired than she'd ever realized. Was it possible for weariness to catch up with a person like that, for all those years of hard

237

labor at the Indian camp to accumulate so she could do nothing but sleep once she got back home again?

Having no answer, she submitted meekly to Jewel's ministrations and allowed the black woman to prop her up in her bed—someone had covered her in the night, although she still wore her clothes from yesterday—and to set the tray of food in her lap. Nothing on the tray looked particularly appealing, not the cornmeal mush laced with molasses or the steaming coffee, but Jewel glared at her until she forced a few spoonfuls of the mush down her throat, and the coffee revived her somewhat.

How odd, she thought. If she hadn't eaten since yesterday, when she'd only managed a few bites of flapjacks, she should have been starving by now. Instead she could barely make herself swallow. Perhaps she was missing the Comanche diet of nearly raw meat and little else, although the very idea of the bloody buffalo meat made her stomach turn.

"You'll waste away to nothing, you don't eat," Jewel warned, and when Rebekah finally looked at her, she saw genuine concern in Jewel's dark eyes.

"I'm all right," she said. "I'm just tired and not very hungry."

"What you got to be tired about?" Jewel challenged.

Rebekah didn't have the slightest idea. All she knew was every bone in her body ached with weariness even though she'd just slept almost an entire day.

Jewel hovered over her until the bowl of mush was nearly empty and Rebekah finally gave up. The coffee had energized her somewhat, however, and when Jewel insisted, she rose and washed and made her way to the kitchen.

"Your pa and the boys are out in the fields," Jewel informed her when she saw Rebekah looking around.

But Rebekah hadn't expected to see them. "Where's MacDougal?" she asked, knowing he wouldn't have volunteered to help with any farming.

"He's gone."

"*Gone?*" Rebekah echoed in alarm, feeling an unreasonable sense of loss. Would he have left to fetch her son so soon? Would he have gone without saying good-bye? "What do you mean gone?"

"I mean he rode out about sunup this morning. Said he was going to look things over. Said he'd be back in a day or two."

"Oh." Rebekah hated herself for feeling slighted because he hadn't consulted her. He should have, of course. After all, he still had some unfinished business to take care of. If he was going to ride anywhere, he should have headed for the plains where her son still waited to be rescued. What else could have been more important than that?

Before Rebekah could think of an answer, the dogs outside started barking, heralding the approach of visitors. Rebekah felt a jolt of alarm and would have bolted from her chair if Jewel hadn't grabbed her shoulders and held her in place.

"You've got to see folks," she was saying softly, gently, in Rebekah's ear. "They won't hurt you none."

Rebekah wanted to argue, but she didn't think she had the energy, so she surrendered to Jewel's superior strength and sat where she was. "Who is it?" she asked, not really caring.

Jewel went to the door and looked out. "Couple ladies from your pappy's church, looks like."

"Cousin Prudence?" Rebekah asked with dread.

"No, some others." Rebekah heard a wagon rattling up outside. Jewel went to greet them, and once again Rebekah heard her speaking in that subservient tone she never seemed to use with the Tates.

In too short a time, the two female visitors entered Jewel's pristine kitchen. One was tall and scrawny, the other short and plump. They were both dressed in black from head to foot, and they both carried bundles.

"Hello there," the tall one said. "I'm Eliza Phipps and this is Pearl Williams." She spoke unnecessarily loudly, and Rebekah wondered if she were deaf.

Rebekah forced herself to stand up and nodded politely. "How do you do?" she said, hoping this was the expected response.

"We're so happy to meet you at last," the short woman, Mrs. Williams, piped in her shrill voice. She too was fairly shouting. "How are you feeling, dear?"

"Fine," Rebekah lied. Her head was starting to ache from the shouting.

"We've brought you some things," Mrs. Phipps informed her with alarming cheerfulness and set her bundle on the kitchen table. Then she turned to her companion and said in a normal voice, "She's awfully thin, don't you think?"

"Oh, yes," the other woman replied somberly and quietly. "But what can you expect? I hear they treat their women like animals."

They both turned back to Rebekah and studied her again. "What do you suppose those things on her feet are?" Mrs. Phipps asked her friend.

"Indian shoes of some kind. Prudence was right." She shook her head sadly.

Mrs. Phipps smiled again with her unnatural gaiety. "Don't you want to see what we've brought you?" she asked, startling Rebekah by shouting again.

"Not everything will fit, of course," Mrs. Williams added, matching her companion's increased volume. "But we know your girl there can sew just fine, so she can fix everything up."

"I'm a little worried about the shoes," Mrs. Phipps confided normally to her friend. "If she's been wearing those things for a long time, her feet'll be just ruined."

What on earth was wrong with these women? Did they think she was deaf? "I can hear you just fine," she informed them.

They both started as if *she'd* shouted at *them*, and their faces creased into strained smiles. "Of course you can, dear," Mrs. Phipps said loudly and slowly. She set her own bundle down and began to unwrap it. Rebekah saw it was a dress of brown homespun.

"This belonged to a lady in our church," Mrs. Phipps reported, shouting again.

Mrs. Williams unwrapped her bundle to produce another dress and a pair of well-worn, black, lace-up shoes. Both bundles contained other things as well, aprons and stockings, a bonnet, undergarments and nightdresses, everything a woman would need.

Rebekah supposed she should be grateful to them. She certainly needed all these things, and the gesture was a kind one. If only they weren't looking at her so strangely.

"Would you ladies like some coffee and cake?" Jewel asked suddenly.

"Oh, yes, thank you," they said, fairly scrambling for chairs, although Rebekah noticed neither of them sat too near her. In fact, it almost seemed they were deliberately keeping the width of the table between themselves and her.

They kept staring at her, too, as she lowered herself back into her chair. No one spoke while Jewel efficiently set out cups and plates, and poured and cut and served. Rebekah looked at the cake Jewel set before her, a snowy white confection with fluffy white frosting, the kind of thing she'd only ever enjoyed on special occasions like birthdays and holidays and for which she would have given a limb during the long years of captivity. Now the sight of it filled her with revulsion since she knew she didn't dare eat it in front of these staring women. In truth, she didn't even want to eat it. The thought of putting anything at all, no matter how luscious, into her mouth made her nauseous.

The two women were eating it with relish, however, and exclaiming over how delicious it was. "Miss Prudence brought it," Jewel explained, giving Rebekah a sharp look that told her she ought to be trying a little harder with her guests. If only she hadn't been so very tired.

"It all must be strange to you," Mrs. Williams observed, her plump cheeks jiggling as she chewed the cake. She didn't speak quite as loudly as before, but she was still using a different tone than she used with her friend, a little slower and more distinct, as if she were afraid Rebekah wouldn't understand if she spoke normally.

"I'm getting used to it," Rebekah said dully, wondering if it were true.

"Well, you look just fine," Mrs. Phipps declared. "Except for being so thin, of course. No one would ever guess . . ." She stopped abruptly and glanced at her friend who dropped her eyes in apparent embarrassment.

"What I mean," Mrs. Phipps clarified, "You don't look as if . . ." She stopped again, at a loss for words.

"Was it really very terrible?" Mrs. Williams blurted, then blushed furiously. "I'm sorry, but we hear such things—"

"How they stake women out—"

"Without a stitch of clothes—"

"And all the Indians take her—"

"Over and over—"

The images bubbled up from the filthy mire of

242

Rebekah's memory, leering faces and putrid smells and pain no one could ever imagine. She tried to push them back down, but the voices were too strong, too loud, and she heard them even though she tried not to.

". . . don't know how any woman could bear it—"

"Their filthy hands—"

"I'd kill myself before—"

"No savage would ever—"

". . . live with yourself?"

"*No!*" Rebekah screamed, clamping her hands over her ears to drown them out. But the questions didn't stop because the women weren't even asking them anymore. They stared at her, dumbfounded, their speechless mouths gaping open stupidly, but she could still hear them, echoing in her head, over and over and over and they wouldn't stop, wouldn't stop, so she ran from them, around the table and out the door and across the dogtrot to her bedroom door which she slammed behind her. She dove for the bed and clamped the pillow over her head, but still she heard them.

"No decent woman would . . ."

"Kill myself . . ."

"Too ashamed . . ."

So she stared at a knothole in the wall, staring until she wasn't there anymore, until she was drifting off somewhere and the voices faded at last and no one could hurt her anymore.

Chapter Nine

Rebekah never learned what happened to her visitors after she had left them so unceremoniously. Jewel never told her, and she never asked. Jewel didn't bother her, either, only coming in to check on her periodically as silent as a cat. Rebekah sensed her presence, but she pretended to be asleep. She didn't eat the food Jewel brought and she didn't come out of her room, not until another night had passed and she was certain they were gone.

Then she just sat in the shade of the dogtrot with the mongrel dogs sleeping at her feet, ignoring Jewel and her father when they tried to get her to eat or come inside, and she watched the horizon for signs of MacDougal's return. She knew the sun was shining because she could see it, but she didn't feel it's warmth because she was somewhere far away, somewhere dark where the heat couldn't reach her and where the light didn't really penetrate.

Sometimes her father would sit beside her and take her hand and speak in that voice he used for praying, but she didn't really hear him, not the words anyway, and if he were praying she knew no one else could hear him, either, at least no one who could do any good.

244

No, she was alone now, alone except for MacDougal. He was her only hope.

He didn't come back for another day, but Rebekah was waiting for him. She heard his shout down where she was in the darkness, and she forced herself back, up and up, until she could see him clearly, until she could almost feel the warmth of the sun, until she was almost free again, except she wouldn't really be free until MacDougal placed her son in her arms again because he was all she had left now, the only thing worth living for in this cursed world to which she had returned.

He rode his horse right up to the house, smiling broadly as if he expected a hero's welcome simply for showing up again. He called her name, and she curled her lips up the way she'd once done when she smiled, although no one would have called her expression a smile, and she waited until he'd dismounted and come to her.

He carried a bundle—would all her visitors carry bundles now?— and he was smiling as if he'd done something of which he was very proud.

"I've brought you a few things," he said, presenting her with the package. "God, the cost of yard goods out here! I got enough for a couple dresses, though. I figure Jewel can sew you some so you won't look like you should be standing out in the field scaring the crows anymore." He suddenly noticed she hadn't taken the bundle from him, and his smile disappeared. "Rebekah?"

She didn't answer him because she didn't know what kind of an answer he wanted. But she didn't really need to say anything yet, because her father had come out of the house and was welcoming him back like the hero he seemed to think he was.

"I've found a spot," MacDougal was telling him. "Near the church, just like you suggested. It's the most logical place for a store and later for a town."

"Looks like you've been visiting someone else's store," her father observed, indicating his bundle.

MacDougal frowned again. His lean cheeks had a few days' growth of whiskers, but he still looked civilized, not at all like the wild man who'd carried her across hell and half of Texas. "I got your daughter some dress goods, but she doesn't seem too interested in them. The last time I got her a dress, she was a lot more excited."

He looked at her like he expected her to remember, but she couldn't. She didn't want to remember, because if she did, her mind might drift back to the past and get lost in all the memories and she might forget what she was going to ask him.

"Come inside," her father said before she could ask it.

MacDougal was looking at her strangely, the same way those women had looked at her, but she no longer cared what he thought. She no longer cared what anyone thought.

Jewel had come to the door and was greeting MacDougal. "You've missed supper, Mr. MacDougal, but if you're hungry, I can warm something up."

"I can always eat one of your meals, Jewel," he said, still smiling.

They all went inside and sat around the table while Jewel bustled about, preparing MacDougal's meal. Zebulon Tate was full of questions, and MacDougal had all the answers.

"I went to the nearest outpost and talked to the trader there. That's where I got the gifts," he said, giving Rebekah a questioning glance, but she wasn't the least bit interested in the bundle he had placed on the table before her. "The trader told me everything I needed to know, although I don't think he realized I'd be his competition until it was too late." He

246

grinned at his own cleverness, but Rebekah didn't grin back and her father only stroked his beard the way he did when he was worried about something.

"They didn't have any shoes," MacDougal was saying, "but I ordered some, so you won't have to wear those ugly things much longer."

He gestured to her feet, and then paused, giving her the opening for which she had been waiting. "When are you going after my boy?" she asked.

Even though no one else had really been making any noise, the entire room went silent as if everyone had even stopped breathing, and Rebekah felt the cold knot of dread forming in her stomach when MacDougal looked away and wouldn't meet her eye.

"I've been meaning to talk to you about that," he said, his voice a little less sure than it usually was, although she couldn't imagine why.

"Then talk to me about it," she said. "I figured you'd want a few days to rest up but winter's coming on. If you wait too long, you might get caught out in a norther or something."

MacDougal quite visibly squared his shoulders, as though bracing himself for a fight. "Have you thought about this? I mean, are you sure you really want to bring him here?"

The cold knot of dread hardened into terror. "What do you mean?" she demanded.

MacDougal exchanged a glance with her father, and she instantly knew they had discussed this before. They had discussed this behind her back and come to some conclusion, a conclusion they knew she wouldn't like. "The boy is happy where is, but would he be happy if you brought him here? Think about it, think about what it would be like for him. He's a half-breed, a bastard. People around here hate Indians—"

"But he's a *child!*" she cried, panic rising up in her

like a black wave.

"People can be cruel," her father said gently, taking her hand in his as if to soften the impact of his words. "They fear what they don't understand, and what they fear, they hate."

She jerked her hand out of his grasp and glared at him until he dropped his gaze, obviously ashamed for his part in this, but he said, "I know how you must feel, but it's what's best for the boy and for you."

"How can you know what's best for me?" she fairly shouted, jumping from her chair so quickly it crashed to the floor. "I expected you at least would understand. You know what it's like to lose a child!"

"But my child was taken by cruel savages. You've left your child with his own family, with people who love him and who'll take care of him—"

"Nobody can love him like I can! Don't you even care about his soul?" she asked incredulously. "He'll be a savage! No one will ever tell him about your precious God! Doesn't that count for anything?"

"I'll pray for him every day—"

Rebekah contemptuously swore one of MacDougal's more colorful oaths, and her father paled visibly. Having silenced him, she turned on MacDougal.

"You promised me!" she wailed. "You said you'd go back for him! You swore on everything you hold sacred!"

MacDougal didn't quail, but his neck reddened and his eyes grew bleak. He opened his mouth to speak, then thought better of it and closed his mouth again.

No one said anything for a long minute, then from the far end of the room, Jewel said, "Maybe he don't hold nothing sacred."

Rebekah gasped in horror. That was it! The truth of it was like a knife plunged into her heart, a

248

betrayal so agonizing, it took her breath. "You never intended to go back for him, did you?" she accused in a hiss. "You lied to me so you could get me away and be a hero, so you could be *the man who rescued Rebekah Tate!*"

She had never hated anyone so thoroughly, not the Indians who had killed her mother and her baby brother, not the braves who had raped her, not the women who had beaten and humiliated her. She wanted to kill him. She wanted to plunge a knife into his chest and cut out his beating heart and crush it between her fingers. She wanted to rip him open and fill his body with live coals and hear him scream while his insides cooked. She wanted to strip every inch of skin from his body and watch while the ants and the flies devoured his writhing carcass. She wanted to watch him die in every horrible way she'd ever seen anyone die.

He was rising to his feet, his cursed eyes appealing, his filthy hands reaching for her. "If you'll just think about it, you'll realize the boy is better off—"

She spat in his face, then she turned and ran, unable to hear another word, unable to look at him another second. She ran outside, straight for her bedroom door and the blessed solitude it offered, but someone was after her, someone was coming.

She threw open the door and tried to slam it shut before he could get in, but she wasn't fast enough or strong enough and he pushed the door back open, flinging her across the room.

But it wasn't a he, it was Jewel who had followed. "Miss Rebekah," she said, reaching out, her dark eyes swimming with the same grief that was tearing Rebekah apart. "He ain't the only man there is! You can get somebody else to go for the boy!"

If only that were true. Rebekah shook her head in despair. "He's the only one who knows where he is or what he looks like. Do you know how big the plains are? No one else would ever find him!"

The two women stared at each other across the room, the horrible truth hanging there, naked and hideous, between them. Then someone started to wail, a high-pitched keening that pierced the silence like a blade. For a moment Rebekah wondered from where the sound was coming until Jewel took her in her strong arms and she realized it was tearing from her own throat.

Jewel's arms tightened around her, pressing Rebekah's face to her bosom, but the awful sound continued, and Rebekah couldn't have stopped it, even if she'd wanted to. It was the primal scream.

"She's going to die," Jewel informed the men two days later.

Sean MacDougal looked at the other faces gathered around the kichen table for the evening meal. The two dark ones, Dan and Enoch, were lowered out of respect for the white man's problems. Zebulon Tate's was pale above his snowy beard, his eyes sunken and shadowed from lack of sleep and despair.

He'd been praying for his daughter night and day, but she hadn't stirred from her bed, even though no one could find a damn thing wrong with her, and nobody could get her to swallow so much as a mouthful of food.

"She won't die," Sean said gruffly, his own voice hoarse from emotions he didn't dare let anyone see. "She's upset, but she'll get over it. She's lived through worse than this."

"Maybe," Jewel said, slapping a plate of food down in front of him, "but always before she at least had some hope that things'd get better, hope she'd get rescued and brought home. Now she's got nothin'."

"But she *is* home," Zeb insisted weakly. "I just don't understand. Why isn't she happy?"

"Why should she be?" Jewel challenged. "What does she got here? A house, an old man who's going to die before too much longer, and a bunch of folks whose idea of Christian charity is to come by and gawk at her like she's some kind of freak."

"They'd gawk at her worse if she had a half-breed bastard kid," MacDougal argued.

"Maybe," Jewel allowed, "but at least she wouldn't care."

MacDougal had no answer for that, so he glared at Jewel, a look that had caused grown men to quake in their boots, but the black woman just glared back.

"She's gonna die. I seen it before at that place where I was at before I come here. They'd take a woman's baby away from her and she'd just lay down and die. Wasn't nothing nobody could do to stop her, neither."

MacDougal's heart was cold in his chest. He couldn't lose Rebekah Tate, he just couldn't, but he also couldn't believe a woman could die like Jewel said. "I'll talk to her," he said, getting up without touching his supper.

"You can talk 'til your tongue falls out, but it won't do no good," Jewel called after him. "Only one thing that'll cure what ails her and that's bringing her boy back to her."

Sean swore under his breath. How had he ever gotten himself into this mess? Everything had seemed so simple back at the Indian camp. He'd get Rebekah Tate home, she'd be happy, she'd forget all about the little red bastard she'd left behind, and Sean would be a hero. His plan for getting her away had worked perfectly. Why couldn't the rest of it have worked equally well? Or even a little bit well?

Damn it to hell.

He paused at Rebekah's bedroom door, wondering if he should knock. Of course, if he did, she might tell him he couldn't come in and then what would he do? On the other hand, he didn't want to catch her in an embarrassing position, either. He knocked.

He waited.

Silence.

He knocked again.

More silence.

He swore and lifted the door latch and pushed the door open a crack. "Rebekah Tate?"

Still more silence.

Was she even in there?

He opened the door farther until he could see the bed on the other side of the room and he could see her lying in it.

"Rebekah Tate?" he called again.

She didn't move, and for one horrible moment he thought he was too late. Charging into the room, his heart in his throat, he fairly ran across the floor, stopping abruptly at the side of the bed, not knowing what to do, but when he'd stood there for a few seconds, he saw the feeble rise and fall of her chest and knew she wasn't dead. He wasn't too late after all.

"Rebekah Tate," he said loudly, figuring she must be asleep.

Not even her eyelids flickered. What the hell?

She looked like a wax statue, pale and beautiful and perfectly still except for her faint breathing. Then he noticed how very thin she was, even thinner than she had been before, as if the flesh had melted off her bones. How could someone who'd been sleeping for days look so drained and exhausted? Terror coiled in his stomach like a snake, and he reached out one trembling hand to touch her shoulder. He gave her a shake.

He might have been shaking a rag doll.

"Oh, God," he murmured as the memories came rushing back. He saw it all so plainly now, the way she'd looked that night, the first time he'd tried to make love to her, the blank eyes, the limp body. And the second time, when she'd almost done it again before he'd forced her back.

"Rebekah Tate!" he shouted, sitting down on the bed and taking hold of her shoulders. "Come back here!" He shook her, hard, until her eyelids did flicker, then he slapped her cheeks, sharp, stinging slaps that sounded like gunshots in the quiet room. He called her name again and again until at last she opened her eyes, those lovely blue eyes that reminded him sometimes of a robin's egg and other times of the purest water he'd ever drunk, all sparkling and clear.

But this time they weren't clear. This time they were dull and empty and glazed and unseeing, and terror sank its fangs into his heart. "Rebekah Tate, listen to me! You can't do this! You've got to come back from wherever you are!"

She stared at him with those awful eyes, then the bloodless lips moved ever so slightly, and in a hoarse croak she said, "Why?"

Because I love you! he wanted to say. Because I need you, and because if you die, I don't know how I'll bear it! But he knew those were worthless arguments. She didn't care about him or his love, and it certainly wouldn't draw her back from where she'd gone.

He could almost feel her growing cold beneath his hands as if the life were ebbing out of her while he watched. How much longer could she go on like this? And how could he sit by and wait for her to die, knowing he had the power to save her?

"Because," he said, knowing he was crazy, wondering if he could even do what he was about to promise, wondering if anyone could, but answering her question in the only possible way, "I'm going to bring your boy back here, and who'll take care of him if you're dead?"

He watched her closely, not even certain she had understood, and at first he was sure she hadn't. Then something flickered deep in her eyes, a faint spark of understanding.

"My boy?" the hoarse voice asked vaguely.

"Your son. *Situ-htsi2 Tukeru*, Little Boy Who Goes To Hunt or whatever you call him. The fat little kid with gray eyes. I'm going to get him, but only if I know you'll be here when I get back, alive and well and strong enough to take care of a wild Indian."

"MacDougal?" she whispered, so weak and pathetic he wanted to die himself.

"What, my darling girl?" he asked, blinking at the unfamiliar sting of tears.

"Are you lying again?"

He felt an absurd urge to laugh, so happy was he to hear the faint echo of her old spirit. "No, I'm not lying this time. I swear it, and this time I'll swear it on your life since it's the only thing that's ever mattered to me."

Her lips twitched slightly as if she were trying to smile but couldn't quite manage it. "I'd believe you more if you swore on your gold."

"Then I'll swear on my gold. Whatever pleases you, sweet girl. And whether you believe me or not, I'm going. I'll leave tonight. It'll take a while, probably longer than it took to get you away because I'll have to hire someone to help me and—"

"MacDougal?" the whispered word was no more than a thread of sound.

"Yes, love?"

She swallowed with difficulty, and her lovely eyes swam with tears. "I'll be here when you get back."

Damn fool. Damn fool. Sean MacDougal kept repeating the words over and over to himself. It was what Zebulon Tate had called him, except Zeb never swore, so he'd just said, "Fool," plain and simple. Sean himself had added the "Damn" about five miles out from the Tate farm. The rest of the way, he'd been chanting the result silently, just in case he was tempted to think what he was doing was in any way sensible.

Now he lay in the tall grass, flies and gnats swarming curiously around his face while he looked down at the Comanche camp below. The band had moved since Sean had last visited them, settling in for the winter in a more sheltered spot, and Sean and his men had had one hell of a time finding them. Time was running out, too. Anyone familiar with the vagaries of the weather on the plains could practically taste the coming change.

Already the grass had cured down to winter feed, and the buffalo were growing their winter coats. In response, the Comanche were hunting relentlessly in preparation for the starving months to come.

Which was, of course, all to the good, since most of the men and a lot of the women were gone on the hunt, leaving just a handful of adults, most of them elderly and feeble, to guard the camp and the children.

The casual observer might not have noticed any movement at all down at the camp, so sparsely populated was it, but Sean's keen eye had identified virtually every inhabitant and carefully noted his or her movements. So far, no one had exhibited any sign of alarm to show they were aware of the outrage taking place at that very moment on the edge of their camp.

Sean could hardly believe it himself, and he'd watched every step of it. The Tonkawas he had recruited at Hopewell's Fort had proved much more competent than Sean had expected, given their dissolute appearance.

They weren't quite as accomplished as Hopewell had promised, but they were Indians, which made them more than adequate for the task at hand. They knew how to sneak up on a Comanche camp without disturbing one blade of grass and how to sneak away again taking half-a-dozen male children with them without making the ghost of a sound. Sean had watched in amazement as the little boys who had been practicing shooting their toy arrows at the edge of the camp had been lured farther and farther away by the gobble of a turkey, then as they had disappeared, soundlessly, one by one, into the tall grass.

Waiting now, Sean tried to trace the path of the returning Tonks, but without success. They seemed to have disappeared into thin air along with the children, and just as Sean had concluded as much, they reappeared behind him, clutching their stiffly terrified captives.

The boys had been trussed hand and foot, and their mouths were stuffed with the pieces of rags Sean had provided, held in place with gags. Sean hated seeing the children tied so cruelly but reminded himself of how dangerous even a very small Comanche could be at close quarters.

"We got 'em," the leader of the Tonks informed Sean. He was a tall man Hopewell had called River, and at the moment he was grinning from ear to ear.

"Let's see if you got the *right* one," Sean said, scrambling down from his vantage point to inspect the captives.

But River was ready. He grabbed the hair of the boy he held, forcing the child's head up so Sean could see his eyes.

Gray as ashes and wide with recognition of the trader who had visited his camp a few months earlier. Sean smiled and said, *"Sitū-htsi̱ Tūkerū?"*

The gray eyes grew wider, this time with hope. The trader knew his name. Surely the man who'd plied these same boys with candy a few weeks ago could mean them no harm now.

The other boys started squirming in their captors' arms, and the Tonks put a stop to the minor rebellion in various ways, none of which was particularly gentle.

"Let's get going before somebody notices they're gone," Sean said, taking the Tate boy from River's arms and carrying him to where his horse waited. The Tonks mounted, too, placing the bound boys before them on their saddles and tying their legs in place. Then they started away, riding single file in each other's tracks as Indians did so no one following would be able to guess the number in their party.

Once out of earshot of the camp, they broke into a gallop, and the ground beneath them became a blur as they covered the miles as swiftly as possible. Sean held his small burden securely, aware the boy was still stiff with terror. There would be plenty of time later to put his little mind at ease, but not until they had separated from the others. He didn't want one of the other boys to overhear and carry back the story that Rebekah Tate was alive and well and that her son was being taken to her.

Sean had timed the abduction carefully. Early afternoon, when the adults would be sleeping off their midday meal and paying little attention to the antics of the youngsters. The Tonks had taken all the boys in the group, so no one could go back to camp and raise the alarm. Now, if all went according to plan, no one would notice the boys were missing until it was time to eat again, giving Sean and his party a good head start on any pursuit.

They rode for hours, alternating running and walking the horses so as not to wear them out. Finally, the sun slipped below the horizon behind them, and the world turned blue and then black, and the stars appeared in the broad canopy of sky. It was time.

River, the leader, stopped his little caravan, and everyone dismounted for a quick bite to eat. The captives got nothing, of course, which was part of the plan to keep them terrified. The Tonks quickly swallowed handfuls of pemmican and mouthfuls of water. They were muttering among themselves, laughing and poking each other in the ribs, and after a few minutes of this Sean understood they were making jokes about what they intended to do with the boys.

"The younger ones are more tender," one of the Tonks was saying sagely. "We will roast them over a slow fire until the skin sizzles and pops."

"I like to eat their hearts and their livers," another said knowledgeably. "So juicy and sweet . . ."

The captive children were quaking in terror since all of them had been frightened by stories of the Tonkawas and their cannibalistic habits. Sean didn't know if the stories about the Tonks eating human flesh were true or not, but he saw no harm in frightening the children as much as possible. Later their fear would make their stories even more confused, so those trying to make sense of what had happened would be unable to.

When Sean determined the men were ready to travel again, he took a small bag of pemmican and a

258

water skin and laid them beside one of the captive boys. "Your people will come for you," he said in his halting Comanche. "We are taking the one with gray eyes to sell to the white man because he is white, but the rest of you are no good to us."

Five pairs of terrified eyes glittered in the darkness, and Sean could almost smell their relief. They wouldn't be afraid of being left alone on the prairie, which had been their home since birth. Given the training they had had, any one of them could have survived alone and made the trip back to their camp. Together and with the certainty a rescue party would be dispatched for them, their safety was guaranteed.

But when Sean turned back to the Tate boy, he saw exactly the opposite reaction. Time to tell him the truth, Sean thought, picking up the boy and carrying him to his horse. The kid squirmed like a snake and bucked like a bronco, making the Tonks laugh at Sean's struggles to hold him still. Plainly he did not intend to be taken alive, but of course, Sean knew many ways short of killing the boy to calm him down.

With some difficulty, he found the boy's shoulder and squeezed in the way an old freighter had once taught him, catching the underlying nerve just right to produce paralyzing pain while doing no damage whatever. The boy went still instantly and gave Sean no more trouble while he tied him onto his horse and mounted behind him.

The Tonks mounted, too, unable to resist a few last taunts at the boys. They predicted the coyotes would pick their small bones clean before their parents found them in the vast reaches of the prairie. Then they lead the way into the darkness, following the stars to the east. Sean's captive risked leaning a little to look back at his fellows who were no more than shadows on the vast prairie. Comanche boys were trained not to cry, but Sean felt a shudder go through the small body as the littlest Tate contemplated his fate.

Suddenly Sean began to think of the thing in front of him as a person. Until now, he'd been merely an object which Sean was retrieving, a gift for the woman he loved. But the body leaning against him was a human being with feelings, someone for whom he had become responsible. It was an odd sensation. Sean had never been personally responsible for another person, except perhaps this boy's mother, and heaven knew, Rebekah Tate was perfectly capable of taking care of herself. This boy, however, for all his training in survival as a potential Comanche brave, was just a small child whose mother was still very far away.

Instinctively, Sean tightened his arm and pulled the boy a little closer to him. Unfortunately, the boy mistook the gesture as a threatening one and went rigid with terror again. Sean swore and relaxed his grip, murmuring what soothing Comanche words he knew. It was probably better for the boy to be a little frightened anyway, he reasoned. He would be less likely to try any mischief.

By the time the moon rose, Sean could see a pinpoint of light behind them, marking the fire the boys had built when they'd finally loosened their bonds. They would be safe from predators now, and if a rescue party was on the way, it would see the fire and go to it.

He might have mentioned as much to his companion, but the boy was fast asleep, fatigue and fear having taken their toll. Lolling limply in Sean's arms, the child seemed even more real and much more of a responsibility. And when he saw the Tonks stopping their horses, he almost panicked at the thought that he would soon be completely alone with the boy.

"This is the place," River told him when Sean had pulled his horse up beside his.

The boy started awake in Sean's arms, but Sean wasn't worried, knowing the boy couldn't understand what they were saying. Sean looked at the ground and saw it was darker than the grass over which they had been traveling.

"You think this'll fool a Comanche?"

"Long enough," River replied. They'd found this rocky stretch on the way out and formed their plan accordingly.

"If I don't see you back at the fort, Hopewell will be holding your money for you. Thank you, my friend." Sean reached out to shake the Indian's hand.

"You should have let us keep the other boys," River scolded. "They would make fine Tonks."

"Maybe, but the Comanche would never let you get away with so many of their sons. They would've hunted you down even if it took the rest of our lifetimes."

"It would have been a good hunt," the Tonk replied. He lifted his hand in farewell, his teeth glowing white in the moonlight as he grinned.

Sean watched the Indians disappear into the darkness. He could still hear their horses' hooves rattling the rocks long after he could no longer see them, but soon even the sounds faded until he and the boy were completely alone.

It probably wasn't safe to remove the gag from the boy's mouth yet since sound carried well on the night air, so Sean left him as he was and kicked his horse into motion, going in the opposite direction from the Tonks.

Their plan was simple. If the Comanche managed to track them this far, they would be much more likely to pick up the Tonk's trail when it left the rocks. The Tonks would be traveling back to Hopewell's Fort, too, but by a much more roundabout route. By the time they got there, Sean and his companion would—or at least should—be long gone.

Of course, there was always a chance the Comanche would pick up his trail as well. Which meant he'd better be taking advantage of this moonlight to put as much distance between them and himself as he could. He urged his mount into a trot.

Later Sean would remember this trip not as a series of events but as a series of ordeals. He and the boy rode almost constantly through the next day, stopping only long enough to rest the horse and feed themselves.

The first ordeal came at the first stop on the first morning. Sean had untied the boy and removed his gag, figuring they were far enough away now for it to be safe. The boy watched Sean like a hawk, his large gray eyes alert to every movement and every nuance.

Sean decided it was time for him to put the boy's mind at ease.

"Do you remember me?" he asked in his rough Comanche.

The boy nodded warily.

"I am a trader."

The boy nodded again.

"I'm not going to hurt you."

Plainly the boy did not believe him.

"I swear," he said, raising his hand and realizing as he did how he had so falsely sworn to this boy's mother. He hastily lowered his hand and went on. "I'm going to take you to your mother."

The boy went berserk. Screaming like a banshee, he took off at a run, chubby legs pumping furiously.

Sean almost didn't catch him, either, and when he did catch him, he almost lost him. Flailing hands and feet, wailing with the most bloodcurdling scream imaginable, he was like an armload of lightning. Sean couldn't even get a grip to deliver one of his painful but harmless holds, so finally he had to clock the boy one right on the jaw.

Instantly, the small body went limp, and Sean carried him back to camp, cursing himself the whole way. At first he couldn't figure out why the boy had tried so desperately to flee at the prospect of seeing his mother again. Then he had remembered the boy thought his mother was *dead*. No wonder he'd panicked! He thought Sean was going to send him to the land of the great beyond, too.

Well, Sean would have to straighten this out right away. This time, he took a few precautions, first, though. After tying the boy up again, he slapped his cheeks gently to rouse him. This, of course, brought back memories of the way he'd slapped the boy's mother, too. "You've sunk pretty low, MacDougal, roughing up women and children," he muttered as the boy regained consciousness.

The gray eyes flickered open, and at the sight of Sean's face, grew wide with terror again, but before the boy could start wailing, Sean said, "Your mother isn't . . ."

But he didn't know the word for dead! Frantically, he rephrased his speech. "Your mother is . . ."

But he didn't know the word for alive, either, and the boy was starting to keen again.

"I took your mother away," he managed.

Something about this statement stopped the boy in mid-wail. "Under the water," the child said tremuously, his eyes frantic.

"No!" Sean exclaimed. "I took her away on a horse, back to the white people." There, that should

263

make everything clear.

Except the boy didn't consider that particularly good news either, especially since Sean apparently intended to take him there as well. It was what the Indians might have considered a fate *worse* than death. The boy was wailing again.

Sean swore and decided he would just feed the kid and forget trying to explain things to him. He'd soon see Sean had no designs on his life, and nothing Sean said would make him happy about going to the whites until he actually saw his mother again. He untied the boy's hands and gave him some pemmican. The boy ate ravenously, reminding Sean of the way Rebekah Tate had been when she was so freshly from the Comanche camp.

The boy was much wilder than she could ever have been, though, having never experienced civilization at all. His mother was going to have a time with him. Sean was glad it would be her job and not his.

Then Sean realized that if he took Rebekah to wife as he fully intended to do, the boy would be *his* problem, too. Why hadn't he thought of that before? God, he must have lost his mind! But of course he had. Only a crazy man would fall in love with a woman who was stubborn enough to starve herself to death and who didn't even want him in the first place. And only a very crazy man would sneak into Indian country and steal a Comanche boy right from his front doorstep and expect to get away with it with both his scalp and his *cajones* in tact.

On that thought, he got the boy back up on the horse, taking the precaution of tying the child in place once more. It was a precaution he decided he shouldn't forget again. As Sean settled into the saddle behind the child, the boy peered at him over his small, brown shoulder.

"What is your name?" he asked.

"MacDougal," Sean said, wondering if this was a gesture of friendship or if the Comanche had some sort of custom about casting a spell on their enemies that only worked if you knew the enemy's name.

The boy tried to repeat it but couldn't get his tongue around the foreign syllables.

Sean touched his own chest and said, "Mac."

"Mac," the boy repeated carefully.

Sean nodded his approval.

The boy touched his own chest and said, *"Sitŭ-htsi̱ Tŭkerŭ."*

Which Sean already knew, and which, of course, was too much of a mouthful for a white man to mess with. What had his mother called him? Something long about going out to hunt. That wouldn't do, either. Sean touched the boy's chest. "Hunter," he said in English.

It took a little more sign language for the boy to get the idea, but finally he'd learned this was his new name. Sean soon had cause to regret the gesture, however, since the boy repeated it about a hundred times before Sean lost patience and shouted him to silence.

After that, the boy was wary but not quite so frightened. Sean should have recognized his behavior as a warning sign.

That night, they stopped and actually made a camp, having found a pile of rocks that provided some cover. Sean didn't risk a fire this far into Indian country, but he did scrape all the pebbles away before spreading their blankets for the night, making the place somewhat more comfortable.

He trussed the boy hand and foot again before wrapping him in a blanket, then tied a strip of rawhide connecting the boy's wrist with his own. If the kid so much as rolled over in his sleep, Sean would know. To his other hand he attached a thong that lead to his horse.

Finally he settled into a light sleep, satisfied he had taken all reasonable precautions. He was wrong, however, and the mistake almost cost him his life.

What woke Sean was the thud of one small Indian boy hitting the ground after failing to execute a jump onto the horse's back. He was already making another try for it when Sean caught him, grabbing him around the waist and holding him at arm's length while the arms and legs thrashed with murderous intent.

If the boy had just been a few inches taller, he would've gotten away clean, leaving Sean stranded afoot in Indian country. As it was, he had somehow untied the rawhide knots that held him without disturbing the tether binding him to Sean. Then he'd released the horse just as neatly.

Sean couldn't remember ever being so furious, and without even thinking, he tossed the squirming boy over his knee and administered several sound smacks to the boy's bare behind.

The thrashing ceased instantly. Indian children are never spanked or disciplined in any way, and plainly the boy was stunned. Taking advantage of his momentary stupor, Sean retied him, and since it was almost dawn, planted him on the horse and started on their journey again.

The next night, Sean took no chances and tied the boy smack up against his side where he could feel every breath the kid took. Sean awoke a few hours later to find small hands gripping the knife he usually kept strapped to his calf beneath his pantleg. Whether the boy intended to stab Sean with it or simply cut his own bonds, Sean never really knew, nor did he ask.

Another spanking cowed the boy sufficiently for Sean to believe he'd have no further trouble. The third night, he tied the boy to him after carefully stowing all weapons far enough away for safety. The boy got his revenge by peeing all over them both.

It was two days before they encountered enough water to wash away the stink of it, and Sean threw the boy into the creek bodily. The child screamed, so terrified was he that Sean intended to drown him the way he obviously thought Sean had drowned Rebekah.

When they were both clean and Sean's clothes lay drying in the afternoon sun—the boy's "clothes" consisted of a leather breechcloth that he'd simply strapped back on after his dunking—Sean had the leisure to consider his young charge.

The boy lay back on the grass, nearly naked and shivering a bit in the early autumn sun. Sean, too, could feel the hint of winter chill, and for the first time he thought about the boy's apparel. How could he take him back to Zebulon Tate's house dressed only in a scrap of leather? He'd have to take care of that when he got to Hopewell's Fort. Hopewell, the old thief, would probably be only too happy to charge him a small fortune for an old flour sack.

There was nothing he could do about the rest of it, though. Even with white man's clothes covering his sturdy limbs, the boy was still as brown as a berry. Or as an Indian. In spite of his light eyes, his high cheekbones bespoke his heritage only too plainly, and even if Rebekah Tate was able to get the boy to sit still for a haircut (Comanche males considered their hair sacred and cut it only for deep mourning), it was still as black as a raven's wing.

If the truth were told, Sean would be doing both the boy and his mother a favor by doing exactly what the boy had expected and drowning him in this very stream. When Sean thought of what lay ahead for them, the ugly remarks, the snubs, the outright

267

hatred, he shuddered. Half-breed. It was the worst insult anyone could hurl, and Rebekah Tate's son would bear the title as long as he lived.

The Comanche would never have cared about the boy's heritage. To them a man was what he proved himself to be, regardless of the color of his skin. Some of the greatest Comanche warriors had been Mexican or even Negro by birth. But Sean could not think of a single American hero who had been anything less than lily white.

Who from that world would befriend him? Whose daughter would marry him? What kind of life would he have?

Sean felt an overwhelming urge to protect the boy somehow and wondered where such an uncharacteristic impulse might have originated. The kid certainly hadn't earned any tender feelings with his behavior of late. Or perhaps he had. In many ways he'd proved himself his mother's son, and if Sean loved Rebekah Tate, as he'd pretty much resigned himself to admitting, then how could he help admiring someone who was so much like her?

The boy was dozing now, his small chest rising and falling rhythmically, proof he was no longer afraid for his life. Or else that he felt nothing but contempt for Sean's ability to kill him. Whatever his thoughts, Sean noticed for the first time how much the boy resembled his mother, his dark skin and hair notwithstanding. He certainly had the Tate nose and mouth and the characteristic high forehead. If you didn't mind the cast of his skin, he was a fine-looking child.

With any luck at all, he'd have a passel of fairer brothers and sisters before too much longer.

The thought made Sean smile, the thought of new babies but mostly the thought of getting them with Rebekah Tate. He'd make her happy, too. The woman who never laughed would learn to once more, and their home would be the happiest one in Texas. And at last Sean would belong someplace to someone.

Sean dozed a bit, too, and when he woke up the sun was setting, cooling the air enough to remind him he was lying naked on the prairie. When he'd dressed, he roused the boy, and they set out again, riding through the last of the daylight.

The next few days were even more eventful. The boy tried no more tricks, but the Comanche seemed to have picked up their trail at last. Sean thought of the bandy-legged man named *Isatekwa* who considered himself the boy's father. He wouldn't give up the chase easily, no more than Sean would if someone had stolen *his* son.

Twice Sean saw the Indians on their trail through his spy glass, and once they were almost overtaken, hiding under a cut bank as the Indians rode by above, sending clumps of dirt cascading over Sean and the boy while Sean held a knife to the boy's throat to keep him from calling out to them.

With the Indians in front of them, however, they were able to break away on a new trail, and when they reached the fort, *Isatekwa's* party had already come and gone in their fruitless quest.

Although Josiah Hopewell had not been exactly happy to see Sean the last time he'd been here—"You son of a bitch! You had that woman with you when you were here before!"—he was overjoyed now because Sean was going to pay him his commission for procuring the Tonkawa braves who had assisted Sean. And, of course, the money Sean paid the Indians would come back to him too when the braves squandered it on whiskey.

Sean was more than happy to see the ugly fort since it marked for him the beginning of civilization and

269

the last leg of his long journey. His companion seemed to feel differently, however.

Sean first noticed the problem when the boy began to twitch in his bonds as they approached the fort. Feeling he still couldn't quite trust the boy not to escape, Sean had continued to tie him on the horse each time they traveled.

Sean asked the boy if he needed to relieve himself. The boy, whom Sean now thought of as Hunter, shook his head and continued to squirm.

"What's the matter, then?" he asked in Comanche.

"Is this the place of the white men?" he asked in a strangled voice.

Oh, so that was it. "It's one of the places. The white men live in many lodges, just like the Indians. If we rode for many moons to the east we would not come to the end of them."

Plainly Hunter did not believe him, but he shuddered just the same. "You will sell me here?" he asked.

The boy was trying so hard to be brave, Sean couldn't let himself laugh, although the temptation was great. "No, I told you, I am going to take you to your mother."

The small body went rigid with fear, and Sean sighed in disgust. He was definitely going to have to get this straightened out immediately. Fortunately, he now had the means to hand.

A shout from the wall of the fort welcomed them inside, and as they rode between the log walls, the boy began to tremble. Sean wasn't sure if he was upset at being inside such a huge edifice or whether he was just expecting to be murdered at any moment. The boisterous inhabitants calling their greetings didn't calm his fears, either.

"I see you found the little bugger," Josiah Hopewell hollered jovially, making his way through the crowd of Indians who normally lounged around the fort and who had now gathered for a better look at Sean's captive. Hopewell peered up into the boy's face, making him draw back in fear.

"I'll be damned," Hopewell declared. "Gray eyes. I reckon you've got the right one, at least. Well, get him down and bring him inside."

Sean dismounted with difficulty, having to push away the curious onlookers to do so. Swiftly, he untied the boy and lifted him from the saddle, planning to set him on his feet. Instead a pair of small arms clamped themselves around his neck, and a pair of small legs locked themselves around his waist, and a small body pressed itself against him for dear life.

"Ah, yes," Sean murmured in amusement. "It's like the philosopher once said, 'One bears most easily the evils to which one has become accustomed.'" Hunter certainly had no love for Sean, but he preferred him to these frightening strangers.

Feeling oddly gratified and not a little disconcerted by the boy's sudden attachment to him, Sean carried him through the crowd and into Hopewell's store. By the time they entered the dimness of the building, the boy was shaking violently, and Sean heard himself whispering, "No one is going to hurt you."

The boy wasn't in a mood to be convinced, however, so when Sean took a seat at one of Hopewell's tables, he found the boy still locked to his torso.

"Would you," Sean said to Hopewell, "please explain to this young gentleman in your best Comanche that his mother is still alive and well and anxiously awaiting him at her father's house?"

"You mean you haven't told him?" Hopewell asked in surprise.

"I tried, but my command of the Comanche

271

tongue is not what it should be, and I'm afraid I've given him a completely false impression of what his fate is to be."

Hopewell laughed delightedly and proceeded to explain exactly what had become of Rebekah Tate. Since Sean understood a lot more Comanche than he spoke, he realized Hopewell was laying it on pretty thick when it came to Sean's cleverness at outwitting the Comanche and helping Rebekah Tate escape. He didn't feel the need to contradict the trader, however. Having the boy in awe of him wouldn't be such a bad thing.

And Hunter was plainly in awe of him by the time Hopewell had finished his explanation. His pale eyes stared up at Sean with unabashed wonder.

"Pia?" he asked tentatively.

Sean nodded. "Mother," he corrected, figuring the boy's English vocabulary could use some expanding.

The boy tried the new word and got it right after stumbling only once. "Mother."

"She wants to see you very much," Sean said, thinking what an understatement it was and wishing he could somehow convey to the boy Rebekah's desperation.

His small face broke into a smile, the first Sean had ever seen on the child's face, and his heart stopped when he remembered Rebekah Tate smiling exactly that way the day he'd given her that godawful dress. He wanted to say something, but a hard lump had lodged in his throat and his eyes felt strange, hot and burning, and for a moment he couldn't imagine what was wrong with him.

Then one of Hopewell's squaws set two heaping plates of stew down on the table in front of them, instantly capturing the boy's attention. Perfectly secure now, he released Sean, grabbed up the plate and slithered to the floor where he squatted, resting the plate on his knees, and began to scoop the stew into his mouth with his fingers.

Sean cleared the lump out of his throat, all sentimental thoughts driven from his mind by the sight of the boy on the floor. Probably he should give him a few instructions in civilized eating procedures, and maybe he would, later. For now he would be satisfied that the haunted look was gone from the boy's face.

Everything about the fort was strange to Hunter, who had never seen any kind of dwelling except a Comanche lodge. He resisted Sean's efforts to get him to sit in a chair unless he was sitting on Sean's lap, a situation that suited neither of them for very long. The squaws doted on him, exclaiming over him and stuffing him with sweets until he was sick in a brass spittoon.

Sean set them to work finding something suitable for the boy to wear, and they managed to scrounge up a very small man's shirt. The shoulders hung almost to the boy's elbows, but one of the squaws hemmed the sleeves and the finished product was more than serviceable. At least Sean wouldn't have to present poor Zebulon Tate with a naked savage as a grandson.

When at last they retired to the room Hopewell had rented them for the night, little Hunter was exhausted but not so exhausted that he'd let Sean put him to sleep up off the ground in the room's bunk. After a few attempts which Hunter resisted in much the same way a cat resists being dunked in water, Sean gave up and spread a blanket on the floor for him.

Sean himself was only too glad to strip down and crawl between the blankets of a real bed for a change. The straw mattress crackled in protest, sending the boy bolt upright in his pallet, but Sean sighed a blissful contentment before he blew out the candle,

273

plunging them into darkness.

He didn't know how much later it was when he woke up to find he was no longer alone in the bed. He recognized his small companion at once, having shared a blanket with him out of necessity for quite a few nights now. Usually, however, the boy slept with his back to Sean, obviously reluctant. Tonight, however, the boy was facing him, a small arm and leg thrown over Sean's body in a near-caress, his head nestled in the crook of Sean's arm.

If Sean had been allowed to choose from among the Tates for a bed partner, Hunter would not have been his selection. Still, he felt a strange sensation in the region of his heart at the feel of the boy pressed up against him, an urge to protect the child the way he wanted to protect the mother.

Few men, he mused, met their sons under such strange circumstances, but Sean knew he'd met his. With a smile, he curved his arm around the boy and held him close.

Chapter Ten

Rebekah wrapped her shawl more closely around her against the chill of the Texas wind. Winter was coming and with it, she hoped, her son.

"You'll get squint lines, you keep lookin' into the sun like that," Jewel informed her from the kitchen doorway. She'd stepped outside to call everyone in for supper, and she picked up the striker and clanged the triangular dinner bell loudly to summon Dan and Enoch from their cabin.

"There's not much I can do except watch," Rebekah snapped when the clanging stopped. "We've cleaned this house three times, we've sewed up every stitch of cloth left in Texas, and we've knitted every inch of yarn you had in the house. What else is left to do?"

"You could pray," her father said, making her jump. She hadn't heard him come up behind her, and now he slid his arm around her shoulders. She stood stiffly under his caress, still uncomfortable with physical contact, even from someone as harmless as her own father.

She tried to smile. "You already do enough praying for both of us."

He didn't smile back. "I wish you'd go to church

with me, Rebekah. Everyone is so anxious to see you and—"

"To gawk at me, you mean," she corrected him bitterly. "I don't like being stared at." After the incident with Mrs. Phipps and Mrs. Williams, she hadn't dared show her face in public again.

"No one will stare at you," he said, patting her shoulder in what was supposed to be a comforting gesture. Rebekah had to fold her hands into fists to keep from throwing his arm off. "They love you, Rebekah. If you knew how many prayers went up for you when you were captive—"

"And you see how much good they did, too."

"They kept you safe. They kept you alive."

Rebekah could have argued with him. Indeed she already had, but he didn't seem to realize she'd been anything but safe when she'd been with the Comanches. And as for being alive . . .

"If I could pray, I'd pray for my son," she said, not wanting to hurt him anymore. "But since I can't, I'll have to depend on you, Papa."

His old eyes were more than troubled as he looked down at her, but he didn't want to argue either. "I pray for Mr. MacDougal, too. I presume you want him back as well."

He smiled a bit, but mention of MacDougal didn't amuse Rebekah. Instead it brought a strange feeling of apprehension. "Only because he's bringing my boy."

Behind them, Jewel made a rude noise, but Dan and Enoch were coming for supper so Rebekah couldn't demand to know what she was snorting about.

Silently they all trooped inside for the evening meal of leftover beans and cornbread. As Rebekah walked by Jewel, the black woman said, "You look right smart in that there dress Mr. MacDougal got you."

Rebekah glared at her, sick and tired of Jewel's constant references to the trader. "All MacDougal did was buy the cloth. If the dress looks nice, it's because you and I sewed our fingers to the bone to make it that way."

But Jewel knew all that. She smiled benignly. "We wouldn't've had nothing to sew if he didn't pick that cloth out special for you, though. It matches your eyes, did you notice?"

"How could I help but notice with you pointing it out every time I wear it?" Rebekah replied crossly.

"I see you wear it right often, too," Jewel remarked as she turned away to start serving supper.

Rebekah opened her mouth to deny the charge, but she knew she would be wasting her breath. Besides, the charge was perfectly true. She wore the dress out of vanity, though, she told herself. Because the fabric MacDougal had given her was the nicest to be had in Texas, it naturally had made up into the nicest dresses. Rebekah didn't feel disposed to wear the hand-me-downs the church ladies had given her, either, since they brought back memories of a very unpleasant scene. So she wasn't wearing this dress because MacDougal had given it to her. On the contrary, she was wearing it *in spite* of that fact. But she didn't think Jewel wanted to understand the distinction.

Rebekah took her place at the table, glancing at the two black men as they sat down. She wondered if she would ever get used to having them around. Even though Jewel was black, too, and just as much a slave as they, she seemed somehow different, not as subservient. Not as much a slave. Perhaps because Rebekah worked right along beside her.

Which was ridiculous when she remembered her father worked right alongside these men in the fields, sweating just as hard as they to bring in the crop that would keep them all fed during the winter. And when they did eat, they ate together at one table like equals. Her father had told her some of the poorer slave owners lived in the same house as their slaves and sometimes even shared a bed with them.

Perhaps it was just that their dark, inscrutable faces reminded her too much of Indians for her to feel truly comfortable in their presence.

When Jewel had finished serving and taken her own seat, everyone bowed for the blessing which Zebulon Tate gave in the voice he reserved for talking to God.

". . . and we thank Thee again for our daughter's safe return and ask Your grace on Mr. MacDougal and the safe return of our grandchild. Amen."

The others murmured, "Amen," and Rebekah stared at her plate, picturing her son's face. How much longer would it be?

Jewel nudged her with the cornbread plate, forcing her out of her reverie, and she concentrated on serving herself. Using eating implements no longer felt awkward, and she had no difficulty at all in restraining the natural urge to gobble. Perhaps this was because of the security she had here, knowing she would receive three meals a day regardless of the vagaries of the weather or how good the hunting had been. No longer at the mercy of the elements, she found her more civilized habits had returned without too much conscious effort.

"You're ready now," Jewel remarked about half-way through the meal.

Since no one usually spoke during meals, everyone looked up in surprise.

Rebekah paused, fork almost to her lips, and frowned at the other woman when she saw Jewel was addressing her.

"Ready for what?"

278

"Ready to see other folks. Ain't she?" she asked the others.

They knew what she meant and so did Rebekah, whose face felt hot with outrage at the unwanted attention. Carefully she lowered her fork and scowled at Jewel.

Jewel just stared right back. "You don't have nothing to be ashamed of. You act just like them other ladies now. Look like 'em, too, in your new duds. And since you started eating again, you ain't even too skinny. What're you waiting for?"

Rebekah was going to tell Jewel to mind her own business, but her father said, "She's right, Rebekah. The longer you hide yourself away, the more people will think you have some reason for hiding."

"I'm not hiding," Rebekah insisted, although she suspected she was. "I just don't want to see any of those people. Why should I?"

Dan and Enoch were concentrating on their food, not even raising their eyes for fear of being drawn into this extremely uncomfortable conversation. Even Zeb seemed reluctant to reply, but he said, "So they won't talk about you, honey. If they don't have any evidence to the contrary, they'll think you're crazy."

"Let them," she snapped, ready to get up and walk out.

"And what about your boy?" Jewel asked casually in between bites.

"What about him?" Rebekah asked suspiciously.

"You gonna hide him away, too?"

Rebekah hadn't given the matter any thought.

"Might have to, you know?" Jewel continued, just as casually. "Folks think his mother's crazy, they might think he's crazy, too. Can't expect him to face all that by his own self, can you, little boy like that? And if you keep to yourself . . ." She shrugged eloquently.

"If you expect to raise him here, he's got to be part of the community," Zeb added, warming to the subject. "He'll have to have friends. He'll have to go to school, to church, to trade, to—"

"All right!" Rebekah cried, overwhelmed by the force of their arguments. They were right, she knew, although she hated to admit it. She thought of Mrs. Phipps and Mrs. Williams and Cousin Prudence. She remembered their eyes and the way they'd looked at her as if she weren't quite human, and she wanted to run away someplace where she'd never have to see anyone like them again. But if she did, she'd prove them right. And she had to protect her son. She sighed with resignation. "What should I do?"

"You could go to church for a start," Zeb said quickly.

"And invite some of them women over to visit," Jewel added.

Rebekah would have rather swallowed live coals, but she nodded stiffly. "Tomorrow's Sunday, isn't it?" she asked with the enthusiasm of one sentenced to die on the morrow.

"All those men ever talk about is the war," Cousin Prudence complained. The men in question had adjourned outside to smoke and replay General Zachary Taylor's victory at Monterey while the women remained seated at the Tates' kitchen table, the remains of Sunday dinner scattered around them.

Mrs. Phipps and Mrs. Williams nodded their disapproval.

"Well, they never should've allowed Santa Anna back in the country," Mrs. Phipps declared. "He'll cause even more trouble, you mark my words. I guess President Polk didn't ask anybody from Texas if the man could be trusted. If he had, he would've known better."

"Mr. Williams said Santa Anna promised to make peace with the United States if they helped him get back in power," Mrs. Williams offered.

Cousin Prudence sniffed. "Man like that would promise anything. Can't trust a single one of those greasers, if you ask me. Anybody knows anything at all about the Alamo knows that."

Jewel was cleaning up around them as they talked, and she wasn't letting Rebekah help, so Rebekah had to sit and smile and pretend to care about what they were saying. This at least was better than church had been, when she'd had to sit and pretend to listen to her father's sermon, knowing every parishioner was watching every move she made.

"Sending the Rangers home wasn't smart, either," Mrs. Phipps said. "Ain't nobody knows more about fighting than Texas Rangers."

"They say even General Taylor couldn't stand the way they killed Mexicans every chance they got, though," Cousin Prudence said.

"Well, I don't reckon anybody who wasn't a Texan could understand," Mrs. Phipps replied. "Nobody who had kin at Goliad where they shot the Texans down in cold blood would criticize, though."

The ladies all nodded grimly, remembering the treachery of the Mexican army in times past. Rebekah tried to share their outrage, but the Mexicans weren't her personal enemies.

After a moment of silence, Cousin Prudence turned to Rebekah, obviously intent on drawing her into the general conversation. "That's a lovely dress, dear. Wherever did you get the material?"

Rebekah tried not to wince. "Mr. MacDougal brought it," she said, the words fairly sticking in her throat.

"Oh my," Mrs. Williams said, delighted. "I hope he plans to stock something equally nice when he opens his own store."

"Where is the store going to be, do you know?" Mrs. Phipps asked.

Rebekah shifted in her chair, fighting the urge to flee now that everyone was looking at her. Somehow she managed to smile pleasantly. "I believe he is going to build it near the church."

Indeed, that very morning her father had pointed out the exact portion of land he was going to deed to MacDougal for the proposed emporium—MacDougal's reward for rescuing Rebekah Tate.

"My goodness," Mrs. Williams exclaimed. "With a store there, we'll practically have a town!"

"I believe that's what Mr. MacDougal intends," Cousin Prudence said authoritatively. "As he explained to me—"

"He said the church was at the crossroads because it was more convenient," Rebekah heard herself saying, rudely interrupting Cousin Prudence who gave her a startled look. Rebekah ignored it. "He said a store should be just as convenient as a church."

Rebekah hadn't really heard MacDougal say these things. He'd said them to her father, though, and Zeb and Jewel had recounted the conversations more than once. Why she felt obliged to explain MacDougal to these women, though, she had no idea. All she knew was she couldn't sit here and let Cousin Prudence talk about him like *she* knew what his plans were.

The women were watching her now, a little wary because Rebekah was speaking so much. Mrs. Williams smiled a little. "Do you know what kinds of things he plans to sell?"

"Everything," Rebekah reported confidently. "Anything you might need and probably a few things you don't, just to get you to spend more money than you should. That's how traders get rich, you know."

The women were gaping at her now, looking as if they'd just seen a stone not only speak but talk good sense. They didn't seem quite able to accept the evidence of their own ears. Rebekah sat back, gratified to have shocked them, and waited for their response.

Cousin Prudence was the first to recover. "I understand Mr. MacDougal used to trade with the Indians," she said tentatively.

"Yes," Rebekah said. "He was what they call a comanchero. The people in New Mexico deal openly with the Indians. They've somehow managed to make peace with them, although heaven knows how they did it."

"Perhaps we should take a lesson," Mrs. Williams offered.

"Pshaw, Pearl," Mrs. Phipps scoffed. "Texans would never lower themselves like that, not after the way those savages butchered so many of our people." Suddenly realizing she might have given offense, she flushed scarlet. "Oh, I'm sorry, Rebekah. I didn't mean . . ." Her voice trailed off. Obviously, she had no idea what she hadn't meant.

"You're right," Rebekah said, not in the least offended. "We shouldn't make peace with them. We should kill them all."

The ladies were surprised, but only Mrs. Williams did not approve the sentiment. She frowned. "But dear, what about your son?"

"He's not an Indian!" Rebekah declared fiercely, making the ladies jump. Behind her a pot clanked loudly in warning, and she drew a calming breath. "My son is a Tate," she said quietly.

"I think Mr. MacDougal is so brave to go back for the boy," Cousin Prudence said, a little too enthusiastically for Rebekah's taste since Rebekah knew her true feelings on the matter. "Can you imagine riding into Indian country like that, much less riding right up to an Indian camp?"

"He's done it before," Rebekah reminded them, unaccountably annoyed at hearing another woman singing MacDougal's praises.

"Mr. Williams said he was crazy to do a thing like that," Mrs. Williams said apologetically.

"MacDougal may be a lot of things, but he's not crazy," Rebekah snapped, equally annoyed at hearing MacDougal criticized. What on earth had come over her? Why should she care what people thought of him?

"Well, crazy or not, I think we all know why Mr. MacDougal went, don't we?" Cousin Prudence said, smiling strangely at Rebekah.

Rebekah felt her face growing hot and wondered if everyone knew she'd gone into a decline like some silly chit over the prospect of never seeing her son again.

"Oh, yes," Mrs. Phipps agreed. "Love has made many a man do impossible things. You're a very lucky woman, Rebekah."

"She certainly is," Cousin Prudence declared. "Not every man would take an Ind—" She glanced uncertainly at Rebekah and amended her statement. ". . . would take someone else's child as his own."

Rebekah felt her earlier apprehension swell into near panic. "MacDougal hasn't taken my son as his own," she insisted.

The ladies exchanged knowing looks. "Not yet, dear," Cousin Prudence said, then deftly changed the subject. "Have you finished your canning yet, Eliza?"

While the other ladies discussed domestic issues, Rebekah seethed silently over their remarks about

MacDougal. All that nonsense about love. MacDougal never cared about anything in his life except his precious money. Even rescuing her had been so he could be famous and make more money.

Except he wasn't going to get any more famous by rescuing her son. In fact, he might just get himself killed. She shuddered at the thought and told herself it was just the prospect of never seeing her boy again that made her blood run so cold. Surely she didn't care what happened to MacDougal. At least she didn't care too much. So why did the thought of his death turn her heart to stone?

The visit seemed to drag on interminably, but finally the Phippses and the Williamses headed for home, satisfied at last that while Rebekah Tate might be a trifle strange, she certainly wasn't as crazy as they had first suspected. This left the Nelson family as the only remaining visitors. Rebekah, weary from so much socializing and no longer worried about giving offense, sought a little solitude by wandering away from the others and seeking the bench at the back of the house.

There she found her cousin Andrew whom she hadn't noticed was missing. He smiled, jumping to his feet. "You caught me hiding."

"Why would you be hiding?" she asked, taking a seat beside him and motioning for him to sit back down. She wouldn't mind company from Andrew.

"I get tired of hearing them talk about the war," he said, taking a seat beside her. "I get the idea they think I should join the Rangers and go fight or something."

"I thought the Army sent the Rangers home."

"They'll go back if the fighting starts again. For all his complaining about the Rangers' lack of discipline, General Taylor doesn't have anybody else who can scout in that country."

"Why would anybody expect you to go, though?"

Andrew frowned. "A good question, since God knows I'm not much good at that sort of thing."

Oh dear, she hadn't meant to insult him. "I didn't mean—" she tried, but he cut her off.

"I know you didn't." He tried to smile again. "I'm just a little quick to take offense I guess. It's my guilty conscience."

"What do you have to be guilty about?"

He laughed mirthlessly. "You mean besides the fact that I'm a worthless do-nothing?"

"You're not worthless!" she protested, remembering how he was the only one except Jewel who had really seemed to feel her pain.

"Thank you, Rebekah," he said sadly, "but I am, at least as far as my family is concerned. I can't farm, I'm no good on the range, I can't shoot, I—"

"Andrew!" she cried. "That doesn't mean you're worthless!"

"So far as my family's concerned it does. Those things are the measure of a man in Texas, and if you can't do them . . ." He shook his head and stared out at the bare horizon, his eyes bleak.

"Can't you learn to do those things?" she asked tentatively, thinking of the effortless way MacDougal seemed to do them.

His broad shoulders sagged. "I've tried, but it must be something you're born with, a feel for the land or something. I do everything, just like my father shows me, but it never turns out right. Maybe I'm just stupid."

"You're not stupid! Papa said you've read every book in the county!"

"But as my father has pointed out many times, book learning won't keep a man from starving to death. And how could I take care of a family if I can't even keep myself?"

Rebekah wanted to comfort him, to somehow ease his pain the way he'd tried to ease hers that first day. Perhaps if she took him in her arms the way he'd taken her . . . But she couldn't do that, not without giving him the wrong idea about her feelings for him.

"Papa says anybody can make a go of it here now that the Indians aren't a threat anymore," she told him. "And somebody as smart as you . . . and if you've got somebody special . . . I mean, you said something about taking care of a family. Do you have a girl, Andrew?"

He smiled sheepishly. "I'm not sure."

"Well, if *you're* not sure, who is?" she teased.

"Maybe I should've said she doesn't know it yet, or at least I don't think she does."

"Then you'd better tell her before somebody else steals her from under your nose."

Andrew frowned. "That's why I haven't told her yet, because there is somebody else, or there might be. Are you . . . ? I mean, Prudence said you're going to marry Mr. MacDougal when he comes back."

"What?" Rebekah asked in confusion. Why were they suddenly talking about *her?*

"Are you? Going to marry him, I mean? He did rescue you, after all, and now he's gone after your son and—"

"No. Oh no!" Rebekah assured him, fighting her instinctive terror of the very idea. "I can't imagine where Prudence got an idea like that, but it's not true. I'm not going to marry MacDougal or anyone else."

Andrew's face brightened, and he smiled broadly. "I reckon that just shows you what a fool I am. Here I've been worried all this time, and all I had to do was ask you."

Rebekah couldn't imagine why this news had made Andrew so happy, but she was glad she'd been

287

able to cheer him up. "So now that we've got my future settled, what about yours? When are you going to propose to this young lady you're so fond of?"

Andrew chuckled. "Right now, I guess." To her surprise, he took her hand. "Rebekah, you know I've always loved you ever since we were kids. And I know I just told you all the reasons why you shouldn't, but I'm going to ask anyway: Will you marry me?"

Too stunned to speak, Rebekah could only gape at him and shake her head in amazement.

"I'm not much of a catch," he went on, not waiting for her reply, "but I'd work hard for you, harder than I've ever worked at anything in my life. I'd take care of you Rebekah, and of the boy, too. And I'll make it up to you, to both of you, for everything that's happened. I'll make you forget it all, I swear, and we'll be happy. You won't be sorry, I promise you."

Rebekah was already sorry, sorry she'd pressed this issue and even sorrier she was going to have to hurt Andrew when she'd only been trying to help. "Andrew, I—"

"Look, I know this is sudden. I can see by your face you weren't expecting it. I should've let you know how I felt before now, but I thought you and MacDougal . . . But now there's no reason why we can't—"

"There's a lot of reasons!" she exclaimed, clutching his hand in both of hers. "I'm not the same girl you loved seven years ago, and I have a child and—"

"None of that matters, not to me. I loved you then and I love you now, and I'll love anything that belongs to you. Give me a chance to help you forget. I owe you that much."

"You don't owe me anything!" she cried. "And even if you did, you've already paid me back a thousand times by being my friend."

"You need more than a friend. You need someone

to take care of you, and your father won't be here forever."

Suddenly her father's dogs began to bark ferociously.

"Sounds like we've got more company," Rebekah observed in a feeble attempt to distract him.

"More people come to see the famous Rebekah Tate," he said sarcastically, and when she winced, he squeezed her hand. "You see, that's why you need someone—why you need *me* to protect you from all that, and I would, Rebekah. No one would ever stare at my wife or talk about her behind their hands or make fun of her child. I can't give you much, but I can give you that."

"Rebekah!" her father called, but she ignored the summons.

Andrew's offer was tempting, so tempting she could almost imagine herself accepting it, except that she cared too much for Andrew to saddle him with the burdens she would bring him.

"Andrew, I—"

"You don't have to give me an answer now," he assured her. "I know you've got a lot on your mind right now, what with the boy and everything."

"*Rebekah!*" Zeb called again, and this time the urgency in his voice made every hair on her body stand on end. "Rebekah, come quick!"

"What could it be?" Andrew murmured in alarm, but Rebekah was already on her feet, hope trembling inside her like a fragile, brittle leaf. Only one thing could possibly be so urgent. Forgetting all about Andrew and his offer, she ran.

Prudence and Cecil and her father were standing in the yard, staring out at the lone rider approaching. Jewel had come from the kitchen to see, and Dan and Enoch were coming from their cabin.

The dogs were silent now, hushed by her father's

command, but they milled restlessly, tails wagging, ears pricked. Beyond them Rebekah could see the rider, the familiar set of the shoulders, the familiar glint of red hair hanging below the equally familiar sombrero. And before him on the saddle, almost swallowed in a faded red shirt . . .

She cried out as her fragile hope blossomed into joy. The rider had stopped before the others, and she raced to them, holding her skirts in both hands and cursing them for slowing her down. MacDougal slid from the saddle, and the boy fairly leaped into his arms, clinging to him in terror while the others gathered around, exclaiming over him.

She burst into their midst, furious at her family for frightening her baby. She reached for him with hungry arms, crooning softly, but her arrival only frightened him more, and he turned away in a panic, clinging desperately to MacDougal and burying his face in MacDougal's shoulder.

"What have you done to him?" she demanded, stricken by the boy's rejection.

MacDougal grinned through the beard he'd regrown during this trip. "That's some greeting, Rebekah Tate. Haven't they taught you any manners at all while I was gone?"

She could only sputter furiously, unable to decide whether to shake MacDougal or try to snatch her son away from him.

And MacDougal just kept grinning. "Maybe you better say something to him. I don't think he recognizes you in that pretty dress."

Automatically she glanced down at her gown and realized how different she must look from the mother the boy had known.

"*Sitū-htsi?*" she whispered.

The small body stiffened, but he didn't move, and she thought her heart would break.

MacDougal said, *"Pia,* Mother."

The boy lifted his head questioningly, and MacDougal nodded. The boy turned warily, his small face suspicious, and he looked at the white woman again.

"I'm here," she said in Comanche, slipping easily back into the tongue she hadn't spoken for several months and holding out her empty arms. "You're home, Little One."

He still couldn't quite believe it. She could see the doubt glittering in his pale eyes, the eyes she'd thought she'd never see again, and she didn't know whether to laugh or to cry.

Then the boy said, *"Pia?"* and when she said, "Yes, my darling, yes!" she was doing both.

The boy lunged for her, and she caught him with the arms she'd thought might never hold him again and clasped him to her pounding heart, closing her eyes against the sheer ecstasy of having him again, of touching him and kissing him and smelling him and tasting him. She ran her hands over him, unable quite to believe he was here and real and whole and safe and with her again.

But he was, and he was wondering why she was crying and why she wasn't dead as he had been told and why she'd sent Mac after him instead of coming for him herself and why was she wearing such a funny dress and what had happened to her hair, and she couldn't get enough of touching him or looking at him until finally she glanced up and saw MacDougal watching her expectantly.

Suddenly, her joy evaporated. What did he want? What would he demand of her now that he had saved not only her own life but her son's as well? Now that he had risked himself not once but twice for her sake? And she didn't doubt for a moment that he wanted something, something much more important than

291

fame or land on which to build a store. He wanted something from her, and his wolf's eyes told her he intended to claim it. Fear tightened like a band around her heart because whatever he wanted, she knew she could not give it, and for a second she couldn't even breathe for the terror of knowing it.

Then her father said, "Rebekah, aren't you going to introduce me to my grandson?"

She whirled instantly, desperately grateful for the distraction. "Oh, Papa, I'm so sorry!" she said breathlessly. The boy had startled at the sound of Zeb's voice and was now clinging to her again, a frightened child facing a group of strangers, all of whom now stood around him. "Papa, this is my son . . ."

She faltered, not knowing exactly what to call the boy.

"I call him Hunter," MacDougal said behind her.

The boy's head jerked up at this, and MacDougal ruffled the child's hair affectionately, then let his other hand rest on Rebekah's shoulder. She felt the touch reverberate through her, but she managed not to acknowledge the reaction.

"'Hunter,'" MacDougal was saying, "is pretty much what his name means in English."

"I think that's a fine name," Cousin Prudence declared, as if everyone were waiting for her approval.

"Hunter," Zeb said softly, his voice rough with emotion, his faded blue eyes swimming with tears. The wind teased at his long white hair and beard, and Rebekah tried to see him through Hunter's eyes. Indian men had little hair on their faces, and they plucked out what they did have, so the boy should have been frightened by the beard.

Except MacDougal had a beard, so maybe he was used to it by now.

Pushing the thought away as she wanted to push MacDougal's possessive hand, she said in Comanche, "This is your grandfather, Little One. My father. He has been waiting many years to see you."

Zeb reached out to touch the boy, but Hunter cringed, and Zeb dropped his hand, mortified. Rebekah wanted to weep for the pain she saw in his old eyes, but MacDougal was more practical.

"Is that the proper way to treat your mother's father?" he demanded in Comanche.

She felt the boy stiffen at the rebuke and saw dismay on his little face. She knew a pang of jealousy over the boy's eagerness to please MacDougal, whom he had known so short a time. Then Hunter straightened his small shoulders and held up his right hand questioningly. MacDougal nodded with approval, and the boy thrust the small grubby hand out to Zeb.

For a moment, the old man didn't know what to do. Then MacDougal explained softly, "I taught him to shake hands."

Zeb's eyes cleared instantly with understanding, and he took the small hand in his much larger one. Hunter shook quite vigorously, making everyone chuckle, which frightened him again because he thought he'd done something disrespectful.

"They're just happy to see you, Little One," Rebekah soothed him, then introduced him to his cousins, Cecil and Prudence. "And this is your cousin Andrew," she said, turning to him.

Cecil and Prudence had taken the boy's hand gingerly, not quite certain how to react, but Andrew had no reservations. He took the boy's hand in both of his and smiled hugely, just the way a prospective stepfather might, Rebekah thought in dismay.

"Tell him I'm very pleased to meet him, pleased and honored to meet my beloved cousin's child,"

293

Andrew said as the boy returned his smile.

When Rebekah felt MacDougal's hand tighten on her shoulder, she knew the situation was getting even more complicated, but she refused to think about any of it just now. She'd sort it all out later, she decided as she translated for Hunter who was too shy to reply to his new cousin.

She saw the slaves hovering at the edge of the group and said, "Jewel, come and meet my boy. Dan and Enoch, you come, too."

Hunter stared in unabashed curiosity at the three blacks. Jewel was the first to approach, and although she held her head high and managed to maintain her dignity, Rebekah saw the tears glittering in her friend's eyes as she took the boy's small hand in her own. Dan and Enoch stared back at Hunter just as curiously. Perhaps they'd never seen an Indian close up just as Hunter had never seen a Negro.

When everyone had shaken Hunter's hand, a moment of awkward silence fell during which no one knew exactly what to do. Rebekah stood holding her son, still not quite able to believe he was really here while at the same time acutely aware that Andrew and MacDougal *were* here and that MacDougal had some claim on her she didn't understand and didn't want to understand and that Andrew at least thought he had a claim on her, too. She couldn't bring herself to look at either of them, especially MacDougal, although he stood so close she could feel the heat radiating from his body and his hand still rested possessively on her shoulder.

Finally Jewel cleared her throat and said, "I expect you two are hungry. Come inside, and I'll rustle up something. Dan'll take care of your horse, Mr. MacDougal."

She strode off toward the house, and the whites followed obediently with Rebekah and MacDougal bringing up the rear and Andrew hovering protectively. Rebekah stepped out suddenly, slipping from beneath MacDougal's hand and almost sighing aloud at the relief of being free of his touch.

"The boy's too heavy for you to carry," MacDougal said, easily keeping pace with her. "He can walk."

She didn't look at him. She didn't dare. "I want to carry him," she said, knowing she should say something, thank him at least, but if she did, she would have to look up into those wolf's eyes, and if she did that, something terrible would happen. Maybe she was just being superstitious. Maybe she just hadn't been among the whites long enough to have forgotten the Comanche penchant for seeing evil omens everywhere.

Or maybe MacDougal really was a danger to her.

The Nelsons and her father had stopped by the front door, and Prudence was making their excuses. "This must be upsetting for the poor child, so many strangers, and it's time we were getting home anyway. I'll come by in a few days to see how you're getting along," she assured Rebekah when she approached. "Andrew, go hitch up the wagon, will you?"

But Andrew didn't obey her instantly. Instead, he took Rebekah by the shoulders and smiled his wonderful smile that made Hunter smile back at him and made Rebekah remember her newest problem. "Now that you've got your son back, you'll have some time to think about yourself and . . . and other people," he added cryptically, since others were listening.

"Yes," she said stiffly, wishing she could have a moment alone with him to settle this once and for all. But Andrew would just have to wait.

"I'll see you soon, then?" he said.

"You're always welcome here, Andrew."

"That's good to know," he said, ruffling Hunter's raven hair again. "See you later, partner," he told the boy. Hunter seemed to understand the sentiment if not the words, and he grinned after Andrew as he loped off to do his stepmother's bidding.

"Good-bye," Rebekah said to Cecil and Prudence, ignoring their puzzled frowns over her exchange with Andrew. "Thank you for coming."

Duty done, she escaped into the house without waiting for Prudence's effusive replies.

Jewel was setting out plates filled with leftovers from the lavish Sunday dinner, and at the sight of the food, Hunter at last felt secure enough to wiggle down from his mother's arms. She released him reluctantly and watched him scamper across the room with mingled pride and wonder that quickly changed to dismay when she saw him snatch the plate from the table, squat down on the floor with it, and begin scooping the food into his mouth with his dirty fingers.

"I figured I'd leave it to you to teach him table manners," MacDougal said in her ear, making her jump. She hadn't realized he'd followed her inside.

She forced herself to look up at him. He seemed no less threatening now than he had outside, but at least he wasn't touching her. "I . . . I don't know how to thank you for bringing my son back," she stammered.

"Don't you?" he asked archly.

She could feel the heat rising in her face and hoped the light was too dim for him to see.

"Your supper's ready, Mr. MacDougal," Jewel informed him, mercifully causing a distraction.

"Thank you, Jewel. I've been dreaming about your cooking halfway across Texas," he said.

"Well, this here ain't nothing much," Jewel demurred. "You wait till tomorrow, I'll fix you up something special."

He grinned that charming grin. "I'm not sure my poor heart, or my poor stomach for that matter, could stand the shock."

Jewel preened under his compliment, and Rebekah wanted to shake her for . . . For what? For liking MacDougal? Why on earth should it matter if Jewel liked him or not? Then she noticed her son still squatting on the floor and realized she had more important things to worry about.

She really should get him up off the floor before her father came in and saw him. Jewel was doing an excellent job of not noticing, but her father would be appalled. Rebekah opened her mouth to speak to her son, but she stopped when she remembered the name she would have to call him.

Suddenly furious, she whirled on MacDougal, who was now sitting at the table, stuffing his bearded face. "And just who gave you permission to name my son?" she demanded.

He blinked in surprise, carefully chewed and swallowed the mouthful of food he'd just taken and said, "I had to call him something, didn't I? If you don't like the name I picked, call him something else."

But she didn't want him to be reasonable. She wanted to pick a fight with him because she wanted a reason to be angry with him. "How can I? You've got him answering to it now!"

"He'll answer to anything if you tell him it's his new name. Comanches change their names all the time."

He was right, of course, which didn't help at all. "And what's that thing he's wearing?"

MacDougal glanced at the boy who was still eating furiously but who was now watching them warily, sensitive to the tone of their voices even though he couldn't understand their words.

"It used to be a shirt. I got it at Hopewell's Fort, where the selection isn't exactly wonderful, if you will recall. By the way, that dress you're wearing looks very nice, if I do say so myself."

This time her face felt like it was on fire. "You had nothing to do with this dress, MacDougal. Jewel made it."

He lifted his sun-bleached eyebrows but said nothing. He didn't have to, since they both knew he'd bought the material now covering her body.

"You've filled out some, too, since I saw you last," he noted with obvious approval. "I reckon I'm not the only one who likes Jewel's cooking."

The fire in her face sizzled over her entire body, and she had an overwhelming desire to slap that smug grin off MacDougal's hairy face. Except she knew she didn't dare get even that close because if she so much as touched him, heaven only knew what might happen.

"Mother?"

At first Rebekah didn't register the strange word coming from the small voice near the floor beside her. No one had ever called her "Mother" before.

Slowly the realization penetrated, however, seeping through her anger and her inattention until it touched an answering chord.

"Mother?" Hunter asked again.

And his name *was* Hunter. It was a perfect name, the one she would have picked if MacDougal hadn't beaten her to it. And he looked so dear and small and frightened hunkering there on the floor, an empty plate balanced on his knees, his face and hands smeared with the remnants of his meal.

Her heart throbbed with love and joy and a thousand other emotions she couldn't name, and she answered him, crooning endearments, and disposed of the plate and scooped him up into her arms again, heedless of his smeared hands and face.

"He's probably tired," MacDougal observed with infuriating certainty. "We've been riding since before dawn this morning. I knew we were close, and I didn't want to have to camp one more night if I didn't have to."

"I know how to take care of my own son," Rebekah snapped.

"Maybe we oughta get him a bath before he goes to bed," Jewel suggested, frowning at the dirty face. "I'll get the tub ready."

"Put it in my room," Rebekah said, and Jewel stole discreetly out of the room, leaving her alone with her son and the man who'd stolen him from the Indians.

And when she saw the way Hunter looked at MacDougal, Rebekah couldn't help wondering if MacDougal had stolen the boy in other ways, too. Well, it didn't matter now. He was here, and he was hers again, and she didn't need MacDougal's help any longer.

Or so she thought until she tried to get Hunter into the tub. Taking off his clothes had been no problem since he'd never been particularly fond of wearing them in the first place. He'd never seen such a thing as a bathtub before, though, or imagined anything as bizarre as a hot bath with soap, and he'd fought all attempts to submerge him until his shrieks drew MacDougal's interested attention.

"He probably thinks you're going to boil him and eat him," MacDougal observed, lounging in Rebekah's bedroom doorway. "Maybe you ought to get into the bath first to show him it's safe."

Rebekah gasped in shock at the very suggestion, and MacDougal laughed aloud at her outrage.

"You've turned white again in a mighty big hurry," he said, grinning. "I doubt *Huuwǔhtūkwa*

299

would've hesitated a minute about taking a bath with her kid."

"I'm not the one who needs a bath, MacDougal," she informed him in exasperation.

He glanced down at himself and shrugged. "You're right at that. I was going to wait until you'd finished with the boy, but I might as well get it over with now." He was already unbuttoning his shirt as he strolled across the floor, and Rebekah jumped to her feet, releasing a naked Hunter who raced right to MacDougal and clung to his legs for protection against the crazy white woman who wanted to murder him.

"What are you doing?" she asked in alarm as MacDougal shrugged out of his travel-stained shirt to reveal the broad chest liberally sprinkled with rust-colored hair. Her heart lurched painfully at the memory of being held against that very chest, and she felt the strength draining dangerously from her limbs.

"I'm going to take a bath, and I'm going to give your son one, too. You're welcome to stay and watch, of course . . ."

Rebekah didn't wait to hear the rest. She bolted from the room, slamming the door shut behind her before MacDougal could remove anymore of his clothes or bring back any more disturbing memories.

She only wished her heart wasn't racing so painfully and her breath wasn't quite so labored. Anyone would think he'd frightened her. Of course, *she* knew she wasn't afraid of him. She just didn't want to see him naked. What woman would?

She didn't go far, though. As a mother, she was obliged to stay near in case her child needed her. Perched on one of the benches beneath the dogtrot, her father's dogs sleeping peacefully at her feet, she waited, ignoring Jewel's occasional curious glances when she walked by the open kitchen door.

When the call came, it wasn't from Hunter, though.

"Rebekah Tate," MacDougal shouted, bringing her running.

She stopped dead in the doorway, however, at the sight of two naked males.

Well, Hunter was naked and grudgingly allowing himself to be toweled dry by MacDougal who wasn't exactly naked but might as well have been for all the flour sack towel around his waist concealed. They were both standing in a puddle of immense proportions which revealed MacDougal had had his hands full in getting one small Indian boy into the tub.

Seeing her shock, MacDougal grinned and said, "I didn't want to put my dirty clothes back on." He wasn't apologizing, just explaining, and Rebekah was determined not to let him see how disturbing his nudity was to her.

"He looks like he's done in," she observed, pointing at her son with her chin, Indian style.

MacDougal nodded cheerfully. "You might have a little trouble getting him into the bed, though. He was scared of the one at Hopewell's Fort, although he crawled in with me eventually. Of course, if you want me to sleep here tonight so he won't be scared—"

"MacDougal!" she cried. She was exasperated and annoyed and not a little shaken because she didn't find the prospect as appalling as she should have.

He straightened from his task, his long, lean body looking impossibly masculine in the flickering candlelight, and when he released Hunter, the boy almost keeled over, fairly asleep on his feet. Rebekah swooped in and caught him up, murmuring imprecations at MacDougal as she carried the boy to the bed and laid him down.

As she had often dreamed of doing, she pulled the

covers over his precious body and tucked them in around his chin, then brushed the damp hair off his forehead and kissed him tenderly. He was asleep before she straightened from the kiss.

"He's a fine boy, Rebekah Tate," MacDougal said from behind her. "I can see why you didn't want to give him up."

She wanted to say something cutting, to remind him how reluctant he'd been to save Hunter and how dare he pretend to care for the boy now, but she couldn't speak because of the lump in her throat.

Then MacDougal's arms slid around her, enveloping her in his warmth and the musky scent of fresh-scrubbed male skin, and the lump in her throat became a leaden weight in her stomach.

"I've been wanting to do this ever since I rode in here," he whispered into her ear. "God, you feel so good."

He felt good, too, more than good. Strong and virile and overwhelmingly compelling. She wanted to lean back into his strength and feel all that bare flesh against her own, even though she knew she didn't dare, not if she wanted to stay free. But he was nibbling on her ear, sending delicious shivers racing over her and robbing her of whatever resistance she had left so when he turned her to face him she was powerless to stop him from kissing her.

His mouth ravished hers, taking everything and giving her no chance to refuse. She'd braced her hands against his chest to ward him off, but the feel of his naked flesh beneath her hands paralyzed her. The skin was cool but the touch scorched her palms and the answering heat raced over her body, settling into her secret places and making her tremble with fear and wanting.

When they were both breathless, he lifted his mouth from hers and said, "Come to me tonight.

I've told Jewel to make me up a pallet in the parlor and—"

"I can't," she said, panic twisting in her stomach.

"I know you don't want to leave the boy, but he can sleep through anything, believe me—"

"I can't!" she tried, but he wasn't listening.

"It won't take long," he was saying with a self-mocking grin. "I just need to hold you for a little while and—"

"No!" she cried and would have wrenched away but his arms tightened like steel bands, holding her fast.

"You can't tell me no, Rebekah Tate," he informed her, his breath warm and sweet against her face. "You're mine now, and I intend to claim you—"

"*No!*" she screamed and this time she did break free, furious and shaking with the force of her rage. "I do not belong to you or anybody else and I never will again! I'm free now and I'm going to stay free!"

"What's the matter with you?" he demanded, planting his hands on his hips and almost dislodging the towel clinging so precariously to those hips. For a second he looked completely baffled, then his fierce eyes narrowed speculatively. "Is it Nelson?"

"Who?" she asked in genuine confusion.

"Your cousin," he snarled contemptuously. "Handsome young Andrew. Has he been . . . courting you while I was gone?"

He had, of course, although the "courting" had been rather recent and awfully brief, and MacDougal saw the truth of it on her face. His own face grew scarlet and his eyes glittered dangerously, but his anger didn't frighten her nearly as much as his passion did.

"Yes," she told him defiantly, "Andrew's asked me to marry him. We were promised to each other when

303

we were children. We've always loved each other."
That much was true, at least, although it wasn't the
kind of love MacDougal was imagining.

"And that's what he meant this afternoon when he
said you could think about yourself now," MacDougal said through gritted teeth.

She nodded, not trusting her voice to respond.

"And what do you think young Andrew would say
if I told him what happened between us out on the
prairie? About how you gave yourself to me and—?"

"I already told him," she lied, finding it easier than
she had imagined, although her own face was
flaming now. "He knows you . . . you forced me
and—"

"*Forced* you!" he shouted, grabbing her by the
shoulders and lifting her to her toes.

Beside them Hunter muttered in his sleep at the
disturbance, and MacDougal lowered his voice to a
vibrating whisper. "I never forced you, and you
know it, you lying little witch. You were the one who
seduced me, and you loved it, too. You loved every
minute of it. Does young Andrew make you feel that
way? Do you wrap your legs around him and—"

"Stop it!" she hissed in panic, feeling her body's
response to his nearness and knowing she had to fight
him any way she could. "You're making a fool of
yourself! Can't you understand? I don't want you!"

Instinctively, she'd said exactly the right thing. He
started as if she'd slapped him, and his hands
dropped from her shoulders. For one terrible second,
she saw the agony in his eyes, so bright and fierce she
winced, but then he turned away and snatched up his
dirty clothes and stormed barefooted and almost bare
naked out of the room.

She heard Jewel's startled cry at the sight of him
and his voice saying, "Wash these, will you?" as he
thrust the clothes into her hands. Then he disap-

peared into the other side of the house, and Rebekah's knees buckled with relief that it was over.

She sank down on the bed beside where her son, unaware of the drama that had just been played out before him, still slept peacefully. Lifting her hands to cover her burning face, she saw they were trembling and closed them into fists and pressed those fists against her aching eyes. She wouldn't cry, not over MacDougal.

At last she'd escaped from her final bond. She was free of MacDougal, and now she would never again have to fear what he would take from her if she had let him have her. She was free, and she had her son, and she didn't have to be afraid.

Why then did she feel like she had lost everything?

Chapter Eleven

MacDougal was gone when she woke up the next morning. Rebekah had gotten Hunter up and dressed and taken him to the kitchen for breakfast, marching him in front of her like a guard to provide a buffer for when she encountered MacDougal. But he wasn't there.

"He left at first light this morning," Jewel informed her. "Said he wanted to get to work on his store. Wants to have it open before Christmas comes."

"His store?" Rebekah asked stupidly.

Jewel frowned and shook her head. "He's a storekeeper. You remember, he was going to open a store out by your pappy's church."

For some reason, Rebekah had expected him to abandon that plan now that she'd rejected him. She'd expected him to return to Sante Fe and ... And what? He'd sold his business there, hadn't he? And he'd rescued her so he would be famous in Texas and so everyone would come to his store here. Why should he change his plans just because Rebekah Tate had refused him herself?

"I see," she said carefully, unwilling to examine her reaction too closely for fear she might discover she was relieved to know he wasn't actually leaving. "So he'll be back again tonight."

"No," Jewel replied, studying Rebekah's expression carefully. "He said he'd be camping out there from now on until he's got a place built. Lots of work to do, he said."

Rebekah should have felt relief at this, at least. Instead she felt . . . Well, she wasn't sure what she felt, but knowing MacDougal was so close made her not only uneasy because she wasn't anxious to face him again, but somehow comfortable, too.

It was habit, she told herself. He'd taken good care of her out on the prairie, and he'd taken good care of her son, too. He'd be a good man to have around if there was trouble.

But what if there wasn't any trouble? a small voice asked.

Then he'd probably make some, she decided, and turned to the task of teaching her wild son to sit at the table for his breakfast.

The next few days passed in a blur of activity, each event a crisis that left Rebekah near despair and her son near tears or actually in tears, even though Comanche boys don't cry. Maybe she shouldn't have tried to do everything at once, she thought to herself as she sat on a bench beneath the dogtrot and leaned wearily against the log wall of the house. It was only nine o'clock in the morning, and she was already exhausted from having finally gotten Hunter's long hair shorn.

Hunter himself was sitting on a bench opposite her, glaring murderously and trying not to cry over the enormous indignity he had endured. But with his dark hair cut short and wearing the shirt and trousers Jewel had stitched for him, he looked almost civilized.

Except, of course, for the moccasins which he had

307

to wear because they hadn't been able to get him any real shoes yet. He was eating at the table, though, and using a spoon most of the time. And he'd accepted the fact he must relieve himself in the outhouse and not wherever he happened to be when the urge took him. The clothes still annoyed him, but since the weather was getting colder, he'd finally acquiesced. He'd surely hated giving up his hair, though, and he wasn't going to forget his mother's treachery, either.

Rebekah sighed and wondered where she would get the energy to deal with the next lesson, whatever that might be, and found herself wishing for MacDougal's help.

The traitorous thought was no sooner born than rejected, but Rebekah's heart was pounding at it just the same. She'd hardly thought about MacDougal since the morning he'd left. Except, of course, each night when she put Hunter to bed and Hunter asked when he was coming back. And each morning when she woke up, and she thought about him before she was fully awake and could stop herself. And at each meal when she remembered how much he enjoyed Jewel's cooking and wondered what he was eating now that he was on his own. And occasionally when she thought about seeing him again and wondered what on earth she would say to him, if she even had a chance to speak to him at all. But except for those times, she never thought of MacDougal at all. Well, almost never.

She thought of him now, though, and the pain in her heart made her gasp aloud. She had barely recovered from the shock when Hunter and the dogs jumped up and started running. The dogs were barking their "visitor approaching" bark and Hunter was yelling, "Mac! Mac!"

Rebekah's poor heart stopped dead in her chest when she saw the lone rider, but it started beating again almost instantly when she recognized the rider as Andrew Nelson instead. She was not, she told herself sternly, disappointed.

Neither was Hunter, since Andrew reached down and pulled him up before him on the saddle and let him ride with him the rest of the way to the house, the howling dogs following in their wake. By the time they reached her, Rebekah had remembered her new problem with Andrew, the one she'd completely forgotten in all the excitement of having Hunter home.

"Andrew, what brings you here?" she asked with forced brightness, hoping against hope that he'd forgotten all about his proposal, too.

"I came to see if you'd made up your mind yet," he replied cheerfully, dashing her hopes.

"Andrew, I . . ." she began, wishing she knew how to refuse him without hurting him.

"Don't worry, I'm not going to push you for an answer," he assured her just as cheerfully. "I also came to see how you're making out." He slid down from the horse and plucked Hunter from the saddle and transferred him to his own broad shoulders, much to the boy's delight.

"This young man told me you scalped him," Andrew reported with mock solemnity.

Rebekah smiled in spite of herself. "I did, or at least Papa and I did, and Jewel and Dan and Enoch helped hold him down. I didn't know you spoke Comanche, though."

"I don't. He used sign language," Andrew said, not bothering to hide his amusement. "Although he's picked up a few words. I thought I heard 'hair,' and I definitely heard 'Mother,' which is how I knew who was responsible for the outrage. This boy definitely needs a father around to protect him."

Rebekah's smile died. "Well, he could use a

309

teacher," she said, skirting the issue. "I've almost forgotten how to read myself, and Papa is so busy with the farm . . ."

"I taught school a couple years," Andrew offered. "Did you know? I didn't have the patience to keep it up, although I could probably handle one small pupil if his mother would help me." His blue eyes held a question that Rebekah couldn't answer yet because she didn't want to see the pain her answer would cause.

"I'm afraid his mother wouldn't be much help to anyone, at least today," she said instead. "Hunter's worn me out. Come, let's sit down."

Following her back to the dogtrot, Andrew sank down on one of the benches and heaved Hunter off his shoulders and into his lap. The boy was giggling happily. "He seems to like me," Andrew observed.

"He's probably just happy to see somebody who's not coming after him with a pair of scissors," Rebekah replied, sitting down beside them.

"Oh, no, it's more than that," Andrew insisted.

"Well, he's probably also happy to see a man," Rebekah allowed, frowning. "He's used to having his . . ." She'd almost said, "his father" before she caught herself. ". . . to having a lot of men around, doting on him and teaching him things. That's the way the Indians raise their children. It's sort of a community project, and I think he's lonely with just me and Jewel here all day."

"He probably misses MacDougal, too," Andrew suggested. "They spent a lot of time together on the trip back here."

At the sound of the name, Hunter's little head jerked up and he looked round eagerly for signs of another rider. "Mac? Mac?"

Rebekah's stomach did a little flip at the sight of his joy, but she shook her head. "No, Hunter," she

310

said firmly. "No Mac."

The little face fell in disappointment, and Rebekah would have taken him into her arms if he hadn't turned away from her in disgust.

"He doesn't understand why MacDougal hasn't come to visit him," she explained to Andrew.

"I expect he's been busy with the store. They say it's coming along well. I can't wait to see it," he added enthusiastically. "I've always been fascinated by that kind of thing. My father usually lets me do the bargaining when we buy our yearly supplies. It's the one thing I'm really good at."

Rebekah resisted the urge to assure him he was probably good at many things. That was something a fiancée would do, and Rebekah didn't want to put herself in that role even accidentally.

"Hey, I know!" Andrew said suddenly. "Why don't we go visit MacDougal's store? I've been wanting to see it, and Hunter's been wanting to see MacDougal, and you look like you could use an outing. What do you say?"

Rebekah's stomach leaped straight up, forcing her heart into her throat. "We . . . we couldn't . . ." she stammered, wishing the idea sounded less appealing.

"Sure we could. Ask Hunter if he wants to go," Andrew suggested. "We could pack a lunch, make it a picnic."

Rebekah knew she shouldn't. She had no reason to want to see MacDougal, but she couldn't seem to stop herself, even though her mouth was dry as she formed the Comanche words. Hunter's face brightened like a sunrise, and he jumped down from Andrew's lap and began dancing and whooping with joy.

"I take it he likes the idea," Andrew remarked, "Let's ask Jewel if she'll pack us a lunch."

"I'm already doing it, Mr. Andrew," Jewel's voice called from the kitchen behind them.

So it was settled. Of course, Rebekah could have told Andrew to take Hunter and the picnic himself and leave her here. It was the most logical thing to do since to go indicated she wanted to spend time with Andrew. So she should have refused, but she didn't. She didn't even consider it, and she refused to wonder why.

They rode in her father's buckboard with the picnic lunch stowed in the back and Hunter sitting on the seat between them. He was so excited, he could barely sit still for the long ride, and he kept plying Rebekah with questions about everything they saw and everything they passed.

Andrew helped, telling him the English words for things and showing far more patience than he'd claimed for himself in helping the boy pronounce them. The closer they got to the site of the store, the more Rebekah began to fidget, too. She was not, she told herself repeatedly, nervous about seeing Mac-Dougal. He was nothing to her now. She didn't have to be afraid of his having any power over her or any claim on her. She was perfectly free, and she had Hunter and Andrew to serve as buffers. Things might be awkward between them because of the way they had parted at their last meeting, but she had no reason to be the least bit apprehensive.

Unfortunately, she couldn't quite convince her stomach of that or the butterflies that were going berserk inside it, but at least she thought she was managing to conceal her agitation.

They could see the store, or at least the beginnings of it, long before they were even within shouting distance, and Rebekah was surprised at how far along the structure was. She was also surprised to see about half-a-dozen men working on it.

"Where did he get all those workers?" she asked.

"I suppose they're farmers," Andrew said. "They

were only too happy to leave their fields when they heard Mr. MacDougal was paying cash money for laborers. As you probably know, cash money is still pretty scarce in Texas."

"I guess he really is in a hurry to get this thing built," Rebekah mused. She wasn't sure how she felt at seeing this solid evidence of MacDougal's intention to stay in her very backyard for the rest of his life, but she knew it did not make her as unhappy as she had expected.

Hunter was literally jumping up and down on the seat by the time they pulled up near the store, and she had to hold onto him until Andrew had stopped the wagon to make sure he didn't jump down and injure himself. The instant she let him go, he scrambled across her lap and down the side of the wagon, yelling, "Mac, Mac!" at the top of his lungs.

She'd seen him, too, of course. She'd recognized him long before she was able to see his face or even make out his red hair or his sombrero. His figure was as familiar to her as the image of her own face, perhaps even more familiar, and she'd had no trouble at all picking him out from among the other workers.

He must have recognized them, too, because he'd stopped work and come down from his ladder and was waiting for them. He caught Hunter up in a bear hug when the boy launched himself at him, and the two of them were chattering away in a mixture of English and Comanche by the time Andrew had helped her down from the wagon.

Her heart was pounding and her knees were trembling as she took Andrew's arm and walked toward him. He looked different somehow. Perhaps it was because he'd shaved off his beard and cut his hair again, but she didn't think that was all. He was dirty and sweaty and covered with sawdust from the logs with which he had been working, but that wasn't it either.

"Good morning, Mr. MacDougal," Andrew called cheerfully. "I hope you don't mind a few visitors."

"I'm always glad to see Hunter," MacDougal replied, looking up at her and Andrew for the first time. When he did, she saw what was different about him. She saw it in his eyes. They were as cold as ice and just as bleak, and even though he was looking right at her, she had the feeling he didn't see her at all. She shivered and pulled her shawl more closely about her, even though the day was only pleasantly cool.

Andrew chuckled at MacDougal's implied insult. "Maybe you'll be happy to see us, too, when we tell you we've brought a picnic that Jewel made up special for you."

By now Andrew was close enough to offer MacDougal his hand, and he did so, forcing Rebekah to drop his arm. MacDougal was still holding Hunter, and he made a little show of shifting the boy to his left arm, then wiping the worst of the dirt off his palm onto his pant leg before taking Andrew's hand. He couldn't have made his reluctance any clearer, but Andrew appeared not to notice, or at least he didn't let it bother him.

"This was Jewel's idea, then?" MacDougal guessed, not looking at Rebekah.

"Oh, no, Rebekah was the one who suggested it," Andrew lied gallantly. "Said Hunter hadn't seen you in a while, and since you were so busy, why didn't we come out."

"Hunter's been wondering where you were," Rebekah added hastily, glad to hear her voice sounded fairly normal even though every nerve in her body quivered with the apprehension she hadn't wanted to feel. "He . . . he missed you."

"I missed him, too," MacDougal said, still not looking at her. "Would you like to look around?" he asked the boy in Comanche.

Hunter nodded vigorously and squirmed to be set back on his feet. MacDougal set the boy down, took his hand, and started off, glancing over his shoulder only at the last minute to add, "You can join us if you like," rather coldly.

Andrew offered her his arm again and leaned down to whisper, "He doesn't seem too happy to see me."

Suddenly Rebekah remembered the lie she had told and almost gasped in dismay. How could she have forgotten she'd told MacDougal she was going to marry Andrew? No wonder he was being so rude. He probably figured she'd brought her new lover along out of spite. How could she have been so stupid?

"He probably heard what a good bargainer you are," she suggested to reassure him.

MacDougal had taken Hunter inside the skeleton of the main building and was showing him where everything would be. Each time he finished an explanation, he'd give Andrew a brief translation, but he never acknowledged Rebekah's presence at all. As they moved around the half-built edifice, the other workers called out greetings to Andrew, who replied, stopping now and then to exchange small talk and to introduce Rebekah. Each time he would say, "You know my cousin, Rebakah Tate, don't you?" and of course they all said yes, sure they did. Rebekah vaguely recalled seeing the men at church, and she nodded politely, ignoring their curious stares and trying not to notice how pointedly MacDougal was ignoring her. And pretending she didn't care.

While Andrew chatted with the men, Rebekah at his side, MacDougal took Hunter back outside and was showing him the outbuildings and explaining how they would get the roofs on them when the time came. The boy was listening intently and asking a million questions.

By the time Rebekah and Andrew caught up with them, MacDougal seemed to have forgotten their presence. He was hunkered down to eye level with Hunter, and they were having a very serious discussion about something. Rebekah could see MacDougal's expression had softened and for that moment he looked like the man she remembered.

But the instant he heard their approach, the softness vanished, and he straightened at once and turned to meet them. "Look, there's no reason for you two to stay. Why don't you just leave Hunter here with me for a day or two, longer if you want. Come back for him when you figure he's worn out his welcome."

It was a dismissal, plain and simple. He didn't want her there, didn't want to see her or talk to her, and what else could she expect? And why on God's earth should she care?

She opened her mouth to say something spiteful right back, but Andrew beat her to it. "I guess it's up to Rebekah whether she wants to leave Hunter here, but we've got nothing more important to do, and like I said, we've brought our dinner with us. I don't reckon Hunter's ever been on a picnic, and I haven't been on one in so long, I almost forget how it's done. I know you want to get back to your work, Mr. MacDougal, but you've got to eat whether we're here or not, why not eat with us? It would mean a lot to Hunter, and besides," he added with his charming grin, "I've been wanting to find out more about your little enterprise here, and this might be my only chance."

Rebekah instantly understood that Andrew's interest in business was far greater than he had led her to believe. Certainly it was more than just casual if he was willing to overlook MacDougal's rudeness to pursue it.

And if it was so important to Andrew, the least Rebekah could do was help him, even if it meant spending more time with MacDougal. "Yes, please join us, MacDougal," she said, hoping her smile didn't look as strained as it felt.

MacDougal thought about it for a long time, so long Rebekah thought she was going to scream, but finally he said, "Just let me go get cleaned up a little. I think under that tree by the church would be a good spot."

Without waiting for an answer, he took Hunter's hand and they walked off toward the tent where MacDougal had his living quarters.

Andrew let out his breath in a long sigh and gave Rebekah a questioning look that she ignored. "This was your idea," she reminded him and headed off toward the wagon.

Together they fetched the picnic basket and made their way to the tree MacDougal had suggested. When they got there, though, they realized they had forgotten to bring any sort of blanket on which to sit. "I'll get one from MacDougal," Andrew said and left her standing under the tree, cursing herself for having gotten them into such an awkward situation.

Sean was showing Hunter how to wash up in a basin when Andrew Nelson appeared in the open doorway of the tent. Sean straightened and glared at the young man, resisting with difficulty the urge to beat Nelson's brilliant smile off his handsome face.

"We'll need a blanket to sit on," Andrew said. "We forgot to bring one."

Sean dried his hands and bent down to pull one of the blankets off his coat. Folding it quickly, he handed it to Hunter and told him in Comanche to take it to his mother. The boy took off at a run. Sean waited until the boy was gone. Then he said, "I don't know what in the hell you're trying to do, Nelson,

317

but you can stop now. I'm not going to play games with you."

Andrew Nelson blinked, and his smile vanished. "What do you mean, 'play games'?"

"I mean that Rebekah told me about the two of you. She can marry whoever she wants, but I'll be damned if I'll sit back and—"

"What do you mean, she told you about the two of us?" Nelson demanded eagerly. "Did she tell you she's going to marry me?"

"Of course she did," Sean said, too angry at first to notice just how happy this news had made Nelson. But when he did, he began to suspect a problem. "You mean she hasn't told *you* she's going to marry you?"

"Not exactly," Nelson admitted, a little embarrassed but too pleased to let it bother him. "I mean, I asked her and all, the same day you got back with the boy as a matter of fact. She seemed awfully surprised, although she should have known how I felt about her, so I couldn't insist she give me an answer right then, could I?"

"And she still hasn't given you one?"

"I didn't want to press her," he explained. "At first I thought the two of you . . . But she told me I was wrong about that, so I don't see any other obstacles. She's worried about the boy, of course, but he's taken to me. I thought she just needed a little more time, but if she's already told you, I guess I don't have anything to worry about." He grinned expectantly, obviously waiting for Sean to agree.

But Sean didn't agree at all. Why would a woman tell her former lover she was going to marry a man when she hadn't even told the man himself? Quickly, Sean thought back to that scene in Rebekah's bedroom when she'd sent him away—the same day Nelson had proposed to her—and tried to remember just what she had said. Except she hadn't said it at all. Sean himself had made the suggestion, and Rebekah had merely confirmed his suspicions, confirmed them a little too adamantly, too, if he'd only noticed it at the time.

Looking back, he began to wonder if he hadn't just handed her the perfect excuse when she'd been looking for any at all to send him away. "I don't want you," she'd said, the words he'd thought had sounded the death knell to their relationship.

But if she didn't want him, didn't want anything to do with him, why was she here? And why had she insisted on staying when he'd given her the perfect opportunity just now to leave?

"Who's idea did you say it was to bring Hunter here today?" he asked Nelson.

"Well, I guess it was mine," he replied, a little surprised by the suddenness of the question. "I've been wanting to see the store and—"

"And you talked Rebekah into it?" Sean insisted.

"Not exactly," Nelson said, obviously puzzled. "At least, she wasn't hard to convince. I guess she knew Hunter would want to see you."

But Rebekah wouldn't have wanted to see him, not after what had happened the last time they were together. So why was she here? Unless, of course, she had really wanted to see Sean in spite of everything.

Now that sounded like his Rebekah Tate. She'd wanted to see him, but she'd come on the arm of the man she supposedly was going to marry. None of it made any sense, which was why Sean was sure it was true since nothing Rebekah Tate did made good sense to Sean. And she hadn't really agreed to marry Nelson at all. So maybe, just maybe, things weren't really over between him and Rebekah. He smiled at the thought, puzzling Nelson even more.

"Look, if you really don't want to be bothered, we

can leave," Nelson offered, but Sean was already shaking his head.

"I guess I've given you that impression, but actually I'm glad for the chance to show the place off a bit," Sean assured him with a smile, once again surprising his visitor with his change of mood. "Just give me another minute to get cleaned up, will you?"

While Nelson waited, bemused, Sean quickly changed his shirt, then combed his hair, slicking it back from his forehead before putting his hat on. Satisfied that he looked presentable but not too much like he was trying to make a good impression, he slapped Nelson on the back and said, "Let's go join the lady, shall we?"

Rebekah sat on the blanket she and Hunter had spread beneath the tree and watched them come, fighting an impulse to jump up and run away. She didn't think she could stand any more of MacDougal's disdain, and if he said anything about her and Andrew getting married, she would simply die right on the spot. How could she have managed to get herself into a fix like this?

But when the two men got a little closer, she could see they were talking pleasantly, and when Hunter ran out to meet them, they both laughed as MacDougal caught him up and set him on his shoulders. Something had happened in MacDougal's tent to put them on good terms, but what could it have been? Rebekah didn't think she even wanted to know.

"This looks delicious," MacDougal declared when he saw the food Rebekah had set out. He was even being pleasant, which was all the more disturbing. "That Jewel sure knows the way to a man's heart."

"His soul, too," Andrew agreed as they both sank down on the blanket.

MacDougal sat Indian style and plucked Hunter

320

from his shoulder to sit beside him, between him and Rebekah. Andrew stretched out on her other side, propping himself up on one elbow.

"Help yourself," she murmured tensely, waiting for whatever new unpleasantness was coming. Life had taught her it was best to be prepared.

The men needed no further encouragement, and she helped Hunter get a sandwich and showed him how to eat it. She took nothing for herself, knowing she couldn't have swallowed one bite.

The silence stretched, Rebekah feeling it more because she wasn't eating and had nothing to do but wait. The men didn't seem to notice, though, and at last Andrew said to MacDougal, "I hope you said something nice to Hunter about his new haircut."

Hunter's head popped up at the sound of his name, and of course he'd recognized the word "hair." He shot Rebekah a black look before turning expectantly to MacDougal.

"I told him that's the way white men wear their hair, and he's a white man now." MacDougal tousled the hair in question affectionately. "He didn't like it much, but he felt a little better when he saw my hair was short now, too." Then MacDougal gave Hunter a short translation that made the boy a little happier. At least he didn't glare at his mother again and went back to eating his sandwich.

After another short silence during which Rebekah began to wonder how much longer she could stand this, MacDougal said, "You haven't said what you think of my store, Rebekah Tate."

Rebekah's throat felt tight, but she managed to force the words out. "It's big," she allowed.

"Is that all?" he inquired pleasantly. Too pleasantly. She didn't trust him when he was being polite.

"No, that's not all," she blurted, unable to restrain herself any longer. "I can't figure out how you expect to make money here. Nobody in Texas has any money, not cash money anyway, and you can't get rich just taking things in trade.''

MacDougal was as surprised as she at the outburst, which was why Andrew was able to answer for him. "Things'll get better, now that we're a state," he explained. "And in the meantime, Mr. MacDougal will probably be happy to take crops in trade for his goods, which he'll freight to the coast and sell for far more than he gave in trade, so that's where the money will come from. Is that about right?" he asked MacDougal.

"Exactly right," MacDougal said, obviously impressed. "Where'd you learn so much about it?"

Andrew shrugged. "I read a lot, and I've always been fascinated by . . . Well, by business, I guess you'd say. One thing I've never been able to figure out though is how you know how much to charge for something so you're sure to make a profit."

The two men launched in to a discussion about profit and loss and a lot of other things Rebekah knew nothing about. She didn't complain though. At least MacDougal didn't seem to be angry anymore, and if he was talking to Andrew, he wasn't paying attention to her, which was just fine.

It wasn't fine with Hunter, though, who had now finished eating and was getting bored. Still discussing the mysteries of trade, MacDougal and Andrew took him off to climb among the logs piled nearby, ready to be incorporated into MacDougal's store. Somehow the two men managed to entertain the boy and talk at the same time, and neither of them seemed to notice they had left Rebekah all alone.

And she didn't mind a bit, she told herself as she cleaned up the remains of the picnic and packed it back into the basket. When she had finished, she leaned against the tree and closed her eyes, or at least pretended to. In truth, she kept them open a slit so she could watch MacDougal.

He was, she admitted, a very attractive man. No wonder she had allowed him to . . . But she wouldn't think about that, wouldn't remember it now or ever because remembering was much too dangerous. No, she would just enjoy looking at him and admire the way he moved and the way the sun glinted off his bright red hair when he took his hat off to wipe his forehead and the way he so obviously doted on her son and the way he had so completely captured Andrew's interest.

Andrew was handsome, too, of course, and tall, but next to MacDougal, he seemed as insignificant as a boy. In some ways even more insignificant than Hunter who refused to allow the men to forget his presence and insisted upon jumping from the highest log into MacDougal's arms time and again until even MacDougal grew weary, deciding to distract him by taking him over to the lowest part of the store wall and showing him how to walk along it, balancing himself while MacDougal and Andrew walked on either side to catch him if he fell.

Hunter would hate to leave, she knew. He'd cry and scream and beg to stay with MacDougal, but she couldn't allow that, shouldn't even have brought him in the first place. There was no point in encouraging him to love MacDougal when he would never be a part of their life.

On the other hand, Hunter needed to be around men. Her father loved his grandson, but he was busy with the farm and had little strength left at the end of the day for the antics of a young boy. Andrew could have helped, of course, but she couldn't expect him to be a father to her son if she wasn't willing to marry him. Since she wasn't—and she'd certainly have to tell him so very soon—that meant Andrew wouldn't be around much, either. And who else would bother with a half-breed bastard?

MacDougal was the only one, but he wouldn't take Hunter without Rebekah, of that she was certain. She would be the price of his attention to the boy, and it was a price she couldn't pay. Despair settled over her, dark and suffocating, and for a moment she knew the panic of helplessness.

But she threw it off, desperate now and knowing she had to do something for her son, something short of giving up herself. Off in the distance, she saw Hunter was now prowling the interior of the store while MacDougal showed Andrew with broad gestures how he intended to lay it out inside. And Andrew was nodding, more excited than she'd ever seen him, responding with gestures equally broad as he offered alternative suggestions.

For an instant she forget her own problems, and her heart ached for her cousin. Poor Andrew, who had yet to find his place in the world, and soon she'd have to dash whatever hopes he might have for happiness with her. The only other thing she'd ever seen him express an interest in was MacDougal's store and . . .

The idea hit her like a physical blow, and she sat straight up in the shade of the old tree. It was the perfect solution, perfect for Andrew and even for her, because if Andrew could make a place for himself here with MacDougal, and if he could finally succeed at something, he wouldn't be quite so crushed at losing her. And if Rebekah had a hand in that success, her own conscience wouldn't bother her quite so much.

When she thought some more, she realized this might even be a solution for Hunter, too. If Andrew worked for MacDougal, she'd have a reason for bringing Hunter to visit and a buffer in her cousin who, she knew, would always protect her.

She would definitely have to be the one to suggest it, though. Andrew might not even think of it, and even if he did, he would never put himself forward since he seemed convinced he was of no value to anyone, except possibly to her. That meant she would have to speak to MacDougal. The prospect made her tremble, but she reminded herself she wasn't afraid of him. What could he do but refuse her, after all? He couldn't hurt her, not unless she let him, and she had no intention of letting him.

So she waited, knowing what she had to do and steeling herself for it as the sun rose high and started its descent. They should be going soon. They'd kept MacDougal from his work long enough, and Hunter was getting tired and cranky.

Finally she called out and told Andrew it was getting late. He waved in reply, and the two men collected Hunter and started back to where she waited.

Their voices carried to her. They were discussing the war as men always seemed to be doing lately.

"It's a hell of a thing to do to somebody like General Taylor," Andrew was saying in disgust.

"That it is, but the politicians weren't about to let a Whig general get the credit for winning the war, especially when they know he wants to run for the Presidency next time. The way I heard it, they disallowed his truce and the fighting was supposed to start again on November 13, which means they must be fighting again by now."

"And what an insult to send General Scott down to take over command, as if Taylor had botched the whole thing instead of whipping their as—" Andrew looked up and realized how close he was to Rebekah and swallowed whatever he'd been about to say.

MacDougal was carrying Hunter, slinging him

around as he walked, turning him upside down until he squealed, then righting him again so he could climb up his shoulder, then plucking him off to upset him again. When they reached the blanket, Hunter was hanging upside down, shouting his protest, with MacDougal holding him by one leg.

"Why don't you just leave him here with me for a day or two, like I said," MacDougal said to her. It was the first time he'd looked directly at her today without animosity, and her heart fluttered in response. "I wouldn't mind."

"No, I . . ." She had to swallow before she could go on. "You're busy here, and there are too many ways for him to get into trouble. You couldn't watch him every minute."

He frowned, but he didn't argue. "He isn't going to be happy about leaving."

"Maybe . . . Maybe we could come back again," she suggested.

MacDougal's wolf's eyes studied her for a moment, and she had the uneasy feeling he saw more than she wanted him to see. "If you want to," he said at last, giving no hint of his true feelings on the matter.

She picked up the basket and handed it to Andrew. "Would you take this to the wagon so I can speak to MacDougal alone for a minute?" she asked.

Andrew's eyebrows shot up in surprise, and for a moment she was afraid he might be stricken with a sudden attack of jealousy and refuse. But she should have known he could deny her nothing. He took the basket, however reluctantly, and started for the wagon, although he did keep glancing back over his shoulder, a worried frown on his handsome face.

But Rebekah couldn't worry about his sensibilities just now. She turned then to MacDougal, whose eyes had narrowed suspiciously, and for an instant she almost changed her mind. He looked so huge and compelling, and something inside her wanted to be compelled, wanted to draw close to him and feel his arms around her again and rest her head on his shoulder and taste his mouth on hers. The urge took her breath, and she was afraid she wouldn't even be able to speak.

Then MacDougal bent down and picked up the blanket, shaking it out a little and wadding it up into a ball. "Take this to my tent," he told Hunter in Comanche. The boy grabbed the blanket and took off at a run, leaving them completely alone. MacDougal looked at her expectantly, all other emotion wiped carefully from his expression.

For a second, Rebekah felt panic welling up, which was ridiculous, she told herself. It wasn't as if they were really alone. Andrew and a half-dozen men were within sight and sound, even if MacDougal was going to do anything to her, which he most certainly wasn't.

She took a deep breath and tried to smile. "Would you . . . ?" she tried, then decided against asking. "You should give Andrew a job in your store."

She'd surprised him. His sun-bleached eyebrows rose, and his brown eyes widened. "Why?" he asked sharply. "So he can afford to marry you?"

Rebekah wanted to swear at her own stupidity. Now she'd have to tell him the truth. She could feel the heat crawling up her face, but she squared her shoulders defiantly. "No, because he needs a job, and you need some help. He's smart, and he knows all about your business."

"And I suppose you'll want me to build a house for him to live in where he can bring his bride, and maybe you'll want me to build it close enough to mine so that on warm nights when the windows are open, I'll be able to hear the two of you moaning in your bed. Do you make all those wonderful noises when you're with him, Rebekah Tate?"

"Stop it!" she cried, then realized others might be listening and lowered her voice again. "Shut your filthy mouth and listen to me! Andrew and I . . . We aren't . . . We aren't getting married," she forced herself to say, acutely aware that her face must be scarlet. Humiliation burned over her like a fever.

He was surprised again or at least pretended to be. "A lover's quarrel?" he asked. "You seemed to be on good terms today, though. Maybe there's still hope."

She thought she heard sarcasm in the words, but she was too furious to decide. "There isn't any hope and there never was. I lied about me and Andrew because I thought it would make you leave me alone."

He stiffened at that, and his face hardened to stone, but for some reason he didn't seem surprised. "Are you that desperate to get rid of me?"

Yes, she wanted to shout, but the admission would also be an admission of weakness, a weakness she knew MacDougal would exploit. "It was a silly lie," she said instead, managing to keep her voice steady. "I never should've involved Andrew in this, but don't take it out on him. Please, MacDougal," she added, the word almost choking her.

This time his amazement was genuine. "Please? I never thought I'd hear that from you, Rebekah Tate."

"I never thought I'd say it to you," she replied, "but this is important. *Andrew* is important, and I can't let him suffer for my stupid pride. You'll need help here, MacDougal. You know you will, and Andrew can help you. Don't punish him because you hate me!"

He smiled then, an unpleasant grimace that made her shiver. "I don't hate you, Rebekah Tate," he said in a ragged voice. "I only wish I did."

She wanted to ask him what he meant, but she didn't dare. Fortunately Hunter returned at that moment, running at top speed and not even bothering to slow down so that he crashed into MacDougal's legs with enough force to stagger him. He caught the boy up in his arms and remonstrated with him in Comanche.

Hunter apologized humbly, then squirmed to be set down again, and grabbed MacDougal's hand, pulling frantically in an effort to get him to go off and play some more.

MacDougal stood like a statue, immovable, his gaze holding Rebekah's, compelling her to say something, anything. She had an overwhelming urge to fling herself into his arms the way Hunter had and to surrender to the strength she knew she would find there. It would be so easy, and sometimes she felt so weak and helpless that she thought it might almost be worth what she would have to give up.

But then she remembered what it was like to be truly helpless and in someone else's power, and she knew she could never endure it again. So instead of giving MacDougal what he was silently willing her to give, she said in Comanche, "Hunter, we have to go now."

The boy froze, shocked for a second, then looked to MacDougal for confirmation. MacDougal's gaze never left Rebekah's face, but he nodded, and instantly Hunter began to howl.

"I told you he wouldn't like it," MacDougal said, turning away from her at last and picking the boy up under one arm. He started for the wagon where Andrew waited.

Hunter kicked and struggled and bawled but to no avail. Rebekah ordered him to stop carrying on, but he was yelling too loud to hear her. At last

MacDougal stopped, lifted one knee, and deftly draped the squirming boy over it. He administered just one swat before the howling ceased as abruptly as it had begun.

The instant she'd realized what he intended to do, Rebekah had opened her mouth to protest, but the protest died in the face of such success. MacDougal stood the boy on his feet, and he instantly ran to Andrew for protection. If Rebekah hadn't been so upset, she might have smiled.

"MacDougal?" she said, taking this one last opportunity before they got close enough for Andrew to overhear them.

He stopped, but he didn't look at her, as if looking at her would be too painful or perhaps just unpleasant. "Yes?"

"Will you give Andrew a chance?" The word stuck in her throat, but she forced it out. "Please?"

She thought he flinched a little, but she couldn't be sure, then he walked on as if she hadn't spoken. Once again she felt her face burning with humiliation. Well, now they were even, she supposed, remembering how she'd sent him away the other night. She followed in his wake.

He was shaking Andrew's hand and smiling. *Smiling*, damn him, as if nothing at all had happened. Andrew was smiling back, although his gaze kept darting to her and the expression in his eyes was uncertain. Plainly he wanted to know what they had been talking about, but she knew he wouldn't ask. He was much too polite. Hunter was pouting but not too seriously because he wanted MacDougal to make up with him before he left.

"We'll have a party when the store opens," MacDougal was telling Andrew. "Be sure to come."

"Nothing could keep me away," Andrew replied. "We'll be there, won't we, Rebekah?"

When MacDougal turned to her this time, his expression was cool, his eyes blank, and no one would ever guess what emotions he might be concealing.

"I'm sure Hunter will want to come," she said dully, wishing she were gone, wishing she had never come, wishing MacDougal would take her in his arms and hold her, and wishing she had never been born. How had everything become so confused?

MacDougal spoke to Hunter in Comanche, warning him to be a good boy and inviting him back to visit and telling him to get Andrew to bring him anytime. Hunter was delighted, although he pretended not to be, and only grudgingly allowed MacDougal to hug him before Andrew boosted him up onto the wagon seat.

"Be sure to thank Jewel for the picnic," MacDougal said to no one in particular, and Rebekah hated herself for wishing he would hug her, too. What was wrong with her? She must, she decided, be losing her mind.

Andrew helped her up into the wagon, and in a few minutes they were on their way. The workmen stopped long enough to yell their good-byes, and Andrew and Rebekah waved back. MacDougal just stood silently and watched them out of sight with his wolf's eyes.

They hadn't gone far when Hunter started to nod off, and Rebekah put him in the back of the wagon where he could stretch out. When he was settled and they were on their way again, Andrew said, "MacDougal told me you're going to accept my proposal."

Rebekah stared at him in horror. "He . . . How could he know such a thing?"

Andrew smiled, a little sadly, she thought. "I was wondering the same thing. He said you'd told him, and at first I was happy, but then I started trying to

331

figure out why you'd tell him and not me."

"I . . ." How could she explain any of this to Andrew, dear, sweet Andrew who'd never done anything to deserve it? "I can't imagine why he'd tell you a thing like that," she hedged.

"I can't either," he replied, "especially when it's not true, is it?"

"Oh, Andrew," she tried, laying a hand on his arm, but he was shaking his head.

"I should have known. And there's no reason why you should marry me at all. I told you myself what a failure I am and—"

"It's not that!" she cried, desperate to make him understand. "And you're not a failure. You're a wonderful person, and you'll make a wonderful husband. It's me, Andrew. I'd only make you unhappy, and I care too much about you to let that happen."

Plainly he didn't believe her. "You'll excuse me if I disagree."

"No, I won't! Listen to me, I understand how you feel, I really do. We loved each other when we were children, and we still care for each other. And you feel guilty because I was taken by the Indians and you survived and nothing bad happened to you. You want to make it up to me, and you want to take care of me now because you couldn't take care of me then, but that's not a good enough reason to marry someone, Andrew. Especially when that someone is . . ." Her voice trailed off because she didn't know how to finish that sentence.

But Andrew did. "Especially when that someone is in love with another man?" he suggested.

"Don't be silly!" she exclaimed, although she could feel the heat rising in her face.

"I don't think it's silly," he said, as solemn as she had ever seen him. "I watched the two of you together

332

today, and it made me remember why I thought there was something between you before. When you told me I was wrong, I wanted to believe you, but there is, isn't there?"

"I'm not . . . in love with him," she managed to say, although her throat was tight and her mouth had gone dry and her heart was thumping laboriously in her chest. She couldn't be in love with MacDougal, she just couldn't.

"Well, he's in love with you," Andrew said, clearly unhappy with the idea. "Or at least he acted just the way I would have if you'd shown up on my doorstep with another man. At first I thought he was just rude. I'm a little slow, but I finally figured out he was jealous, at least until he found out you hadn't told me you'd marry me."

Andrew was wrong, of course, but she didn't think she could convince him of that. All she could do was ease the blow. "It doesn't matter how he feels about me because I'm not going to marry him, either. I'm never going to marry anyone, Andrew. There's a lot of reasons, and you wouldn't understand most of them, so I won't even try to explain. But you don't have to be jealous of MacDougal because he's not the reason I can't marry you."

"No, because *I'm* the reason you can't marry me," he said dully.

"Yes, because you're a fine man and you deserve to be happy!" she cried, clutching his arm with both hands now. "You don't really love me, Andrew, not the way a man should love the woman he marries! You're kind and noble, and you want to do the right thing. You said it yourself: you want to protect me. But I don't want to be protected. I don't want anything from anyone except to be left alone. And you should have a woman who will love you and not just need you. Can you understand the difference?"

Andrew smiled grimly. "Sometimes the difference isn't really important, especially when the only other choice is being alone when it's the middle of the night and you reach across the bed and nobody's there."

"But that's just it, Andrew," she told him grimly. *"I never want anyone to reach for me again."*

He went rigid beside her, and she knew she'd shocked him, but she wasn't sorry. He had to understand. She thought he did until he said, "Never is a very long time, Rebekah."

She thought about that later when she really was in her bed, alone in the dark. Hunter was sleeping nearby on the trundle bed her father had made for him, and the sound of his regular breathing comforted her. She wouldn't really be alone just because she didn't have a man. She would always have Hunter. The farm would always be his home. When he married, he would continue to live here, and she'd watch his children grow up, too.

But would that be enough?

Several weeks passed before she saw Andrew again. He'd been hurt and angry when they parted, and she'd been dreading their next meeting. But when he rode up to the house one evening in mid-December just as they were sitting down to supper, he seemed to have forgotten all about her rejection.

He was grinning from ear to ear when he jumped down from his horse, and he actually picked Rebekah up in a bear hug and swung her around exuberantly. "I've come to invite you to a party," he told her when he'd set her on her feet again. "MacDougal's store is finished, and he's going to have the biggest party this country's ever seen!"

"And hello to you, too, stranger," she scolded him,

only half in jest. As relieved as she was to find he'd apparently forgiven her, she found herself more than a little annoyed to see him so excited about MacDougal's business, especially when she hadn't heard a thing about it.

"Oh, excuse me," he laughed, not the least bit chastened. "Hello, Cousin Rebekah, and how have you been keeping yourself?" he asked with mock solemnity.

"Not as well as you, apparently. What on earth have you been up to that's put you in such good spirits?"

"I'm working now. I thought you must know since it was your suggestion, or at least that's what Sean claims. He hired me to clerk in his store. We've been setting it up, and Rebekah, I don't know how to thank you."

He babbled on excitedly, telling her all about it as he followed her into the kitchen to join the others, but Rebekah couldn't hear him for the roaring in her ears. *MacDougal had done what she'd asked!* She could hardly believe it, and she knew she should be happy, or at least gratified. Instead she felt, well, jealous. *Sean*. Andrew had called MacDougal *Sean*, and she felt absurdly, irrationally jealous!

"We aren't officially open, of course," Andrew was saying when she forced herself to hear him again, "but we've already had a lot of customers. Sean lets me handle them, and he only jumps in if he thinks I'm giving them too good a deal. He says I'm pretty good. It's my honest face, he says. It makes people think they can put one over on me."

She smiled perfunctorily, wishing she could feel as happy as she should that Andrew had recovered from his broken heart and finally found a place where he could use his talents and feel like a success. Instead all she could think was that Andrew got to see *Sean* every day, while she only caught a glimpse of him on Sundays in church. But this was crazy! Anyone would think she *wanted* to see MacDougal when she most certainly didn't. In fact, the less she saw of him, the better. Right?

"Saturday is the big day," Andrew told them as he joined the Tates for supper. "Sean's going to have music and dancing and all the whiskey you can drink. Well, all the whiskey the men can drink," he corrected with a laugh. "And lemonade for the ladies and the children."

"Sounds like fun," Jewel remarked, although she was looking at Rebekah, reminding her *she* should have said it.

"Yes, it does," Zeb agreed. "We'll be there for sure. I think I'll ask the ladies from the church to supply some cakes for refreshments."

"Good idea," Andrew said.

Rebekah listened woodenly while they made their plans. All she could think about was seeing Sean MacDougal again.

Chapter Twelve

They could hear the music from a mile away, drifting across the air like a siren's call. Hunter heard it first and started jumping up and down on the wagon seat. Rebekah had to hold him in place, just as she'd had to hold him the last time they'd visited MacDougal. This time, however, things would be different.

This time her father was driving the wagon, and their slaves were sitting in the back, anxiously awaiting their own party which would be held separately from their masters' but at which they would see others of their kind and enjoy a few hours of relative freedom. Rebekah could certainly understand the attraction.

Even Zeb was tapping his foot in anticipation. Rebekah felt only apprehension, and not just at the prospect of seeing MacDougal again. There would be strangers here, not just the people from her father's church, distant cousins, and friends of the family. Everyone was coming to see the man who had rescued Rebekah Tate, and of course they'd want to see Rebekah Tate, too. And her half-breed son. Her father seemed to think this was a good thing. Rebekah was sure it wasn't.

Although they arrived before noon, they were not the first, not by a long shot. Dozens of people were milling around the newly completed store and outbuildings, and the Tates' arrival attracted little attention except from Andrew who detached himself from the crowd and came loping over to help Rebekah out of the wagon.

"You're late," he told them. "The party's been going on for hours already. People were here practically at dawn."

His face was flushed and his eyes shone with excitement and pleasure, making him even handsomer than usual. Or perhaps it was the new air of confidence with which he held himself that made the difference. Just as she'd suspected, Andrew had found himself here among the dry goods and dickering. Unfortunately his success had cost her a partner in misery. Somehow she knew he would never be quite so sympathetic to her problems as he'd been before, and her heart felt like a leaden weight in her chest.

"Promise you'll save me the first dance," Andrew said when he'd lifted her from the wagon seat.

"I don't remember how to dance," she said, trying to match his smile with one of her own.

"Don't worry, I'll teach you. It'll come back to you in no time," he said, then turned to her father and shook Zeb's hand.

"Looks like half the people in the state are here," Zeb said. "Come on, let's get a look at them all." He ushered his slaves forward and left Andrew to escort Rebekah and a suddenly shy Hunter.

Hunter was clinging to her skirts, peering suspiciously out at the unfamiliar crowd from beneath a fringe of raven hair. When Rebekah looked down at him, her heavy heart contracted at his apprehension. Of course he was afraid, and he didn't even know why

338

he should be.

"People have been asking for you," Andrew said, pulling her hand through the crook of his arm and patting it reassuringly when she flinched. "They're curious, Rebekah. You have to expect that."

"MacDougal should've sold tickets," she said bitterly. "Ten cents to see the Indian squaw."

"It's not like that," Andrew said, patting her hand again. "You'll see."

Rebekah didn't think she wanted to see, but Hunter had spotted MacDougal and taken the matter out of her hands.

"Mac! Mac!" he cried, racing toward the tall man who stood in the center of a circle of admirers.

MacDougal's gaze found the boy at once, and Rebekah saw it flick up to take her in for just a second before it returned to the boy. Confident of his welcome, Hunter charged into the circle of men, straight for MacDougal who caught him up in his arms.

The men were chuckling, and one of them said, "Who's your little greaser friend, MacDougal?"

Rebekah's breath caught in outrage.

Andrew must have heard because he said, "It's a natural mistake. He's so dark . . ."

And he was, of course. No one would take him for a white child, not with that jet black hair and coppery skin. Only his light eyes revealed his true heritage.

"This, my friends," MacDougal was saying, "is Hunter Tate, the young man I've been telling you about. And here comes his mother, the lady you've all been waiting to meet."

Rebekah's step faltered as all eyes turned to her. For a second she knew sheer terror and wanted nothing more than to run as fast and as far as she could. But, as if sensing her reaction, Andrew slipped his arm around her shoulders and held her fast for their inspection.

"Say something," Andrew hissed behind his fixed smile.

"How do you do?" she managed through clenched teeth.

The men who had been staring at her so tensely suddenly relaxed, and several of them murmured greetings.

"I've been telling them a little about our adventures," MacDougal said. She hated his smug confidence and the way he held her son as if he had the right. She wanted him to feel as vulnerable as she did.

"Did he tell you about how he saved my life when the snake bit me?" she asked perversely, hoping to make him appear a braggart.

But instead of nodding their assent, the men shook their heads in denial, and their eyes lit up in anticipation. "Wasn't it enough you saved her from the Indians?" one of the men exclaimed.

"How'd you come to be bit by a snake, Miss Tate?" asked another.

"It . . . it crawled into my bedroll one night," she said, shivering involuntarily at the memory. Andrew's arm tightened around her slightly, and she thought MacDougal's jaw clenched a bit.

But then he was smiling again. "And I couldn't let her die of snakebite after I'd gone to all the trouble of kidnapping her, now could I?" he said, drawing their attention back to himself.

"What'd you do, suck out the venom?" one man asked.

"No, I killed the snake and used the raw meat to draw it out," he explained. "Old trick I'd learned back when I was a freighter."

The men started asking questions, and Andrew leaned down and whispered in her ear, "Let's get some lemonade."

340

She nodded, only too glad to escape. Clustered around the refreshment table were some of the women from her father's church who greeted her and exclaimed over her dress, which was the one Jewel had made from the rest of the fabric MacDougal had provided. It was just a simple round dress, the kind virtually every other woman there wore, but the fabric was fine wool, teal blue in color, and so dear as to be considered an impossible luxury by those on the frontier. The full skirt accented her narrow waist, and the fitted bodice showed off the curves she'd acquired since she'd been eating Jewel's cooking regularly.

Rebekah knew she cut a fine figure. At least she didn't have to be ashamed of the way she looked, even if she owed her appearance to MacDougal's generosity, and she answered the women's questions about the construction of the dress with more confidence than she had faced the men.

Time crawled by, and the only thing that saved Rebekah's sanity was Andrew's attention. Although he was busy greeting each family that arrived and making important contacts with each potential customer, he never neglected Rebekah, always making sure she wasn't alone before going back to attend to his duties. The other women were kind, too, making small talk with her when they could think of something to say.

Still, more than once Rebekah found herself with nothing better to do than search out MacDougal's familiar figure in the crowd. Like a magnet, he seemed to draw her gaze, and more than once he glanced up to catch her watching him, too. Each time, she turned away, embarrassed, and each time her gaze had been drawn back again.

She just hoped he thought she was merely keeping an eye on Hunter who had stayed with MacDougal as if he, too, were drawn by some mysterious force. She was telling herself not to look at him again for about the tenth time when she heard his voice directly behind her.

"Maybe you ought to get Hunter to play with the other children," MacDougal said.

She'd jumped at the sound and tried to convince herself it was only because she was surprised. But when she turned and saw him so close, her pounding heart lurched painfully as if she'd experienced some sort of loss. Probably she just didn't like seeing her son so happy with MacDougal. Unwilling to analyze her reaction further, she steeled herself against it.

"He doesn't know any of the other children," she said, trying to smile but not quite succeeding.

"Kids don't need to be formally introduced," MacDougal said. "Just take him over and turn him loose." He nodded toward where about a dozen youngsters were playing a spirited game of tag.

"He won't be able to talk to them, either," she protested. "They'll laugh at him."

"Then he needs to learn how to deal with it," MacDougal said.

She wanted to hit him, probably because she knew he was right and she didn't want to admit it and she didn't want to see Hunter hurt even though she knew she couldn't protect him. Or maybe she wanted to hit him for another reason entirely. Instead she reached for Hunter and took him, protesting, from MacDougal's arms and set him on the ground.

"Would you like to play with the other children?" she asked in Comanche.

He frowned and looked up at MacDougal questioningly. MacDougal grinned and nodded. "Go play," he told the boy.

Hunter seemed a little disappointed, but his gray eyes lit up when he glanced over at the other children.

Rebekah knew he'd missed the rough and tumble of playmates. She took his hand and led him away, feeling oddly reluctant to leave MacDougal even though she didn't really want to be near him. She had to grit her teeth to keep herself from looking back at him, too.

Rebekah took Hunter to where the children were playing away from their elders and out of harm's way. Their young voices were like discordant music, and the closer they got to them, the more excited Hunter became. At last he dropped Rebekah's hand and started running toward where the others were racing around. He careened into another boy, almost knocking him down. Rebekah opened her mouth to call out a rebuke, but before she could form the words the other boy had given Hunter a shove in return and they'd run off together, instantly fast friends.

For a moment she stood there, anxious and worried. Hunter didn't know how to play these games; he could only speak a few words of English; he knew none of these children. But she soon realized he was doing fine, much better than she because he was oblivious to his own problems.

Knowing she couldn't leave him completely, she glanced around and saw a few other women standing underneath a tree nearby. Other mothers, she supposed, keeping an eye on their offspring.

Warily she wandered over to them, ready to move on if they didn't accept her. But one of the women knew her from church and introduced her to the others. Rebekah nodded stiffly at the introductions, not even hearing the names.

"That's your boy, isn't it? The dark one?" one of the women asked. She was short and rather stout, her homely face pockmarked and her small brown eyes far from friendly.

"Yes," Rebekah said. "His name is Hunter."

"Is that his Indian name?" the woman said.

"Bertha," one of the others scolded, but she ignored the rebuke and stared expectantly at Rebekah.

"That's his *name*," Rebekah said, furious but trying not to let it show.

Bertha's small eyes narrowed even more. "He's a wild one," she said, glancing meaningfully at Hunter who was rolling playfully on the ground with another boy.

"He's a boy," one of the mothers said. "They're all wild. Rebekah, did you get the fabric for that dress from Mr. MacDougal?"

Rebekah explained, haltingly, how MacDougal had found the fabric at someone else's store but that, yes, he did intend to stock equally nice things.

"I'm so glad Mr. MacDougal decided to settle here," the same woman exclaimed. "We've needed a store here for a long time. Until now, the closest one was a day's ride away. That meant three days just to do our shopping, and if you forgot to put something on the list, you'd just have to do without for six months."

The other women agreed, and the discussion moved to the usual complaints of women suffering the hardships of living on the frontier.

Rebekah started to relax, feeling that perhaps she might be able to endure the rest of the afternoon, when the women were distracted by screams from the children.

The children were gathered around two others who were rolling on the ground, but this time there was nothing playful about the encounter. The boys were plainly fighting and the larger one was getting the worst of it.

Rebekah needed only a glance to tell her the smaller one was Hunter. She raced toward the fracas, the other mothers on her heels.

344

Pushing her way through the throng of children, she found Hunter sitting on the other boy's chest, raining blows on his unprotected face. Blood flew everywhere, and the larger boy's howls were deafening.

Rebekah grabbed Hunter around the waist and plucked him, still swinging, off his adversary. As the other mothers descended, the children scattered to make way.

"Oscar!" one of the women shrieked, and Rebekah's heart sank when she saw Bertha kneeling beside the injured boy, cradling his bleeding head to her ample bosom.

"Oscar hit him first," a little girl with flaxen braids announced, "and called him a dirty redskin."

"He's a filthy savage!" Bertha screamed furiously, her round face mottled with rage. "Decent people aren't safe with animals like that around! You should've left him where he belongs, with the rest of his kind!"

Rebekah felt her cheeks growing scarlet with her own rage, but from the expressions on the faces of the other mothers, she would get no sympathy from them. Hunter was still flailing his arms and legs, and she gave him a warning shake to make him stop. He stopped, but his gray eyes were fierce when he glared up at her.

"Come on," one of the women was saying to Bertha. "Let's get Oscar down to the creek and wash off that blood before it stains."

With difficulty they got Oscar on his feet, and Rebekah saw he was at least half-a-head taller than Hunter and many pounds heavier. The boy was still howling his distress, and Rebekah suspected he wasn't hurt nearly as badly as he wanted his mother to think. The blood seemed to be coming only from his nose, hardly a serious injury. Rebekah watched through narrowed eyes as Bertha led Oscar, tottering on his thick legs, down to the creek. The other mothers gathered up their children and spirited them away, leaving Rebekah alone with Hunter.

She set him down on his feet and looked him over to see if any of the blood staining his shirt belonged to him.

"Are you hurt?" she asked in Comanche, glad no one could hear that her son didn't speak English and have one more reason to hate him.

"He hit me first," Hunter insisted, his small face twisted in outrage.

"I know, Little One. I know it wasn't your fault." She wanted to take him in her arms and tell him everything was going to be all right, but she knew that would be a lie. For every person who grudgingly accepted them, there would be another like Bertha or her son who would hate them on principle alone.

Rebekah waited to go to the creek until the women and children who had been there had rejoined the growing crowd over by the store. No one was near now except a few men who'd wandered away from the others and seemed to be enjoying the contents of a jug which they passed from hand to hand.

Ignoring them, she walked Hunter down to the water and, moistening her handkerchief, she wiped the blood from his hands and face and tried her best to get the worst of it from his shirt. Pleased to see he didn't seem to be injured anyplace, she didn't notice they were no longer alone until someone asked, "You're that Tate woman, ain't you?"

She looked up in surprise to find the three men who had been sharing the jug now clustered around her. Up close, she saw they weren't farmers. They looked more like drifters, ragged and unkempt, and up close she saw they were drunk. She rose slowly and moved Hunter behind her.

"What do you want?" she demanded, fighting the

panic surging through her. She'd been in this situation before, surrounded by men who despised her, and she knew what they could do, knew what they *wanted* to do, but she'd die before she'd submit to it again.

"Sure it's her," another of the men said. "Don't you see the kid? A half-breed for sure."

"Well, now, who would've thought she'd be such a looker?" the first man observed, grinning to show rotting teeth. The others chuckled drunkenly, and Rebekah backed away instinctively, even though she knew the creek was behind her and she had nowhere to go. Hunter's hand tightened around hers.

If she screamed, would anyone hear her? The music and the noise from the crowd was awfully loud. And even if they did hear, would anyone come to help *her?*

The men were still chuckling lewdly. "She can put her moccasins under my bed anytime," one of the men said.

"Hell, she prob'ly don't even need a bed," the first man said. "The Injuns just do it on the ground, don't they, girl? She's prob'ly used to it that way. That's prob'ly how she got that there youngun, ain't it? Wallowing in the dirt with some buck. Bet she'd be glad to have a white man for a change. How about it, girl? We'd all be glad to oblige you."

They laughed uproariously at this, and Rebekah saw her chance. "Go get Mac," she told Hunter in Comanche, and the boy darted away, easily alluding the clumsy grab one of the men made for him as he skittered past.

"What'd you say to him?" the first man demanded. He was no longer laughing.

Rebekah smiled, hate roiling within her. "I told him to go play with the other children so I could be alone with you boys."

She'd thrown them, she saw. They had expected her to be frightened, and they no longer looked so confident or quite so drunk either. Their red-rimmed eyes were darting wildly.

"What's the matter?" she taunted, reaching into her pocket. "I thought you boys wanted a little fun. Which one of you wants to be first?"

"She's got somethin' in there," one of the men said nervously, pointing to her pocket.

"It's a knife!" another cried, backing away.

"Damn Injun," the first man snarled, but he, too, was backing away.

"I can show you things the Comanche taught me," she said, moving forward now as they moved away. "Comanches are really good with knives. I saw a man skinned alive once . . ."

They were running now, fleeing in fear, and Rebekah stared numbly after them, her own heart pounding in terror and her knees growing weak now that the danger was past.

Someone was calling her name, and she looked up to see MacDougal jogging toward her, Hunter at his heels. She had never been so happy to see him, and when he grabbed her by the arms, she didn't even object to his touch.

"What's going on?" he demanded. "You're white as a ghost, and Hunter said some men were bothering you."

"They were, but . . . they're gone now."

Hunter threw his arms around her legs, and she was glad for the extra support. She leaned her head against MacDougal's broad shoulder, savoring his strength for a moment and drawing on it to renew her own.

"What happened? Who were the men?"

"I don't know," Rebekah said after she'd swallowed down the last of her terror. "I never saw them before.

They looked like drifters or something. They . . . they were just insulting."

She lifted her head from his shoulder and met his gaze. His wolf's eyes were glittering with anger. "Tell me who they were, Rebekah Tate."

"I told you, I don't know. I doubt they'll hang around very long, either." She managed a small smile.

MacDougal blinked in surprise. "What did you do to them?" he asked suspiciously.

"Not a thing," she said quite honestly. "For some reason they thought I was dangerous and decided to move along."

"Dangerous?" MacDougal echoed incredulously. "What made them think that?"

"I have no idea." She could feel the weight of the comb in her pocket, and her smile widened.

MacDougal shook his head and smiled back at her, his brown eyes glowing now with what might have been pride but which was probably only relief. "Well, at least I didn't have to rescue you again. You've already made me too famous, Rebekah Tate. A man can only bear so much before it gets to be a burden."

"You should've thought of that before you saved me the first time, MacDougal," she replied. Suddenly she was very happy, although she could not have said why. MacDougal's hands felt so very right on her arms, as if his touch alone had the power to lift her sadness, and his musky, masculine scent filled her senses. She hadn't been so close to him for such a long time, and every nerve in her body tingled in response until she longed to close the small space between them and feel the length of him pressed up against her and . . .

"Mother?"

Hunter's small voice broke the spell and brought

Rebekah to her senses. "Yes, Hunter, I'm all right," she assured him, then translated into Comanche so he was sure to understand. "Thank you for bringing Mac, though."

When she looked up, MacDougal was still smiling, only the expression in his eyes had changed again. This time it was speculative. "You sent the boy for me," he mused, and the hands still holding her arms gentled ever so slightly. "Why not for your father or Andrew?"

"I . . ." She hesitated, not sure she could explain why, even if she thought she should tell him, which she didn't. His wolf's eyes already saw too much, and if he knew how much she'd missed seeing him these past weeks or how jealous she was of poor Andrew just because he worked at MacDougal's store or . . .

"You're always the one who saved me in the past," she managed. "I figured I should stick with what I know works."

He looked as if he wanted to press the issue, but someone shouted something incomprehensible, then other voices took up the call. They both turned to see a body of horsemen approaching. Rebekah counted about twenty men riding in a group. They were all dressed like the rest of the men at the party, which is to say in every possible way. Some wore broadcloth suits, others wore work clothes, and still others wore parts of what might once have been military uniforms.

From their attire, they could have been any random group of men, but everyone knew they weren't. At first Rebekah thought they looked in some way familiar until she realized it wasn't their actual appearance that was familiar. No, she had never seen these men before, but she recognized them because they all rode like MacDougal, tall and straight and confident and cocky, as if they were certain even the Devil himself couldn't cause any trouble they weren't perfectly prepared to handle. This air of confidence proclaimed what they were.

"Rangers," MacDougal said, confirming her guess, although Rebekah was certain he had never set eyes on the men before either.

"What are they doing here?" she asked, unable to take her eyes from the riders.

"Let's go find out, shall we?"

He took her arm and led her toward where the crowd awaited the arrival of the newcomers. Although everyone was watching the Rangers now, Rebekah remembered she might not be very welcome to join the other women, so as they approached the others, Rebekah said, "I need to go find Papa," and slipped away before MacDougal could protest. Holding Hunter firmly by the hand, she skirted the crowd and found her father and her cousin Cecil lingering around the fringes.

Hunter wanted to be lifted up so he could see what was going on, so she gave him to her father who put him on his shoulders. She was too far away to make out the faces of the men, and their bushy beards made them look remarkably similar anyway. But as they drew near, they stopped their horses, and one man rode out ahead of the others, obviously the leader.

He lifted the brim of his hat and wiped his brow on the sleeve of his shirt. "I'm Ben McCulloch," he announced, and a gasp went through the crowd at the mention of one of the living legends of the frontier. "My men and I are on our way back to Mexico, but we decided to stop by here first. We'd like to meet the man who rescued Rebekah Tate."

Rebekah's breath caught at the mention of her name, and a buzz went through the crowd. Sean had been working his way through that crowd, and now it parted for him like the Red Sea opening for Moses.

351

He stepped forward and held out his hand.

"Pleased to meet you, Captain McCulloch. Sean MacDougal, at your service."

McCulloch dismounted in one fluid motion and took MacDougal's hand.

"Can you imagine?" Cousin Cecil whispered in awe as the two men shook hands, and only then did Rebekah realize the magnitude of this honor. These Rangers, the men who were considered the bravest among all the exceptionally brave men who had settled Texas, had come to pay tribute to Sean MacDougal.

To *her* Sean MacDougal. Her heart swelled in her chest, and she wondered why she should feel so proud. He wasn't really hers, after all. And heaven knew, she'd helped in her own rescue. MacDougal wasn't completely responsible. But when she remembered how he'd saved her from the snake and how he'd held her when she was frightened and how he'd buried those poor people after the Indian raid and how he'd hidden her when the Indians had practically run right over them . . .

She didn't know she was crying until a tear slid down her face, and she reached up quickly to catch it before anyone else saw. How ridiculous! She didn't have a thing to be crying about, even if she were in the habit of crying at all, which she certainly wasn't. Still, she had to blink to keep any more tears from falling, and something had tightened around her heart and was squeezing it painfully.

Captain McCulloch had told the rest of his men to dismount, and one by one they were stepping forward to shake Sean's hand. This was what he'd wanted, this was even more than he'd wanted, and she thought he must now be finally happy. Except he didn't look particularly happy. In fact, he looked almost grim, but perhaps that was just his way of hiding his true emotions. A triumphant grin would be unseemly, after all. Rebekah found herself smiling for him.

"I thought you boys got kicked out of the army," Sean said as he handed Captain McCulloch a jug of special blended whiskey he kept as his own private stock. The two of them were alone in Sean's office, a small room off the store where he kept the books and tended to the paperwork of storekeeping.

McCulloch took a swig of the whiskey and shuddered with pleasure. "Well, General Taylor was only too happy to let us go when our enlistment was up, if that's what you mean. I even heard he asked the President not to send him any more Rangers, but that was when he thought the war was over. Now I expect he'll be happy to see us back again."

He passed the jug to Sean who took a sip and passed it back again. "What was it he had against you boys in the first place? Seems like he would've been glad for the help."

McCulloch grinned through his beard. "Oh, he was. He just couldn't get used to how many Mexicans died when we were around."

Sean grinned back. "Isn't that the whole point? To kill them before they kill you?"

"In battle, yes, but you'd be amazed how many greasers bit the dust even after the truce was declared."

"They all died accidental, I guess," Sean said, amused.

McCulloch shook his head solemnly. "Well, you know, a lot of our men were prisoners down there a time or two and got treated real bad by some of those folks. We figured our government should understand that when some of these same folks was found shot up or hanged that they'd just been hit by a fit of remorse for their past bad behavior and had laid violent hands upon themselves to make amends."

Sean could just imagine the exasperation of the regular army over such activities. "Then General Taylor was just upset by all those suicides."

"He's a kind-hearted soul," McCulloch agreed. "But a hell of a soldier. We call him Old Rough and Ready, and we'd be proud to call him a Ranger. That's why we're heading back. We figure he got a raw deal from the government when they canceled his truce, and we want to help put an end to Santa Anna once and for all."

"I wish you success," Sean said, slightly envious of the man's opportunity.

"And I wish you would join us," McCulloch said, his deep-set blue eyes twinkling.

"What?" Sean asked, certain he had misunderstood.

"I need a few more men. We—the men and I—we heard about you, and we talked it over. We'd like to have the man who rescued Rebekah Tate in our company."

Sean was stunned. *The man who rescued Rebekah Tate.* It was the title he'd wanted. It was the title he'd known would buy him everything he'd ever dreamed of: fame, success, and most of all, respect. And now he had it all, including this tribute from the most highly respected men in Texas. After all the years of being an orphan, a nobody, at last he was somebody very important indeed.

Why, then, didn't he feel happy?

"I see I've taken you by surprise," McCulloch said.

"Shock is more like it," Sean said, trying to smile. "I'm honored," he added quite truthfully. "It's just . . . this is a bad time for me."

"I know. You've just started your business," he

agreed. "Christmas is coming, too. The men hated to leave home, but it has to be done."

Sean nodded. He should have been thinking about the store and who would run it. Instead, all he could think about was Rebekah Tate and how she'd felt when he touched her just a few minutes ago and how she'd leaned against him and how she'd smiled at him. It was the first time she'd spoken a friendly word to him since he'd come back with Hunter. It was the first time he'd let himself believe there might be a chance with her. How could he leave her now? And why should he? He had nothing else to prove.

"There's no way I could be away from here for a year. That's the length of enlistment, isn't it?"

"For the Army, yes, but we're not regular army, and we figure we'll stay six months instead."

"Will the Army let you do that?"

"If they need us bad enough, they will."

"It's not my war," Sean argued, a flimsy argument because he could only think of one real reason not to join McCulloch and he didn't want the Ranger to know a woman was holding him back.

"You're an American now, and a Texan. Of course it's your war," McCulloch argued right back. "The greasers want to take Texas back. Where would your business be then?"

"They won't take Texas back even if they win, which they won't."

"You're sure of that?" McCulloch challenged.

Sean had no answer, so he said, "Would you like to meet Rebekah Tate?"

McCulloch's face brightened. "She's here? Hell, yes!"

Finding her was more difficult than Sean had expected. He'd thought she'd be with the other women, but she was sitting in her wagon as if she'd been hiding. She slid off the wagon gate and straightened her dress and her bonnet when she saw them approaching. Sean felt a surge of pride at the sight of her. Her golden hair was gathered now under her bonnet, but her blue eyes shone and her satiny skin glowed. She was, he was certain, the most beautiful woman in Texas, even without the fine-looking dress. *Especially* without the dress, he thought, smiling inwardly. And it wouldn't be long now before he claimed her as his own.

She wasn't smiling when they approached, and Sean thought she looked a little wary, which was only natural, he supposed. "Rebekah Tate," he said, "I'd like to introduce Captain Ben McCulloch of the Texas Rangers. Captain McCulloch, this is Rebekah Tate."

"How do you do, Captain?" Rebekah asked, giving him her hand.

McCulloch pulled off his battered sombrero and sketched a little bow as he shook her hand. "It's an honor, Miss Tate. You're a legend in Texas, you know."

"No more than Ben McCulloch is," she countered solemnly, making Sean wish he knew what thoughts were going on behind her sky blue eyes. She didn't seem particularly pleased.

"Don't believe a word of it, ma'am," McCulloch told her. "Most of it's lies, anyway."

Her lips twitched, and she smiled almost reluctantly. "I doubt it. The Rangers wouldn't have made you a captain otherwise."

He smiled back. "I think if folks knew what you'd been through, they'd make you a captain, too."

Her beautiful eyes widened in surprise, but her smile only faltered for a moment. "Maybe you're right," she said, surprising Sean. She didn't like to speak of her past, especially not with strangers.

McCulloch still held her hand, and Sean felt the

sudden need to inform the Ranger of his own position in Rebekah's life. "Where's Hunter?" he asked, lifting his hand and resting it familiarly on the back of Rebekah's neck. He felt her slight start but didn't think McCulloch noticed. Indeed, the man instantly dropped Rebekah's hand and stepped back a pace, silently acknowledging Sean's prior claim.

"He's with my father. He wanted to meet some Rangers," she said, giving McCulloch another smile.

"They'll want to meet him, too," McCulloch said. "And you, too. It'll be something to tell their grandchildren."

Sean could almost smell her resistance. For some reason she didn't want to go back to the crowd around his store, probably for the same reason she had been hiding out here at the wagon. Maybe she was more upset about the incident down by the creek than she'd let on. Sean had an urgent need to soothe her fears, whatever they might be. "I'll take you over," he said, thinking his presence would help, at least.

Her gaze darted to him, then back to McCulloch again. "I'd be happy to meet your men," she said, although Sean knew she wasn't really happy about it at all. When had he learned to read her so well? He wasn't sure, but he wasn't particularly curious about it, either. The important thing was that he could.

As they walked back toward the store, Sean took Rebekah's arm and McCulloch answered her polite questions about why he was returning to Mexico. His explanation was less colorful than the one he'd given Sean, though.

When they were almost there, McCulloch glanced meaningfully at where Rebekah's hand rested on Sean's arm. "I've asked Mr. MacDougal to join our company, Miss Tate."

Rebekah stopped in her tracks, forcing the men to

357

stop, too, and her fingers tightened on Sean's arm. Her eyes were troubled when she looked up at him. "You're going to Mexico with them?" she asked. She didn't look at all happy about it, and Sean felt a weight lifted off his heart.

He started to tell her he had no intention of going, but McCulloch said, "He hasn't given me an answer yet. Maybe he needs to talk it over with somebody first."

"I should think so!" she said, more outraged than she had any right to be. "He's got a store to run, after all."

"Oh, Andrew could probably run it as well as I could now that everything's set up," Sean allowed, testing her.

Was that alarm he saw in her lovely eyes? Gratified, Sean decided he really did want to talk it over with her, that and other things as well, and if she was worried about keeping him here, well, he knew exactly how she could persuade him to stay. "We'll talk about it later," he said, and he had to bite his lip to keep from grinning over her troubled frown.

Rebekah endured meeting the other Rangers who had already encountered Hunter and her father. When the introductions were over, she asked her father to take her home. Sean wanted to protest, but he knew he wouldn't have an opportunity to speak with her privately until the party was over, which probably wouldn't be until morning.

"Maybe I can come by in a day or two so we can have that talk," he said as he helped her up onto the wagon seat.

"That would be fine," she said. She didn't really look at him, but he thought her fingers lingered just a second too long on his before she released his hand.

As he had expected, the party didn't break up until the wee hours of the next morning, and the Rangers lingered until daylight. Before they rode out, Mc-Culloch took Sean aside. "If you decide to join us, you can catch us up later. We'd be proud to have you, Sean MacDougal."

Sean watched them go with profound regret. Any other time, he would have sold his soul to serve with these men. They'd found him too late, though. His soul already belonged to someone else.

At the Tate farm, all anyone could talk about was the Rangers, and Rebekah wanted to scream. She supposed it was only natural for people to be impressed by them, of course. They were most impressive.

But all Rebekah could think about was Captain McCulloch's invitation for MacDougal to join them. She spent most of the next day thinking about it, sitting unhearing through her father's sermon and refusing offers of hospitality from would-be friends after the service because she wanted to be alone to think some more.

MacDougal had said he'd talk to her about it, but he made no effort to approach her at church. How long would he wait? The Rangers had ridden out, she knew, and if he wanted to join them, he should go now. And what if he decided he didn't have to discuss it with her at all? He certainly didn't need her permission, and she'd already told him he had no place in her life.

What had she been thinking? How could she have done such a stupid thing? At the time her reasons had seemed fine. Now she couldn't even remember what they had been. Now she couldn't even imagine her life without MacDougal, and she didn't want to try.

Of course, she couldn't give up her freedom, either. The thought of being owned by a man again, even if that man was MacDougal, was too terrifying to even contemplate, but she still needed MacDougal in her life. After a day of thinking, she'd finally figured out the perfect solution, too: she would simply give him what he wanted.

It was so obvious, she didn't know why she hadn't thought of it before. She would give him her body, and she would get what she wanted in return: the promise that he would always be there when she needed him. She'd only be giving what others had already taken by force, and if she remembered correctly, she hadn't even minded submitting to MacDougal. In fact, she'd rather enjoyed it, if "enjoyed" was the proper word, and she knew MacDougal had, too. They would both be happy. Except she would have to see him soon or it might be too late.

Somehow she waited through the long afternoon and sat through supper. When she was sure it was late enough—Andrew had stayed at the store to clean up after church, and she didn't want to arrive before he had gone—she asked Jewel if she would see to putting Hunter to bed.

Jewel's dark eyes narrowed. "You going someplace?" she asked, plainly believing the only possible answer to such a question was "no."

"I'm going for a ride," Rebekah replied, ignoring Jewel's gasp of surprise.

"This time of night? Who's going with you?" Jewel demanded, but Rebekah was already outside and moving toward the barn. "Massa Zeb!" she heard Jewel calling, and thought, *Tattletale*.

Her father caught up with her just as she finished saddling the old mare. "Where are you going?" he asked, his weathered face creased in concern.

"I'm going to see MacDougal," she said, having decided the truth was less shocking than any lie she could dream up.

"This time of night?" her father said. "Can't it wait until morning?"

"No, it can't," she said, wondering what she would do if he forbade her to go since she had no intention of allowing him to stop her. "I need to speak to him in private, and tomorrow the store will be full of customers."

"You can't go out there alone," he pointed out. "What will people say?"

Rebekah cast him an exasperated look, remembering the men who had insulted her by the creek. "Papa, I don't have a reputation to ruin. I was with the Indians, remember? I've got a bastard child. It doesn't matter in the least what people say about me now."

He grabbed her arm when she would have mounted the mare, and she turned to him impatiently, ready to shake him off if necessary. But when she looked into his eyes, she saw not outrage but concern. "Do you know what you're doing, Rebekah?"

She almost sighed in relief. At least he wasn't going to lecture her or try to change her mind. "I know exactly what I'm doing, Papa. I need to see MacDougal, that's all."

He let her go, but his eyes were still troubled. "Be home before dark," he called after her as she rode away, and she didn't dare look back. Did he know why she was going and what she planned to do when she got there? And if he did, why had he let her go?

She didn't worry herself over the answers, though. She had too many other things to worry about.

By the time she saw MacDougal's store in the distance, she'd been over the matter so many times, her brain felt like mush. Time and again she'd tried to come up with a speech that told MacDougal what she wanted him to know, and each time she'd failed. No one, it seemed, had ever thought to invent the words necessary to convey the plan Rebekah had in mind.

But maybe she wouldn't need any words at all. If she remembered correctly, once MacDougal started kissing her, they didn't need to talk to communicate. Memories she'd suppressed stirred to life again, memories of his hands on her naked flesh, of his mouth on hers, of his body forcing hers to yield, and of her body surrendering in delirious ecstasy.

Her stomach fluttered and her heart began to pound, and she shifted restlessly in the saddle. Her nerves tingled, anticipating his touch, and she shivered. Soon she'd be in his arms, and she could lose herself there, forget all the pain of the past and the uncertainty of the future. She'd bind MacDougal to her without being bound herself. The sensation of her own power was intoxicating, and she laughed aloud, startling herself and the old mare who looked back at her quizzically.

Careful, she told herself. MacDougal would sense if she were too cocky. No, better to hide her confidence and her power. He wouldn't appreciate her gloating, and besides, there was no need for him to suspect she was trying to manipulate him. Better if he thought she simply couldn't stay away from him, which was, she admitted, pretty close to the truth.

She was almost there now, near enough to see no signs of activity from the store and no extra horse in the corral behind it. For a moment she wondered if MacDougal were even there. He might have gone to someone's house for Sunday dinner. Maybe he wasn't back yet. Maybe . . .

Then she saw him standing in the doorway of the

one-room cabin he had built for himself. He wore work clothes, but his shirt was unbuttoned, and he was bareheaded, as if he were relaxing at the end of the day. Instinctively, she waved, but when he didn't wave back, she lowered her hand self-consciously. Was something wrong? She'd thought he would at least be happy to see her, but he wasn't even coming forward to greet her.

She rode right up to his cabin, her heart pounding now in apprehension. He was watching her, his wolf's eyes unreadable, his face expressionless. His red hair was slightly tousled, as if he'd been running his fingers through it, and Rebekah felt her own fingers aching to do the same. She wanted to jump down off her horse and run to him, but he looked too forbidding somehow.

Swallowing, she tried to smile, thinking she knew what might be inhibiting him. "Is . . . is Andrew still here?"

His brown eyes narrowed suspiciously. "Is that why you came, to see Andrew?"

"No!" she exclaimed, horrified to have given him the wrong impression right off. "I . . . I just wanted to make sure we were alone. You said we should talk, but you didn't say when so I—"

She didn't have to explain anymore. He was already coming for her, plucking her off the horse into his arms, and his kiss silenced the rest of her explanation.

Oh, God, she thought surrendering to his plundering mouth, how could she have thought she could ever live without this? She wrapped her arms around his neck, clinging desperately, opening her mouth for his sensual assault and luxuriating in the feel of his hard, masculine body against hers.

The kiss went on and on while his hands moved over her, relearning her curves, reclaiming his possession of her, and she reveled in his touch and the riot of sensation it caused in her. This was everything she remembered and more; *he* was everything she remembered and more. What a fool she'd been to send him away when they could have had this!

When Rebekah thought her knees would no longer hold her, MacDougal broke the kiss for just a second while he bent down and scooped her up into his arms. Clinging to his neck, she protested weakly, "My mare!"

"She won't wander far," he murmured quite logically before he captured her mouth again.

He was taking her inside which was what she'd expected, what she'd wanted, so she didn't protest again. He sat her on her feet then, and although he was still kissing her, his hands were intent on other things.

She felt the ribbon of her bonnet sliding free, and the bonnet fell from her head. Then he started on the buttons of her fine wool dress, and she had to help when the task proved too difficult for a man distracted. He'd want her naked, of course. He'd said once it was better that way, and she didn't mind obliging him. If only she'd thought about this part, though, she'd have worn something easier to get out of!

Finally they had to stop kissing entirely so Rebekah could pull her arms free and let the dress and then her petticoat slip to the floor. Except for her shoes and stockings, she now wore nothing more than her chemise which covered her to her knees, but when she met MacDougal's eye, she could have sworn he could see right through it. Indeed, the heat from his gaze fairly scorched her as he slipped out of his unbuttoned shirt and reached for her again.

When he lifted her this time, she caught a glimpse of the cabin, bachelor neat with a mud-and-stick fireplace and a homemade table and chairs at one end. She only had time to form an impression, however, before MacDougal laid her on the bunk that took up the opposite end of the room.

He laid her down gently, almost reverently, then stood and began to remove the rest of his clothes. She looked away, self-conscious, kicking off her shoes so they fell off the end of the bed. In another minute he joined her on the bunk, taking her into his arms and smothering her with searching kisses that swept away the moment of awkwardness and sent her blood racing when she touched the heated flesh of his naked back.

When she was limp with wanting, he stripped off her stockings and chemise, leaving her as naked as he. She reached for him again, but he did not come to her at once. Instead he held her away, so he could look at her. His burning gaze brushed her throat, her breasts, her belly, and below, and she felt it like a physical touch that stirred the flames of passion she had so long suppressed. What a fool she'd been to deny herself!

When he whispered her name, she went to him, wrapping her arms and legs about him, desperate to experience all of him, the silken flesh of his back, his hair-roughened legs, the cozy nest of his chest, the fevered depths of his mouth. She touched him with all of her, her lips, her hands, her breasts, her legs, her hips. Need roiled in her, the need to touch and be touched, to hold and be held, to possess and be possessed.

She wanted to tell him, but there were no words for how she felt or at least no words she knew, so she showed him with her body instead, clinging to him while his hands stoked the fires of desire into a raging inferno.

When she could no longer even think of speaking,

he entered her, sliding into her like a sheet of flame that surged through her body, igniting every part of her. Desperate now, she sank her teeth into his shoulder while her nails raked his back and her hips churned beneath his, frantic for the release that would send her soaring. He met her thrust for thrust, as frantic as she, as desperate as she, his breath coming in ragged gasps, his weight crushing her, holding her helpless while he gave her everything she wanted and more.

At the end, she cried out, an incoherent sound she had meant to be his name. The spasms of release convulsed her in waves of pleasure so pure she could see the colors of it swirling behind her eyelids. Then she cradled him through his own release until he collapsed on her, weak and spent and sated.

They lay like that for a long time, limp and gasping. MacDougal's breath was warm against her face and smelled of pipe tobacco and him. She savored it, drinking in his fragrance so she could hold the memory until the next time.

She was silently congratulating herself on how easily she had accomplished her goal when he said, "Was there another reason why you showed up here tonight?"

She opened her eyes and turned her head so she could see his face. He was too close for her to really see him properly, but she thought he was smiling slightly.

"You said you wanted to talk to me about going to Mexico with the Rangers," she reminded him.

"Ah, yes," he murmured. "I'd forgotten."

"Forgotten?" she echoed in outrage, pushing him away so she could focus on his face.

Reluctantly he rolled off of her, and instantly she felt the chill of the evening air on her passion-slicked body. MacDougal reached down and pulled up the quilt that had been folded at the foot of the bed to cover them both.

"How could you have forgotten?" she demanded when she was buried beneath its folds. "He only asked you yesterday. I was afraid you'd already gone!"

"Were you now?" MacDougal asked, plainly delighted by the prospect. "And what would you have done if I had?"

"I . . ." She hesitated, not certain of her answer and even less certain she should reply at all. "Well, you didn't, so what difference does it make?"

"None, I guess," he allowed, propping himself up on one elbow so he could look down at her, "although you could have said you'd have ridden after me and dragged me back again."

"Has anybody ever succeeded in getting you to do anything you didn't want to do?" she challenged.

"As a matter of fact, no, but you stood a pretty good chance of being the first since I'd much rather do what we just did than ride off to Mexico. I just wasn't sure I still had the choice."

MacDougal was the only person in the world who could make her blush, Rebekah thought in annoyance as she felt the heat rising in her cheeks. "Well, I guess you do have the choice," she said, primly adjusting the quilt over her naked breasts.

"And I assume this visit means you've changed your mind about wanting me and that you'd prefer I didn't join the Rangers," he added, grinning.

"Yes, er, no, I mean, I don't want you to join the Rangers," she stammered, wishing she could get up and put her clothes back on. This discussion was awkward enough without being naked.

"Rebekah Tate, you never cease to amaze me," he remarked, stroking her hair. "One minute you send me packing and tell me you're going to marry another man, and the next you come riding up to my front door to seduce me. I wonder why I ever imagined marriage would be dull? Marriage to you will probably be the most exciting adventure I've ever had."

Marriage? Rebekah tensed in distress. She hadn't said anything about *marriage*. Of course, she supposed it was only natural for him to assume she'd want that. He'd probably be relieved to learn it wasn't necessary. "I . . . We aren't getting married," she tried, not surprised to hear her voice sounding strained.

His eyebrows rose and his smile disappeared. "I know I haven't exactly asked you yet, but I did notice how much you seemed to enjoy our little encounter just now. And forgive me if I presume, but I had the distinct impression that was exactly what you came out here to do, too."

"It was," she admitted, too mortified to look him in the eye as she did so.

"Then wouldn't marriage be the next logical step?" he inquired archly, obviously convinced he was right. "That is, if we enjoy each other's company as much as we apparently do and if we wish many future opportunities to . . . ah . . . indulge ourselves?"

"Not . . . necessarily," she offered, still unable to meet his eye.

"What?" He was genuinely confused.

"We don't have to be married to . . . to do what we just did. I mean, we aren't married now, are we?"

She glanced at him to check his mood, which she discovered was growing hostile. Quickly, she went on. "We don't have to get married. We can just . . . meet whenever . . . whenever we want and . . . and be together and . . . and then go on like we are now." She checked his expression again and found he was now scowling. "You don't have to marry me," she hurried on. "Not when this is all you really want." She gestured to indicate their bodies in the bed. "I don't mind," she assured him. "I don't want to be married anyway."

"And what if this is *not* all I really want?" he said, surprising her.

She stared at him, trying to read his expression and tell if he was teasing her. He didn't seem to be. He seemed angry, although she couldn't imagine why when she was offering him everything his heart could desire. "What else is there?" she asked.

"There's *love*, for one thing," he fairly snarled, making her jump. "But maybe I'm dreaming. Maybe I was a fool when I thought that just because I'd fallen in love with you, you'd fallen in love with me back."

For a moment she didn't understand. Then she remembered what he'd called it when two people came together. "I'll make love with you!" she assured him. "You said you could tell I . . . I liked it. I'll come to you whenever you want!"

"I'm not talking about *making* love!" he exclaimed in exasperation, throwing off the quilt and jumping to his feet. "I'm talking about being *in* love, about caring for somebody more than you care for anyone else, even yourself. About wanting to be with that person every day and every night. About spending your life with that person and sharing everything, all the important things and even the unimportant things. That's what I'm talking about."

The picture he painted terrified her. She couldn't do the things he said. She'd be too vulnerable, too helpless and powerless, like the fifteen-year-old girl the Indians had taken. She'd had no defense then, and if she loved him, she'd have no defense again. He could hurt her, hurt her beyond bearing, and if he did, she knew she would die.

Rebekah felt as if someone had placed a pillow over her mouth. She could hardly breathe, and she began to tremble beneath the blankets. "No," she whispered, but he didn't hear her.

He was pulling on his pants with quick, jerky motions, talking as he worked. "Do you think I just want somebody for a quick roll in the hay every now and then? Is that what you think? Is that what you want?"

Her eyes burned as if she wanted to cry but couldn't, except she certainly didn't want to cry. She didn't want to shake, either, but she was, so badly that MacDougal suddenly noticed.

Instantly his expression softened. "Are you all right, Rebekah Tate?"

She pushed herself up, clutching the quilt to her breasts and casting about for her chemise. She found it lying on the floor beside the bed and snatched it up. Awkwardly, with unsteady hands, she pulled it on over her head, then struggled to her feet.

Her knees felt like jelly, but she staggered over to where the rest of her clothes lay and began to put them on.

MacDougal watched her warily, hovering as if he wanted to help but didn't know how. Somehow she managed to get her dress buttoned. Her feet were bare, but she couldn't take the time to find her stockings or put them back on. She shoved her feet into her shoes and headed for the door.

MacDougal grabbed her arm. "Where are you . . . ? My God, you're shaking like a leaf! What in the hell is the matter with you?"

"*Let me go!*" she cried, and shocked by her vehemence, he released her instantly. "I'm leaving, and don't try to stop me! What you've had of me is all you'll ever have, and if it's not enough, then too bad.

I don't love you, MacDougal, and I'll never love you!
Nobody's ever going to hold me prisoner again!"

With that, she lunged out the door and ran for her
mare who, as MacDougal had predicted, had not
wandered far. She was in the saddle in an instant,
almost before MacDougal had gathered his wits and
followed her.

"Come back here!" he shouted, running for her.
"Rebekah Tate!"

But she ignored the cry and kicked the mare into
motion. The old mare didn't like running, but
Rebekah soon had her trotting briskly enough so that
MacDougal's shouts died in the distance.

The wind tore at her hair and whipped away the
tears that coursed down her face. She didn't know
why she was crying. The world wouldn't end if she
never made love with Sean MacDougal again. That
was all she had lost because she didn't love him,
because she would never let herself love any man,
because she would never belong to any man again.

But if that were true, why did her heart feel as if
someone had torn it open with a knife?

Chapter Thirteen

Sean was packed and ready to go when Andrew arrived for work the next morning.

"'Morning, bossman," Andrew called, striding up to the front door of the store after he'd put his horse away.

He stopped when Sean didn't return his smile or his greeting.

"Is something the matter?" Andrew asked warily.

Sean wished he knew how to answer a question like that. "No, not if you really want to prove what a good storekeeper you can be," he said, somehow managing a grin.

Andrew frowned as if he'd heard something in Sean's voice he didn't like. "You already know I do. If you're worried—"

"I'm not worried about you," Sean said. He turned and led the way into the store which was now stocked with neatly stacked piles of goods that filled the shelves down the entire length of the building. He kept going until they were in the small room that served as an office. Sean took a seat at the desk and motioned for Andrew to take the other chair. He noticed Andrew kept looking around suspiciously. When his gaze finally settled on Sean, Sean said,

"How would you like to run this place all by yourself?"

"Is this some kind of a joke?" Andrew inquired, clearly not amused.

"Not at all. Remember I told you McCulloch asked me to join up with them and go to Mexico? Well, I've decided I will."

Andrew's mouth dropped open, and he gaped at Sean incredulously. "Are you serious?"

"Absolutely."

Andrew shook his head as if to clear it, or perhaps he was simply denying Sean's statement. "This is crazy! Why would you head off to Mexico when you've got this place to run?"

Sean tried to make it sound logical. "Andy, if Ben McCulloch invites you to join the Rangers, you don't refuse."

"The hell you don't!" Andrew exclaimed. "Nobody's forcing you to go. They probably don't even need you, and God knows, you don't need them. Damnit, Sean, you're the man who rescued Rebekah Tate! You don't have to prove anything to anybody ever again! And speaking of Rebekah, what do you think she'll say when she hears about this?"

Sean stiffened at the mention of her name, but he thought he concealed his reaction very well at least until Andrew scowled at him.

"This is about her, isn't it?" Andrew guessed.

"No," Sean lied, but he didn't fool Andrew who knew him pretty well by then.

"Is this some crazy plan to impress her or something?" Andrew demanded. "Because if it is, you're going to a lot of trouble for nothing. She's already impressed with you as any idiot can plainly see. Oh, I know you've had your troubles, and I've done my share to make things tough for you, too, but it's been hard for her coming home, what with everything being changed, and then getting the boy back and trying to get him settled and all. If you'll just give her a few more weeks, I know she'll—"

"It's too late," Sean told him coldly. "She was here last night."

"Here! You mean she came to see you? Alone?" Clearly Andrew was shocked by such immodest behavior.

Sean could have shocked him even more, if he'd wanted to blacken Rebekah's name and if he wanted his friend to think him even more of a fool than he already did. But of course, he didn't want to do either of those things. Instead he said, "She came to talk to me. I thought we'd get things settled at last now that she's finally admitted there wasn't anything between the two of you, but that's not exactly what happened."

"Then what exactly did happen?" Andrew prodded when Sean hesitated.

"She said she didn't love me and she never would and she'd never marry me," Sean admitted bitterly. "So much for your argument that she just needs more time."

"So you're going off like some lovesick fool to get yourself killed," Andrew snapped in exasperation.

Sean was halfway out of his chair, ready to pound Andrew into a greasy spot before he caught himself. To his credit, Andrew did little more than blink in surprise before he reached up, clamped a hand on Sean's shoulder, and forced him back into his chair. "Easy, partner," Andrew soothed. "I don't think I'm the one you're mad at, anyways."

"You're right," Sean agreed, sagging weakly in the chair, "and I'm not . . . I'm not going to get myself killed, at least not if I can help it." He'd started to deny that he was a lovesick fool, too, but he figured Andrew would give him an argument there. He might've won it, too.

"And who's going to take care of Rebekah and the boy if you don't come back?" Andrew challenged.

Sean smiled sadly. "I figured with me out of the way, you would—"

"Oh, no!" Andrew cried, throwing up his hands in protest. "You can count on me to run the store, but that's all! Rebekah was finally able to convince me we don't belong together, and I'm not going to put my head in that noose again! Listen, Sean, I don't care what she says, if you could just see the look on her face when she talks about you, you'd know she's crazy about you!"

"Crazy, maybe," he allowed, thinking of the way she'd come to him last night and the way she'd been in his arms, wild and passionate and sweet and loving . . . Except she hadn't been loving, not really. That part had been a lie, or at least an illusion.

"Sean, you're the man who rescued her!" Andrew insisted, desperate now. He was losing the argument, and he knew it. "Doesn't that make you responsible for her, somehow?"

Sean felt his heart grow cold in his chest. "No, it doesn't, and damnit, I don't want to go to my grave as 'The man who rescued Rebekah Tate.'" There, he'd said it aloud, and although Andrew seemed surprised, he wasn't actually shocked, which meant it didn't sound as silly as he'd feared. "I want to do something else in my life besides that, something important, something that matters."

"That matters," Andrew argued weakly. "And what you did for the boy. There's not another man alive who could've—"

"No!" Sean fairly shouted, making Andrew jump. "There's a hundred men could've saved her and the boy both. You know it and I know it and everybody else does, too." Andrew was shaking his head, but

375

Sean ignored him. "I'm going to Mexico and do what has to be done. Now should I close down the store or can you run it by yourself?"

They argued some more, but finally Andrew surrendered in the face of Sean's implacable will. When Andrew had accepted his fate, he listened once more as Sean went over everything he'd already explained a dozen times. Luckily Andrew had paid attention the other times because he wasn't paying attention this time. All he was doing was wondering how he was going to explain this to Rebekah.

"Does she know?" Andrew asked when Sean had finished his instructions.

"Does who know what?" Sean asked in a good imitation of bewilderment.

"You know damn well who. Did you tell her you were going?"

"She'll hear about it soon enough. Here," he said, handing Andrew a flour sack containing the articles of clothing she had left behind in her haste last night. He'd drawn the bag shut and hoped that Andrew wouldn't look inside and wonder how Sean came to be in possession of Rebekah's bonnet and stockings. "These things belong to her."

"Sean, it's almost Christmas," Andrew tried. "Can't you at least wait until—"

"If I don't leave now, I won't be able to catch up to McCulloch and his men," Sean replied. Christmas, he'd almost forgotten. He thought of the velvet cloak he'd ordered for Rebekah when he thought he'd be wrapping it around the shoulders of his future bride. The pain in his heart convulsed into an aching emptiness which he supposed he'd always carry. He reached up and brought the cloak down from the shelf on which he had placed it. "Give this to Rebekah Tate for me, will you? For Christmas?"

Andrew snatched the folded garment from Sean

and swore eloquently, using words Sean would have sworn he didn't even know. "And what am I supposed to tell her when she asks me why I let you go?" he demanded, furious now. "And if you think I'm going to break the news to her if you get hurt or killed, you're even crazier than I thought! She's not *my* woman, Sean MacDougal!"

"She's not mine either!" Sean shouted back. "And that's her choice, not mine, so you can tell her anything you want or nothing at all, suit yourself—if she even cares, which I don't figure she will."

He stomped out of the store and went to saddle his horse and load his gear. Andrew didn't follow him, but when Sean was ready to ride away, Andrew came out, looking as forlorn as if he'd lost his best friend.

He reached out to shake Sean's hand. "You're a fool and an idiot and if you get yourself killed, I'll never forgive you," he said grimly.

Sean couldn't help smiling, although he suddenly realized he was losing more than Rebekah by riding away; he was leaving a friend, and God knew he had few enough of them in this world. "I'll be back before you know it, and you'll probably have so much fun running my store into bankruptcy, you won't even notice I'm gone."

"If that's what you're counting on, you'll be disappointed," Andrew said, managing a smile of his own. "I plan to make more money than you ever dreamed, so you'll know once and for all which of us is the better trader."

"You've got a deal," Sean said, reluctantly releasing Andrew's hand.

Andrew's smile faded. "Do you want me to say anything to her? Tell her anything?"

Sean considered, trying his best to ignore the throbbing emptiness in his chest. "No," he said at last. "There's nothing else to say."

Andrew stood and waved for as long as Sean could see him. He tried not to look back, but he couldn't seem to help himself. Something about the raw wooden structure drew his gaze like a magnet. What was the matter with him? He'd left his store in Santa Fe without a qualm. He supposed if he'd been a more philosophical man, he might have said it was because then he'd been going to something while this time he was going away from something.

Except, of course, that without Rebekah Tate's love, he had nothing.

"You ain't going to stop eating again, are you?" Jewel inquired as she scraped Rebekah's virtually untouched dinner onto a plate for the dogs.

"I'm just not hungry today," Rebekah protested, carrying some dirty dishes to the dishpan and dropping them in. The men had gone back to work after the noon meal, and Hunter was outside playing with the dogs, leaving the two women alone in the kitchen.

"You ain't been hungry since you went to see Mr. MacDougal night before last," Jewel reminded her. "When you gonna tell me what happened between you two?"

"When and if it ever becomes any of your business," Rebekah replied, wishing she had the stomach for treating slaves with the contempt Cousin Prudence used. Rebekah couldn't imagine Jewel questioning Prudence about her private affairs.

"It's my business if you get sick again," Jewel went on, undaunted, "since I'm the one's got to take care of you, and now there's the boy to see to, and if you ain't able, why—"

"I'm not going to get sick again!" Rebekah exclaimed, exasperated. "And you don't have to worry about Hunter. I'm perfectly capable of taking care of him myself."

Jewel humphed her disgust and continued to scrape the dishes. She didn't say anything else on the subject, but she didn't have to. Rebekah could feel her displeasure like a physical chill in the air.

She told herself she didn't care what Jewel thought. Jewel was just a slave, and an uppity one at that.

Except, of course, Jewel was also her friend, her only female friend, and possibly also the only person to whom she could talk about Sean MacDougal.

Heaven knew she couldn't talk to her father about him. The night she'd come back from MacDougal's, half-dressed and distraught, she'd stolen into her room before he could see her and ask embarrassing questions. He'd known something was wrong just the same, though. She could tell from the way he watched her all the time now as if he were waiting for her to tell him about it.

Nor could she talk to Andrew, who would most likely be shocked and who would certainly never understand how she could lie with a man but not want to marry him.

Truth to tell, Rebekah couldn't understand it herself, and the confusion was driving her to distraction. She wanted to cry all the time, but no tears came, no matter how miserable she felt. She wanted to crawl into her bed and pull the covers over her head and hide, but when she did, she couldn't stand the lonely silence or the memories that haunted her there.

The only person she really wanted to see was Sean MacDougal, which meant she must truly be losing her mind because he was the one person she couldn't be with, not ever again, at least not the way she wanted to be with him.

And God help her, she did want to be with him, more than she wanted to be alive. In fact, without him, she didn't know if she could stay alive. But when she thought about his terms, the price she would have to pay, she felt that invisible pillow closing over her face again, and her breath came in shallow gasps as if she really were suffocating.

But she wasn't ready to tell Jewel all this, even though Jewel was the only person who might understand. Maybe in a few days when the pain had faded a little and Rebekah thought she might survive the telling, then she would speak of it. But not yet.

She and Jewel had just finished cleaning up the kitchen when the dogs began to bark, announcing a visitor. Before she could stop it, Rebekah's heart leaped at the absolutely ridiculous thought that the visitor might be MacDougal. But of course it wasn't since MacDougal had a store to run and wouldn't be riding around visiting people in the middle of the day, and he wouldn't be riding around visiting *her* at any time at all, not after the way she'd behaved at their last encounter.

So she didn't bother to go to the door to see who might be coming, and in a minute, Hunter came racing inside, announcing in his broken English that his cousins were here.

Thinking he meant Andrew, Rebekah stepped outside eagerly, but to her disappointment, she saw Prudence and Cecil instead riding up in their wagon.

Prudence called a greeting and waved her lace handkerchief. Rebekah lifted her hand in acknowledgement, telling herself she'd been silly to expect Andrew since he now had a store to run, too. She tried to smile at Prudence when she came bustling forward after Cecil helped her down from the wagon seat.

"I hope we're not interrupting your dinner," she

said, her homely face flushed from the brisk Texas wind.

"We just finished the dishes," Rebekah said, "but if you haven't eaten, I'm sure we can—"

"Oh, no," Prudence said, waving away the suggestion with a flick of her handkerchief. "We already ate with Andrew over at the store. We took a meal to him so we could have a little visit and find out what happened to Mr. MacDougal."

"Happened?" Rebekah echoed in alarm, feeling as if someone had kicked her in the stomach. "What happened to him?"

"You mean you haven't heard?" Prudence said, obviously delighted to be the bearer of fresh news. "He left yesterday morning. The first we heard was Andrew sent us word last night he wouldn't be coming home because he had to stay at the store all the time now and would we bring his things over and—"

"Where did he go?" Rebekah demanded frantically, hoping she wouldn't have to lay hands on Cousin Prudence and shake the story out of her.

"You mean Mr. MacDougal?" Prudence asked coyly, and Rebekah had to curl her hands into fists to keep from slapping her.

"Of course I mean Mr. MacDougal," she said through gritted teeth.

"Why, I can't believe he didn't tell you," she lied, obviously thrilled to believe that very thing. "He went to Mexico, my dear. He joined the Rangers."

There was more, of course. Prudence had a lot to tell her, but Rebekah could no longer hear her because unbearable agony had swallowed her up.

"Cold, ain't it?" one of the Rangers remarked.

"Cold enough to freeze spit on a stove," another

agreed, setting off a series of comparisons as each man tried to outdo the others with cleverness at describing the unusually frigid weather.

When somebody colorfully described what might happen if a man relieved himself in this weather and the stream froze, Sean smiled behind his shaggy beard—all the men wore beards, even the soldiers, since the hair kept their faces warm, and besides, they never had much hot water for shaving.

The mental exercise of describing the freezing February wind didn't do a thing to temper it, but it did provide some distraction from the endless boredom of waiting for General Santa Anna and his army to make their appearance. And everyone, especially the Rangers, was more than bored.

The truce made at Monterey had ended in mid-November by the President's order, but except for a few minor, accidental encounters, the Mexicans and the Amercian had yet to fight again. The Rangers—twenty-seven in number by the time they reached the border—had arrived in Monterey on New Year's Day to find General Taylor had moved on. They finally tracked him down a few days later at Saltillo, a short distance west of Monterey.

True to his word, McCulloch had refused to agree to a one-year enlistment, and General Taylor, desperate for the Rangers' unique services, had violated regulations and signed them on for a period of six months. They had spent the next six weeks riding around Mexico with the American troops while Taylor tried to decide what to do now that General Scott had arrived sending him orders to retreat to Monterey and to transfer the bulk of his troops to Scott for Scott's use. Since this would leave the city and Taylor's remaining forces completely vulnerable, nobody wanted to obey these orders. Currently they were camped at Agua Nueva, waiting.

Morale had plummeted, especially among the Rangers who had come to fight, and even more especially with Sean MacDougal, who was beginning to wonder what had ever possessed him to imagine he could win any glory at all riding with soldiers, for God's sake.

The men were distracted from their ruminations on coldness by a rider quickly approaching their camp. Seeing it was Ben McCulloch, they all rose expectantly from their spots around the sputtering fire and waited while McCulloch dismounted and tended to his horse.

"Well, boys," he announced when he approached the fire at last, pausing to rub his hands together briskly over its warmth, "looks like we'll get to see a little action at last."

"A fight?" one of the men inquired hopefully.

"Not yet," McCulloch said, "but we've got something to scout at least. Old Rough and Ready's had word that Santa Anna found out about his orders," he explained, using the nickname the troops had given General Taylor. "Seems Scott sent some snot-nosed lieutenant with the orders, and he got himself captured and killed, so now Santa Anna knows we're supposed to go back to Monterey with less than half our forces. Naturally he's on his way to wipe us out. One rumor says the whole Mexican army is moving up from San Luis Potosi, and another has 'em sneaking up east of here to hit us in the rear. Old Rough and Ready is sending some regular troops to scout to the east, and we're going south."

"What troops is he sending?" somebody asked.

"May's Dragoons, about four hundred of them."

Everybody chuckled at the thought it would take four hundred troops to do the same job in one spot that it would take twenty-seven Rangers to do in another.

"I reckon he figures that's too many soldiers to capture," somebody else remarked. Everyone laughed heartily at that, remembering how the Mexicans had captured almost a hundred American troops without a shot being fired just a few weeks ago while they'd been checking out a similar rumor.

"I'm sorry to say, you can't all go, though," McCulloch continued. "Well, it don't take all of us to find the whole Mexican army," he argued when they protested. "I'm leaving about ten of you behind, just in case the general needs you for anything before the rest of us get back."

The men waited grimly as McCulloch named the men who would stay behind, and Sean released the breath he had been holding when his name was not called. At last something to do, although a chilly ride across thirty-five miles of desert should not have been very attractive.

"We'll dress like Mexicans," McCulloch explained. "They're sending over some stuff they got from some prisoners, serapes and sombreros. That way, even if they see us, they won't take us for Americans."

It was a good plan, Sean thought, and for the first time since he'd left Texas, he felt his blood begin to race with excitement. He'd had too much time of late to think and remember and regret. Now at last he'd be too busy to even recall Rebekah Tate's name.

As they rode out of camp a short time later, Sean glanced around at his companions and thought again how understandable it was that the Mexicans had named the Rangers *"Los Diablos Tejanos,"* The Texas Devils. Surely they looked like they'd ridden straight out of hell with their unkempt beards, stringy hair, and travel-stained clothes. Even in disguise their eyes betrayed them, cool, hard, and merciless. God help any Mexicans who crossed them, although He hadn't seen fit to help a great many to date.

"Do you really think Santa Anna's out there?" Sean asked McCulloch as they rode.

"He's someplace. If I was him, I'd be there right now. He's got to figure he's put Taylor on the run, and knowing what Scott's orders were . . ." He shrugged eloquently.

"The Army doesn't like soldiers who don't obey orders, though," Sean said, thinking of the contempt in which the Rangers were held by the regulars because the Rangers in turn took little notice of Army regulations. "Is Ol' Rough and Ready going to be in trouble when this is all over for not doing what Scott told him to?"

"Not with the people who count. Americans don't like following orders either, and if he can convince the people that President Polk sent Scott down to steal the glory of the Monterey victory so Taylor wouldn't be a hero, then he'll have their sympathy."

"And their votes," Sean concluded. "And if he can whip Santa Anna right here, he'll be the next President of the United States."

"That's what I hear," McCulloch agreed.

Everyone, it seemed, had their own plans for this war.

It was dark when they reached La Encarnación, but the Rangers had no trouble finding the army camped there. Their fires stretched for miles, as far as the eye could see and probably a lot farther.

Huddled in the folds of their borrowed serapes, the Rangers swore softly and eloquently at the sight.

"How many of them bastards are there?" one asked.

"I reckon it's our job to find out," McCulloch said, his voice betraying no hint that he was in the least bit awed by the sight before them.

"Maybe we could just ride up and ask 'em," one of the men suggested. "Save ourselves a lot of trouble."

"Oh, you know how greasers are. They'd probably just lie," McCulloch replied lazily. "Come on, boys, we've got some more riding to do."

Somehow none of the men were surprised when McCulloch led them on, right up to the edge of the camp, past the weary pickets, calling a greeting in perfectly accented Spanish, and into the very camp itself.

Sean felt his nerves prickle and the cold sweat forming beneath his clothes as he looked around at the thousands of Mexican soldiers trying to sleep beside the fires that stretched to the horizon. If a single one of those soldiers looked up and identified the seventeen men riding slowly through their camp as Americans, every one of the Rangers would be dead in seconds.

But as McCulloch had probably guessed, not a single one of them expected to see a troop of *Los Diablos Tejanos* riding through their camp. Not even Texas Devils would dare such a feat. And so they rode, unmolested, slowly past campfires and sleeping men and snoring pickets and grazing horses and silent artillery pieces, and they counted the fires and the men as best they could in the dark.

And when they were back where they'd started and the stars told them it was near midnight, McCulloch stopped them where they could not be overheard. "I reckon we'd better get back and tell Old Rough and Ready what we saw here. Frank, I'm putting you in charge," he said to Frank Gates, a man who practiced law back in Texas when he wasn't needed for other things.

"Does that mean you're not going with us?" Gates asked. His voice betrayed no concern, only curiosity.

"I'd like to get a look at this bunch in the daylight, make sure we counted right, but there's no use in all of us staying." Or, he might have added, possibly

386

getting killed by the almost twenty-thousand hostile troops who would most likely recognize them for Rangers in the light of day.

"You going to stay alone?" Gates asked, disapproval in his voice.

"I'll keep one man with me," McCulloch said as calmly as if he had been discussing needing company for an errand to town.

"I'll stay," Gates offered, and a murmur of other offers echoed his. Sean MacDougal's was among them, although he could not have explained why he wanted to put himself in such a dangerous situation.

"I know you're all wanting to be heros," McCulloch said, teasing them, "but I need somebody I *know* won't spook." He hesitated as if he were looking them over in the flickering light of hundreds of fading campfires. "Somebody who's got the nerve to ride up to a Comanche camp and steal one of their own right from under their noses. I need the man who rescued Rebekah Tate."

Sean straightened automatically in his saddle as all of them turned to him. Every nerve in his body leaped to attention and for a second the blood roared in his ears. Only he knew his answering smile held bitterness at the irony of McCulloch's reason for selecting him. "I'll make sure you don't nod off and forget why you came, Ben," he said.

"Make sure he don't get lost on the way back, neither," one of the others said. "Taylor'll be mighty put out if he's got to come looking for you." It was the closest any of them could come to admitting they might never see either of them again.

"Better get going if you expect to get any sleep before this bunch shows up tomorrow. Tell Taylor he can expect them at Agua Nueva by nightfall."

"*Adiós,*" the men murmured to each other. No one

387

moved, though, not for a long moment, and their reluctance to leave was almost palpable. Then McCulloch said, "Go on, now," and Gates led them off.

Sean and McCulloch sat their horses as they watched the others ride away at a walk. They'd leave the camp and cross the picket line leisurely so as not to arouse suspicion. Once out of sight, they'd whip their weary horses to a gallop and race back through the night across the thirty-five miles separating them from the American forces to deliver a most unwelcome report. The Mexican army, it seemed, outnumbered the Americans four to one.

And at the moment, however, they outnumbered the two remaining Rangers ten thousand to one.

Rebekah gazed up at the midnight sky and pulled her velvet cloak more tightly around her against the frigid wind. Once again she hadn't been able to sleep, and the only comfort she found was stroking the softness of MacDougal's last gift to her and standing under the same stars she knew shone down on him, wherever he was.

She heard her father's footsteps as he came out of his bedroom and moved up behind her. He didn't speak, sensitive to her need to be alone, yet needing just as much to comfort her. His hands settled on her shoulders, and he squeezed gently to let her know he was there.

"What will I do if he doesn't come back?" she asked into the silence.

"He'll come back," her father assured her. "His business is here. That will always draw him."

"If he's alive," she said, bitter with the knowledge that he might even now be lying under Mexican soil and that if he were, she had only herself to blame.

The one thing that kept her sane was the certainty that surely she would know if something had happened to him. Surely her heart would have shattered with the loss. She sighed in despair. "I wish I could still pray."

"You can," Zeb said gently. "All you have to do is try."

But Rebekah shook her head. Prayer only helped if you believed it did, and she knew it didn't. Long ago she'd prayed for protection from the Comanches. MacDougal didn't need the kind of help she'd gotten in reply. "Hunter was asking for him today. I don't know how to explain why he isn't here. He could have at least said good-bye to Hunter."

"He would have had to see you again, though, and I gather he didn't want to, which was why he left in the first place," Zeb said. He'd never pried, never tried to get her to tell him what had happened between her and MacDougal, but she could hear the silent question behind his words. *Tell me, I'm your father. I can help.* Except he couldn't. No one could.

"He wanted me to marry him," she said. The reason sounded so pathetic she wanted to cry, except crying was another thing she was no longer very good at. "I just . . . I couldn't."

Her father's hands tightened on her shoulders. "I see," he said, as if he really did. She waited, feeling the wind whipping against her cloak, trying to tear it from her body. After a few moments, he said, "I can understand after what you went through. You think you don't want a man to . . . to touch you ever again." His voice was strained. He'd never spoken of such things to her before, and she marveled that he would now. "But marriage is different from . . . from what you experienced, Rebekah. When a man and a woman love each other—"

"But that's just it, Papa! He wants me to love

him!" She wrenched free from his grip and whirled to face him. "I don't care about . . . about the physical part of it! That's not it at all. He wants me to be his wife, his property. He wants to own me, body and soul, and I can't do it! I can't ever let anyone own me again!"

"Rebekah!" Zeb exclaimed, taking her by the shoulders once more. "That's not what marriage is! A husband doesn't *own* his wife. If anything, they own each other, or rather they belong to each other. A man cherishes his wife and protects her and adores her with his body. I think that's what Sean would like to do for you, if you could only let him."

She wanted to believe him, but she was still frightened. No, she was terrified, so terrified she wanted to scream. But even more frightening was the possibility of losing Sean completely.

"If only he was here so I could talk to him," she wailed.

"If he was, what would you tell him?" her father asked softly.

What *would* she tell him? "I'd . . . That I was sorry. That I'd never meant to hurt him. That . . ."

"That you love him?" he prodded when she hesitated.

Suddenly her eyes filled with tears. "I don't want to love him. It hurts too much."

"Of course it does." Zeb smiled. "Every joy carries a price. But whether you want to or not, I think you do."

She couldn't deny it, but, "I told him I didn't. I told him I'd never love him. That's why he left. That's why he . . ." Her voice broke, and her father pulled her into his arms. She buried her face in his shoulder and fought the welling tears while he patted her back as if she were a child.

"It's not too late to make things right."

"But he's gone!" she protested, pulling out of his embrace.

"He'll be back."

"He's fighting a war! Anything can happen! And if it did . . ." She could hardly say the words. "If it did, he'd never know that I . . . that I lov—" Her voice broke on a sob, and once again she collapsed into her father's arms.

"You could write him a letter," he suggested when the storm of weeping had passed.

"He'd never get it," she said into his shirt.

"He won't get it if you don't write it. Andrew said there's folks going south all the time that pass by the store. Any one of them would carry it for you."

"What could I say?"

"Say what you told me here tonight. Tell him you want him back. Tell him anything you like, but quit torturing yourself over it, Rebekah."

He was right, she knew. But what if it was already too late?

Sean glanced at the hundreds of dying campfires that stretched out behind him, then turned to Ben McCulloch. The other Rangers were out of sight, and he and McCulloch were alone among twenty-thousand men who wanted them dead. The silence was like a roar. "Where are we going to light?" Sean asked to break it, hoping his voice didn't betray the tension radiating through him.

McCulloch seemed unaffected. He might have been at a church picnic. "I figured we'd settle on that hill over there. In the daylight we should be able to see everything from that high up."

Sean nodded and waited for McCulloch to lead the way. They rode slowly, trying not to wake the soldiers sleeping everywhere, rolled in ragged blankets on the cold ground. Sean tried to match McCulloch's calmness, but his shoulder blades were twitching expectantly, waiting for a bullet to smash through his body, and the cold sweat had turned clammy.

No one had chosen the top of the hill for a resting place, preferring the more sheltered spots below, so Sean and McCulloch had it to themselves. Indeed, when they felt the icy cut of the wind, they wished themselves elsewhere, too.

After tending their horses—and leaving them saddled in the event they had to make a hasty withdrawal—they settled down to wait.

"You can sleep if you want," McCulloch said. "I'll take the first watch."

Sean couldn't help chuckling. The thought of sleeping while surrounded by the entire Mexican army was, quite simply, hilarious. He just shook his head, and the two of them wrapped up in blankets and settled down to wait.

"Do you have any family, Ben?" Sean asked after a few minutes.

"No, never had the chance to marry. You?"

Sean waited for the shaft of pain to subside at the thought of the bride he would never have. "No," he said. "I was a foundling, grew up in an orphanage."

"Seems like you could have a family now, if you wanted. A wife and a kid, too, if I ain't mistaken."

"You're mistaken," Sean said coldly.

"Oh," McCulloch said, stiffening. "Sorry."

Sean wondered if McCulloch thought he didn't want a half-breed bastard for his son. "It's not my choice. It's the lady's."

"Oh," McCulloch said again, this time with real comprehension. He considered the problem. "Maybe she just needs more time. She was only a kid when they took her, and she hasn't been back very long."

Sean smiled grimly. "Why is it bachelors are always such experts on women?"

McCulloch took the hint and settled back again. Both men stared in silence at the glowing embers of a thousand fires winking at them like a thousand red eyes. If he didn't think about it, Sean could almost forget the men sleeping below would like to see him dead, that a single word or gesture could betray him, that he and McCulloch were literally begging to be murdered where they sat.

And would he mind so very much if it came to that? What had he left in this life? Money, fame, his work. Not so long ago, these things had been all he'd wanted, more than he'd ever hoped to achieve. Now he knew the folly of his ambition. What good was success without someone with which to share it? What good was money unless you could use it to make someone you loved happy? What good was fame if the only person you'd ever loved in this world wouldn't love you back?

Was that why he'd come to Mexico? Had he been hoping he wouldn't have to go home at all? That some willing greaser would put a bullet in his skull so he'd never have to feel the agonizing emptiness again?

If so, then here was his chance. All he had to do was stand up and shout and a *thousand* greasers would be happy to oblige him. He thought of the hapless lieutenant who'd been caught carrying Scott's orders to General Taylor. He'd been roped off his horse and dragged to death. Not a very pleasant way to die, if there even was such a thing, but preferable to the kind of suffering Sean knew American prisoners endured at the hands of the Mexicans. Was that what Sean wanted, oblivion from the suffering? The oblivion of death?

Hell, no! he thought, straightening unconsciously.

"You see something?" McCulloch whispered, straightening himself.

"No," Sean hastily assured him. "I just . . . I thought of something."

"Better if you don't think at all," the captain replied. "Takes your mind off what's going on around you."

Sean had to agree this was good advice, considering the circumstances. Still he couldn't help wondering if maybe, just maybe . . . He was a fool to hope. God knew, he'd been disappointed too many times already.

Then he pictured Rebekah Tate's face, as he had so many nights of late. Her flawless skin, her sky blue eyes, her golden hair, her soft, sweet lips. Even if she never loved him, he'd always want her. And she wanted him, too, as he well remembered from their last night together. Of course, it wasn't enough. It would never be enough, but at least it was something. A reason to keep going. A reason to go back and try again. A reason to hope that someday . . .

And a reason to stay alive until that day.

Sean pulled the blanket more tightly around him against the chill wind and glared out defiantly at the slumbering Mexican army. *God damn you all*, he thought and settled back to wait for dawn.

The night was long and still and frigid and full of unseen terrors, and neither of them so much as closed his eyes. But at long last they saw the faint hint of the sun on the horizon. As the first fingers of daylight stretched across the sky, the buglers' rude blasts roused the soldiers, and the men staggered from their blankets, bleary-eyed and stiff.

Sean and McCulloch watched, their own eyes grainy from lack of sleep, as thousands of Mexicans stretched and relieved themselves and gathered firewood and went about the task of fixing themselves some breakfast and getting ready to march.

"I don't see much of a supply train," McCulloch remarked.

"Seems like they're each carrying their own food. Wonder how Santa Anna plans to keep an army going with no grub."

"Maybe he plans to take our army's," McCulloch offered, making Sean grin.

"Maybe he'll be real disappointed," Sean replied.

They rose, too, and made ready to travel, watching carefully as they adjusted their saddles and rolled their blankets, their eyes studying and counting, always counting. The fires were even clearer in the daylight, especially since the Mexicans were burning green wood and sending up billowing clouds of smoke. And in the daylight they could see how many men shared each fire. Six on average, which when multiplied out by how many fires they'd estimated last night, gave them a pretty accurate accounting of the enemy's forces.

Soon the smoke filled the sky and lay over the land like a fog, seeming to swallow the whole Mexican army.

"Let's get the hell out of here," McCulloch suggested, and Sean agreed with alacrity.

They mounted and started their horses down the hill at a walk, past men eating, men walking, men arguing. Near enough to reach out and touch, only partly hidden by the smoke. If one of them looked up, if one of them wondered at Sean's red hair or McCulloch's blue eyes, if one of them called out a challenge . . .

They rode, plodding along, each hoofbeat like the roar of thunder, heralding their progress to the waiting hoards. But the waiting hoards were devouring their breakfasts.

They rode, through the swirling smoke that

burned their weary eyes and blinded them and concealed them but only partially.

They rode, on and on, past fire after fire, soldier after soldier. One cursed them when they passed too close, and Sean murmured an apology in Spanish. One asked where they were going so early, and McCulloch murmured something in Spanish about scouting.

They rode, on and on, to the edge of the camp. The fires were behind them, but the pickets were in front, the camp guards assigned to warn of intruders. They stood and challenged the riders, raising their guns, the long barrels dull in the smoky light.

One shot and . . .

But Sean waved lazily and McCulloch repeated his lie about scouting, and the gun barrels lowered again. The men went back to their breakfasts, and Sean and McCulloch rode on.

"What the hell's going on?" Sean wondered aloud hours later when the American camp came into view. Men swarmed like ants in the noonday sun, packing and pulling and hauling and saddling.

"I reckon our men got back last night," McCulloch said. "They must've scared the old man because, unless I miss my guess, this looks like a retreat."

Sean swore. "Then we'll probably be going back to Monterey to hide, and General Scott will get his way after all."

McCulloch grunted, and they rode on through the bustling camp, straight to General Taylor's tent. At their approach, a young lieutenant started shouting, having recognized them, and General Taylor ducked out of his tent to see what the commotion was about. The young man was pointing and jabbering something about how they'd made it back and how it was a miracle.

Sean wasn't paying much attention. He was too busy looking at General Taylor. The man never ceased to amaze him. His face was lined and haggard as if it had been carved from stone by an unskilled hand. And no casual observer would have recognized him as the commander of the American Army because he never wore a uniform. Today he was clad in a ragged shirt, baggy linen trousers, and an old brown coat.

When he saw who his visitors were, he nodded once as if he'd fully expected to see Ben McCulloch approaching his tent, and spit a dark stream from the chaw of tobacco lodged in his cheek. "Good morning, Major," he said, using McCulloch's military rank.

"Did my men make it back all right?" McCulloch asked, dismounting. Sean followed suit and found his limbs stiff from the long, hard ride.

"Every one of them. They said you'd found Santa Anna."

"Yes, sir. MacDougal and I spent the night in their camp so we could see what they looked like in the daylight. We'd counted the fires the night before, and this morning we counted the men. We figure there's about twenty thousand of them."

Taylor nodded as if that was about what he'd expected to hear. "Very well, Major, that's all I wanted to know. I'm glad they didn't catch you."

While Sean marveled at the general's calm acceptance of their accomplishment, McCulloch glanced at the activity going on around him. "Are we retreating?"

Taylor's craggy face cracked slightly in the semblance of a grin. "No, Major, we're pulling back to Buena Vista. General Wool feels we can make a better stand there. With these unseasoned troops, we thought we'd better have something like mountains protecting our flanks."

McCulloch nodded and turned to Sean. "I guess we'd better find the rest of our men."

"And get something to eat," Taylor advised as they remounted their horses.

"He's not exactly what you'd expect a general to be," Sean remarked when they were out of earshot.

"No, he's more like a Ranger, don't you think?"

Sean had to agree.

The army's withdrawal to the hacienda of Buena Vista took the rest of the day, and the troops camped that night on their intended battlefield. The generals had chosen a spot called La Angostura, The Narrows, where the road to Saltillo passed through a narrow valley at the foot of the Sierra Madres. Usually the valley drained toward Saltillo, but this time of year the channels and washes through which the mountain runoff would course were dry, making deep, steep-banked, dry gullies in a herringbone pattern of ridges and ditches. Such terrain would be impossible for artillery and difficult for cavalry to cross, and would render infantry ineffective.

The Rangers' troop, known officially as a Spy Company, had been assigned along with the Dragoons to the rear of the line where they would support the infantry and cover the gaps between the infantry formations.

Weary from their sleepless night and all-day ride the next day, Sean and Ben McCulloch slept late on the morning of George Washington's birthday. They were awakened around eleven o'clock by the stir in camp caused by the arrival of General Santa Anna's messenger under a flag of truce. Within a few minutes, an account of his message had spread through the ranks.

"You are surrounded by twenty thousand men," Santa Anna had said to Taylor, and the Rangers congratulated themselves on the accuracy of their estimate, "and cannot in any human probability avoid suffering a rout and being cut to pieces with your troops; but as you deserve consideration and particular esteem, I wish to save you from a catastrophe, and for that purpose give you this notice, in order that you may surrender at discretion, under the assurance that you,will be treated with the consideration belonging to the Mexican character," which the Texans knew only too well, "to which end you will be granted an hour's time to make up your mind, to commence from the moment when my flag of truce arrives in your camp."

Those who saw General Taylor's reaction when the message had been translated reported that it was both colorful and profane. He dictated his reply to his assistant, Major Bliss, who no doubt took liberties with interpretation because the official response read, "I beg leave to say that I decline acceding to your request."

Hoots of laughter went up as word of the reply passed through the ranks, and the troops settled in for a fight. It started about three o'clock that afternoon but never amounted to much, just a little skirmish with some Mexican troops who tried to capture the high ground on the American flank. At sundown the Americans held their positions, and the men lay on their arms and slept where they were without fires in a freezing drizzle in that woodless country.

The morning dawned bright and clear, however, and the American troops were awakened by reveille sounding in each of the different Mexican units.

"What the hell're they blowing so many horns for?" one of the Rangers demanded in annoyance.

"He's waking each of his units up separately so we'll hear how many there are," Sean explained, stretching his cramped limbs and trying to get his teeth to stop chattering.

Some of the men had found some dried weeds and built a small fire. Sean huddled around the feeble flame with the rest of them, trying to absorb some of its warmth.

Then a shout went up among the troops, and everyone ran to look at what had caused the disturbance.

"Holy Mother of God," someone next to Sean murmured. Indeed, he had to agree the sight was awesome.

Santa Anna had drawn his infantry and his cavalry up in a single line while his combined bands played religious music. Sean remembered how worn and dispirited those troops had looked in their own camp. But from this distance the Americans couldn't tell that the splendid Mexican uniforms—red, green, yellow, crimson and blue—were just as ragged as their own. They watched as priests in magnificent robes passed benedictions down the lines of troops. The sight was meant to impress, and the American troops were impressed.

"Too bad they can't fight as good as they look," Sean reminded the other Rangers. "They've never beat Yankee troops yet."

"Maybe you've forgotten the Alamo," Frank Gates, the Ranger second in command, remarked with some amusement.

"The Alamo don't count," another of the Rangers said. "And look how long it took for all them greasers to take a handful of Texans. MacDougal's right. We'll lick these bastards, fancy uniforms or not."

Still, watching the pageantry, every soldier in the line was tense, weary from a near-sleepless night on the frozen ground, and wondering how they could win against so formidable a foe.

The battle began at full daylight with a simultaneous attack on the narrow road which marked the American right flank and on the plateau which marked the American left.

The Rangers, on the left, saw little action until around nine o'clock, when the American line began to cave in toward where they were stationed in the rear. Suddenly everything was confusion as unseasoned men with little training and no combat experience broke ranks in a disorderly retreat and ran, racing for the shelter of the hacienda three miles behind the lines.

"What the hell?" Sean shouted over the din.

Beside him, Frank Gates was trying to catch his rearing horse. "We'd better get moving," he yelled. "Looks like they turned our flank!"

Having no combat experience himself, Sean had no idea what that meant, but he could easily see the colorful Mexican troops swarming over where the American line had been just a short time ago. He grabbed his own horse and was just about to mount when something bumped his right leg. Glancing down, he saw nothing, so he thrust his left foot into the stirrup and swung up.

The motion sent pain lancing through his right thigh, and when he was in the saddle, he looked down to see blood soaking through his trouser leg.

"You're hit!" Gates called, now in the saddle, too. He brought his prancing horse up beside Sean's to examine the wound. "You got something to tie it up with?"

Sean was already pulling off his bandana and cursing enthusiastically. This was all he needed, although he had to admit a bullet in the leg was a lot better than a bullet in the skull.

"Ride back to the rear and find a surgeon," Gates was telling him as he tied the bandana around the wounded leg. The fiery agony was spreading up to his hip and down to his knee. "But whatever you do, don't let them put you in a wagon with the wounded. If the greasers break through, the first thing they do is lance the wounded!"

Sean lifted his hand in silent thanks for the advice, turned his horse to the rear, and followed the scores of fleeing American troops. All around him men yelled, horses screamed, guns boomed, cannon roared, but mostly men ran in mindless terror through the smoke, scrambling up and down gullies and racing across the plateaus.

Sean rode in their wake, fighting the pain and the dizziness, his eyes searching for something resembling a surgeon's wagon. But he saw only more carnage and confusion, the thunder of guns, the cracking of rifles and muskets, billowing, blinding smoke that reminded him of the Mexican camp two mornings (had it only been *two* mornings?) ago. Yells and shouts and in the distance the screams of men who were being run down and lanced by the Mexican cavalry.

His leg throbbed and his head swam, but he clung to his saddle. Damnit, he wasn't going to die, not now, not when he'd already decided he was going to go back and find Rebekah and make her . . .

Then he saw the strangest thing. General Taylor astride his favorite horse, Old Whitey, calling orders, stopping the fleeing men, turning them.

Sean shook his head. The general shouldn't have been in the thick of the battle, but there he was on his magnificent white horse and behind him came his son-in-law, Jeff Davis, leading his volunteer troops, the Mississippi Rifles. The Mississippi troops let loose a storm of lead that stopped the enemy attack and began to push them back.

Seeing the tide turning, Sean and hundreds of other American soldiers cheered, and Sean kicked his horse with his good leg and rode into the fray. A huge Mexican loomed up before him, a scarlet sash draped across his chest, brandishing a gleaming sword. Sean pulled his pistol and fired. Instantly, a crimson rose bloomed on the scarlet sash, and the Mexican cavalryman keeled over and plummeted off his horse with a crash. Sean turned, pistol ready, but the battlefield began to spin. He blinked furiously, but the spinning only got worse, and in the next second, the ground rushed up and hit him in the face.

The next thing of which he was aware was an unfamiliar voice urging him to his feet and rough hands helping him back into his saddle. "Go to the hacienda," the voice told him, pointing his horse in the right direction and giving the animal a slap to send it on its way. Clinging to the saddle with both hands, Sean rode.

By the time the walls of the hacienda came into view, Sean was reeling in the saddle again. The pain in his leg alternately burned and throbbed, and he prayed it would keep him conscious until he reached the safety of the walls.

So intent was he on his purpose, he didn't realize he was riding into danger instead of away from it until it was too late. By the time he saw that the horsemen lining up before the walls were preparing a cavalry charge, he was between them and the attacking Mexicans who had somehow skirted the entire American Army and were preparing to take the hacienda itself, Taylor's base of operations.

Knowing he was in mortal danger, Sean still couldn't seem to move. He felt as if he were under water. Everything was blurry and seemed to be happening much too slowly. Using every ounce of strength he had left, he whipped his horse with his hat, racing for the American line as the Mexicans came on behind him. After what seemed a lifetime, amid shouts of men and the roar of guns, he finally broke through the American line and galloped through the gate someone was holding open for him.

It slammed shut behind him, and someone caught his horse and then caught him when he fell from the saddle. For a moment his vision cleared, and he saw the hacienda was full of American soldiers, some of them the guards that had been posted here but most of them the deserters from the morning's battle who had sought shelter.

From outside the walls they could hear the clash of sabers and the screams of dying men. He looked around and saw there was a walkway at the top of the wall. "Give me my rifle!" he shouted, and someone thrust it into his hands. In the next second he was hobbling up a ladder, heedless of the agony of his leg, knowing only that he had to reach the top.

Helping hands reached out to pull him up the last few rungs, and he saw he wasn't the only one who'd had the idea. Already dozens of soldiers lined the walls, and they had begun firing, picking as targets the brightly colored Mexican uniforms below.

The Mexicans had ridden right through the charging American line, lancing mercilessly. The screams of the dying filled the air, even above the roar of the guns, and Sean took careful aim, firing just before a Mexican could thrust his lance into a fallen American soldier. The Mexican screamed in agony and flew backwards off his horse.

Reloading rapidly, Sean found another target and just as quickly dispatched him. Beneath the withering fire from the walls, the Mexican forces shrank and ran, splitting in two. Half of them went east, back the way they had come. The other half went west, circling the entire American Army in their flight back to friendly lines.

Sean watched in wonder, his rifle resting on the wall because it had grown unbelievably heavy.

"You're hit!" someone cried in alarm, and Sean looked around to see who he was talking about.

But everyone seemed to be pointing at him, and when he looked down, he saw his pantleg was soaked in blood. How strange. He couldn't even feel the pain anymore. In fact he couldn't feel anything. And why was it getting so dark? Surely the day wasn't over yet.

He raised his head to ask somebody just as the blackness claimed him completely.

Chapter Fourteen

Rebekah looked down at the letter over which she had been slaving for two days. For someone who could express herself in two languages, she realized she simply didn't know the words in any language to explain how she felt or what she wanted to tell MacDougal. If he were here, of course, she would simply whisper, "If you still want me, I'll marry you," then kiss him and he would take it from there.

Writing it all down, of course, was much, much harder, and she knew she still didn't have it right. But since she probably never would, this would have to do. Before sealing it, she read it over one last time.

"Dear MacDougal," the letter began. She'd agonized for hours over what to call him. "MacDougal" sounded much too formal, but she couldn't bring herself to say "Sean" since she'd never called him that to his face even though it was a much more appropriate way to address the man she had finally admitted she loved.

"I don't know how to tell you all the things I have to tell you." That much, at least, was perfectly true. "Maybe when you're home, I'll be able to explain it to you, but maybe not, because I'm not sure I understand it myself. Anyway, I want you to know that I'm sorry for the things I said. I lied before when I said I didn't want you and I was going to marry Andrew, but then, you already know that. What you don't know was that I lied the last time, too, when you asked me to marry you. About not loving you, I mean. I can't explain why I lied. I was just too afraid. I'm still afraid, but if you still want me and if you can forgive me, I'll marry you when you come home. Just please come home, MacDougal, even if you don't want to marry me, so at least I'll know you're all right and nothing happened to you down in Mexico because I'm more afraid of that than anything.

"I miss you terribly, and Hunter asks for you every day. Please be careful and take care of yourself and don't get shot. Come home soon.

Love,
Rebekah"

When she had finished reading it, Rebekah laid the letter down on the kitchen table, put her head on her arms, and wept.

The Cathedral in Saltillo was a vaulted masterpiece of wood and plaster and stained glass, a gorgeous place of worship. The perfect place in which to marry blissfully adoring young couples, to christen their babies, and to bury the dead.

More than a few dead had been buried from the cathedral in the weeks following the battle of Buena Vista, too, since General Taylor had appropriated it as a hospital for his wounded.

Sean MacDougal was determined not to be among the men carried stiff and cold from the church, however. Since his wound had healed over, he stood in no immediate danger, but he knew that could change at any time because he still carried a musket ball in his thigh. Left there, the lead would eventually poison and kill him.

In spite of that danger, the surgeon was reluctant to operate and remove it, however. The physician claimed he couldn't locate the ball and it was too dangerous to slash Sean's thigh open and just go looking for it. So for more than a month, Sean had been hobbling around on a pair of crude crutches one of the men had fashioned for him, helping to care for the wounded soldiers less fortunate than he.

One of those men was Frank Gates, who had ridden into the hacienda at Buena Vista through the thunderstorm that had struck toward evening of the day when Sean had been shot. Frank had caught a bullet in the shoulder, and although the wound had healed well, Frank had recently learned his left arm would always be stiff from the damage the bullet had done.

"At least it's my left arm," Frank had feebly joked after learning his prognosis. "A lawyer only needs one arm anyway. As long as I can write, I'll be in business."

Sean had sought to cheer him up by taking him on a stroll through the picturesque town of Saltillo. The cathedral in which they were billeted was only one of many gorgeous buildings in the city, and the residents were unusually friendly to the Americans, probably since no battles had taken place there and General Taylor had been most considerate of the citizens since making the city his headquarters after the battle.

The two men made slow progress through the dusty streets since Sean had to stump along on his crutches, but at least Frank seemed a little more cheerful by the time they got back to the church. There they found a visitor waiting for them.

"McCulloch!" Sean shouted in greeting when he

recognized the familiar figure on the church steps. The tall Ranger waved his acknowledgement and hurried down to meet them.

He shook their hands and exclaimed over how well they both looked. "I just had some news and thought you boys'd like to hear it. Vera Cruz surrendered this morning."

Having left General Taylor in northern Mexico, General Scott's forces had turned their attention to the south and the taking of the capital. The first step in that quest had been a blockade of the port city of Vera Cruz. From there it was only a short march to Mexico City. With Vera Cruz fallen, the war would be over in a matter of months.

"Too bad you boys won't be around much longer. I also had word Sam Walker brought along those new revolving Colt pistols I was telling you about when they landed at Vera Cruz. All the Rangers there got two apiece, and we'll get ours before too much longer, but I don't reckon you boys'll be around here then."

"Do you know something we don't?" Sean asked.

"I don't think so, but since you're both fit to travel, I expect they'll be mustering you out and sending you home before too much longer."

The three men sat on the church steps and discussed this prospect without much enthusiasm. McCulloch, of course, seldom showed any emotion at all, and Frank was less than happy at being discharged as an invalid, even though he seemed perfectly willing to go home. Sean, of course, had no home to which to go, not really, and the prospect of renewing his ongoing battle with Rebekah Tate in his weakened condition held little appeal.

When McCulloch had finished telling them all the latest Army gossip, he rose to take his leave, then said, "Oh, I almost forgot. A letter came for you." He reached into his coat pocket and pulled out a rather dirty and crumpled missive.

It took a minute for Sean to realize McCulloch was handing the letter to him and not to Frank. "Me?" he asked, still not reaching for it.

"Has your name on it," McCulloch confirmed, his lips stretching into one of his rare smiles. "A lady's handwriting, too. God knows how it ever got to you. A messenger brought it to camp this morning. I almost opened it myself since it has my name on it, too, but then I happened to think there wasn't nobody who'd be writing to me."

Indeed, the envelope was addressed to Sean in care of McCulloch's Texas Rangers. The handwriting was certainly feminine, and although Sean had never seen Rebekah's, he would have bet his life the letter was from her.

He took the letter gingerly from McCulloch's fingers and stared in wonder at the fragile piece of paper. How many people had carried it from Rebekah's hand to his? Across hundreds of miles and how many weeks? And what had driven her to write him a letter in the first place?

A dozen possibilities came immediately to mind, none of them pleasant. A death. His store burned to the ground. Andrew sick or hurt or worse. Or little Hunter.

He felt the cold sweat forming under his shirt as he stared at the paper in his hand, the same sensation he'd experienced when he and Ben had been left alone in the Mexican camp. His apprehension must have shown because Frank hastily rose from his seat on the steps and said, "I'll walk a ways with you, Ben, so Sean can read his letter in peace."

Once again, Ben McCulloch said his good-byes to Sean, but Sean barely nodded in acknowledgement. As soon as he was alone, he very carefully broke the seal and spread the stiff paper open. The message was short, much shorter than he'd expected, and it began, "Dear MacDougal." He knew then it was from Rebekah Tate, even before he saw her name penned neatly at the bottom. He skimmed the few words anxiously, looking for the ones he most feared, and because he was so afraid to see what he didn't want to see, he didn't comprehend a word of what was really there until he got the bottom where he saw she'd signed it, "Love, Rebekah."

Love? That didn't make sense. Quickly he reread the message, and this time he saw what was there, what she had really written, and when he did, it made less sense than ever. Rebekah Tate apologizing? Rebekah Tate missing him? Rebekah Tate agreeing to marry him?

He read it over a third time and then a fourth. By the fifth time, he was beginning to believe it, and after the sixth, he whooped loud enough to bring Frank Gates running back, cradling his sling with his good hand so he wouldn't jar his shoulder.

"What is it?" Frank demanded in alarm.

"We're going home, partner," Sean announced, stuffing the letter into his pocket and hoisting himself up onto his crutches. "But first I've got to find that sawbones and get him to cut this hunk of lead out of my leg. A man can't walk down the aisle on crutches, now can he?"

"Aisle?" Frank asked, helping Sean with his crutches. "What are you talking about?"

"I'm talking about getting married. Miss Rebekah Tate has finally consented to become my wife, and I figure I'd better get myself back to Texas before she has a chance to change her mind."

Frank was slapping his back and congratulating him as they limped into the sanctuary. Inside, Sean bellowed for the doctor whom they found taking a

411

much-needed rest in a room behind the altar.

"I want you to operate on my leg, Doc," Sean informed him.

The physician, a once-portly man who had lost some flesh from the strain of caring for far too many patients at once, glared at him through bloodshot eyes. "I've told you before, I can't just go digging around in your leg. If we wait a while, the lead might work its way to the surface and then—"

"I know exactly where it is right now," Sean said. "I can feel the damn thing every time I move. I'll point and you cut, and if you don't do what I tell you, my friend here will shoot you, won't you, Frank?"

Frank Gates nodded obligingly, vastly amused.

The doctor scowled but showed no fear at the threat. "It's your leg, so I suppose if you don't mind me carving it up, I won't mind doing the carving. We'll do it tomorrow morning."

"I can't wait," Sean replied. "I've got to get home as soon as possible, so we'll do it right now."

The doctor rolled his eyes, but he pushed himself out of his chair. "Whatever you want, Mr. MacDougal, but God help me if I ever have to deal with civilian soldiers again."

The operating table had once served the priests for a dining table and had been set up in one of the myriad small rooms surrounding the sanctuary. The doctor's only preparations were to strap Sean to the table so he wouldn't be able to squirm too much and to give him a piece of leather to stick between his teeth.

"Are you ready?" the doctor asked, holding his scalpel poised over the spot where Sean had insisted the musket ball had lodged.

Sean nodded, fixing his eyes on the surgeon's face, and clenching his teeth on the leather. Behind him, Frank Gates clamped his hands on Sean's shoulders just as the surgeon sliced into the living flesh.

The searing agony exploded in his leg and swept over him, choking off the scream that formed in his throat, filling him, drowning him. A red haze covered his eyes, but he could still see the surgeon's grim expression as he labored over his torturous task, digging, delving into the ragged, quivering tissue as the warm blood poured out. Sean fixed his gaze on the man's sweating face, watching and watching, fighting and fighting, as for the second time in his life the darkness hovered at the edge of his consciousness, beckoning him into oblivion. But he fought it, clinging to the pain as he clung to life, savoring the agony, reveling in it until every nerve in his body swelled, straining against the skin until he thought he would burst into a million pieces.

And then the doctor's face suddenly brightened, and he cried, "Got it!" and lifted his blood-drenched hand to show Sean his prize: a pitted, crusted, mutilated scrap of lead.

Rebekah's heart leaped when she heard the dogs barking their warning at an approaching visitor, and she chided herself for hoping. Andrew and her father had explained over and over to her in the weeks since she had sent her letter that Sean couldn't return from Mexico until his enlistment was up. Since that wouldn't be for months yet, she knew this visitor couldn't be Sean. But she ran to the door, hoping just the same, and leaving Jewel working unconcernedly over the supper preparations.

Hunter was calling her, pointing to the wagon. She squinted in the spring sunlight, trying to identify the two men on the wagon seat. For a moment she'd thought . . . but no, the man with his arm in a sling wasn't MacDougal, and the other, the one driving, was only a boy.

"Who is it, Mother? Who is it?" Hunter demanded in his newly perfected English.

"I don't know, dear. They're strangers." Except the man with his arm in a sling seemed somehow familiar. Perhaps he was a distant neighbor, someone she'd seen once or twice.

He was remarkably unkempt, however, she noticed as the wagon approached. His beard hung down his chest, his hair was badly in need of a trim, and his clothes looked as if he'd fought a war in them.

Suddenly her blood went cold as she realized why he looked so familiar. He was a Ranger. She'd known it instinctively, just as she'd recognized the men who'd ridden up to MacDougal's store that day without ever having seen them before. And if he was a Ranger, he could have only one reason for coming here.

She grabbed Hunter by the shoulders. *"Anáa!"* he protested, slipping back into Comanche, probably because he'd forgotten the English equivalent of "Ouch." He tried to squirm free, but she held him fast, needing to touch him because she was suddenly so very afraid of what this man had come to tell her.

The boy driving the wagon—he looked to be about fifteen or sixteen and seemed inordinately curious about her and Hunter and everything else, peering around while pretending not to—pulled the horses to a stop.

The man with his arm in a sling lifted his battered hat with his good hand and nodded a greeting. "Good afternoon, Miss Tate. I'm Frank Gates. We met a few months ago at Sean MacDougal's store."

She managed to nod back although she had no memory of this man in particular. All she could think was that he didn't look as if the news he'd brought her were good. Her heart was pounding a

414

tattoo against her ribs.

"I was with McCulloch's Rangers," he tried, obviously concerned that she didn't know who he was.

"MacDougal?" she forced, forcing the word through her cottony mouth, and Hunter echoed, "Mac?"

Frank Gates frowned and glanced over his shoulder uncertainly. "Well, yes, that is, I've brought him home, but you see . . ."

He glanced over his shoulder again, into the back of the wagon, and then Rebekah knew what it was he was trying not to tell her. MacDougal was back there. Lying in the bed of the wagon. Not moving and not speaking. Which could only mean one terrible, utterly unspeakable thing.

"No!" she cried as the blood rushed from her head. She clamped both hands over her mouth to hold back the sob and swayed as everything began to swirl around her.

"He's not dead!" Frank Gates shouted in alarm when he saw her distress. "He's in bad shape, but he's still alive!"

He was scrambling down from the wagon seat as quickly as he could with the use of only one arm, but Rebekah was no longer paying any attention to him. Galvanized by his words, she was running to the wagon, Hunter at her heels.

Clasping the wooden side, she peered over it and saw him, Sean MacDougal, the man she loved. He lay as still as death, his long red hair and straggly beard spread around his head, but his face was flushed with fever, not pale and cold, and as she stared, she saw his chest rose and fell unsteadily.

"MacDougal!" she called in anguish, and he stirred slightly in response.

Beside her, ignored, Hunter was clambering up the wagon wheel so he could see, too, and once at the top, he didn't stop, but swung himself over the side and

415

onto the wagon bed beside him.

"Mac's sick," he announced, hunkering down beside him.

"Don't touch him!" Rebekah cried and raced to the rear of the wagon. Frank Gates was already there, unlatching the tailgate and lowering it for her. "What happened? What's wrong with him?" she demanded as she hoisted herself over the end and scrambled up.

"He took a musket ball in the leg at the battle of Buena Vista," Gates explained.

"But that was almost two months ago!" she protested, knowing he would have died long since if he'd been this sick from the bullet wound.

"He was all right at first," Gates explained. "And the surgeon wouldn't take the ball out right away. He was waiting, you see, until . . . Well, anyway, then Sean got your letter."

Rebekah started and turned back to Gates, appalled. "My letter?" she asked, knowing instinctively she'd caused this somehow.

"When he found out . . . Well, what you had to say, he wanted to come home right away, so he made the surgeon operate that very day. Everything was fine, but he wouldn't wait until the wound had healed. As soon as he could sit a horse, he started out. I went with him to make sure he was all right, but of course he wasn't. After about two days, he started running a fever. When he couldn't ride anymore, I hired this wagon and Billy here to drive it and—"

"Why didn't you stop somewhere and let him rest?" she cried in outrage.

Gates looked guilty, but he didn't drop his gaze. "Because he wouldn't let me."

Of course, she should have known, she thought, looking down at MacDougal's wasted form. His eyes were sunken, his lips dry and cracked from the fever.

416

Tentatively, she reached out and touched her fingers to his forehead, only to jerk them away in fright.

"He's burning up!"

"Is it a fire, Mother?" Hunter asked in alarm, looking around for the danger.

"No, not a fire," she replied, too distracted to explain the idiom. "Mac is very sick. Hunter, will you run out and find Grandpa and tell him Mac is here. Tell him to hurry!" she called after him since he'd already jumped down from the wagon and was racing away.

"MacDougal, can you hear me?" she asked softly, leaning down and wanting to kiss him but not daring to for fear she might hurt him. "MacDougal? Are you awake?"

His eyelids fluttered, then lifted with apparent effort. His eyes were bright with the fever, the pupils large and black, and he couldn't seem to focus until she said his name again.

"Rebekah Tate? Am I dreaming?" he asked hoarsely.

"No!" she told him, gently touching his cheek. "I'm here. You're home now, MacDougal, and I'm not going to let you out of my sight again."

A ghost of his old grin flickered beneath his mustache. "You might not have a choice this time," he said.

Despair clamped its icy grip around her heart, but she forced herself to smile. "Don't think I'm going to let you get away now that I've finally got you back. I'm warning you, MacDougal, if you die, I'll . . . I'll *murder* you!" she said, remembering how he'd made the same threat to her so long ago.

This time he grinned in earnest. "Didn't I tell you she was a hell of a woman, Frank?"

"That you did, partner," Gates agreed, but MacDougal's eyes had closed and Rebekah didn't

417

think he'd heard the reply.

She felt the tears welling up, hot and stinging, but she wouldn't surrender to them, not now, not when Sean needed her so much. Carefully, so as not to disturb him, she lifted the ragged blanket under which he lay. She saw the bloody bandage on his leg and smelled the scent of decay, and her heart died within her.

No! she railed at the God in whom she no longer believed, and she knew beyond knowing that this was a punishment for her unbelief. The God she couldn't love had been jealous of the man she could love and was taking him away.

Except she wasn't going to let MacDougal go without a fight, even if she had to fight the Almighty Himself.

"Jewel!" she shouted, but the black woman was already beside her, peering over the side of the wagon at MacDougal's ravaged face. Her expression told Rebekah she comprehended the situation.

"I'll put some water on to boil," Jewel said. "Where do you want to put him?"

"In my room," Rebekah replied without hesitation.

"I'll get everything ready."

From a distance they heard her father's shout, and Rebekah looked up to see him running across the field with Dan and Enoch behind him.

Within minutes, with their help, MacDougal was tucked up in Rebekah's bed and divested of his dirty clothes. Now Rebekah, Jewel, Zeb, and Frank Gates stood around, examining the festering wound Rebekah had exposed while outside Hunter protested loudly to Dan and Enoch at having been excluded from the consultation.

"I don't know no remedy for that, Massa Zeb," Jewel said, shaking her head in dismay when she saw

418

MacDougal's wound. "Hot rags'll help some, but when it gets black like that . . ."

"I know something," Rebekah remembered. "The Indians made a poultice for bullet wounds, but they used a cactus that doesn't grow around here. If we had some . . ."

"I'll get it for you," Frank Gates said.

Rebekah gaped at him. "You're wounded yourself!"

"I'm healed up now," he said, shrugging beneath his sling. "I'll probably have to wear this the rest of my life, but the wound itself is fine. You just draw me a picture of the cactus you want and I'll fetch it for you."

The quest was impossible. Even if he could find the necessary ingredient, it would take days of hard riding. No matter what he said, he probably wasn't up to it, and even if he was, by the time he got back, it would probably already be too late.

Rebekah opened her mouth to protest, but before she could, Frank Gates smiled at her. She recognized that smile and the steely determination in his cold, gray eyes. Wolf's eyes, just like MacDougal's.

"You'd do this for him?" she asked.

"After what he did for all of us, I'd be proud to," Gates replied.

"What did he do?"

"I'll tell you when I get back," Gates promised. "Or maybe I'll let him tell you himself. If he starts talking before I get back, ask him how he liked sleeping in the Mexican camp. It's quite a story. Now, if you'll show me what that cactus looks like and pack me some grub and loan me a fresh horse . . ."

Within an hour, Gates was gone again, and so was the boy Billy and his wagon. Jewel and Rebekah worked over MacDougal, cleaning his wound and cutting away the dead flesh and keeping a steady

419

supply of hot compresses coming.

The sun set, and Zeb put Hunter to bed in his room. Andrew arrived shortly afterward, having been summoned. At the sight of him, Rebekah burst into tears and collapsed into his arms.

He comforted her as best he could, patting her back while she sobbed against his shirt front, and when she was calmer, he asked forlornly, "Aren't you happy to see me?"

She laughed through her tears. "I'm sorry," she said, stepping out of his embrace and using the handkerchief he gave her to wipe her face. "I've been wanting to do that ever since they brought him in this afternoon, but I've just been too busy. When I saw you . . ." She shrugged helplessly.

"I know," he offered. "You didn't think I'd mind if you cried all over me."

"I'm sorry," she said again, this time for a different reason. "It seems like I'm always using you for something."

Andrew smiled, not the least bit offended. "Believe it or not, I like it. For a long time I felt completely useless. The whole time you were gone, in fact. But since you've been back, well, things have been a lot different. What can I do now?"

Rebekah wasn't sure, but she said, "Maybe if you talked to him. I don't know if he can hear you or not, but sometimes he responds when I talk to him. Tell him about the store, about how much money you've been making for him." She smiled wanly. "If that doesn't get through to him, nothing will."

So Andrew sat beside the bed and talked, explaining everything that had happened in the four months Sean had been gone, while Rebekah alternately held Sean's hand and put hot compresses on his leg and cold ones on his head.

When Andrew left, much later, Rebekah pulled

out the trundle bed and lay down on it, fully clothed, and spent the night fitfully dozing in between her ministrations to Sean.

The next few days passed in a blur of activity as she alternately napped and tended to Sean because no matter how much argument there was, Rebekah would allow no one else to care for him. Somewhere in there, surprisingly soon and much sooner than Rebekah would ever have dreamed, Frank Gates returned. From the looks of him, he hadn't slept or even rested, but he had found the cactus and brought her back a bagful of it.

Almost from the first application of the freshly made poultice Rebekah cooked up, Sean's wound began to improve. The flesh stopped dying and the fierce redness faded to a gentle pink. Still his fever raged, however, day after day, until Jewel despaired and wouldn't even meet Rebekah's eye anymore. Her father prayed almost constantly now, kneeling by the bed during his frequent visits, laying hands on Sean's burning body so the strength of his spirit could pass through.

Rebekah watched the ritual numbly, remembering the chants and rattle of the Comanche medicine men as they tried to frighten away the evil spirits and thinking her father's prayers were no more effective. If there was a God, he'd decided to punish her, and nothing anyone could do now would save Sean.

She knew that, but still she fought for him, working blindly now, going through the motions that had been so futile up to now, afraid if she stopped she would have to lie down and die, too.

Early on the morning after everyone else had given up hope, Rebekah woke with a start, wondering what had disturbed her. Instantly alert, she turned on her trundle to see if Sean had called her in his sleep as he sometimes did in his delirium. Sean was still, but

Hunter was there, looking small and sweet in his flour sack nightshirt, his little feet bare and his hands stretched out in front of him, resting on Sean's naked chest.

Her breath caught when she realized he was imitating his grandfather, laying hands on Sean the way Zeb did when he prayed. Hunter wasn't kneeling. He couldn't have reached Sean if he had been, but when Rebekah listened, she heard he was praying, imitating the words he'd heard so often.

"Fill him with Thy healing power. Restore his strength." Stilted phrases whose meanings he could not have understood. Then she heard the piping voice catch on a sob and begin to plead. "Please don't let him die! Please don't let him die!"

Rebekah was there in a moment, catching the boy to her, cradling him as he wept out his anguish. "I don't want Mac to die," he told her between sobs.

"I don't either," Rebekah soothed him, unable to promise anything more. She took him to the trundle and lay down with him, cuddling him, as grateful for the comfort of his small body as he must be for hers.

"Grandpa says you should pray, too," Hunter said between sniffs. "He said only the white man's God can save him, but you won't ask Him."

Anguish twisted her heart. "I don't think it would do any good. The white man's God doesn't listen to me anymore."

"Grandpa says He would if you would just try," Hunter argued.

If only it were so simple, she thought in despair.

She held the boy for a few more minutes until Jewel came in with Rebekah's breakfast and took him away. Through the closed door, she could hear them talking as they crossed the dogtrot to the kitchen.

"Why won't Mother pray like Grandpa says?" the

boy asked her.

"I think she prays in her own way," Jewel replied.

Her own way, which was to do everything she knew to keep MacDougal alive in spite of God's determination to kill him. She could taste her own bitterness, and sighing, she threw her arm over her eyes and lay like that for some time, wallowing in her despair.

But she couldn't quite lose herself because something was teasing at the back of her mind, something she should have noticed, something she should have seen but didn't, something she should know.

Slowly, so slowly, but much faster than she wanted, the truth came, creeping up like the horrible slimy monster she knew it to be until it had its clutching tentacles wrapped around her throat and she couldn't even breathe for knowing.

And when she wasn't breathing anymore, she heard it. The awful, deafening silence where she should have heard the rasping, labored gasps of a dying man.

MacDougal!

She scrambled up to her knees and stared in horror at the motionless figure on the bed. The flush of fever had vanished from his face, leaving it pale. The tense, restlessness of delirium had quieted, leaving him perfectly still.

As still as death.

"No!" she screamed, covering her face with both hands as her whole body convulsed in agony. "You can't let him die! You can't!" she railed, closing her hands into fists and shaking them toward heaven. How would she bear it? How would she live? She'd never even told MacDougal she loved him!

"No!" she cried again as the tears came, flooding her eyes and coursing down her cheeks. "Please, You can't!" she pleaded in anguish. "Don't punish him because you're mad at me! Punish *me!* Let me die instead! Just please, please don't take him!'' Her voice broke on a sob, and she covered her face again, weeping uncontrollably into her hands.

Which was why she almost didn't hear the question.

"Could you cry a little quieter? You're making my head hurt.''

At first the words didn't register, and when they finally did, she raised her head and looked around to see who had come into the room. But she was still alone. Alone with MacDougal.

MacDougal?

Her gaze snapped back to him, but he lay just as he had before, still and pale and silent. Carefully, cautiously, Rebekah moved off the trundle and crawled across the small strip of floor separating her from MacDougal's bed until she was mere inches from his face.

His eyes were still closed, his face was still pale, but now she could see it wasn't yet the waxen whiteness of death. And this close she could see the slight rise and fall of his chest as the air moved in and out of his body.

He wasn't dead!

At least not yet, she reminded herself. "Mac-Dougal?'' she tried, her voice hoarse from weeping. His eyelids twitched, and she tried again, louder this time. "MacDougal!''

This time the eyelids rose, and he blinked a few times before he actually focused on her face. "Why are you crying?'' he asked weakly.

"MacDougal!'' she almost shouted, scrubbing the tears from her face with frantic hands. "Do you know who I am?''

This time his lips twitched as if he were trying to grin, and she could see them perfectly since her father had shaved off his long beard days ago. "Aren't you Rebekah Tate?" he asked, amusement twinkling in his eyes. "Unless your name's MacDougal by now. Did we get married yet?"

"No! Not yet," she told him, wanting to laugh and cry and dance and shout but still too afraid to do any of those things. "You've been too sick, but as soon as you're well, we'll have the biggest wedding you ever saw!"

He sighed. "I'm glad we aren't married yet," he said, really grinning now. "I wouldn't want to miss my wedding night."

"Oh, MacDougal," she said, laying her hand on his stubbly cheek. "Your fever's gone!" she exclaimed, quickly moving her hand from his face to his neck to his chest to check. Everywhere his skin was cool to the touch.

She threw back the blanket and peeled off the bandage on his leg. The wound was still an angry shade of red, but the flesh around it no longer burned against the infection.

"If you want to touch me, you've missed an important spot," he murmured.

Suddenly aware that he was naked—a situation of which she had hardly been aware until that moment—and that the spot to which he referred was plainly visible and just a few inches from her hand, Rebekah blushed furiously and quickly pulled the blanket back over him.

"How do you feel? Do you hurt anywhere?" she asked to cover her unexpected embarrassment. How strange. She'd felt not the slightest bit uneasy all these days when she'd tended to his most intimate needs. Why should things be different now?

But they were very different, and Rebekah's face burned hotter when her gaze met his and she saw he was laughing at her shyness.

"I hurt everywhere," he told her. "But I'd probably feel a lot better if you laid down here beside me for a little while so I can be sure I'm not dreaming."

Ever so carefully she slipped into the bed beside him, cautious not to jar his leg or any other part of him. But he surprised her by wrapping his arm around her and, with more strength than she'd thought him capable, pulling her face to his for a kiss.

The kiss was so sweet, so familiar yet so new, that Rebekah was crying when he lifted his mouth from hers. "Oh, MacDougal, I love you!" she whispered fiercely.

His eyes lit up like the morning sun, and the color rushed back to his pale face. "I love you, too, Rebekah Tate. It was almost worth dying to hear you say it, too."

She laid her fingers over his lips. "Don't say that! Don't ever say that! You aren't going to die. I—"

She stopped. She'd almost said she'd made a deal with God to keep him alive, that she'd offered herself in his place. The memory of that moment echoed through her like a chime, and the sacred truth of it was the pure, golden tone. She'd prayed. She'd spoken to the God whose existence she had so long doubted, because she knew now that she'd never really doubted. She simply hadn't wanted to believe because she'd been so angry and so bitter. And her father had been right. The instant she surrendered her foolish pride, Sean had been healed. And God wouldn't hold her to her silly bargain. As her father had told her many times, He just didn't work that way.

"You aren't going to die," she repeated more firmly. "Because if you do, I'll *murder* you!" she added, laughing through her tears. "Do you remember I told you that the day your Ranger friend

426

brought you here?"

He smiled. "I thought I dreamed it. I've dreamed a lot of things, and I'm not sure what's real and what isn't. Did you ever crawl into my bed without a stitch of clothes on and—"

"I most certainly did not!" she informed him in mock outrage. "But if you're starting to think about *that*, you're in much better health than I thought, and maybe I should get out of this bed before you take advantage of me."

She made as if to go, but his arm tightened around her, holding her in place, and she chose surrender over struggle.

"Tell me again," he said.

"Tell you what?"

"That you love me."

The words were more difficult to say this time, perhaps because she could see how very much it meant for him to know. But miracle of miracles, she was somehow no longer afraid. "I love you."

"I'll never hurt you," he promised, his brown eyes glowing. "You don't have to be afraid of that."

"I know. I . . . I wasn't afraid of *you*."

"What were you afraid of, then?"

What *had* she been afraid of? She'd never actually tried to figure it out. "I guess . . . I guess I was afraid to care too much. I'd lost everything I ever cared about, my mother and my brother and my home and for all those years, my father and the only life I'd ever known, and then I almost lost Hunter, and loving him was scary enough. I couldn't stand the thought of loving you, too, because if I lost you . . . Oh, MacDougal, I wanted to die when I thought you weren't going to make it! Especially because I'd been so mean and told you all those lies about how I'd never love you or want you. They weren't true, none of them! I do love you and I do want you, and I think I

427

always have."

"Then you'll have me," he said, smiling triumphantly. "Of course, if I was any kind of a gentleman, I'd be warning you that I'll probably be a cripple or at least walk with a limp, but instead I'm going to promise you a wonderful life. I'll build you the biggest house in Texas, and you'll never have to turn your hand because you'll have as many servants as you need, and when the time comes, we'll send Hunter back East to the best schools. So even though parts of me might not work as well as they used to, you'll never be sorry you married me."

"I wouldn't be sorry even if we lived in a buffalo-skin lodge and I had to slave for you every day," she said, planting a kiss on his smiling mouth and snuggling blissfully into the delicious warmth of his body. "And I have a feeling that your parts are going to work just fine."

"You may be right. In fact," he added, lifting the blanket and peering beneath it to check, "I think a certain part of me is working *too* well."

"Why, Mr. MacDougal, I was right!" she said coyly. "You *are* going to take advantage of me."

He sighed and closed his eyes. "If only I could. I'm afraid the effort is a little more than I could manage right now, though. But," he added, lifting one eyelid to check her reaction, "if *you* wanted to take advantage of *me,* I don't think I'd be able to do a single thing to stop you."

"But I have to tell everyone about your recovery!" she protested without much sincerity. "Papa and Hunter and Jewel and your friend Mr. Gates who's been waiting all this time, and Andrew will want to know and—"

He silenced her with a kiss, and Rebekah decided everyone else could wait a few more minutes to hear the very wonderful news.

Author's Note

I hope you enjoyed reading about Rebekah Tate's adventures. The idea for this book came from the true story of Cynthia Ann Parker, who was kidnapped by the Comanches as a child. She grew up among the Indians, married a Comanche chief, and bore three children. Her life was perfectly happy until the Army attacked the camp where she was living and "rescued" her, returning her and her young daughter to her Parker relatives. Although Cynthia wanted nothing more than to return to her husband and her other children, the Parkers—believing they knew what was best for her—held her prisoner until she and her daughter died, the victims of civilization. Her son, Kwana (Quanah), became the last great Comanche war chief and his band was the last to surrender to the U.S. Government when the slaughter of the buffalo left them starving on the plains. He was never defeated in battle.

Being a typical writer, I couldn't help wondering what might have happened if Cynthia had been rescued earlier in her captivity, while she still might have wanted to return to her white family. And, of course, what might have happened to her son if she had raised him as a white man. The result of these musings is this book and the ones that will follow.

Sean MacDougal's adventures in the Mexican War are based on actual events. Texas Ranger Capt. Ben McCulloch and "another man" really did spend the night in the Mexican army camp in order to better determine the size of the enemy's forces. Their estimate was exactly accurate. What they didn't know was that on the grueling march from that camp to meet the American forces at Buena Vista, Santa Anna lost approximately five thousand of his twenty thousand soldiers to death, disease, and desertion, which helped cut the odds somewhat. Still, the Americans were outnumbered three to one, and they didn't actually win the battle at all. After the second day's fighting, Santa Anna determined he'd suffered far too many casualties and simply withdrew, claiming victory. General Taylor's "That's all I wanted to know, Major. I'm glad they didn't catch you," is exactly what he is reported to have said to McCulloch upon his return.

The Americans claimed victory at Buena Vista, too, and their claim stuck since Santa Anna was the one who retreated. This battle lost Santa Anna the confidence of his people and his army and marked the turning point of the war.

Col. Jefferson Davis, later president of the Confederacy, really was Gen. Zachary Taylor's son-in-law. For two years, Davis had courted Taylor's daughter Knox, but Taylor refused to allow his daughter to marry a soldier. Finally Davis resigned from the Army, and he and Knox were married. Seven weeks later she died of malaria, so Davis was then free to lead a troop of volunteers from Mississippi in the

Mexican War and help save the American forces from an ignominious defeat at Buena Vista.

The details of Sean's wound are based on the experiences of Lt. Samuel French who was shot in the leg during the battle of Buena Vista. Afraid of being lanced by Mexican soldiers if he allowed himself to be placed in a wagon with the other wounded, he stayed on his horse for most of the day, riding behind the lines in search of a surgeon. During his quest, he encountered both the heroic charge of Jefferson Davis and his Mississippi Rifles that stopped the American rout, and the fight at the hacienda. Carried to Saltillo after the battle, he spent forty days hobbling around on crutches with a musket ball in his leg because the surgeon refused to operate. Finally in exasperation, French told the surgeon he could show him where the ball was, and the surgeon removed it in much the same way as I described Sean MacDougal's operation.

I'd like to offer a special thanks to the Wycliffe Bible Translators' Summer Institute of Linguistics for compiling the world's first Comanche/English Dictionary. It was my source for the proper spellings of Comanche words and names. Any mistakes are my own misinterpretation of their text.

And to those of you who noticed, I did indeed spell "Monterey" incorrectly. At that time in history, the name of that city was spelled with only one *r*.

Wild Texas Wind is only the first volume of the Tate family saga. The next book will begin about twenty years later and will tell you the story of Hunter Tate, the woman he comes to love, and how he deals with the U.S. Government's determination to exterminate the Comanche people. He does what I imagine Kwana Parker would have done if he had been raised as a white man. I hope you'll watch for it.

Meanwhile, please tell me how you liked this book. Write to me at:

Victoria Thompson
c/o Zebra Books
475 Park Avenue South
New York, NY 10016